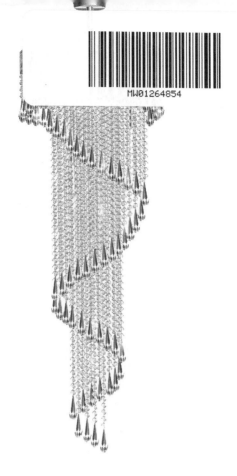

CHANDELIER
DREAM

USA TODAY BESTSELLING AUTHOR
VANESSA FEWINGS

Chandelier Dream
(Chandelier Sessions)
Copyright © 2023 Vanessa Fewings

Cover Design by: Hang Le
Cover photo: YAYImages from Depositphoto
Formatted by: Champagne Book Design
Editor: Debbie Kuhn

ISBN: 9781733774215

DEDICATION

To
Lauren Luman, Paramita Patra, Lupita Gonzalez
for reading this one in advance!

Also for

Amber Vasquez, Melissa Williams, Melissa Becci, and
Victoria Bullock for sharing your love of the ENTHRALL
SESSIONS
and all you do on BookTok!

"Without darkness, nothing comes to birth, as without light, nothing flowers."

—May Sarton

CHANDELIER DREAM

CHAPTER ONE

Stella

THIS WAS *HIM* PROVING HIS POWER—THAT MUCH WAS obvious.

Summoning me, knowing I was desperate for answers. Knowing how distraught this would make me.

Cruel, really.

Shielding my eyes from the midday sun, I peered through the side window of the helicopter and saw that we were heading for a superyacht. As we closed in, its name became visible: *The Hades*.

A chill swept over me.

The craft floating on the Pacific waters below, about thirty miles out from the California coast, was the definition of extreme luxury.

My stomach lurched as we set down on the helipad. As the rotating blades slowed, I eased off my headphones. The pilot and I had spoken little.

I watched him climb out and then I scooted closer to the door, offering him my hand. He assisted me onto the roof of the yacht.

He motioned for me to continue alone down the stairs. Fear gave way to courage with each step as I descended. A February breeze ruffled my hair, and I dragged my fingers through the dark strands, hoping to restore my appearance.

You can do this.

I held on tightly to the railing until I stepped onto the deck.

"Welcome, Ms. Adair," said the man in the pristine uniform. "Petty Officer Klein."

"Stella."

"This way, please." He strolled ahead of me along the portside.

The officer had sun-weathered skin and the proud stride of a seagoing man. I wondered how well he took orders from my brother, the captain of *The Hades*, considering AJ was twenty-two when he'd first qualified to skipper a yacht.

I wondered if Klein knew anything about him, but he marched ahead too fast for me to ask.

Once we turned the corner ahead, I recognized the owner of the yacht from his photo.

Lance Merrill sat at a round dining table. He was handsome in a silver fox way, with salt and pepper hair and a neatly trimmed beard, looking distinguished in his sweater and cream pants. The expensive sunglasses perched atop his head only added to his suaveness.

He stared back at me coldly.

A man of extraordinary taste—or so AJ had told me. Merrill was an oil baron with money to burn. My brother didn't like him, but the pay was good.

Merrill remained seated.

Officer Klein offered his boss a polite nod, then left us alone at the table set for two.

Merrill nursed a drink in a tumbler, sipping from it as he assessed me over the rim of his glass, his gaze trailing over me.

It made me feel dirty.

At least I looked the part of a guest on this floating palace. I'd ditched my usual jeans and T-shirt for this blue summer dress with delicate pumps. I was carrying my favorite Coach handbag, the one I kept stored away because I never went anywhere. Other than work, but that didn't count.

My heart was pounding already.

Without waiting for an invite, I pulled out the chair opposite him and sat, placing the handbag at my feet. We would never be equals, but I needed him to see I was serious about finding my brother.

Silver cutlery and fancy plates were set before me. If they were for my use, I'd never be able to eat anything. Too nervous.

A manila envelope rested on the table to Lance's left. I felt a rush of hope that maybe he'd learned something important about my brother.

Merrill's lack of warmth caused my forearms to prickle. Still, he was a busy man, and all this was a great inconvenience to him—he made that apparent.

I tried to assess how tall he'd be when standing, and guessed he used his height to intimidate. The signate ring on his pinky finger, bearing an ornate insignia, screamed old money.

We assessed each other as strangers do.

"May I?" On his nod, I reached for the glass of water and brought it to my lips to quench my thirst.

"Thank you for accepting my invitation," he said with a Texas drawl.

"Of course." I set the glass down.

AJ had shared little about Lance, other than to say he was a chauvinist who refused to hire female crew members. He paid well but there were caveats—staff did things his way or they were fired.

AJ rarely saw him, apparently.

I cleared my throat. "AJ's never done anything like this before, which is why I'm so worried about him."

Lance swirled the liquid in his glass.

"He's a good man," I added. "A hard worker, as you must know. He's been your skipper for several months."

Merrill's eyes remained cold and indifferent.

I continued, "I was hoping you might have some news? Or might have heard from him?"

Lance set his tumbler down next to the envelope.

His gaze darkened. "I imagine his actions have caused great disruption in your life."

True.

Over the last week, every waking thought was about my brother. I continually blamed myself for not detecting anything amiss during our last call, or sensing he was in trouble. I was supposed to be the older sister he could tell anything to.

A server appeared with two salads. He refused to make eye contact with me as he set the smaller plates before us. Lance requested the steward come back with a bottle of chardonnay—like drinking might be a good idea. I was tactful enough not to make a thing of it.

"You probably know we share a house in Burbank," I began. "Just us. With our busy schedules we cross in the night."

"Both parents dead," he said.

"Yes." Though most people broached that subject with a little more tact.

"What about you?"

"How do you mean?"

"What do you do?"

"I'm a makeup artist. I work at Save Face at the Burbank Mall. Occasionally do weddings. That kind of thing." He didn't need to know I wanted to launch my own stylist business. That would elicit more questions about why I'd not managed to do it so far. Something always got in the way. The disappearance of my brother would put it on hold indefinitely.

He went on to say, "What did your brother tell you?"

"About?"

"Working for me."

"He loves it."

I wondered if AJ would be able to work for Lance after this. Disappearing without a trace might ruin his reputation as a reliable employee. Maybe he'd gone on a bender? But that was so out of character for him. Maybe he'd lost his phone. Maybe he was in a hospital and couldn't reach out.

"Have you or your crew heard from him?" I asked. "At all?"

"What are you asking of me?"

"To help me find him," I said with an edge of frustration.

"I'm a busy man."

"Sir," I continued, "you have the resources."

He looked amused, running his fingertip around the rim of the tumbler.

"You own oil refineries in Texas."

"And Dubai," he added.

Exactly. "You can afford to hire someone to locate him. Please, I need your help."

He drew in a deep breath. "Your brother was a great captain. Reliable. To a point."

I froze, sensing bad news.

"Unfortunately, AJ became a problem."

My flesh crawled at his words.

With the worst timing, the steward reappeared and poured two glasses of wine. I needed him to go away.

He was shooed off with an arrogant wave by Lance. "We may have a solution."

I exhaled in relief. "Thank you."

"Wouldn't want to see your brother turn up dead."

For some reason, that comment had me turning my gaze toward the vast ocean. Or maybe it was because I'd followed his line of sight.

A *threat?*

No, impossible. I'd read that wrong.

"Why would you say that?" I asked, my voice sounding weak.

Lance slid the manila envelope across the tablecloth toward me. With a nod of permission from him, I reached inside and slid out a piece of paper. A name was written in bold ink:

De Sade.

"Why are you showing me this?"

"This is who you'll be meeting."

"Why?" *He knows something about AJ?*

"He must never learn of our arrangement."

"Arrangement?" Adrenaline surged through my veins. "Who is he?"

Get up.

Get off this boat.

I'd find my brother another way. Every cell of my body was warning me Lance couldn't be trusted. He showed no compassion, no normal response to any of this.

He pointed to the name. "De Sade is your brother's way out. Via you, of course."

"I don't understand."

"Seduce him. Report back to me everything he tells you."

My glare told him to fuck off.

He pushed up. "Walk with me."

Managing to stand despite shaky legs, I followed him back along the starboard side and then walked along beside him. I'd been right about him being tall—right, too, that he seemed to enjoy towering over me.

The helicopter pilot was waiting at the base of the stairs.

I was being ushered away.

Lance picked up the pace. "The illusion of choice fascinates me."

AJ, what did you do?

"There seems to be a misunderstanding, Mr. Merrill," I said.

"Not as far as I'm concerned."

"How do you mean?"

"I'm moving you to a temporary location."

"What's going on?"

Lance softened his expression. "An improvement on your house on Olive."

He knew our address. *Of course he does,* came that soothing inner voice. *He's your brother's boss.*

"I'm not going anywhere except home."

"We expected you'd need convincing."

Following his gaze toward the upper deck, I drew in a sharp breath and my heart squeezed with relief.

Thank God.

My brother was safe.

But AJ appeared quietly distraught. I could see the fear in his eyes. He didn't move, didn't rush to greet me. Behind him stood a sinister man with tattooed arms.

Confusion set in as I tried to understand what was happening. I took a step forward to go to him.

Lance grabbed my arm. "Don't make it worse."

"He needs me."

Lance's grip tightened.

"What happened to him?" I felt chilled to the bone, not knowing why they weren't letting him come to me. I searched for the words to persuade Lance to let us reunite, trying to figure out what to say to not make this worse.

The pilot ascended the metal steps up toward the helicopter.

"I won't leave without my brother," I snapped.

"That's not up to you." Lance turned to face me. "I demand loyalty. When someone breaks that rule, I take appropriate action. As you can see with your brother, who has made some serious errors in judgment."

"What did he do?"

"That's confidential, for now."

"Let him go!"

"Nothing will happen to him. If you're compliant."

"He's innocent."

"More on that later, Stella." Lance gestured to Klein.

The petty officer was a man seemingly compliant in all this. He'd changed out of his uniform and now wore a suit.

"Escort her to Marina Del Rey," said Lance. "Settle her in."

Panic shuddered through me. "What's there?"

"Tell no one about our arrangement, Stella. Or you'll never see AJ again."

"I'm not leaving without him," I snapped.

"Stella, I'm giving you both a way out."

An engine roared to life, blades cutting through air, slicing my nerves, threatening to separate me from AJ.

I turned to Lance. "Please, I'll do anything."

"I know."

"Don't hurt him."

"That's up to you." Lance gave me a sinister smile.

A man with a lust for cruelty.

This aspect of him my brother had failed to share.

I stared up at AJ. *Stay calm, AJ. I'll come back for you. I'll do whatever it takes.*

"Do as I ask." Lance drew my focus back to him. "Then AJ goes free."

"What do I have to do?"

Lance gestured toward Klein. "Get her off my yacht."

Klein motioned for me to walk with him.

"I'm not leaving!"

Lance glanced at his wristwatch. "If you'll excuse me." He strolled off as though he'd not just torn apart my world and threatened my brother's life.

In a blur, despite trying to resist the manhandling, I was forced back up the metal steps and shoved into the back seat of the helicopter.

When I glanced back toward the upper deck, AJ was gone.

Panicking, I tried to imagine what my brother had done to rile up such a dangerous man. I shoved Klein's hands off me when he tried to secure my seatbelt. He gave up and climbed into the front seat beside the pilot.

The rotating blades whirled faster and louder.

I leaned forward to get Klein's attention. "It's all a mistake. Something easily clarified. Let him go. I'll sort it out."

He peered over his shoulder. "Let's discuss this when we land."

Fuck him.

And his boss.

Once we landed, the first thing I planned to do was get away from him.

CHAPTER TWO

Stella

THIS ISN'T HAPPENING.

It was a nightmare I could never have envisioned. I'd always believed that at twenty-four, I'd have my life together.

Yet even as I wanted to deny it was happening, I followed Officer Klein around the luxury penthouse from room to room as he gave me the grand tour.

The helicopter had landed back at Marina Del Rey Airport. We'd driven here to Dorchester House in an unmarked SUV.

They weren't letting me go.

My life before this hadn't been perfect, but it had been a good one. For me, a five-day week at the mall. AJ, a hard-working ship's captain, often away for long periods of time.

Mom and Dad might be gone but we continued their legacy of working hard. Our great-grandparents had immigrated from Armenia. We'd proudly honored their sacrifice by thriving as second-generation Americans. We'd inherited their dark hair and olive

skin. We'd inherited their sense of family and their longing for a simpler life.

Home wasn't that far away. An hour's drive in good traffic. I just
had to persuade Klein to let me go.

Keeping my distance from him, I ran through the things I'd do
if he tried to touch me.

The chill of the air-conditioning made my limbs ache. The dress
I'd put on for the meeting was too skimpy for this apartment.

AJ, make this go away.

When he was in town, we'd often argue over the cost of keeping the house at a frigid temperature. Now, I regretted our disagree-
ments over the small things—and I'd give anything to turn back time.

Klein was giving me the grand tour like he wasn't my captor.
I played along as though there was nothing unusual about a creepy
guy showing me around my prison.

Discreetly, I scanned the rooms for a landline.

Klein led me back into the living room.

A cream-colored couch at the far end had matching armchairs.
A clear glass table in the center reflected the glare of the light fixture
above. The décor had a lackluster style even though no expense had
been spared, screaming, "Don't get too comfortable."

The full-length windows facing the ocean were a saving grace—
the only good thing about this penthouse.

I miss you, AJ.

He'd love this view, being attracted to anything that had to do
with the ocean. The vastness of the watery expanse reflected his depth
of character, his ability to remain calm during any situation—staying
serene through any kind of storm.

Without him, I was drowning in that endless blue.

I wrapped my arms around myself, trying to get warm. "I don't
understand why I'm here."

Klein's sinister presence loomed behind me.

Finally, he spoke. "You'll settle in. This place has the best view
in Marina Del Ray."

"What about my job?" I said bitterly.

"We sent your employer a message letting them know you'll be out for a while."

I pivoted to face him. "You had no right."

"We're handling the details."

Now no one would report me missing.

My back straightened. "I can do more from home."

Klein shook his head. "There's no negotiating with him, I'm afraid. This is your home for now."

He moved toward the glass dining table, which had eight chairs around it as though this place entertained guests when it wasn't housing captives.

Klein rested his hand on a book that lay on the table. "This will guide you through this compelling experience."

I stalked towards him. "What experience?"

"You've been found useful."

"How?"

"Luckily, Mr. Merrill found a purpose for you. You'll work for him."

"Does my brother owe him money?"

"No."

"Then why is this happening?"

"Stella, you'll appear to have lived here for some time, for at least a year. Feel free to fill in the other details however you wish."

"Tell me what's going on!"

"You've already been provided with your assignment."

"The name I was shown?" *De Sade?* Wouldn't they give me any other details to make sense of this madness?

"You can't force me to hurt anyone," I said. "I don't have it in me."

"If we wanted that done, we'd hire a professional." He looked smug. "Someone who never leaves a trace."

I shuddered at the way he'd offered that up.

Klein handed me the book. "This will cover everything you need to know to accomplish your goal."

I walked closer to take a better look, examining the gold embossed cover: *A Submissive's Rule Book.*

My face blanched at the content.

A shiver of uncertainty ran through me. "Is Lance forcing me to become his lover?"

"Goodness, no." Klein responded with surprise. "Not *his*."

I won't have sex.

With anyone.

With distaste, I threw the book on the table. "This is…" Words failed me, panic rising in my chest. "I refuse."

Klein gave me a sympathetic look. "What would happen to AJ?"

I know very well what would happen.

"Help me. Please. Get me out of this."

"Your naivety is extraordinarily appealing. Which is the reason Mr. Merrill has chosen you, I imagine." He gestured toward the bedroom.

"I'm not going in there with you!" I bit out.

He looked disgusted.

I hugged myself tighter. "What's in there?"

"The appropriate dress for tomorrow night."

"I'm going out?"

He gave a shrug. "You may leave the penthouse. However, the consequences of you discussing this situation with anyone have been described."

Yes, they'd made that clear.

I rallied my confidence. "Are you staying?"

"No." He reached into his jacket pocket and brought out a phone, setting it on the table. "For you."

"Bugged?" I jested darkly.

"It is."

But of course. There was no way I'd be given free rein to call for help.

I inhaled sharply. "You prepared this place before I arrived on that yacht?"

He ignored that. "We'll provide more orders tomorrow."

"Orders?"

"Right before you make contact with De Sade."

"Who is he?"

"I'll allow my boss to fill you in on the details."

Klein didn't seem to sense my vitriol. Or maybe he'd grown used to hate. He worked for *him*, that's all I needed to know. But then again, so did my brother. But in my heart, I knew AJ hadn't suspected Merrill was corrupt when he'd been hired.

Klein continued. "Familiarize yourself with every appliance. It's important you know where everything is and how it all works."

"I already hate it here."

He ignored that and strolled toward the remote control resting on the coffee table. He picked it up and directed it toward the TV on the wall. The screen lit up with streaming apps.

"Make yourself at home." He set the remote down. "If there's something you need just let me know."

"My freedom."

"My number's in the phone. The fridge automatically restocks by sending an email out to your local store. They'll leave your supplies outside. Don't communicate with them. We will know."

"What you're doing is illegal, Officer Klein."

"We're aware of that, my dear." He seemed unperturbed. "I'll provide you with your door code. No key required."

"You just take orders from Lance Merrill without questioning them?" I gauged his response.

"For those in his employment, his generosity knows no bounds."

"This is about money to you?" I said, not caring.

"Goodness, no."

It was about power.

"He's a monster," I said flatly.

"Don't let him hear you say that." Klein shook his head. "He considers himself the quintessential gentleman."

"Gentleman?" I repeated sourly.

"He keeps his promises."

That threat caused me to shut my mouth.

"Try on the dress you'll be wearing tomorrow. I need to know if it fits. It's in a box on the bed. Shoes, too."

"How do you know my size?"

"We made a visit to your home in Burbank."

Dread made my chest squeeze tighter. Nausea welled up in my throat at the knowledge I'd been violated by this creepy man who'd gone through my things.

He strolled nonchalantly toward the window. "Read the book, Ms. Adair. Memorize the rules. You'll need to appear convincing." He peered out at the water.

"Why not find someone who's into that sort of thing? Someone who won't give themselves away."

He held my frosty gaze in the window's reflection. "It's better to have someone you own in these kinds of situations."

Own?

Tears stung my eyes, but I refused to let him see me cry. My glare sent silent shards of hate his way.

I couldn't wait for this man to be arrested, to be in court when his conviction was rendered, and I could look into his eyes and see fear.

Finally, Klein turned to face me. "*The Hades* has hosted everyone from presidents to royalty. Mr. Merrill has some of the most influential friends in the world."

They're above the law.

"Tomorrow will be your first visit to Pendulum," he said. "And, Stella, we want you to make the best impression possible."

CHAPTER THREE

Stella

THE ELEVATOR DOORS OPENED ONTO THE EMPTY FOYER OF Dorchester House.

I can't do this.

Yet my feet reluctantly moved toward the exit.

I felt self-conscious in this mini sequin dress. The price tag I'd ripped off proved it was worth a fortune.

This penthouse, these clothes, a reminder that no expense had been spared for what that devious man had in mind. This Alexander McQueen clutch purse made me look like I was going out partying. If anyone glanced my way, they would see no sign of coercion.

When Klein had warned me that I was owned, this was what he meant. They knew I wouldn't do anything to endanger my brother.

Paranoia had set in. I feared they were watching me. I'd scoured the rooms for cameras, not finding any but feeling no less reassured.

I'd hardly slept in that mammoth king-sized bed, tossing and turning under satin sheets with my head denting that perfect pillow.

For tonight, I'd not been in the mood to spend time on my

makeup, merely adding light mascara and eyeliner. I'd washed my hair and then blow-dried it—with a natural shine it fell straight down my back.

Glancing at the blindfold in my hand, I wondered at what point I was meant to put it on, hating the idea of not seeing the dangers around me.

Do what he asks. You have no choice.

What if the man I was meant to be with didn't find me attractive? Our deal was contingent on me following through on seducing some stranger.

A stone of granite settled in my chest at the thought of it.

I should never have accepted the invitation onto *The Hades*. But if I hadn't, I knew what the consequences would have been.

A sleek limo waited at the curb.

Stepping out into the night air, I drew in a breath of courage and walked toward the car. Klein sat in the front seat appearing eerily calm.

A uniformed chauffeur opened the back passenger door and motioned for me to get in.

"I need a second," I said, feeling hesitant to get in.

"We don't want to be late," he chided.

Exhaling slowly, trying to calm my nerves, I lowered my head and climbed into the back of the car.

The chauffeur closed my door and joined Klein in the front. The car navigated away with the quiet engine of an electric vehicle. I glanced back at Dorchester House as though seeing that luxury building for the first time. Strange to feel that tug pulling me back.

Anywhere but here.

A soprano's voice rose out of the speakers, as though Klein wanted to squeeze even more drama out of the night.

Until now, I'd not questioned if *I'd* live through this experience.

I wiped my sweaty palms over the seat, swiping my DNA over the leather. These people would probably think of that, too. Make sure I was disappeared without a trace.

The car took the ramp onto the 405 Freeway. I made a note of the direction, fingernails digging into my palms so I could remain focused. It was a coping mechanism, I suppose—my brain trying to stop me from having a panic attack.

If I screamed, if I pounded on the window, I'd get myself killed. Sitting back, I kept reminding myself that I'd been through so much already. Losing our parents at an early age had made me independent. Being the big sister, I'd learned to take the hits for both of us. But this—this was beyond anything I'd ever experienced.

Within an hour, we took the exit toward Manhattan Beach.

"Miss." The driver turned to glance back at me. "Blindfold on, please."

Reluctantly, I lifted the strip of material and secured the blindfold around my eyes. Maybe this was a good sign I'd be permitted to leave. If I didn't see anyone's faces, then I couldn't be a viable witness.

I tried to keep my breathing steady and even, tried to make sense of what I'd read in the book they'd given me. I'd skimmed through it, but had been unable to focus, reading about sensuality and submission, unable to comprehend what was being asked of me.

I didn't date—not since college. This was going to be hard for me, having to kiss a man I didn't even know.

The car came to a sudden stop.

Not being able to see was worse than I'd imagined. I heard the sound of the car door opening, Klein telling me to hold out my hand and feeling him grasp it, not wanting him to touch me but being reliant on him.

All I had to do was not fall to my knees. Not make a scene. Not draw attention.

"Steps coming up," warned Klein.

With the tip of my heeled shoe, I tapped each step as we ascended to feel the next.

"Door's straight ahead, Ms. Adair," said Klein.

Again, his eerie politeness that never fit the situation.

I heard a large door closing behind us.

Music was playing—Moby's "I Love to Move in Here."

Was this a party?

Peeking below the blindfold, I glimpsed a hardwood floor. Raising my eyes to peek above the top, I could see the glass blown ornaments decorating the space and made out a stained-glass ceiling of blues and oranges and reds. A light fixture behind it brightened the design.

What is this place?

Fingers tugged my blindfold down. They'd caught me spying.

"Stella," said a voice, with that familiar Texas accent.

I moved my head in his direction.

"You look divine," said Lance, his accent a contradiction; friendly, welcoming, yet beneath his warmth I heard a sinister undertone.

"This way." Lance took my arm and led me forward. "You wore the dress," he said quietly. "Looks good on you."

Like I'd had a choice.

Conversations rose over the deep bass of the heady music. A young woman being escorted didn't rouse any suspicion here. Maybe he'd done this before.

We walked for a few minutes, around corners and along noisy hallways. For a few seconds, I thought I heard a couple having sex.

The sound dimmed.

"Take off your blindfold," demanded Lance.

Easing it off, I blinked, my eyes trying to adjust to the dimly lit room.

Lance stood beside a young woman who was dressed in a bodice, her outfit making it clear she was a "submissive." Her dark brown hair cascaded over her shoulders. She wore a glittered masquerade mask, but her interest in me was obvious.

Coming out of this frazzled trance, I was again reminded that Lance held my brother's life in his hands.

I dropped the blindfold to the floor. It was passive-aggressive, but I didn't care.

He stared at it. "You will be afforded all you need to perform your best."

"You never mentioned—"

He snapped up his hand. "Just do as you're told."

In glided a middle-aged woman wearing a silver filagree mask, her brunette hair in a chignon. An elegant bow at the neck of her blue silk blouse and her pencil skirt gave off business vibes.

She assessed me. "New submissive?"

"Yes." Lance watched her reaction. "How are you, Jewel?"

"This needs to go through me," she said, her eyes not leaving mine.

Lance appeared smug. "Heard there's going to be a change in management."

"We'll see," she said. "Not everyone is in agreement with the takeover."

"How far have they gotten?" he asked.

The subject seemed to bother her. "A handshake deal."

"Can you stop it?" he said.

"Let's discuss this outside," she said tersely, glancing back to make sure he was following.

They left the room, closing the door behind them.

I looked to the stranger for reassurance. "What's happening?"

"You're being presented in The Key Chamber."

"What happens in there?"

"You'll be blindfolded again. Remain still. Don't say anything."

"No one touches me?"

She appeared surprised. "That's up to Master Merrill."

Lance was into this lifestyle himself, apparently.

"What's your name?" I asked.

She strolled over to an ornate cabinet. Reaching in, she pulled out a leather collar and a clothes hanger and carried them over to me. "Turn around."

I traced my fingertips over the collar. "I have to wear this?"

She helped me clip it in place around my neck.

I pivoted to face her. "Tell me your name."

"We don't share names."

"Then how do I find you again?"

She looked sheepish. "I was ordered not to talk to you."

"By Merrill? Did he tell you why I'm here?"

"My advice, don't speak unless spoken to."

"Do you want to be here?" I asked her.

"Of course," she said, unconvincingly. "Take off your dress."

"Why?"

"We don't wear dresses here."

"Maybe we should ask Lance."

"He wants you in your underwear. I'm tasked with preparing you."

Not wanting to get her into trouble, I complied, reaching for the catch at my nape, unclipping it and shimmying out of the sparkly material.

She took it from me and slipped it onto a hanger.

I glanced down at my skimpy thong and lacey bra. "I don't get a robe?"

She flashed me a look of surprise as she hung my dress inside the cabinet. "All you have to do is obey."

"Is that what you do?" I watched her reaction, wanting to ask if Lance had something on her, too.

"Don't make him angry, okay?"

"How long have you been here?"

Lance startled us both when he came back into the room.

I folded my arms across my chest to cover my skimpy bra.

"Out," Lance snapped at the girl.

The submissive scurried away without hesitation—the one person who could help me.

With her gone, I turned to him. "This man I'm meeting…"

Lance smirked. "He'll be gentle, at first."

At first?

My forearms pricked. "Why are you making me do this?"

"I have my reasons."

"Is he dangerous?"

"Not in the way you think."

"What does that mean?"

He clenched his jaw. "Submissives never ask questions."

"I'm only pretending to be one," I blurted out. "How long do I have to do this?"

"Until I say otherwise."

"What if De Sade finds out you made me do this?"

"I would advise you not to tell him."

Running would be the wisest decision, but even if I got away, I'd gain my freedom but not AJ's. That would be impossible to live with—knowing I could have saved him by doing what Merrill asked of me tonight.

If I could just wrap my head around what he wanted me to do, I'd come out the other side.

Lance motioned for me to step closer. "Did you read the book?"

"Yes."

"Yes, sir," he corrected.

"Sir." I took a deep breath.

He rested his hands on my shoulders. "Look at me."

An unceasing dread was made worse when I felt his clammy touch on my bare skin. His tall frame towered over me as his eyes traveled over my body, assessing my worthiness.

Doubt crashed through my thoughts. "What if he doesn't like me?"

"He will."

My old life was out of reach, all those ordinary things I'd taken for granted. Maybe I'd never leave the house again. Maybe I'd become a recluse.

I was already halfway there. Too timid to live. Too afraid to die. Those college years still haunted me.

Lance stepped back and pointed to my clutch. "You'll find some red lipstick in there. Put it on."

I hadn't even thought to check inside the purse. With trembling hands, I unclipped it and brought out the gloss, smearing it on my lips.

"Blindfold back on, Stella."

I knelt and retrieved the strip of fine material, glancing up at him as I rose.

His expression was one of fierce pride.

CHAPTER FOUR

Jake

"F OR FUCK'S SAKE," GREYSON RASPED, THE PRESSURE OF my forearm against his throat.

I'd cut off his air.

"Carrington," he managed to squeeze out. "Cease this behavior."

He always did sound old-fashioned. That Oxford education he'd garnered as an American in London had left him with quirky traits—like his penchant for dicky bows and threesomes.

Like me, he wore a masquerade mask, but we'd been to enough events for people to know who we were, regardless.

My best friend was a delicious pervert. He had this young Marlon Brando look about him. Same hair, too. Kind of preppy in a seductive way, which made the submissives dizzy.

I pressed harder.

His pupils dilated with pleasure. He liked what I was doing. I savored this heady combination of control and dominance.

"That's not what this is," I said. "And you fucking know it."

This renowned architect spent hours creating structural masterpieces.

I'd even commissioned Greyson to design my Mulholland home. He'd crafted towering walls and captivating spaces that ushered in the sun during the day and, at night, welcomed the moon. The guy was a genius, and his brilliant mind made him somewhat eccentric. He came from old money but never made it a thing.

He was also a wily bastard.

I had him cornered against the wall, overpowering him with my tall, muscular frame to punish him.

Music by Moby was being blasted throughout Pendulum, a backdrop to our playful rivalry.

Greyson tried to talk.

Lifting my arm, I let him have the air he needed.

"You don't feel the same way about her as I do," he said. "De Sade!"

He rarely called me that—preferring to use Jake or my last name.

Calling me De Sade was his way of deferring to me as a senior Dom. He also knew I secretly hated it.

I stepped back. "You were allowed to fuck Amelia. At no time did I say steal her."

"It just happened." He caressed his throat. "Amelia wants me as her Dom."

Greyson had fallen for the submissive gifted to me by Pendulum during negotiations. Mainly because I'd taken the lead during the meetings.

She'd been entrusted to *me*.

I'd made the mistake of letting Greyson have a taste of Amelia a week ago. He'd fucked her at my place during a meeting with two senior VIPs from Enthrall.

I'd used Amelia to entertain them.

Apparently, one taste of her wasn't enough.

"Amelia should have come to me first," I reasoned.

"You intimidate her."

"Me?" I acted surprised.

"Anyway, you're married."

"Rylee's my ex."

"You act like you're still married."

"What can I say? She's a hard habit to break."

"You still love her." He shook his head. "That makes things hard on the subs you take on."

Running my fingers through my hair, I realized he may be right.

"Where did Rylee go, anyway?" he asked.

"She has a session with Jewel Delany."

He looked intrigued. "Who's playing Domme in that scenario?"

I smirked. "Why? Want to watch?"

Greyson's expression grew serious. "You're going to have to get used to Amelia being mine. She's not coming back to you."

"Seriously?"

He stepped past me, away from the wall. "You just provided a fine demonstration of what you're into."

I let out a sigh. "Treat Amelia right," I said, relenting.

The look on his face told me he'd already fallen in love with her. Of all the men I knew, he'd be the best fit for her. He was perfect for an ingénue looking for love, perfect for a sub who wasn't into pain.

Greyson adjusted his bowtie. "I'll definitely treat her better."

"I imagine you will," I said, grinning.

"The minute they fall in love with you, you dump them."

"Not true." It was, but I wasn't in the mood to admit it.

I'd used Amelia to entice Lotte, to inspire empathy. Her protective traits were of value to us. She was the kind of gifted Domme we needed at Pendulum.

But it had backfired—seemingly spurring Lotte on to make a lifechanging decision. She was now in a serious relationship with a Cole brother and living her best life.

"Let's head back," he said.

"Changing the subject?"

"We won't accomplish much if we're dick waving in here."

That made me chuckle.

"I need a drink," he added.

We left the private chamber and headed back toward the ballroom with the bar. He opened the door and gestured for me to go on ahead, giving me a rueful glance as though wondering if I'd forgiven him.

"You love it when we fight," I told him.

He adjusted his pants, proving my assertion that he was addicted to drama. His erection had just been pushing against my thigh so there was no hiding the truth.

"Can you believe this place is ours?" he said.

"The ink isn't dry on the contract yet," I said cautiously.

"I'm still looking for an interior designer for this place."

Greyson loved to create inspiring scenes, as he called them.

I wrapped an arm around his shoulders. "It's going to take all our resources to pull Pendulum from the brink."

"They're resistant to change."

"They have no fucking choice."

"They're used to getting anything they want."

We didn't want them setting up the same club in a different location. That would defeat the objective. We wanted to shatter its current reputation and put it on the map as a club to be respected—not the viper pit it was now. We didn't need places like this ruining our reputations.

We strolled through the nearly empty ballroom.

Along the far wall stretched a long glass window allowing guests a view into a private chamber. Other members could observe the play on the other side, but only the elite got to enter.

Lights were dimmed. A St. Andrew's Cross was positioned in the center of the room.

Inside, seated in two rows of chairs, were twenty tuxedo-clad billionaires. The crowd in there collectively owned enough money to possess half the world.

Greyson and I approached a masked Atticus Sinclair, who was just as fascinated with what was about to go on behind the glass.

The three of us stood shoulder to shoulder, peering in, seemingly here for the thrill of it.

Atticus held his tattooed hands together as though purveying the scene with authority. His ink always piqued interest in his new patients, but when this brilliant surgeon saved their lives, they considered his hands sacred.

He'd been checking out the lower chambers. Perhaps his quiet mood reflected what he'd seen.

"Find anything interesting?" coaxed Greyson.

Atticus pointed upward. "How many floors?"

"Eight," I said, "with one underground."

"I think there might be ten instead."

"No, there's nine," said Greyson, and with his eye for structure, he'd know.

Atticus' expression showed he was unconvinced.

"Why would they keep a floor hidden?" I asked, watching his reaction.

"Exactly," he said.

Atticus scared the subs to death. I suppose we all did from time to time.

We all shared a mutual respect for our professions—Atticus the talented surgeon, Greyson, a master of skyscrapers, and me, the retired football player.

They were both Carolina fans, the team I'd played for. We had that passion in common, too. They'd watched me play football long before they'd met me.

Before my fate was sealed during a game by way of a three-hundred-pound linebacker who broke my neck.

Their friendship was the only reason I was walking now. Their constant support helped see me through the worst time of my life. They'd told our mutual friend Cameron Cole and he'd visited me in the hospital. That uncannily brilliant psychiatrist saved my life in his own indomitable way. Cole had known just what I'd needed to help me walk again.

But that was years ago.

They also respected the fact that I'd pushed that world far away. Hell, this former quarterback didn't have one thing on display at home to remind him he'd even won a Super Bowl.

We'd invited Cameron to join us in this endeavor to turn Pendulum around. Because if anyone could see the chess moves before anyone else, it was him.

He would never step foot in here, which was the arrangement we had agreed upon to protect Cole and his family's tea empire at all costs.

It was just us three navigating these hallways and secret sessions as best we could.

Our attention was drawn to the back of the chamber, where a door opened and a lone submissive was escorted into the room.

The blindfolded young woman, clad only in her underwear, was led by a Dom into the center to stand before the St. Andrew's Cross. Her lacey bra and thong gave the impression she'd stepped in off the street.

The sight of her tall, lithe frame sent a visceral shockwave through me. *God*, her mouth was plump and so damn kissable. She was a raven-haired seductress, her olive-hued complexion exquisite.

I couldn't tear my gaze away.

"They're going to auction her," said Atticus.

For some reason, a feeling of uneasiness swept over me.

I needed to see her eyes. I was desperate to tug that strip of silk off her face that prevented me from seeing into her soul.

Atticus squeezed my shoulder. He shared my concern. The woman seemed out of place, dressed down to appear innocent. Alone in a room with a pack of wolves.

That rough looking Dom towered over her, his tuxedo stretching uncomfortably over his immense physique—the suit obviously off the rack and not tailored. It led me to believe he was staff. The VIPs were known to fly in their tailors from Europe on private jets. This guy with his ill-fitting suit wasn't one of them.

But the striking submissive standing beside him appeared demure, her high cheekbones flushing brightly, her glossy raven hair falling straight over slim shoulders.

What kind of man would put a leather choker on that slender neck? It deserved to be draped in diamonds. Even without seeing her eyes, she had slain me.

I had to fight the urge to smash through the glass and claim her.

"Have you seen her before?" asked Greyson.

I shook my head. "No. I'd have remembered."

CHAPTER FIVE

Jake

THE INGÉNUE HAD EVERYONE FIXATED ON HER. NOT JUST me.

The room had fallen quiet.

All three of us were considered lions at Chrysalis, that Bel Air manor resting high above a canyon. But here at Pendulum, those men reigned supreme as kings of dark fuckery. Interfering with an elite's pursuits could end in ruin.

We'd always considered ourselves knights in shining armor ready to save the vulnerable. But there were limits to what we could accomplish.

The Dom behind the glass was giving a monologue over why *this one* was special. We could all see that. Didn't need to hear his banal words.

But why blindfold her?

My gut told me not to walk away. Not to pretend I was compliant in anything sinister. We might be willing to get down and dirty, but there were lines we wouldn't cross.

"I'll go in," I said.

"We should all go," said Atticus.

"We need to handle this tactfully." I shared a glance with them to make my point.

Greyson was right, these members were used to doing things a certain way, however they wanted.

There might be consequences for going against them, but after seeing the way that woman was trembling, I didn't have a choice.

"Good luck," Atticus said, with an edge of humor.

With a nod of conviction, I walked away from them and entered the side door.

I strolled casually toward the Dom, who was introducing the submissive like she was the greatest find—because she was.

I was unsure just how he intended to showcase her. Not waiting to find out, I motioned for a break in the theatrics and scanned the audience to rule out any chance of a sudden threat. I half-expected one of them to stand up and make a scene.

None of them moved.

I turned my attention to the Dom. "Can I have a word?" I ignored the stares from the audience.

The Dom tensed. "Afterwards."

There wasn't going to be an afterwards.

"What's your name?" I asked, closing the gap between us.

"Chase," he said with a smirk. "And I already know who you are."

"Great." Then maybe he'd guessed he'd be the first to be fired. "We need to talk."

His eyes reflected a spark of arrogance.

The young woman was close to perfect for a sub in the way she stood straight and still, but the way she hugged herself proved her uncertainty.

Unless that was an act.

"I'm not negotiating with you," I told him.

He turned to the audience. "Give us five minutes, gentlemen."

They rose from their chairs with a cacophony of annoyed

rumblings and then ambled out, finally giving us the room. There would be plenty more scenes for them to enjoy.

So, fuck 'em.

After the last man left, I zeroed in on the brunette. "Take off your blindfold."

Her Dom looked pissed off.

"I respect that this is your session," I said, trying to placate him. "But we observed doubt."

He shot a glance at Atticus and Greyson on the other side of the glass.

"I'm not afraid," she said softly.

A strange thing to say.

I tugged at the strip of material covering her eyes. "Take this off."

The submissive eased the blindfold off her face and blinked at me, showing pure vulnerability. Her almond shaped eyes and slender nose were exquisite.

I stared at the achingly beautiful creature.

She had an innocence mixed with a rare sensuality. And all she was doing was standing there. She'd be a goddess in the making with the right training.

They'd tried to make her appear ordinary. But there was nothing ordinary about her.

She scanned the chairs, wide-eyed and seemingly panicked— maybe just now realizing the danger. She swallowed hard when she saw Atticus and Greyson peering in through the glass.

"They're with me," I said. "What's your name?"

"Um…"

"Stella," the Dom answered for her.

She forced a weak smile—out of fear or respect or self-preservation. She was hard to read. I'd always had the ability to ascertain the goodness in someone. Beneath all the mystery, I could sense she was special. He'd been right about that.

"Is she yours?" I suppressed my envy.

When he remained silent, I added, "Then who?"

"Hear you're now a senior Dom here?" he said, drawing out the tension. "Master De Sade," he said with indifference.

Stella inhaled sharply, causing us both to snap our attention over to the wildly blushing girl with the prettiest eyes.

It wasn't an unusual response when a sub heard my name. I'd garnered enough of a reputation with my penchant for pain, which was why they called me *De Sade*. It was a reference to the Marquis de Sade, a French nobleman. In my fucking defense, I was a much better man than that historical figure. But the name had stuck, and I'd been unable to shake it.

I ignored his jibe at me.

Because *she* drew my focus like a violent sunrise, a blinding beauty scorching me with the vision of her.

"How long have you been a submissive?" I asked her.

Stella's brows furrowed as she glanced at the Dom, waiting for him to answer.

"I'm talking to you," I snapped.

"Long enough," said Chase.

Movement on the other side of the window caught my attention. I noticed a figure walking behind Atticus and Greyson. Lance Merrill had a submissive crawling beside him. His curiosity had been aroused as to what was going on inside this chamber.

Stella would no doubt attract his interest, too.

Great, that's all we needed—him barging in and claiming her.

After divorcing his crazy wife, Lance had taken a break from his political aspirations. He'd been left with enough time on his hands to cause more chaos—and had earned the nickname "Pinhead" from Hellraiser, for the obvious reasons.

Lance paused in front of the glass and glanced in at the scene. The expression on his face was strangely one of satisfaction. To my surprise, he decided not to enter the room, but turned and led his submissive away.

I focused on the girl again. "You're scared. That's why we halted this."

Her Dom shrugged. "You like them scared."

That wasn't true.

I had a penchant for pain, but rarely inflicted it on unseasoned subs. My kind of session was reserved for distinguished women mature enough to communicate their boundaries.

I gazed at Stella. "Are you aware of what this room is reserved for?"

She didn't respond. Either she was shy, or someone had ordered her into silence.

"What were you told?" I pushed for an answer.

She turned to Chase.

"Look at me," I said. "This room is reserved for auctions."

A puzzled expression crossed her face.

A multitude of questions streamed through my jagged thoughts. I wondered if she had any idea of the type of debauchery he'd had in mind for her.

She had to know, right? Only my gut told me she was out of her depth.

"We need to resume the session." Chase's focus swept over the empty chairs.

"I've seen no evidence that she's ready," I said.

He tapped her left arm to get her attention. "Down."

Stella knelt slowly, her expression one of confusion mixed with fear. Her eyes filled with tears that verged on spilling, triggering a protective response in me.

Chase looked down at her. "Our new lamb."

To the slaughter. That's what he meant, the fucker.

"I want it to be him," she said softly, peering up at me.

This wouldn't be the first time a sub had thrown herself at me. Right up until they discovered my wicked ways.

Chase's smile didn't reach his eyes. "Let me call the gentlemen back in."

The men about to return weren't gentle. Which meant anything could happen to her.

"It's over," I told him. "Session's cancelled."

He glared at me in anger.

I considered giving her to a dominatrix for the evening. "Where did you train?" I asked.

Her teeth were chattering. "You wouldn't know him."

"She's from a private house," said Chase.

None of this rang true.

"Up," I ordered.

She sprang to her feet clumsily. "Sir, choose me."

Her plea caused my dick to harden. She was like forbidden fruit, with the kind of beauty poets tripped over themselves to describe.

"You don't own this place yet," said Chase.

"Get the fuck out."

He turned and stormed off.

After he left the room, Stella appeared even more frazzled. "Does that mean I'm yours?" she asked softly.

"You don't want to be mine," I said. *Not really.*

This submissive may look like my type, but when the truth spilled out during a session, she'd undoubtedly crumble—proving useless to a Dom like me.

As though needing a second opinion on the matter, I turned to face Atticus and Greyson, who both shook their heads *no.*

CHAPTER SIX

Stella

I T WAS HIM, THE MAN I WAS MEANT TO SEDUCE.

He'd reacted with a searing protectiveness, his manner so fierce I'd almost forgotten to be afraid of him.

Once Chase had left, De Sade relaxed a little. I guessed his age to be around forty. But a young forty, because he looked fit beneath his tuxedo.

He led me out of the auction chamber and guided me into an empty private room, different from the one Lance had taken me into. The dark furniture and gentlemen's club décor gave off an old boy's vibe—the smoky air thick like the tension.

I'd not expected De Sade to be tall and handsome, with broad shoulders and a wide chest. His tuxedo fit him perfectly. Even with his mask, I could see his chiseled cheekbones and strong jawline. His dreamy brown eyes pierced through me.

I'd felt the pulse of his strength in that room. His interest in me seemed just as compelling as my interest in him. It was the way his brows furrowed in fascination. The way his eyes reflected concern as he assessed me. He'd genuinely cared about what they might do to me.

He reached out to tip my chin up and then withdrew his hand. "What the fuck are you wearing?" he growled. "This isn't in the dress code."

"I was told to wear this."

"By whom?"

"Another submissive."

"Name?"

"She refused to tell me."

"That doesn't sound right, Stella."

Maybe it was his cologne. Or his toned physique beneath his flawless tuxedo, but he was awe-inspiring. He had the kind of presence that caused everyone to look his way when he entered a room.

He gave me a stern look. "You have no idea how close you came…"

"To what?" I cringed after I said it.

"Exactly."

In the seconds I had to catch my breath, I considered how I'd gotten here. How my life had imploded in the worst kind of way. I was inside a place filled with people and yet I'd never felt lonelier.

I needed him to tell me everything would be okay. I had the uncanny desire to crush myself against him as though he alone could save me. Like this man would know how to make my problems disappear.

I had to accept the searing truth that the only person who could save me was *me*.

De Sade's cufflinks glinted beneath the lights, shining like a beacon of hope.

I breathed in his expensive scent, recalling his show of kindness— and wondering what he'd done to make enemies.

He brushed a strand of hair out of my face, his fingers sending a tingle into my scalp. "You've gone quiet."

Closing my eyes, I sank into this lie. "I'm glad it's you."

"Want to sit?" De Sade gestured to a high-backed chair.

I shook my head.

The door remained partially open. He'd done that to make me feel safe, or so I'd assumed.

Maybe, just maybe, he didn't deserve Lance's wrath.

"Am I yours now?" I whispered.

He came closer. "Well, you're certainly turned on by me."

I snapped my gaze down and saw a damp spot on my panties. He seemed to find it endearing—my body reacting to him with desire.

It made this easier, I suppose.

He nudged me backward, trapping me between him and the wall, caging me in with his muscled arms on either side of my head. He had an impressive height and build—the kind of body any woman would be drawn to.

"Where did you come from?" he asked huskily.

His tone of voice caused every cell in my body to feel electrified. "I live in Marina Del Rey."

"That's not what I meant."

It would be so easy to get lost in his dreamy brown gaze.

His jawline flexed with sensual tension. He made me go weak when he dragged his teeth over his full bottom lip, as though he wanted me, but was trying to resist.

His heavy-lidded stare devoured me. "Talk to me, Stella."

The way he spoke my name caused a shiver to run up my spine, prickling the fine hairs on my forearms.

He noticed my response. "You've been in the scene a while?"

"Two years." I broke his stare.

"Keep talking."

"Nothing else to add."

"I get to say if you stay or leave Pendulum."

"No, you don't."

"Excuse me?"

"It's not like you own the place," I teased.

"Soon."

Which meant he was obsessed with this scene and was no better than Lance Merrill. He, too, was a man to watch out for—and be afraid of.

"Give me a reason to let you stay." He ran a fingertip up my arm.

It set my skin alight with invisible sparks. I suddenly realized I was trapped in here with a stranger.

These were the consequences of my actions. Coming here had set off a chain of events. Lance had made it sound like I'd have to work hard at grabbing this man's attention. Yet De Sade seemed just as fascinated with me.

He was charismatic in the sexiest way. The kind of man I'd never meet in normal life—because he lived in a different stratosphere. Sure, AJ mingled now and again with clients, but we were under no illusion that we'd be considered anything but staff.

"Let's try this." He tilted his head thoughtfully. "What are you into?"

"In bed?"

His smirk widened into a grin, and he looked even more gorgeous.

"Um…you know."

"No, Stella, that's why I'm asking."

"What are you into?"

"This is about you."

"I'm a voyeur," I burst out.

Just watching would also keep me safe from being touched by strangers.

"That obsession we can feed," he said.

I reasoned I could ask him to take me home if it became too much. De Sade had to want to see me again. Because I was determined to make this work, have Lance see I was compliant. I had to make De Sade like me.

Want me.

"Are you going to take me now?"

He curled his knuckles and brushed my cheek. "You mean fuck you?"

I shuddered at the thought of having him inside me.

"That's a curious question."

"I like you." I brushed my fingers over his hand seductively.

"Does someone own this cunt?" he said. His hand pulled away

from my touch and glided down to caress my panties, his fingertip stroking the thin material over my clit—sending a pang of pleasure there.

"I asked you a question." He flicked my clit. "Who owns this?"

I steadied myself. "Me."

"For now."

Why did he have to say it like that, with that seductive voice in that masterful tone?

"I know you've heard of me, Stella."

I felt a sensual stirring deep in my belly. An unfamiliar excitement at the way his eyes roamed over my body. His control reminded me of what I'd read in that book. This was the kind of domination people craved.

And for the first time, I got it.

He leaned in. "I can smell your arousal."

My clit flooded with pleasure as though his touch had returned to my panties. Yet he merely seduced with his voice.

"If I fuck you, it will be hard," he warned. "Do you like to be taken by force?"

"I'm not ready," I blurted out.

For that. *I meant for that.*

"What were you doing in that room, then?" he said flatly.

"Obeying."

"No Dom right now?"

"No, sir."

"Let's rectify that."

"Why?"

"Because you need someone to watch over you."

"Why not you?"

He reached for my hand and led me across the room. I scurried along beside him, trying to keep up with his long strides.

We ended up in a female changing room, where twenty or so submissives were sitting at vanities with mirrors and scattered makeup here and there before each one. They were getting ready for something.

A few of them glanced our way. It was impossible to read their faces behind their filigree masks. All were dressed differently than the submissive Lance had tasked with getting me ready.

"Everyone out!" De Sade ordered.

The room emptied quickly.

Against the far wall stood a clothes rack with nothing but bodices in every size and color. Some were ornate, others simple.

De Sade gestured to them. "Find your size."

Stepping forward, I sifted through them until I found one that might fit. Lifting it off the rack, I showed it to him for his approval.

"Turn around." He unclipped my bra, his hand warm on my spine, and then threw it down, leaving me vulnerable.

I hugged the bodice to my chest to cover my exposed breasts.

He tapped my arm to have me turn around. "Let's keep your panties on."

"You like this one?" I said, trying to hide my nervousness.

"Arms up."

I obeyed, revealing my pert nipples, and hoping he'd not detect my shyness. I was unused to bearing it all or having a man I'd just met touch me.

Not since…

I remembered those college years when my love life had begun and ended in a matter of weeks over the cruelest lie from a boyfriend who never was. Karl had dated me for all the wrong reasons.

I pushed that awful memory away.

With the ease of a man who'd done this many times before, De Sade dressed me in the beaded bodice. He tucked my breasts beneath the material with a gentle hand. A shudder of arousal slithered to my pussy when his palm brushed over a nipple.

"Turn around," he ordered.

I spun to turn my back on him.

He secured the satin bindings along my spine, tugging the strip of silk, pulling me back now and again.

"Who gave you this collar?" he asked.

"A submissive."

"Usually, it comes from your Dom. Chase didn't try to claim you?"

"No."

"The guy's an idiot."

Lance had ordered Chase to take me into the Key Chamber. To deliver me into the arms of De Sade. A secret I was forbidden to share.

"Who did you say you trained with?" De Sade patted my ass when he was done.

I spun around. "Why do you need to know?"

"Why do I sense you're untrained?"

I raised my chin. "I am trained."

"Offer me yourself," he said, a glint of mischief in his eyes.

"I'm yours, sir."

Doubt crossed his features. "Who brought you here?"

"I came alone."

The music stopped, and then changed to something ethereal.

"What exactly do you like to watch?" His gaze narrowed. "Specifically."

"What turns you on?"

His thumb caressed my cheek. "Blushing?"

"Choose what you want me to see."

He hesitated and then said, "Okay, we can do it that way."

I bit my lip in doubt. I didn't belong here. He had to see that. Whatever he was about to show me was probably erotic.

"You may walk." The tip of his tongue rested at the corner of his mouth.

"Where?"

"That's me saying you don't have to crawl."

"Right." Glad of that, I said, "After you, sir."

"Walk beside me," he said. "I need to keep an eye on you."

We strolled side by side down a hallway.

He paused and gave me an amused smile. "You've already broken several rules."

"Which ones?"

"I shouldn't have to tell you."

A flash of intuition hit me. "I'm meant to kneel before we enter the room, and crawl in?"

"Clearly."

"Do you want me to?"

"No." He gestured for me to proceed. "In you go."

"You first, Master."

That seemed to please him. But he motioned for me to enter first anyway. He peered at me beneath his long lashes, seemingly enjoying this.

Swallowing my doubt, I went into the room.

Exquisite music met me as I entered a darkened chamber. I tried not to gape in surprise at the exotic scene of four musicians playing in the center, three violinists and a man sitting in a chair playing cello—all of them wearing latex. The hypnotic sight of them was as mesmerizing as their instruments.

De Sade came to stand beside me.

And then I saw them, at the back of the room.

Several naked women were making out with each other on a table, their moans beginning to rise above the string quartet. They were unabashedly having sex in front of a crowd of twenty or so smartly dressed men.

One of the gentlemen had a submissive at his feet sucking him off.

A woman on the table had her legs splayed while two of the women pleasured her. They were leaning in and taking turns at her pussy.

It was impossible not to be turned on at the erotic sight of them. I'd heard of such parties, but never considered I'd ever be able to attend one.

De Sade's intensity burned through me. He was watching my reaction.

CHAPTER SEVEN

Stella

I TURNED MY BACK ON THE EROTIC SCENE THAT HAD ME blushing wildly.

Pretending to be more interested in what was happening at the bar, I recognized the two guys who'd avidly watched me from behind the glass twenty minutes ago. De Sade had reassured me they were with him, and I'd tried to judge what kind of man he was from the look of his friends. One of them, the one with ink on his hands, appeared intimidating.

De Sade continued to study me with intensity. "That's your type?" He'd caught my line of sight.

"His name's Atticus."

"I want to stay with you," I said.

"Sure you don't want an introduction?" asked De Sade.

A shudder went through me. I couldn't move, couldn't breathe. Couldn't see anything but spots floating in my vision. "Not tonight, sir," I managed to say.

"Maybe I'll watch."

I swallowed hard. "Watch what?"

"Him choke you."

"I wouldn't like that," I blurted out.

"What do you like?"

"What are you into?" I held my breath.

"Dark play."

My vision blurred. A cold sweat broke out on my forehead.

He took my hand and led me in the opposite direction.

"Where are we going, sir?"

He continued to lead me at a fast pace through the building, all the way to the foyer, which I recognized. The colorful glass ceiling threw beautiful shadows over the entrance.

De Sade shrugged out of his tuxedo jacket and wrapped it around my shoulders. It swamped me, covering my body completely. Which was a good thing because he took my hand again and pulled me out into the warm night air. Any car driving by might see me.

I felt relieved to be out of there, but at the same time a part of me wished I'd had the courage to explore a little more.

"Where are we going?" I shivered with uncertainty.

"Home."

"Okay."

"Yours." He guided me toward a yellow Lamborghini.

De Sade opened the passenger door and I climbed in, admiring the shiny interior as I settled on the comfy seat. I pulled on the seatbelt and then became mesmerized by the gorgeous, intimidating man strolling around the front of the car.

He gave me a heart stopping smile.

Maybe I had successfully seduced him. It was hard to tell from his demeanor.

De Sade climbed in. "Marina Del Rey?"

"Yes."

He hung his head. "Why can't it be closer?"

"I can Uber."

"Let's hope you're interesting."

"Feeling is mutual. You spoiled my fun."

"Nice try, Cinderella."

I shot back. "Nice car."

"I think so."

"What woman could resist a man who drives a 'Prickster 900.'"

He realized I was joking. "You've certainly rallied your courage."

"I feel safe with you."

"We need to work on that." He peeled off his mask and threw it into the back of the car. God, he was even more handsome than I'd imagined. His nine o'clock shadow gave him a dangerous edge.

I racked my brain, trying to recall where I'd seen him before. "Have we met?"

"Doubt it." With the press of a button, he started the engine.

The Lamborghini took off.

He pushed another button on the front panel and Mick Jagger's voice came out of the speakers. Apparently, he was into The Rolling Stones.

"Showing your age," I said.

"I liked you better when you were scared," he shot back.

"You're into that, then?" I pushed. "Scaring young women."

"I'm into bitches who keep their mouths shut."

"If that's you flirting with me," I said, my voice husky, "might have to try harder."

He gave me a sideways glance and it was so damn seductive; he oozed sensuality.

De Sade turned the music up, making it impossible for us to talk. He drove along the freeway with the ease of a man comfortable with fast cars and changing lanes at breakneck speed.

I suddenly recalled who he reminded me of—Jake Carrington, that Carolina quarterback who'd fallen off the face of the earth a few years back. De Sade looked a little older than him but had the same build.

I had to strategize to make sure this wasn't our last interaction, even though I was a little nervous about having to explore his kink. I turned to glance at his backseat and saw the plastic container with the football stickers.

Oh, my God.

De Sade was Jake Carrington.

"What's that?" I said, raising my voice over the song blaring from the speakers.

He turned the music down.

"Football gear." He used the rearview mirror to look at what I was referring to. "On weekends, I teach football to inner city kids."

It was too late to pull back on my surprise. "So, you're not all bad, then?"

"'Bout ninety-nine percent of me is high-grade wicked." He winked as he navigated off the freeway. "What street?"

"Ocean Front Way." I pointed toward the tall building.

"Nice." He glanced my way. "How long have you lived there?"

"A while."

"Live alone?"

"Yes," I answered, feeling anxious.

"I'll escort you to your door," he said, as though he'd sensed my uneasiness.

"Where do you live?"

"Mulholland."

"That's a great area."

"If you don't mind the traffic." Tension flexed along his jawline. "Are you at Pendulum hoping to snag a sugar daddy?"

I'd given myself away that I didn't belong. "No."

"I'm not judging."

"You're more my type." I threw him a flirty glance. "And you're not a billionaire."

"How do you know that?"

"I know where I've seen you before."

"This can be our little secret." He arched a brow. "Don't make me hunt you down and end you."

I ignored the threat. "Why do they call you De Sade?"

"No reason." He didn't sound convincing.

"I know this much—you're a man who knows what he likes."

"I like extraordinary experiences."

His words sent a shiver through me. "So do I."

"Is that so, Stella?" He slowed the car and pulled up outside the building, gliding into a guest parking spot. "What's your last name?"

"Adair." I unclipped my seatbelt. "Will I see you again?"

He flinched. "I'm not looking for a sub."

"Maybe I can change your mind?"

"The scene we just witnessed appeared strange to you." His fingertips tapped the steering wheel, as though he were lost in thought.

"Why do they call it Pendulum?"

He looked surprised. "You don't know?"

I turned in my seat to face him.

"No comment." He opened the driver's door and strolled around the front of the car to let me out. There were only seconds left for me to read this man right. To sense what I could do to keep him interested in me.

I took his hand, and he helped me out onto the curb.

We entered Dorchester House through the front entrance. Jake looked around, eyebrows raised as though impressed with the luxury setting. No expense spared here.

I was glad no one else was around to see me in his jacket, wearing little else but the bodice I'd walked off with. I hadn't remembered to retrieve the dress Lance had forced me to wear, and I really didn't care.

De Sade punched the elevator button and the doors slid open. He followed me inside and the doors closed.

"You own a place here?" he said.

"Yes." I'd never been comfortable lying.

He seemed to catch my reaction.

I stared at him. "Tell me what you want. I'll do it now."

"Cameras." He pointed upward.

I bit my lip.

"You're into that?" he jested.

I hesitated to answer.

He shook his head, amused. Probably because he'd seen no evidence of my kink. I was just a scared little girl swamped in his jacket.

Reaching for his hand, I brought it up to my mouth, seductively suckling on each finger.

"Careful, Stella."

This was easily the most daring thing I'd done in years.

He leaned in as though to kiss my throat.

Ding.

The elevator stopped on my floor.

He pulled away as the doors slid open.

We walked forward to the door of the penthouse. I used the code to enter and led him into the living room.

I felt a jolt of terror that I'd lured Jake here only for him to be attacked. If we stayed by the door, I could let him out quickly if we were surprised by someone.

He scanned the room and then turned his attention back to me.

"Thank you for this." I let his jacket slip off my shoulders and handed it back to him seductively. "What should I do about this bodice?"

"Keep it." He slipped his tuxedo jacket back on.

"I appreciate the lift home. Quite a 'Prickster' you have there."

Taking two steps forward, he trapped me between him and the front door. "Be more careful next time."

"I like risks."

"You mean like this?" He reached down and his thumb ran the length of my pussy through the material, caressing my labia, his touch causing my clit to swell. I'd never been so turned on.

His hand moved away. I needed it back on that perfect spot.

This was something I could do.

Reaching down, I shimmied my thong over my hips. Then stepped out of them, leaving myself bare down there.

Jake studied me. "That could be construed as consent."

"It is," I said breathlessly.

He cupped my face in his hands and leaned down to kiss me. "I can't."

"Why?"

He stepped back, his face showing the disappointment he was feeling.

"Thought you were divorced?"

He looked intrigued. "Who told you?"

"Can't recall."

"Convenient."

"A sub mentioned it," I said quickly, trying to cover my deceit.

Maybe he was the only person who could help me get my brother back. Maybe he'd have the resources to protect me. But right now, telling him why he was here would be a perilous move.

I turned up the seduction with a sultry gaze, psyching myself up to have sex with a stranger. "Kiss me."

He glanced around the room as though looking for clues. "Boyfriend?"

"No."

"That surprises me."

"I need this," I whispered. "I need you."

"Stella, are you asking me to make you come?"

A whimper escaped my lips.

"Spread your thighs."

I widened my legs so his hand could slip between them, inhaling sharply at the touch of his finger finding my clit again.

I braced for discomfort, which was always inevitable.

"Only good girls get to be fingerfucked," he teased. "After your lack of obedience tonight, you have to earn it."

My frantic nod gave him permission to do it anyway. His touch offered the right amount of pressure on my swelling nub.

He circled my clit slowly, sparking pure pleasure—a sensation I'd never experienced before.

Peering down, I watched the hypnotic motion of his steady flicking, mesmerized by the shimmer of his Cartier wristwatch. The way his white sleeve peeked beneath the fine material of his black tuxedo. The way he honored what I'd asked for, what I needed.

"Sir, I want more."

"Then spread your legs wider." He made it an order.

I obeyed. Lulled by the intense pleasure, my head fell back against the door, eyes closing, my arousal dampening his fingers as my sighs grew louder.

"Hands by your sides."

I did as he asked and tried to recall what I'd read to make me more convincing as a submissive. "Thank you, sir."

He dipped a fingertip into me.

I clenched it.

"Your cunt's tight, but responds well," he purred in my ear, withdrawing his finger in a cruel tease. "Hands on your labia to spread them for me."

Stunned with how slutty my behavior seemed, I did as he asked, my fingers easing back my folds with a shockwave of blossoming pleasure.

He slid two fingers inside me. "How does that feel?"

I'd been waiting for the discomfort, but it never came. He merely glided gently in and out, knowing the exact pressure to use, the right pace, the rhythm making me heady as his finger pressed against that exact right spot, making my thighs tremble.

The blinding orgasm snatched my breath away as I stared into the mysterious eyes of a man who was keeping me enraptured. We held each other's gaze as I shared this experience with him. I'd never come this hard, or this long.

His fingers slowed, causing the pleasure to intensify. His thumb slid to my clit, and he delivered a crescendo of pleasure.

"Oh, God," I moaned at this enduring orgasm.

I came harder, my toes curling, my body racked with tremors as though awakening for the first time. Shuddering and shaking, I reached up to grip his arm for support, feeling boneless as he continued to strum.

Euphoria made me grin.

"You didn't ask for permission to come."

My smile faded. "Sir?"

"Your pussy is responsive, but your behavior is appalling," he said, his voice deep and commanding.

"Sorry, sir."

He withdrew his hand. "If I had more time, I'd spank you."

His words sent me into sensual oblivion, my eyes fluttering at how good this game felt. Unable to speak, I tried to catch my breath.

He suckled on his wet fingers.

I didn't know it could feel this good. That a man would know how to make a woman come in such an epic way.

Jake reached out and played with a strand of my hair. "Never compromise on your pleasure, Stella. If he's not making you come, don't fake it."

"Who?"

"Whoever is lucky enough to call you theirs." He glanced around. "What is it you do?"

"Makeup artist."

"Are you an influencer?"

"No, not yet. Maybe one day when I'm more confident." I cringed at hearing myself say it.

He seemed to mull over what I'd said.

"I have to see you again," I blurted out.

He sighed. "I'm afraid that's not going to happen. Honesty is essential in these kinds of games."

"I want to play again."

He gave me a smug smile.

I suppressed my embarrassment. "What do you do?"

"Along with some friends, we purchase companies and turn them into multi-million-dollar franchises."

"Is that club one of them?"

"Pendulum is a totally different animal."

Swallowing hard, I fought the urge to beg him.

"Excuse me." He reached for my arm and pulled me aside so he could get to the door. "It was great to meet you, Stella."

He gave me a look of sympathy, and I realized that I'd failed to seduce him.

Instead, he'd seduced *me* with the ease of a gentleman who had his own secrets and obsessions.

"Jake, I want to give you my number."

"I'd run if I were you." He opened the door. "Enjoy the rest of your evening."

"What am I meant to do now?" After he'd delivered the kind of intimacy reserved for lovers.

"Take a bath," he said. "Count your lucky stars you escaped Hades."

Wait, did he mean the club or Lance's yacht?

He walked out the door and strolled down the long hallway without looking back.

I called after him. "You know where I live. If you're ever in the area."

He stepped into the elevator and turned to face me. I held his gaze until the doors closed.

It was as though neither of us wanted to part, but we had no choice.

Yet I couldn't move from where I stood in the open doorway— like it was possible to mentally persuade him to return.

As my adrenaline dissipated, I closed the door and hurried over to the window where I could see Jake's parked car.

A minute later, he strolled toward his Lamborghini. As he opened the car door, he glanced up toward my floor and found my window. Then he shook his head as though trying to clear his mind.

His sports car took off.

The man I was destined to seduce was one of the most gorgeous men I'd ever met. A part of me was relieved that he'd gotten away.

Now all I had to do was face the tyrant who'd set me up with him.

CHAPTER EIGHT

Jake

I RETURNED TO PENDULUM HAVING LOST THE EVENING TO chivalry. Strolling down the corridors with Harry Styles' music rocking the mood, I once more mused at how time had lost its place here.

The dark delights it offered were too many to count.

Temptation comes in many forms. My new favorite one was elevating a new submissive to the heights of precious sin.

I'd had fun watching Stella's response in her penthouse, savoring her pleasure as she came. The way her jaw had slackened, her eyelids heavy as she'd whimpered through her climax.

Without asking for permission to come—I'd noted that, too.

I'd mastered the art of judging which ones were worth risking everything for, and she might be that woman. Still, Stella Adair was too sweet an ingénue to get close to—as much as her exquisite body and face taunted me.

Anyway, I still clutched at the idea of rekindling what Rylee and I once had. It was a love I'd grown dependent on. She'd been there when my life had spiraled out of control on that fateful Sunday, imploding after a career-ending injury.

Both she—and this lifestyle—had saved me. Maybe that's why letting her go was so difficult. She'd stood by me.

Just as I had crimson tastes, Rylee had complicated needs, too. Which made us a tangled couple.

We'd trusted each other to do the right thing. Given each other the freedom to make decisions without repercussions. Our marriage had burned hot and heavy. Though in the end, our mutual needs had driven us apart.

Her exotic desires and my passionate kinks clashed from time to time. But we kept coming back to each other.

Love and hate were the same as far as I could tell. Two extremes provoking the same emotions, the same sense of aliveness.

I didn't like the idea of Rylee being here at Pendulum, to be honest. But saying that to her would make me sound like a sexist asshole.

I found Greyson and Atticus in one of the first-floor chambers. Two pretty submissives knelt before Atticus, their masks off.

They were peering up at him respectfully, deep in conversation with him—which you didn't see much around here. He was asking them questions about Pendulum.

Atticus glanced at me and then resumed his gentle interrogation. He was asking how long they'd been here.

Not that far away, a female dancer twirled around a pole in time with Harry Styles' "Watermelon Sugar."

Greyson sat back, distracted by the erotic beauty who glided around the pole with a feminine grace. This was probably the extent of his fun tonight, since he'd fallen in love with Amelia.

He looked at me as I approached. "How did it go?"

I sat beside him. "Got Stella home safe."

"Were they about to auction her off?"

"Yes."

"You two looked good together."

"Interesting coincidence, right? Or am I paranoid?"

"Coincidence," he reasoned.

I'd wanted to believe that.

"Do you regret it?" His gaze was once again on the dancer. "Trying to turn this place around?"

"Do you?"

He threw a warm smile at the dancer and whispered, "Instead of enjoying her on that pole I've convinced myself she's a spy for the other side."

I felt it too, these sinister undertones all around us.

The dancer hung upside down with her legs splayed, holding that pose for a beat and making eye contact with Greyson. Only he'd committed himself to Amelia, and what that dancer couldn't know was he was also loyal as hell.

"Could be construed as a 'come fuck me' dance," I said, amused.

He agreed with a nod. "Atticus is making progress."

I studied the submissives at our friend's feet. "That's good."

"He needs to separate them," he added. "Talk to each one alone."

"He's gaining their confidence."

"By the way, Rylee left." Greyson watched my reaction.

"Did you tell her I was coming back?"

"Yes." He gave a nod. "I don't know how, but she found out you left with a sub."

"I was rescuing her."

"I told her that."

My back straightened. "She's more likely to play with others," I reasoned. "Hence the session with Jewel Delany."

"Couldn't do it," he said, shaking his head. "Share my lover with anyone."

"No, Greyson, once you've stolen them you keep them all to yourself," I shot back.

He smirked. "You can't keep them all."

"Touché." He'd scored a solid point.

"How are your fencing sessions going with Cameron?"

"I'm shit."

"Let me guess, he breaks you down with defeat. Then gets you to talk."

"Something like that."

"Let's see if Cole is open to having lunch tomorrow at the yacht club."

"Sure, we can brief him on where we are."

"Which is nowhere." He shifted in his seat. "The contract has stalled."

"Let's get it moving again."

"You gotta tell Cole about Stella."

I could, but I just didn't want him telling me she was a walking, talking, sensual ruse to distract me—a woman tasked with stopping us from owning this place. We'd all agreed that being open to those kinds of tactics was wise.

I changed the subject. "Working on anything interesting?"

"I'm designing…" He paused, looking uncomfortable. "Well, I haven't won the bid."

I stared at him. "What is it? You can trust me with a secret."

"It's not that, it's just…" He looked away. "It's a football stadium."

I tried to suppress the dread that came out of nowhere, like a direct hit to my chest. That reaction didn't make sense. Not after I'd dedicated half my life to the sport.

"Stella was quite something." Greyson pulled me back from the brink.

"I'm glad you got her out of here. She didn't seem to be enjoying herself."

"There was something about her," I said softly.

Her nature contradicted her body language, like she wanted intimacy but was afraid of it at the same time. If they were going to insert a woman into my life, a dominatrix would have been a better lure.

Not some sweet newbie submissive.

Which was partly the reason I'd left Stella at Dorchester House instead of enjoying more time with her.

Grayson nudged me in the ribs. "You're thinking of Rylee."

I hadn't been, but I gave a nod anyway.

"Go home and talk to her, Jake."

"What about you guys?"

Greyson smirked. "I think we'll cope."

CHAPTER NINE

Jake

AFTER MIDNIGHT, MULHOLLAND DRIVE WAS RELATIVELY quiet. Though it could have been better lit, for fuck's sake. Coming at me from the opposite direction were occasional cars with drivers who insisted on taking the sharp turns too fast. It made me question why I chose to live on this dangerous road.

As I navigated up my driveway, I turned off the blaring music so as not to annoy my neighbors. The view of my modern mansion never got old. Crafted with architectural glass and surrounded by towering trees, this Greyson Grantchester architectural masterpiece had three stories and a basement to rival any mancave.

I clenched my fists around the steering wheel when I saw a red Porsche parked out front. Rylee had invited someone over. Maybe someone from Pendulum.

I got out and approached the sports car, peering in through the driver's side window looking for clues. Nothing I saw revealed the owner's identity.

Annoyed, I made my way to the front door. We played hard but we had rules—the most important one being that if we wanted to sleep with someone else, we talked it through first and gave the other permission. We were in an open relationship, but there were caveats.

I had thought that main rule had remained in force. But maybe it was just me who needed to know she'd always come back.

Perhaps this rule was getting old for us both.

We'd divorced for a reason.

Once inside, I reset the alarm and listened for the sound of voices. Rylee's bodice and spiked boots had been discarded on the stairway.

That hurt.

She couldn't wait to get to one of the bedrooms. A stark display of passion waiting to be unleashed.

I didn't have a right to be jealous. We'd both broken the rules tonight. Those intimate moments with Stella shouldn't have happened. But she'd captured my imagination and possessing her for that brief time had been a thrill I'd missed.

But I'd not kissed her, no matter how much I'd wanted to. A kiss shows affection. A kiss hints that there's more to come between you.

I knew I needed to calm down before I went searching.

Inside the living room, I slipped out of my jacket and lifted it to my nose, breathing in Stella's delicate vanilla scent.

I should have tasted her at least, licked the dampness between her thighs, her sex silky against my fingertips, her clit responsive.

Get a fucking grip, Carrington.

She's gone.

I threw my jacket over the back of the sofa.

At the liquor cabinet, I uncorked the bourbon, the aroma of caramel hitting the air. I took a sip of the amber liquid, welcoming the burning sensation in my throat.

I'd craved this.

My mind drifted to earlier in the evening as I recalled Stella's wide eyes as I'd made her come, her youthful innocence mingling with her sensuality. Like a pure offering of femininity that I was struggling to forget.

I'd done the right thing in taking her home, getting her out of

Pendulum. Though clearly the best move of the night was getting myself out of her penthouse.

Rylee would understand my motive in rescuing Stella.

Cameron Cole would have the answers to why I'd played the hero tonight. He'd say that by saving Stella, I was somehow saving a part of myself. Or something like that.

I sensed *her* before I saw her.

Turning, I found Rylee standing a few feet away, wearing lacey panties with her pert tits exposed. Her exotic beauty was mesmerizing.

I smiled. "Glad you got home safe."

"Don't start."

I let out a sigh of frustration that she'd misinterpreted my show of affection.

She stepped closer. "You went home with someone."

"Who told you that?"

"Did you?"

"I dropped a submissive off safely. Then went right back to Pendulum. You'd left by then, but I texted you." Another sip of bourbon warmed my throat.

"I thought the point of being there was to assess the place?"

"We're covert."

"Did you fuck her?"

"No, Rylee, I did not."

"You make the rules. Then you break *your* rules."

They'd originated from both of us. Long discussions on boundaries and what lay between.

Seeing her naked and flushed almost made me forget about the Porsche outside.

I rubbed the back of my neck in frustration. "You could taste her fear." Bad choice of words.

"Your favorite flavor."

"I got her out of there, Rylee. You'd have done the same."

"Did you kiss her?"

"No."

"You're lying."

"I didn't kiss her. I drove her home. Don't have her number. I'm never gonna see her again."

The truth was kind of twisted but then again, my ex-wife was up to something, and I wasn't ready to show my full hand yet.

I hated seeing Rylee hurt. She'd been the one I'd run back to when Shay had shut down on me and shut me out. I'd bounced between the two of them because I trusted them the most. *Loved* them the most. Shay had met Rue and seemed happy now, but the loss of him still weighed heavily on me.

When I'd lost Rylee, he'd been my solace.

Back to square one, I suppose. Where Rylee and I played mental games to push each other's buttons. Maybe we were too scared to separate for good. Or maybe we were just addicted to the dopamine hit we delivered for each other—like she seemed to be wanting from me now.

She suckled on her bottom lip, trying to arouse me.

The person upstairs had no idea they were causing this much grief.

Mistrust shimmied between us.

Rylee and I complemented each other as well as fire and ice. We couldn't be together. Couldn't be apart, either. Rylee understood my darkness. Craved it, too.

"Silent treatment?" She brought me back to the present.

"I was thinking about how to make it up to you." I gestured to another glass, offering her a drink. "I've upset you. Didn't intend to."

A good line. Out of character for me, but then again, my therapist had told me saying things like that could placate a woman.

Sadness flashed across her face. Rylee could always read my lies.

I let out a sigh. "Whose car?"

"He's always admired you."

We'd narrowed it down to a *he*.

"Just tell me he's not in my bed?" I said flatly.

"Our bed."

I felt a jolt of annoyance. "I love you. But you bring out the cruel in me, Rylee."

"You bring out the bitch in me."

"Are you here post-fuck?" I asked, looking her up and down with disgust.

"Yes."

I shrugged. "I finger-fucked Stella. But that was it."

"Stella?" She made the name sound like a curse.

"She needed to come. I was happy to oblige."

The anger in her eyes turned to arousal. Rylee reached for my hand and brought it to her mouth, opening her soft lips and suckling on my fingers.

"Other hand," I said darkly.

She pushed my arm away and stepped back. "I want to meet her."

"I'm never seeing her again."

"I hate loving you this much."

"Your beauty paralyzes me," I admitted softly. "We're both fucked."

Her expression softened. "Pour me champagne."

"What are we celebrating? Our foray into madness?"

"Don't."

"I'm happy you're happy," I said, my tone amused. "As long as it's not Lance Merrill in my fucking bed." My grin widened at that insane joke.

She didn't react.

Her response caused an invisible blunt force trauma to my heart.

"Don't say anything," she whispered. "Just let him leave."

I set my glass down on the cabinet and sprinted toward the stairway, taking three steps at a time toward the upper floor, needing to see for myself that this was only a cruel lie.

I flew down the hallway, stopping short at the bedroom door.

My throat closed tight.

In. My. Fucking. House.

Lance Merrill stood beside my bed with its ruffled linen sheets, securing his cufflinks as casually as a psychopath after a kill.

I swallowed hard as he reached for his tuxedo jacket and dragged it off the back of a chair, fury racing through my veins.

This is what revenge looked like—him taking aim at me because of what we were trying to do with Pendulum.

Was this the first time they'd slept together?

He gave me a look of triumph. "Your wife's an impressive fuck."

Rylee bumped into my back, and then rested her hand on my arm. "Don't do anything you'll—"

I shrugged her hand off.

She moved by me and stood between us, trying to block me from reaching Merrill.

She didn't know I'd be coming home.

Or maybe she did.

I glared at her. *What have you done?*

Had she finally sliced through this thin thread tethering us and what we'd had together?

The agonizing thought of losing her completely was like a poisonous snake recoiling and striking me again and again and again.

I lunged at him.

Rylee wedged herself between us.

Lance appeared unperturbed. "How about a session, Carrington?"

Rylee spun round to face him. "No!"

"Saw your dungeon," he said. "Rylee gave me the grand tour. The whole place is impressive, but that room stole the show. Greyson's one talented guy."

"You don't want to be alone with me in my dungeon," I chided, stepping past Rylee.

He shrugged. "How about you take me for a spin in there?"

"He doesn't want that," snapped Rylee. "Neither of you are in any state of mind to go in there."

Lance gave me a smug smile. "Your wife's pussy tastes amazing."

I threw a punch and it landed on his jaw, knocking him backward. I ignored the pain in my hand.

"Stop it!" screamed Rylee.

My fist throbbed, but it felt good to see the look of stunned surprise on his face. Lance regained his balance and caressed his mouth, examining the smudge of blood on his fingertips.

He licked his bottom lip. "Looks like the session's begun."

I seethed. "Get out."

He ignored me and turned to Rylee. "I'm surprised you still live here. He's volatile."

"Shut up," she bit out.

He sidestepped her. "I'm ready for that breakfast you promised, sweetheart."

Panic flashed in Rylee's eyes. She pivoted to watch my reaction. I wondered if they'd talked about me. If she'd let anything slip that might be construed as private, sacred conversations. Or if she'd shared any details about Pendulum. Had she made me professionally vulnerable?

Centering myself, I dug deep not to take the bait.

During a high-stakes football game, when my team had relied on me, I'd kept my cool. I'd been known for that. But this was a game of emotions—of ownership and control.

Lance took a cruel pleasure in destroying lives. And now he'd gone after me by going after my woman.

He'd tainted what was good about us. Ruined what we'd had left.

For the first time in my life, I felt the urge to kill. It contradicted my nature, of always trying to do the right thing—but that principle was about to be smashed to smithereens.

"Maybe this will help clear your head," said Lance.

"My head has never been clearer."

"You really are making some questionable decisions lately."

He meant owning Pendulum.

Rylee's expression was filled with sadness. "Lance!"

"I need you to leave," I told him.

As he strolled by me, he clenched his teeth as though he'd read my mind and was aroused by my reaction.

He walked out of the room and I stepped into the hallway to make sure the fucker left. He was aware of the psychological carnage he'd leave behind. Smug in his privileged world of getting what he wanted. Nothing was out of bounds for him.

"What were you thinking?" I snapped at Rylee.

"He told me he'd make things easier for you."

"At Pendulum? You believed him?"

"We do this all the time. You and me. Have fun. Just because it's him—"

"Exactly, it's him!"

I walked down the hall and leaned over the banister. Rylee followed me.

Lance continued down the stairwell, descending all the way to the basement. He had no intention of leaving.

I snapped a hand up to Rylee. "I'll deal with you later."

Feeling territorial, I raced down the stairs, quickly reaching the basement. I took a few seconds to contemplate if proceeding after him was madness.

Which it clearly was.

Lingering rage made me follow him inside the chamber.

Lance strolled around, assessing the setting. "Your wife is obsessed with my dick. Might want to talk to her about that."

I closed the door behind me.

And locked it.

He stood beside the St. Andrew's Cross. His challenging dark gaze rose to meet mine. "Show me the worst you can do."

Rylee's fists slammed against the chamber door.

Ignoring her, I focused on the silver fox leaning casually against the torture device. Handsome, yes, but if evil could be channeled through anyone, it would exist in him.

"You really want the headache of owning Pendulum?" Merrill slipped out of his jacket and proceeded to unbutton his shirt. Like I hadn't just watched him dress upstairs after he'd taken *my* woman. His sculpted torso was a sign of his fitness, but his head remained in psycho territory.

He examined the St. Andrew's Cross and its silver-plated cuff. "Great craftmanship."

"I like to think so."

"Italian?" His smile widened and he lit up the room with a devilish smirk. "Now this, there's no getting out of."

He was right about that—those metal cuffs were professional grade.

"The deal is still pending, apparently?" he said.

"I'm not discussing Pendulum."

"I hear you kidnapped one of our subs tonight?"

He'd eavesdropped on my conversation with Rylee. That's what he'd done. Or maybe someone else had told him back at the club.

"She wasn't ready," I said, defending Stella. "I took her home. That was it."

"But you like them scared."

"Not as much as you."

"They're sweeter that way, don't you think?"

Which was why he'd been thrown out of Enthrall. That, and the fact he made everyone's lives miserable.

He beamed at me and for a second it looked genuine. "You're more like me than you care to admit."

"You'd like to believe that."

"I merely provide the thrill everyone seeks."

I glared at him.

"I fucked Rylee *before* we left Pendulum. Did she tell you? In front of an audience." He shrugged out of his shirt and threw it down. "A rare delight. Having everyone watch her cunt accommodate me."

He might as well have shot me in the heart.

I watched him slip his wrist through the open metal cuff as though inviting me to close it. He did the same with his other wrist, gliding it through the open cuff, as though waiting for me to lock him in so he was powerless to defend himself. Antagonizing me. Offering his vulnerability.

Tempting me to do anything I wanted to this masochist.

Me, the ultimate sadist.

A match made in Hell.

His scheming shouldn't be a surprise. He'd try to sabotage what we were trying to accomplish with that club.

Bring light into the darkness.

Lance looked smug. "You were headed for greatness, Jake. If that injury hadn't taken you out, I imagine you'd have ended up in the Hall of Fame. Now you're just a washed-up baller. No one remembers you."

Staring down at my hand, I realized I'd picked up the leather whip. My fingers tightened around the strap.

Lance braced himself. "I'm curious to learn why they call you De Sade."

CHAPTER TEN

Stella

FROM A TABLE FOR TWO, I PEERED BEYOND THE WINDOW IN quiet agony at the view of the superyachts in Marina Del Rey's harbor.

AJ was on one of those. Out at sea, and not that far away.

I had to push thoughts of him out of my mind, because if I didn't, I'd fall to my knees and beg someone, anyone, for help.

But instead, I shoved down my feelings, trying to suppress my fear. Just as I'd done all those years ago when our parents had died. At sixteen, I'd been left to take care of a fifteen-year-old AJ. Two teenagers trying to prove we could make it.

My brother was not that far away and yet he was still out of reach.

Having to look at those boats was a cruel reminder. Maybe that was the point. A location chosen to remind me Lance held all the power.

I'd never envisioned being able to visit an exclusive club like this, a restaurant filled with wealthy diners. The spoils of their accomplishments were floating palaces in the harbor.

Maybe one of them belonged to Jewel Delany—the woman who'd invited me to lunch here. I'd ask her about that later. For now, I'd remain respectful until I worked out how she knew Lance. Did she work for him?

Jewel's silk blouse and pencil skirt enhanced her sophistication. Fine gold necklaces were draped around her slender throat. A Birkin handbag rested on the empty seat beside her. Her wavy, shoulder-length brunette hair was styled in that classy way middle-aged women tended to like.

She'd ordered us both the Caprese Salad and a bottle of sparkling water. Throw in a couple of glasses of chardonnay and you had yourself an overpriced lunch. Having skipped breakfast, I was hoping my stomach wouldn't growl.

Last night, I'd failed to convince De Sade to stay in the penthouse. After he'd left, I'd paced the living room waiting for Lance Merrill to storm through the door to berate me for my failure.

Only that didn't happen.

The rest of my night involved tossing and turning and getting very little sleep.

This morning, I'd received a text from Lance telling me I'd be meeting with Jewel Delany. He'd sent a car to drive me from Dorchester House to the restaurant. A mere eighteen minutes' drive.

I only had one item in my wardrobe that I guessed would be suitable—my sundress from my old life. I'd been wearing it at the time of my kidnapping. I was free to come and go, I'd been told, but I was still a prisoner.

I wondered if Jewel knew.

She raised her eyes from her phone. She'd been texting back and forth with someone, giving me the chance to study her. Mirroring her, I lifted my linen napkin and spread it across my lap.

I recognized her from Pendulum. The woman who'd stormed in on Lance and me while I'd been receiving his orders. Jewel had walked out without speaking to me, which made this invitation intriguing.

"Lance always finds the quiet ones," she said in a sultry voice.

I decided to come right out and ask. "Do you work for him?"

"No."

Maybe she outranked him or something?

"Did he ask you to talk with me?"

"I called this meeting." With a manicured fingernail she tapped the base of her wine glass.

"Why?"

"I assess every submissive prior to entry." She gave me a thin smile. "A few manage to slip through—like you."

"I'm not going back."

She lifted her glass of chardonnay like a toast. "Yes, you are."

I sipped my wine, wondering how much she knew about my situation, the liquor heating my cheeks.

"Stella, I've agreed to introduce you to some very influential VIPs."

That got my attention.

"The correct response is, 'I'm honored, ma'am.'"

"I'm honored, ma'am."

"Better."

"I still don't think I'll return, though. But thank you."

"Mr. Merrill assured me you will."

I tried to hide my panic.

"How did you meet him again?" she asked.

"Through a submissive," I lied.

She mulled that over and then continued with, "Did you see any activities that appealed to you at the club?"

I sat back, recalling the room with the musicians playing beautiful music with the odd anomaly of women fucking in the background. Like it was normal to get it on in front of all those people. "The music was nice."

Recalling the erotic live act, I felt myself becoming aroused again, like an awakening of my senses. Part of me had wanted to stay and watch.

Jewel appeared amused. "We have plenty of time to discover your fetish."

"Don't have one."

"Let's circle back to explore what turns you on."

A crazy conversation for brunch. I hoped no one was eavesdropping. "How long have you been into this?" I munched on a baby carrot.

"No eating with your hands, dear."

I dropped the tiny vegetable onto my plate. It had been meant as salad décor, but I'd felt rebellious.

Jewel set down her fork. "I can see we have our work cut out with you."

From her disapproving glare, I sensed I had little to no etiquette.

Her face slid into a scowl. "You're scheduled to be showcased at Pendulum."

"I'm not into that."

"It's not an invitation."

The small hairs on my forearms prickled. This conversation was heading in the wrong direction.

Thinking quickly, I tried to change the subject. "Nice place. If you're into such things."

"You have an attitude." She lowered her gaze. "Can't wait to see it spanked out of you."

I felt a rush of adrenaline at the idea of doing that to someone else. Me in control, not her. Me with the whip and the quick retorts.

I reached for the carrot again and watched her reaction. Then quickly glided my hand toward my fork, picking it up and using it to cut off a piece of mozzarella cheese. I took a bite of the delicious morsel my body desperately needed. No wonder I'd lost weight. I couldn't recall my last meal.

"Use your knife," she whispered.

I reached for it, playing along.

The concierge escorted four impressive looking men across the dining room to a table not far from ours. They settled next to the window.

One of them was so handsome it made me gawp at his striking chestnut eyes and intelligent demeanor. The men on either side of him were just as handsome. I recognized one of them from his tattooed hands.

I inhaled softly.

Jake was with them—the man who'd pulled me out of Pendulum last night. His beautiful dark eyes were unforgettable.

This was no coincidence.

I felt a shiver of arousal, recalling the way he'd touched me inside the penthouse. The way he'd made me come. The memory made my face flame.

I turned my attention back to my salad, hoping Jewel hadn't noticed my reaction to the men. But she was too busy reading something off her iPhone.

"You're a busy woman," I said.

She peered up. "You have no idea."

"What do you do when you're not at Pendulum?"

Her eyelids fluttered and she held my gaze. "I'm in the business of controlling people's lives. In all forms."

"Sounds sinister."

"Trust me, it is."

"Are you a publicist?" There were plenty of those in this town.

"What I do is morally fuzzy."

"And you admit to that?"

She smiled as she chewed on a piece of bread.

I stole a few more seconds to ogle Jake Carrington, his dark hair ruffled, dressed down from when I'd last seen him in a tux. He wore cream-colored slacks and a linen shirt. Mingling with his wealthy boat buddies, he was seemingly a lot more relaxed than he was at Pendulum.

I hoped he didn't look my way.

Then he did.

His eyes narrowed with an intimidating force, sending a jolt of panic through me as though I'd been caught doing something wrong. His eyes tracked toward Jewel and then his gaze returned to me.

I pushed up. "I have to visit the restroom."

Jewel glanced down at her phone. "When you get back, we'll have that talk."

That should have scared me, but I was too busy trying to avoid being caught scurrying out of the dining room by one of the most intimidating men I'd ever met.

Head held high, refusing to look his way, I strolled past Jake's table with my heart racing, afraid he might think I was stalking him. Sensing his attention hadn't left me for one second, I drew in a sharp breath, desperate for fresh air.

I hurried toward the brighter sunlight.

Pushing a door open, I stepped out onto the boardwalk into a balmy breeze. Taking a second to regroup, I was relieved to be away from that stifling affluence of rich people oozing arrogance and waiters scurrying around like they were serving royalty.

Jewel had her phone to distract her. She'd hardly notice me gone. At least I told myself that. Moving toward the edge of the balustrade, I gripped the handrail, feeling small compared to the towering yachts.

"Hello, Stella," said a deep voice from behind me.

Oh, crap.

I drew in a deep breath before turning to face *him*. "Oh, hello."

I walked toward Jake and tried to move around his towering frame to avoid talking with him.

He stepped in front of me. "What are you doing here?"

I peered up at him. "Having lunch. You?"

He shook his head with disapproval. "Strange coincidence."

"I didn't know you'd be here."

He folded his arms across his chest in disbelief.

Jake was still the best-looking man I'd ever met. The memory of him would forever be etched in my mind. I felt a connection with him despite us being strangers—despite how he'd touched me last night. A shiver of remembrance crowded my thoughts. We'd shared the kind of intimacy reserved for lovers.

"Pretty dress," he said, frowning at my pumps.

The left shoe had been scuffed when I'd been "persuaded" to enter the penthouse. Klein had insisted I go in with a shove.

"You know there's laws against stalking." He arched a brow.

"I promise not to press charges," I said.

"I'm serious."

"You'd like to believe that." I stepped forward. "Bet one of those—" I glanced over to the harbor "—dick waving yachts is yours."

"I'd rather waste my money on other things. Like a private body-guard to keep the marauding fans away."

A gust of wind blew locks of hair across my face. I blinked frantically, fighting my hair, trying to maintain composure.

"You even command the weather," he said softly.

"What are you talking about?" Yet my heart was racing fast at his flattery.

Years ago, I'd have reassured myself that we were dating now, because of what we'd done in the shadows. But now, I was older and wiser and had let go of those old-fashioned morals.

"I didn't think I'd see you again so soon," he said, his voice husky.

I blushed at the memory of him, sensual feelings unfurling like a dark dream.

"I deserve to be here as much as you do." I poked his chest. "In fact, you should be treating me with the same respect as all the other members in there."

"Members," he repeated, lips curling at the edges.

Through the window, I saw the men at his table deep in conversation. They turned their attention toward us with suspicious expressions.

"Don't look at them," he said dryly. "Look at me."

A rush of excitement surged into my chest and spread to my limbs, making everything tingle. His voice, his demeanor, *hell*, everything about this man screamed control. I imagined him as a quarterback behaving much like this during a game; intense, precise, and determined.

I wanted to disappear into the ground and yet I rallied my courage. "You and I move in the same circles, clearly."

Amusement spread over his face, his striking eyes crinkling as he gave me a wry smile. Superiority dripped off him, his confidence dangerously alluring.

"I told you yesterday, you and I—"

"Actually, I was hoping I'd never see you again," I said impulsively.

He made me nervous.

I pointed to the restaurant. "I'm having lunch with a friend."

"I wouldn't call her a friend." His demeanor had changed.

"You know her from Pendulum?"

Jake tutted. "We don't mention that name." He shoved his hands into his pockets. "How often do you meet with her?"

"This is the first time."

"What do you know about her?" Seeing my confused expression he added, "Jewel's the oldest daughter of Jim Delany."

I reacted with a jolt of recognition.

He gave a nod, confirming Jewel's father was the world-renowned media mogul who owned a news station. All she'd just told me came into sharp focus. *Morally fuzzy* being an unreasonable way to describe destroying lives with a mere news headline.

Lance had arranged my meeting with her. He had to know Jake would be here, too. Maybe this was Jake's usual haunt for Sunday brunch.

Jake's gaze narrowed. "Why do I sense you're naively making your way around the scene?"

Again, I was making a mess of things. He was right, me being here appeared suspicious. Me walking away would solve that.

"I have to go." I tried to walk around him.

He held out his arm. "Not so fast."

An invisible jolt of electricity hit me in response to his bossiness.

It was easy to misinterpret his flirting as genuine interest when he was merely playing with me like a mouse.

I wanted to go home, *my home*. The one I was forbidden to visit. Fall onto my bed and cry this situation away. My life had imploded and no amount of distraction by mysterious handsome men would steal back my happiness.

And joy—I doubted I'd ever feel that again, too. Even after AJ came home and we both put this nightmare behind us.

Thoughts of him caused me to freeze.

What if they'd already hurt him?

I glanced through the window to make sure Jewel couldn't see us talking, just in case she reported this back to Lance, told him I'd failed my mission.

"Come here." Jake sensed my concern and led me further down the boardwalk. "Has Lance Merrill contacted you?"

"No." I didn't want him to see my face when I lied, so I turned toward the boats.

"You know who he is?"

"Why?"

Jake waved that off. "If you come across him, avoid him."

I wished this sound advice had come before AJ had taken the job on *The Hades*.

"I didn't recognize you in ordinary clothes," I said, trying to change the subject.

"Baby, there's nothing ordinary about me."

"Actually, I agree with you on that one. You look hot for a man of your age."

"If I had the time or desire, I'd find a suitable punishment for that remark."

"If I had the time, I'd take you up on that," I flirted back.

"You look pretty when you come." Jake tilted his head, amused.

I went to speak but no words came out.

"We've discovered the off switch," he joked. "I'll set that to memory."

"If you're divorced, why are you wearing a wedding ring?"

He peered down at his hand as though surprised to see the silver band. His fingers twisted the ring up and over his knuckle, gliding it off. "Right." Then, as though it was the most natural thing in the world, Jake tossed his wedding band into the air. It plopped into the water.

Gawping, I watched his reaction, which was flat. He held up his hand again. "Not married."

A heaviness settled in my chest. "Why did you do that?"

He came closer, towering over me.

I raised my hands in defense. "Don't blame me."

"We're responsible for our own actions, Stella."

My skin tingled in anticipation, as though some part of me would want more time with him, other than doing it because of Lance's bidding.

He brushed a strand of hair behind my ear. "I recall everything about last night."

Cheeks flushing wildly at his intense gaze, I asked, "What did your ex-wife do to piss you off?"

He shook his head as though not wanting to discuss it.

"For you to throw your ring away?" I added.

His flat smile seemed out of place.

I blinked up at him. "Looks like your life is complicated."

"You're outspoken," he said. "For a submissive."

My lips trembled even as I forced myself to keep it together. Because that's not who or what I was. I pined for the chance to meet this man without the lies.

"Who trained you?"

What the fuck. "I'm not a pet."

"Would you like to be?"

Heart racing, I fell into the truth he needed to hear. "Yes."

"You haven't shown evidence you deserve a Dom of my caliber," he said arrogantly.

"You haven't given me the opportunity." I raised my chin in defense.

"Is that something you'd like?"

"I want to deserve you. Show me how. Show me what you like."

Jake gave a wave of reassurance to the men behind the glass that he wouldn't be much longer.

"I'm keeping you from your friends," I said.

"You're forgiven." He gave me a dazzling smile.

"I'm going back to Pendulum." I watched his reaction to see if I'd spiked his protectiveness. "Maybe I'll see you there?"

He lowered his gaze. "No, you're not."

"I am." I stepped closer. "If you see me there, claim me."

"I've wasted enough time rescuing you from that place. Next time, you're on your own."

"With you I feel safe."

"There's your answer. You're out of your league, little girl."

"Jewel's going to introduce me to some very important people there."

He seemed to mull that over. "You wouldn't want me as your Dom."

Impossible not to think about those minutes I'd spent with *him* inside Pendulum and then, later, at Dorchester House. More time with him meant more pleasure.

His expression remained serene. "Go finish your lunch with Ms. Delany."

I held his stare. "What could I do right now to persuade you?"

"Oh, I don't know, be obedient." He gave a devilish smirk.

I bowed my head.

He opened the door and motioned for me to go ahead of him. "In."

We continued toward a private smaller dining room. The lights were dimmed, and I saw the place was empty.

I was hit by a rush of adrenaline, my heart racing with excitement. I shouldn't be enjoying this, but I was.

After he closed the door behind us, I fell to my knees and turned my palms up, resting them on my lap—recalling this pose from *A Submissive's Rule Book*.

"An improvement," he said.

"I'll dedicate every waking hour to pleasing you, sir."

Jake swaggered closer and towered over me like a man who knew this game well, using silence to win me over with an edge of danger.

He rested his hand on my head. "What level are you?"

I searched my thoughts to recall the answer from that book. Nothing came to mind.

"Level one?" he suggested.

"Yes, level one."

He blew out a breath as he peered up toward the ceiling.

Inwardly, I cringed at the misfire.

"How did you end up on those waters, Stella?"

"What do you mean?"

"There are sharks and then there are megalodons."

"Jewel seems reasonable."

"Define reasonable in our world."

"I don't understand."

"Get up."

Pushing to my feet, I steadied myself. At my feet blue swirls on the carpet made a busy pattern. I focused on the elaborate design.

"What happened to your shoe?" he said.

"How do you mean?"

"Did you fall?"

"No." Standing straight, I put my hands behind my back and held them there, guessing this was what he meant. If Jake stroked my pussy like he'd touched me last night, I'd faint from the pleasure.

"Stella," he whispered my name with an unfamiliar empathy.

"Sir."

"There are no levels."

I cringed at my stupidity. I'd been easy to trick.

"Pity," he said. "I'd have offered you blinding pleasure in way of a reward when you responded well."

"How do I convince—"

"Stay away from the scene for now. This is non-negotiable. If I see you at Pendulum, I'll personally escort you off the premises. Am I understood?"

Squeezing my eyes shut, I felt the shame of having fucked up.

With a casual nod, he walked away and exited the room, leaving the air thick with tension. His aura remained. Air rushed from my lungs in a mixture of relief and regret.

I bit back frustration, feeling that familiar craving—a simmering need for what he offered only to have him rip it away. As though this experience might be something I'd have wanted before all this, before being coerced.

He'd teased me with more of what my body had experienced last night.

"…*blinding pleasure.*"

And then he'd snatched it away.

The door flew open.

I braced myself, hoping to see Jake return.

Instead, it was a waiter who jolted to a stop when he saw me.

"I was just leaving," I said, scurrying out. "I got turned around."

When I reached the restaurant, I saw Jake back at his table. I couldn't make eye contact with him. Couldn't have him see my embarrassment from crushing on him.

I gave Jewel a fake smile as I rejoined her, now armed with the knowledge I was having lunch with a Delany—the daughter of one of the most powerful titans in America. The puppet master of politicians, making and breaking careers with a single headline.

"How did it go?" she asked.

"I'm sorry?"

"With Carrington?" She narrowed her eyes. "You disappeared at the same time."

"Just talked."

"About?"

"An opportunity."

"Go on."

"He doesn't think I'm ready to become his sub."

"No one is, dear."

"What does that mean?"

"You like him?"

"Yes." I said breathlessly.

"He rejected you?"

I slid my fork away and then moved it back across my plate hoping she'd change the subject.

"He rejects subs who chase after him," she said. "Don't take it personally. He has rare tastes. His demands are excessive."

"I can imagine."

"No, you can't imagine what he's into. Blood spills."

"During a session?"

"Though he can be a mindful Dom, I hear."

"I figured out what it is you do," I said.

"Carrington warned you about me?"

"He told me who your dad is."

She leaned forward. "I've earned my status at that news station."

"How do I know you won't run a story on me?"

"Don't take this the wrong way," she said. "But you're nobody."

"What about him?" I looked toward Jake's table.

"There's a code we go by in our society. We respect that we each have exquisite tastes and honor our privacy."

"Seems like joining then would be a good way to stay safe."

"You're a fiery minx, aren't you?"

Intrigued, I wanted to ask if her family knew about her passion for kink.

"How well do you know Lance?" I asked.

She shook her head. "Keep your distance from him."

"Why do you say that?"

She leaned forward. "I once heard that a sommelier—" She paused. "Do you know what that is?"

"A wine specialist?"

"Well, this French sommelier working on Lance's yacht brought him the wrong vintage."

"Did he fire him?"

She looked surprised. "No, dear. He threw him overboard."

"Please tell me he could swim?"

"Have no idea." She sat back. "But I'm telling you this so you'll stay away from Lance Merrill."

I tried to catch my breath.

Lance was a psychopath.

Jewel looked thoughtful. "Want more of my advice?"

"Sure."

She gave a nod. "Want to be his?"

"You mean date Jake Carrington?"

"Men like him don't date. They fuck. Don't embarrass yourself by looking for love, either. Not with them."

"What happened between Jake and his ex-wife?" I waited to see if she'd answer.

"They're still together." She gave me a thin-lipped smile.

But Jewel hadn't witnessed him throwing his wedding ring into the harbor.

The news they still loved each other painfully squeezed my heart, as though discovering the man I wanted could never be mine.

But we'd never been destined for anything close to that. And if Jake ever found out I worked for Lance, he'd probably kill me himself.

Lance had called him "a mark." That's all he would ever be to me. I'd been tasked with something unethical, using Jake for some unknown purpose. If Jake was still seriously into someone else, then maybe, just maybe, betraying him wouldn't be too bad for him.

"Can you help me?" I asked her. "Seduce him?"

Jewel's expression turned thoughtful. "De Sade savors putting subs in dangerous scenarios. Let's show him you'd be a sublime experience. A sensual appetizer of sorts."

CHAPTER ELEVEN

Jake

I REJOINED THE OTHERS IN THE RESTAURANT.

"I ordered you the salmon," said Greyson. He waggled his eyebrows over the fact I'd disappeared for a few minutes.

"You couldn't wait?" I pulled back my chair and sat beside him.

"I'm starving." He shared a smirk with Cameron and Atticus.

Stella's delicate perfume had followed me out of that room, haunting my senses with every passing second. I'd had to leave, otherwise God knows what I'd have done. I'd probably have agreed to make her mine, as though I were spellbound in some way from her enticing beauty.

I didn't need any more complications.

Out of the corner of my eye, I saw her walk by, returning to her table where Jewel sat patiently waiting for her.

I wasn't concerned Stella would share anything about me. We were all too locked down to worry about that. To be honest, we had more dirt on Jewel than she had on us.

Greyson nudged my arm. "Isn't that the submissive you rescued last night?"

Cameron sat forward, analyzing that bombshell.

Yes, thank you. I'd already clocked that coincidence.

I whipped my napkin off the table and laid in on my lap.

"What's her name?" asked Cameron.

"Stella." God, even her name did it for me.

"She's having lunch with Jewel?" Cameron's tone turned serious.

The world closed in around me.

As friends, we had each other to help figure things out, but it also meant they'd be in my business when all I wanted was to live a delusional life.

"Thank you." I gave the waiter a warm smile as he poured wine into my glass. "Bit early for this."

"It's brunch," griped Atticus. "Shut the fuck up and stop complaining."

"You're in a mood." I studied him.

We all went silent until the waiter left our table.

Atticus shook his head. "It's bad, guys. Many of the subs at Pendulum are being coerced."

We all let that revelation have its moment. It was a stark reality no one wanted to hear or have to deal with. Somehow, he'd made that den of vipers sound worse.

Atticus sipped chardonnay as though needing to cleanse his palate. Seeing him rattled like this only rattled us more. He was like Cameron—rarely lost his cool. A good trait for a surgeon to have. But if he and Cole were unsettled, we were all fucked.

I glanced over at Stella's table wondering if she was also being coerced. The thought of anyone hurting her caused a wave of protectiveness to flood through me. She remained deep in conversation with Jewel.

And then she glanced my way.

I broke her gaze like I'd brought down a sword on that unsettling connection.

Delany's attendance at Pendulum could become a scandal for her family. But as the Delanys controlled much of the news, they had the power to dissolve a story. But it didn't make Jewel any less of a threat.

"Coincidence?" asked Cameron.

I shot him a look. "Stella being here?"

"What did you talk about just now?"

"She wants a Dom."

Cameron's expression turned thoughtful. "She wants that man to be you?"

"You're bruising my ego." Deep down I knew it was true.

Stella had come into my life too easily.

"Let's focus on why we're here," said Cameron.

Greyson's jaw tightened with frustration. "There's been a hold up on the contract. But maybe that's a good thing."

"Really?" Atticus flinched. "I just told you there are women who need our help, and you want to back out?"

"Didn't mean that." Greyson glared at him. "It gives us more time to research the place."

"I concur," said Cameron.

As a silent partner, our brilliant psychiatrist would be somewhat protected.

"We get them all out," I said. "No one gets left behind. We do everything we have to. Are we in agreement?"

Cameron set his fork down. "Atticus, go on."

Atticus, my closest friend and confidant, gave me a troubled look. "We have to talk."

They were all staring at me.

Atticus took a sip of water and said, "What happened between you and Lance last night?"

I was stunned they knew. "Who told you?"

"It's true?" snapped Atticus.

Defensively, I sat forward. "When I got home last night, Lance was at my place."

"Why?" asked Cameron.

"You didn't call to tell me this?" said Atticus. "I need to know this shit."

"Rylee had sex with him," said Cameron, realizing before the others.

I cringed, preferring this admission had come from me.

Maybe Cole had read my expression. Or maybe the rumors had surfaced and were doing the rounds. This should have been no one's business. Yet, quite suddenly, it was.

"Wily bastard," said Cameron. He had his own reasons to hate Merrill.

His gaze met mine. "What happened? After you found him in your home. Having fucked your ex?"

"Seriously?" I snapped at him.

Cole was known for pure honesty but that hit hard.

Taking in their concerned expressions, I continued. "We argued."

Cameron grimaced. "Lance riled you up on purpose."

I had a sinking feeling in my gut. "How did you hear about it?"

Movement caught my eye—the beautiful vision of Stella Adair strolling toward us in what was quite possibly the worst timed interruption in known history. Her expression morphed into concern when she read our faces.

She made eye contact with me looking for reassurance, offering me something balled up in her palm. I reached out and took it from her, closing my fist around what felt like her thong.

Embarrassment flashed across her face, confirming my suspicion. I shot a quick glance around the restaurant, but no one looked our way. Jewel observed us with the serenity of a woman who'd done worse in public.

"For you, sir." Stella kept her eyes on me.

"Thank you," I replied flatly.

She reached for her hem.

"No." Cameron gave a sharp command. "We're in the middle of something."

Stella swallowed her shame.

She was too new at all this to comprehend we condoned such behavior, encouraged it, even. We needed these erotic moments that often expanded into so much more. Atticus and Greyson and I could be filthy, fucking subs at the same time and bringing them over to the dark side of sharing.

Stella had never experience any of that.

"Listen, beautiful," I said. "You did well. Now return to your table."

She'd locked her gaze on me.

"Shall I order you a drink?" asked Greyson.

"Tomorrow night," I told her. "I'll come to Dorchester House."

"Thank you, sir," she said breathlessly.

"Now go," I said.

Backing up swiftly, Stella turned and walked back to her table.

Cameron blinked, clearly fascinated by her interruption, and turned to face me as though to say *she'd been paraded before us.* Especially for me.

It was hard to tell who to trust. Though now I had an excuse to spend more time with her and suss out this beauty. More than this, from their nod of agreement, I could tell the others approved of my Marina Del Ray plans tomorrow to find out exactly what was going on.

Staying away from Stella before had been a challenge. Now, I had a reason to own her. If only for a while.

It was either me or she'd be thrown to the wolves.

"I'll control her," I reassured them.

"We know you will," said Cameron.

"Can we get back on track?" I asked firmly.

Cameron jabbed a finger at me. "Make sure Rylee knows she's playing with fire. Lance is a confirmed narcissistic psychopath. He'll incinerate her."

"Bit extreme," said Greyson.

Cameron's brows furrowed. "Not extreme. People with psychopathy don't just function in society but thrive. In terms of navigating a career it's a powerful tool. Trust me, in your life you've encountered more psychopaths than you care to know."

"Why would you invite him into your dungeon?" asked Atticus, eager to get the subject back on track.

"I didn't," I said.

"What was Rylee thinking?" Atticus continued. "No one likes him."

All I could think of was that she believed I'd taken home a sub from Pendulum. Her kneejerk reaction was to hurt me back.

I'd fucked up.

"Lance demanded a session with me," I said flatly. "I refused. The conversation became heated."

"Where did this conversation take place?" Cameron watched me carefully.

"The dungeon."

"Lance antagonized you," said Atticus.

My attention became torn between them and Stella. I had to resist the urge to lift her panties and breathe in her scent. My dick hardened with the mere thought of her.

This wasn't me. I didn't fantasize about subs. I took them, hard. Acted out my desires and got them out of my system. But something about Stella had my thoughts returning to her.

I tucked her thong into my pocket. They watched me do it. Either her timing to interrupt us was genius or madness.

Cameron turned serious. "Talk us through what happened?"

I hated having to revisit last night after Rylee's betrayal. "Nothing to tell."

"Well, something happened," demanded Cameron.

I reached for my wine. "The session Merrill wanted didn't happen."

Atticus let out a sigh. "There's been a complaint about you to the Board of Directors at Pendulum."

I sensed where this was going. "I punched him. That was it."

Groans of frustration emanated around the table.

"He personally complained?" I asked.

"We talked about this," said Cameron. "Everyone must be on high alert for saboteurs."

"Rylee was my witness," I said. "Ask her."

Greyson's eyes filled with concern. "She joined the Board, Jake. She's with them."

"She's not with them."

Atticus rolled his eyes. "Be careful what you tell her."

I shot him a glare like he'd gone insane. Rylee was eccentric, but she could be trusted with the big things. Or maybe that was wishful thinking.

"Lance's complaint against you is being investigated," said Atticus. "It could slow things down."

"You stay away from him," demanded Cameron.

I felt annoyed that he'd managed to provoke me.

"Lance has influence at Pendulum," Greyson reminded me.

"I punched the fucker too, once," admitted Cameron. "If it makes you feel any better."

Atticus agreed with a nod. "I'd have killed him."

We could always count on him for his ability to make us feel better by denigrating himself. Atticus saved lives—he didn't take them. But maybe, just maybe, he was capable of what no one else had the stomach for.

"I take full responsibility for letting him into Chrysalis." Cameron sighed heavily.

"How did Lance get by you?" I asked. After all, he'd have undergone a substantial psychological profile with the good doctor here, as did all members.

Cameron considered his words. "Merrill was able to sustain normalcy during our interview, as many narcissists do. Think of it like a survival mechanism. They move about the world faking their way into people's lives."

"He's gotten worse since his wife left him," offered Greyson.

"She kept some semblance of control over him," agreed Cameron. "But I fear he's escalating."

"His psychopathology is worsening," said Atticus. "He's going to kill someone if we don't deal with him."

"Let's engage them with caution," said Cameron. "Focus on what we can. They've made their next move."

"Now we make ours," I said. "Let's close on the contract by the end of the month. Then fucking throw Merrill out of Pendulum for good."

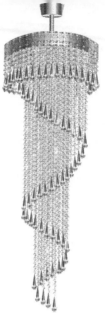

CHAPTER TWELVE

Stella

MY FIGHT OR FLIGHT RESPONSE HAD BEEN TRIGGERED, my adrenaline spiking, causing me to tremor uncomfortably.

This enduring rush had been caused by the man standing in the center of the penthouse. Jake Carrington was taking in the surrounding décor as though drawing on what he might learn about me.

He stood poised in a casual navy-blue T-shirt, wearing Levis that fit him flawlessly, showing off his height and well-rounded butt, the denim taut across his muscular thighs.

Just as he was getting to know me, I was also learning more about him, too. Beneath those sparks of power lay an introspective man. He seemed particularly interested in the books neatly lined on an ornate shelf.

None of them mine.

I'd discovered clothes in my size in what was meant to serve as my bedroom. A wardrobe full, designer labels dripping off blouses and skirts and jeans and sweaters. A stark reminder that none of this was real.

Lance had thought of everything. My clothes back home wouldn't do. Not when I was pretending to have money. The exclusive brands lent a dash of authenticity to my story.

I'd chosen this Ralph Lauren blouse and skirt but went barefoot, trying to give the impression I was comfortable here—acting like all this luxury was familiar.

Usually, at this time of day, I'd be home from my long shift at Save Face, having survived another busy Monday at the mall. I never thought I'd miss it. But I did. Because back then, my life had felt controllable.

I kept going over and over in my head how I could have done things differently, upset with myself for not being there for AJ when he needed me. Maybe I could have prevented all of this.

"Great view," Jake said, his sultry tone brought me back into focus.

I felt a rush of exhilaration even as I stood here anticipating what came next.

"I researched the name De Sade," I admitted. "It means *of pain*."

Some part of me wasn't ready to learn why he was called this.

He picked up a vase. "A Daum Coral."

I guessed it was expensive.

"From Bergdorf Goodman?" he added.

I had no idea. "A gift." I peered down at the contract laid out on the glass dining room table.

"Ready to sign?" Jake's voice cast a spell, sending me reeling each time he spoke with that remarkable sensuality.

I turned to the last page, wondering if a lawyer had actually drawn this up, if it was even legally binding. Jake had made me read it in front of him. All five pages. Intimate details about what he wanted to do to me.

I was to be his possession.

"We can make adjustments," he said. "But pushing your boundaries is important."

I whispered, "Once I've signed this?"

"You're mine."

I found his words comforting, like an unseen mystery, and yet terrifying on the highest level. A contradiction—like him.

This wasn't my world. Even as I forced myself to make it appear like I belonged.

"I'm a busy man, Stella."

I reached for the pen he'd place beside the contract, turned to the last page and pressed the nib to the line.

Was I really doing this?

The agreement stipulated that he could do anything to me. I knew why we needed this contract—to prevent me from suing him later. Pausing briefly, I peered up to study his expression and saw his dark irises dilating as though even this turned him on.

I was willingly stepping inside his metaphorical cage, and it seemed as though I was having an out of body experience, observing myself signing the contract with the sweep of a pen.

Done.

I belonged to him.

The flood of arousal I felt made the decision easier, this facet of myself fascinating. I was turned on by the idea of him pleasuring me again. A remarkable comfort considering I'd been in this fight or flight state since Friday.

Intensity shimmered off him.

"Stella." His tone was dark.

"Sir?"

"I'm waiting."

Heart pounding, I tried to guess what came next.

A wry smile curled at the edges of his full mouth. "Pour your master a drink."

"Of course." I scurried over to the liquor cabinet and searched the labels for something he might like. "What's your poison?"

"The expensive one."

I should have known that. After all, I was supposed to be the person who'd purchased the liquor. Only I rarely drank alcohol and had none at home. Maybe if I'd worked in a bar. Or came from money.

Maybe if I wasn't full of deceit.

"Something wrong?" He stepped closer.

"Cognac?" I guessed the contents from the ten-year-old label. "Yes, of course."

Reaching for the Cognac, I uncorked it with a pop and poured a good amount into a glass. Then turned and offered it to him. "Sir."

His brows rose at the amount in the tumbler. "Ice?"

I glanced at the liquor cabinet as though it should be there.

He took the glass from me and strode toward a doorway, glancing back. "Kitchen?"

"That way." It should be me getting him ice.

I chewed my lip as I second guessed whether I should say something. His lingering stare sent a shiver through me.

He disappeared, and I felt it immediately—the air seemed to chill as though the room itself knew the intensity of his loss.

I'd intimately gotten to know this place but what I'd not considered was him questioning me about it. I was being presented as a sophisticated woman who moved in these circles. But I was still me, the modest girl from an ordinary life trying to pull off this fake persona. Glancing left, I saw my reflection in the long wall mirror and pulled back on this look of confusion.

I could be someone else for a while.

Spend time with this handsome stranger. Let go and surrender and be all he wanted me to be. I could be *that* woman. It wouldn't be the first time I'd had to be strong during a difficult situation.

I could hold my head high and get on with things because what else was there to do but move forward, the days falling into each other as I kept my life afloat.

Like the time I'd been seduced by Karl Smith, beloved jock amongst the seniors at Glendale Community College. I'd crushed on him for months after I'd first arrived at that place.

And then one day, in early spring, Karl had noticed me. He'd talked to me in the hallways and would sometimes join me at lunch. He'd made me feel special.

Because why me, right?

Why the plain girl with the straight hair and olive skin, a contrast to the privileged blondes with their wealthy families equal to Karl's status.

Every Thursday, I'd joined half the college watching him from the bleachers as he played soccer, as tough as a gladiator wearing that extraordinary uniform.

Strange that Jake equally loved football. They were similar but different—Karl a boy and a bully and Jake an unknown entity still.

Anyway, I'd lost my virginity to Karl. The pretty boy with an ugly heart.

Only to discover I'd been nothing other than a team bet. A way for those boys to entertain themselves at my expense.

After that, I'd lost all self-esteem. Lost my nerve to date again. I'd walked the college hallways every day with shame in my heart, feeling the burn of disapproving students who laughed at me behind my back that I'd fallen for their joke.

I'd not reported him because I'd not wanted to bring more attention onto myself.

There'd been no consequences because the privileged rarely suffer for the harm they cause. A sore life lesson that still hurt to this day.

Jake had that same confident swagger. But he didn't lead me on to think this was something more.

Was I now no better than, Karl offering up a story of deceit?

Maybe Jake would come to understand why I'd done this. Maybe he'd forgive me.

He strode back in, and I sensed he'd been gone longer than necessary.

"Did you find it?" I tied to swallow my doubt.

Had he guessed this wasn't my place? Had he looked around while I'd been standing here dazed. Had he seen all those clothes? I made a mental note to strip them of their expensive tags.

"Surprisingly, the ice was in the freezer." He walked toward me. "You're not having anything?"

"No."

"You drink?"

"Sometimes."

He lifted the tumbler to my lips. I sipped the rich liquor and swallowed the heat. "I prefer wine," I said hoarsely.

"Then say that."

"I want to please you," I whispered.

"You do that by letting me please you. That's what a submissive is."

"I know," I said defiantly, earning a glare from him.

"Tell me more about yourself."

"Are you usually this boring?" I chided, trying to throw him off the trail.

He took a sip of cognac. "Safe word?"

"Diamond."

"Contraception?"

"The shot." I got it because some part of me wanted to date again, but nothing had prepared me for a man like him.

He used his finger to motion for me to turn around. Clutching my arms to my sides, I did as he ordered.

I heard the window blinds being closed by him and then the sound of his glass being set on the table.

"You have quite the collection of books," he said.

I heard him sliding one of them off the shelf.

"Where in Italy did you visit?"

He'd probably seen there were a few on foreign travel. I had never gone anywhere.

"I'm hoping to go this summer," I lied.

"Make sure to visit the Uffizi in Florence."

"I want to," I said wistfully. "So much."

"Maybe I'll take you."

I spun around, wide-eyed at that suggestion. He twirled his finger and had me turn away from him again.

I felt a rush of excitement.

Had he really meant it, that he'd fly us both to Italy? But, of course, I reasoned that this is what this kind of man did. They played with you awhile and then ghosted you, moved onto the next pretty challenge.

"Stand straight."

I did as he ordered, staring at the painting on the wall of a horse rearing up in rebellion.

"Take off your clothes."

I obeyed, sliding out of my blouse and skirt. Reaching around, I undid the catch to my bra and threw it down, the chill making my nipples pert. Then I eased my panties over my hips and down my legs, stepping out of them. The heady arousal I was feeling made my breasts swell.

I lowered my arms to my sides as though standing completely naked in front of a man was something I did all the time.

He slid one of the books back onto the shelf. "Cold?"

"No."

With him being fully clothed, my nakedness made me feel even more exposed and vulnerable. I couldn't look him in the eye.

"Something you want to tell me, Stella?"

Swallowing hard, I tried to grasp what he meant. "Sir?"

He closed the space between us and came around to face me, pressing his wide hand around my throat. "I could fuck it out of you."

"Have I done something wrong?"

"You tell me."

"Kiss me," I pleaded.

His expression turned dark.

"My cunt is yours," I whispered.

Jake's lips crashed down onto mine, forcing me to yield, forcing my lips to open as he possessed my mouth.

His fierceness was both terrifying and arousing, making me forget I was meant to have no feelings for this man, making my surrender seem natural, as though I'd been waiting for this exact moment during my entire existence.

The way he placed his other hand against my lower back and pulled me toward him in a tight hug caused pleasure to surge into my breasts as they pressed against his firm chest. His erection pressed into my belly. He was already hard, his size intimidating, his strength impressive.

He suddenly let me go.

I came up for air, shuddering, because I'd never been kissed in such a way. It was like he genuinely cared for me. If he'd sensed this reticence, I'd given myself away. His intelligent eyes studied my every micro expression with intensity.

Reaching for his hand, I turned and led him out of the room and along the hallway—until I reached my bedroom.

A good submissive was like a geisha girl. I'd learned that much. Dedicating herself to a man's desires and satisfying his needs, pouring energy into pleasing him, ensuring his days and nights were arousing.

In turn, he spoiled her.

Because it was also about the submissive being nurtured.

Perhaps I'd never be able to relax around him enough to feel the benefit of this agreement.

My stomach twisted in knots.

Not looking him in the eye helped. I was frightened he'd read this dread and end this charade.

I reached for the bottom of his T-shirt and lifted it up, dragging it over his head and flinging it onto the bed. Next, I reached for the zipper on his jeans and pulled it down, lowering to my knees to strip him of his pants. Peering up, I saw his pupils dilate with want.

The familiar scent of his rich cologne wafted over me. I leaned forward to tease him with a kiss on his left thigh, and then his right.

I was unsure whether he'd like me to take him in my mouth.

"Up," he said.

I rose and continued to undress him, taking my time as though this would prolong the moment before he took me. Before his substantial girth entered me and brought discomfort.

I'd granted him permission to do anything to me, left myself open to all kinds of experiences. Nothing would be off limits.

The thought made me let out a small sob.

"You're looking to be punished severely?" he said.

I tried to read what I'd done wrong. Had something not met with his approval?

Nothing about this scheme made any sense. Another submissive should have been chosen, someone who wouldn't arouse suspicion. Someone who could give him everything he wanted and more.

I tried to read his meaning. "What happens now?"

"We begin."

CHAPTER THIRTEEN

Jake

S TELLA LEANED OVER THE EDGE OF THE BED WITH HER BARE ass pushed out, ready for a hard palm to land on her cheeks— ready for the punishment she'd earned for her rebellion or naivety. It was hard to tell with her.

I mean, she'd begged me for this on more than one occasion. Yet her body language contradicted her desires.

She clenched the duvet like her life depended on it, glancing back a few times to prove she was nervous. Any other sub would have widened her thighs because they'd know that along with the strikes, came the promise of a climax.

Stella's palms should have been placed flat on the duvet. Her posture welcoming, her obedience clear.

Like she'd been fucking trained.

It made me wonder what her end game was. She'd consented to this so there'd be no accusation of me taking her without permission. It was in writing now. Protection at the highest level.

If she was for real, which I doubted, even though I wanted that to be true, then Stella was playing a dangerous game. Even hardened submissives found me too much to handle. Her choosing me didn't make sense.

Greyson would have been a better fit if he'd been open to this. Atticus rarely connected emotionally with submissives. But they loved him anyway. Me, I'd been hailed the complicated one. The sadist into an equal measure of masochism.

Playing with a newbie wasn't something I did.

Yet this young woman emanated innocence in the most intriguing way, with the promise she could become more. I found her devastating beauty alluring—a detour from my usual taste. Her perfume reminded me of lilacs and roses mingling in the most intoxicating way.

I'd keep Stella out of Pendulum. If anything good came out of this, it would at least be that. She didn't seem to belong there.

But I'd have my fun with her.

"It's just fucking, Stella," I clarified. "You know that, right?"

"Spank me already." Her tone sounded nervous, like she wanted to get it over with.

"That's not how this works," I teased, running a hand over her buttocks, tracing circles, arousing her by gliding my fingers down her spine and then lower still, until I reached her sex, where I was greeted by tautness. Dampening my fingers, I explored her more, her thighs trembling as I inserted two fingers deep inside her.

Usually, I'd have tied her up and fucked her into oblivion. But something told me that could wait. Stella needed time to adjust to the intensity—if she ever proved she was even capable of enduring it.

Gently at first, I fingerfucked her, starting off at a slow pace. She dampened my hand as I pounded her faster, her eyelids growing heavy.

We were both entranced by the sticky sounds of my fingers pumping into her pussy. It was tighter than most, proving she didn't even insert toys all that frequently. Someone heavily into our kink would seek all the toys.

Continuing to tease her, pressing against her G-spot, I felt her pussy spasm against my fingering. I changed position so that my right hand could meet her ass in just the right way.

"Ready?"

"Yes."

"Say, 'thank you, sir.'"

"For what?" came her quick retort.

Smack.

She cried out, but as I pleasured her with my other hand, she slid back into a trance, clawing at the duvet, eyes wide and mouth pouty. "I like it!" she said breathlessly.

"Of course you do."

She shuddered as she moved away from my heated palm. Then she repositioned herself so her butt met my hand, asking for more.

Setting a steady pace, I spanked her harder, using my ambidextrous skills to navigate these movements with ease. She was getting wetter by the second, thighs trembling and hips rocking.

How long had it been since I'd spanked a sub this gently? Couldn't recall ever having to wait for them to adjust to the severity—because that's what I offered. A shock to the senses that stole all thought. All resistance. All consciousness.

My usual practice would have been to throw Stella onto the bed, tie her up with her legs spread and force orgasm after orgasm.

If I did that to her, she'd beg for leniency.

Maybe she was a sub in desperate need of clit play. That would relax her. Bring her over to my dark side. Unending pussy spanking to train her up to our soaring standards. Her anus was no doubt virginal. We'd work on that later. Or never at all.

When her ass cheeks were covered in red marks, I finally relented and stepped back, watching her catch her breath as she stared off as though tranced out. Any other sub would have looked at me like I'd lost my touch.

But Stella remained stunned over this basic punishment.

"Up," I demanded.

She slid off the bed and stood once more to face me.

"Assume the position."

Her back went ramrod straight and her arms came down by her sides. She still didn't get it.

"Let me show you what I mean by that," I said.

"Thank you, sir."

"When I say those words, reach down like this and spread yourself open." Reaching low, I eased her labia apart to show her.

Stella's hands replaced mine as she followed my instructions. She trembled in response to me easing her folds out so that her clit protruded.

At any of the clubs we visited this was how someone like her would be showcased to onlookers as a sign of consent, of giving herself over.

Her thighs were damp, at least, in a sign of arousal.

Stepping back, I studied her. "Stay that way."

She eased back her labia like a flower welcoming the light to its pink bud. She gave a shudder, her breasts trembling, proving she enjoyed this pose as she entered subspace.

My eyes traced over every part of her. The way she stood tall, shoulders back, her limbs long like a model's, face flushing, jaw slack. "Very good. Hold that pose until I say otherwise."

Having this exquisite creature obey me felt sublime. I'd forgotten the thrill of having a newbie surrender.

It had been such a long time since I'd done this.

She was never destined to be mine, I reminded myself.

Her nipples were beading, her breasts pushed together as she shook slightly from the way she was revealing herself.

I craved her tits, wanting to suckle her nipples, but we weren't there yet.

Her pussy probably tingled with pleasure and that was where we'd stay focused, for now. I stepped forward and rested a fingertip on her clit.

She shuddered in response to my touch.

"Don't let go," I ordered when I saw her fingers slip a little. "Hold that pose for your Dom."

"Yes, sir."

"Better."

She peered up at me in awe.

Circling my fingertip on her pulsing clit, I observed her ache of pleasure, both in her expression and in the way she responded at this slow cycling.

"That nice?" I asked with a dangerous edge to my tone.

She managed a nod, leaning forward slightly.

"I have rules," I said, slowing the revs even more. "Certain tastes. We can explore those later. For now, I will give you what you clearly need."

"Thank you, Master."

"A lesson." I pulled my hand away.

She looked frustrated that I'd stopped pleasuring her before she'd been allowed to come.

This moral high ground was slipping. Still, if Stella was doing all this against her will then I was no different to her masters at Pendulum.

"Do you have a bathtub?" Upon her nod, I added, "Show me."

We headed in that direction, her in front of me. We entered through the bathroom ensuite and there sat a free-standing, claw-footed tub. Kneeling beside it, I turned on the faucet to let the water fill it.

I reached for the bottle of bath bubbles and poured in a copious amount. Froth swirled and new bubbles appeared, the scent of almonds and lilies.

"Where did you get this?" I asked, half distracted.

"Harrods," she said, wide-eyed.

"You visited?"

"No, I bought it online."

I studied the label and memorized it.

Her place was tastefully decorated but to be honest, I saw nothing of her here.

A gut feeling hit me as I took in the room, making me weary. My intuition was warning me to be on guard.

When the tub was filled, I assisted her into it. She settled into the warm water, seemingly soothed by the heat and pleasant aroma.

"This is aftercare," I told her.

"Yes, of course."

Reaching for the blue sponge, I used it to wash her, gliding it over her throat and down her breasts, all the way between her legs. Then I stepped back so she could enjoy her bath.

I stared down at her. "I've observed that you have low self-esteem." She looked away.

"Want to tell me what happened?"

She gave a telling smile. "Maybe one day."

"One day when you trust me more?"

"I don't want to think about that now. This is the best I've felt for a long time."

"Carl Jung brought attention to this unusual mode of therapy."

"Seriously?"

"I have a friend who specializes in it. If you're ever interested in meeting with them."

"I don't need that," she said.

I sat on a seat close by, taking in her striking beauty and secretly feeling jealous of all her future lovers. Giving her away would be a sublime pain.

After her bath, I took her hand as she stepped out of the tub. She waited while I grabbed a towel and held it open for her, wrapping it around her body.

"Where did you get this?" I tapped the towel.

"So many questions."

"Where?"

"Target," she said quickly.

"Love that store." I peaked at the Hermès label.

The most innocuous things give people away—and they are oblivious to the fact. I felt no anger for what she was doing here, just intrigue. And I was concerned that she'd attracted the attention of a bad element.

"Get dressed in your bodice."

"A bodice?" She looked confused.

"Yes."

Stella left the bathroom, disappearing inside the walk-in closet. I followed her in and leaned against the doorframe while she searched for that item of clothing.

And that was when I knew for sure.

Stella had trouble finding her bodice.

Finally, she slid the top drawer out of the central cabinet and perused the collection of bodices inside as though trying to guess which one would be best.

"The red one," I commanded.

Her brown eyes filled with uncertainty. "What happens after I put this on?"

"You'll see." I said, coming up behind her.

"You gonna to tie me up?"

"Not here, no."

"At your place?"

"Let's prepare you for your fetish." Upon her frown, I reminded her what she'd told me. "To watch others."

"Right."

"You should also be prepared to be watched yourself."

She peered over her shoulder at me. "Watched while…"

"Fucking."

I assisted her into the bodice and secured the silk ties down her spine, now and again caressing her red ass cheeks as though they beckoned a kinder touch. "Turn around."

She faced me, breasts pushed up, appearing as pre-fucked perfection with her waist smaller than before, emphasized by the boned corset design holding her in.

I lifted a strand of hair off her shoulder, twisted it around my finger and tugged.

"When the time comes, I'll secure you with a chain above your head with your wrists bound, completely immobilized. I'll strip you naked out of this in front of everyone."

She swallowed hard.

"I'll flush your skin with strokes of a whip to warm you up. If you're a good girl, I'll place my fingers on you like this—" I lowered my hand and eased apart her labia on both sides to view her clit better. "This way we can all enjoy looking at your pussy." I ran a fingertip along her folds. "A few hundred people will get to enjoy this."

She drew in a sharp breath as though surprised. "Are you taking me back to Pendulum?"

"You'd flourish there." A lie but it evoked the right reaction.

"What happens now?"

"You kneel. For an hour. After that, you go to bed. You need to become acclimated to wearing a bodice during sessions." I watched her carefully, waiting to hear her protest that she'd already done this.

"Are you staying?"

"No. This is where trust comes in. Don't touch yourself. Don't make yourself come until I grant you that privilege. Understand?"

She looked up at me earnestly.

With a gesture, I motioned for her to get to her knees. Aroused, Stella easily slipped back into subspace, tranced out and willing to please, a divine feminine lure. A woman I could never allow myself to fall for.

Stella was still the enemy.

I left her like that, dutifully kneeling, posed flawlessly as a submissive, learning the art of obedience.

A lesson she'd clearly never learned before.

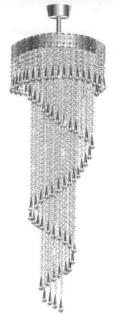

CHAPTER FOURTEEN

Stella

I JOGGED ALONG THE VENICE BEACH BOARDWALK, HOPING TO blow out the cobwebs in my brain, trying to suppress any lingering thoughts of Jake.

My knees were sore from where I'd knelt on the bedroom carpet for an hour last night. As though Jake had not left the penthouse. As though he'd know if I disobeyed. Denial of pleasure was a delicious tease.

I'd hoped a run would reduce the sexual tension I was feeling.

My face felt flushed from sprinting fast along the pathway that ran along the beach. Soon, a sea of people would crowd the area. For now, I had the space to burn off stress without the risk of running into skateboarders, or roller bladers, or tourists ambling along as they visited the shops and restaurants, yet to open.

Pausing, I took a few seconds to soak in the ocean view. Out on that very water, not that far away, my brother was being held captive. I wanted to swim out to him and do whatever I could to help.

Feelings of futility were carried away on a whipping breeze that dragged my hair across my face.

Sometimes devastating things happen in life. The kind of events that make you ask yourself, *Will this break me? Do I have what it takes to survive?* And then, all at once, you realize there is no other way but through.

A million thoughts like these were racing around constantly in my mind. Sucking in deep breaths, I pushed away the feeling of agonizing helplessness.

I'd never be able to shake this dread—not until AJ was safe. And even then, I'd be left with the constant fear it could happen again.

I hated feeling so weak, so useless. I detested this inability to do more than fret.

Last night when I was with Jake, those feelings had disappeared for a short time.

A part of me had wanted those unfolding moments to belong to *him*—and him alone.

After that soothing bath, I'd obediently put on the bodice and knelt as he'd ordered me to in the center of the bedroom, feeling aroused and spellbound. Then I'd climbed into bed and fallen into a deep sleep until morning.

I recalled Jake's presence right before he'd left, wanting him to finish what he'd started. Only he'd denied me that pleasure.

For some reason, I'd obeyed.

You're falling for him.

I needed to cleanse my thoughts. Needed to clear my heart from these swirling emotions, this uncanny feeling that Jake was a good man beneath his dark ways.

Dripping sweat, I took a swig from my bottle of water.

Farther down the beach were bare-chested men playing volleyball, having fun, their laughter and cheers carrying over the breeze. Maybe if I survived this, I'd be willing to date again. That thought had never crossed my mind until now.

Jake had set alight a desire in me to be around an interesting man. Not him, obviously, but someone just as interesting.

A man who knew how to touch a woman—how to leave a person craving more.

Strangely, he'd become a pleasant distraction. Even as guilt burrowed deeper inside me. I had inserted myself into his life for sinister reasons.

Taking another sip of water, I read the graffiti on the wall next to me. The colorful squiggles made no sense. Maybe a gang had left its mark. Or rebellious teenagers had burned through their frustrations with crazy art.

A sleek town car parked nearby appeared out of place. No other cars were brash enough to take up space that was meant for the public. My stomach twisted when the car cruised toward me, stopping a few feet away.

I sensed an evil presence in that town car.

A figure with a familiar face exited the vehicle, causing my flesh to chill. Lance Merrill strolled toward me wearing a striped suit and his usual smug expression. The showy billionaire stood out amongst the beach-going crowd.

"I called in on you at the penthouse," he said, with that Texas lilt.

I wondered how he'd found me.

"Thought I'd make the most of living near the beach," I said, sounding calmer than I felt.

"Nice to see you're keeping that body in shape."

Creep.

"How was your lunch with Jewel?" he asked.

"Fine."

"Just fine?"

"Did you tell her to train me as a submissive?"

"Every admission goes through her."

I narrowed my gaze on him. "Looks like you broke the rules."

"She approves of you. Sees your potential. So that's behind us at least."

"How's my brother?"

"I hear good things about him," he said vaguely, probably in case I was wearing a wire.

"Tell him I love him."

He answered with a nod.

I glanced around to make sure no one else could hear. "I spent the evening with Jake."

"Good." He stared at me. "Anything to report?"

"He's not sharing much."

"He will."

"I don't think this is going to work."

"Give it time, Stella. Eventually he'll let something slip we can use."

I stepped closer. "I don't like being followed."

"You run every morning at this time," he said. "It was easy to guess you'd keep to the schedule."

I held back a hostile response for my brother's sake.

He could see I wasn't convinced. "We don't need to follow you. Not unless you give me a reason."

A strange thought came to me—the desire to get him on his knees begging for mercy. Me standing over him with my power reinstated. Wielding a whip and chastising him.

"It's going to take a while for De Sade to trust you," he continued. "You need to build that organically."

"How much longer am I expected to do this?"

"Until I say otherwise." He sneered. "Don't look at me like that, Stella. This will inject some excitement into your dull life."

"You know nothing about me."

"Your brother's been enlightening me."

"Under duress."

"Careful, Stella."

Threatening *me* now? I didn't say it.

"You work for me. I'd appreciate respect."

"If it's respect that you're after, maybe don't go around kidnapping people."

"I have no idea what you're talking about."

I wanted to roll my eyes.

"You can't help but be defiant." He almost sounded amused.

"Well, I doubt any other woman could pull this off. You're asking a lot."

"You have a choice."

There was no choice. I had no control over the consequences that followed, either.

He gestured. "Walk with me."

Dripping sweat after my run meant I'd not be welcome inside his car. The only good thing about this.

Reluctantly, I walked beside him.

He glanced at me. "How's he treating you?"

"Like a gentleman."

"The sex?" He watched me carefully.

"You want the sordid details?"

"Sordid?" He scoffed. "From the look of you he's not revealed his sordid side."

I looked dead-ahead, recalling nothing that could be considered too kinky. I mean, some couples probably spanked each other all the time.

Lance looked triumphant. "Clearly, he's not shown his true self yet. You don't forget something like that."

"Are you going to tell me more?"

"I'll leave it for you to figure out."

"He seems decent." I let that serve as a jab.

"Don't go and fall in love with him."

"Why not? Might make this easier."

Lance studied me as though suspecting I'd already fallen. "He's still in love with his wife."

"He's divorced." I wasn't going to share what he'd done with his wedding ring.

"They're still fucking. A lot from what I gather."

"Good to know." It shouldn't upset me but for some reason it did. His old relationship was so profound, Jake couldn't let her go.

Lance walked in step with me. "Things became complicated for them since I fucked her."

"His wife?" I softened my tone. "As long as he doesn't find out."

Lance paused. "I made sure he did."

"Why?"

"I'm ten steps ahead of him. I want to keep it that way."

Lance had thrown Jake's life into chaos. And from the look of things, I was part of that plan.

Jake's ex had been his closest advocate. It made me wonder if I was placed into his life to undermine him. To plant a seed of doubt.

"Am I being used to distract him?" I asked.

"I need intel, Stella."

"What kind?"

"There are four men taking over Pendulum. I know the names of three. They have a silent partner. Find out who he is."

"Why would they remain unknown?"

He shrugged. "Maybe they're high profile."

"I take it you don't like Jake?"

"Trust me, the feeling's mutual."

"Can you tell me more about him?" I couldn't help wanting to know more about the man who'd entered my life as though summoned by my darkest dreams.

"He had an impressive start as a quarterback. Right up until tragedy struck."

"What happened?"

Lance tucked a hand into his pocket as though this was just an ordinary stroll. "A few years back, his team was close to winning the Super Bowl. He was hit hard by a defensive end and the fall broke his neck. Jake lost the game along with the ability to walk."

My stomach lurched. "So, he learned to walk again."

"Went through intensive physical therapy in Switzerland."

Thank goodness he'd recovered from that tragedy. But I knew well enough that something like that forever affected your life.

Lance continued. "Supposedly, after that Jake developed an even greater taste for pain."

"You'd think he'd have had enough of it."

"The brain is a complicated thing."

Yours more than most, I thought.

"Recently," added Lance, "he's become obsessed with owning a club that's close to my heart."

"You have a heart?" I said sarcastically.

"What has he shared so far?"

"He's close to owning Pendulum."

He glanced away, annoyed.

"I don't think this scheme will work. Please, Lance, can we find another way? If you let AJ go—"

"I can see his disappearance is causing you concern."

"He's my life."

Merrill watched the volleyball players with a cool indifference. Both of us stared as they threw a ball back and forward over the net, sand covering their feet, all of them seemingly fit and happy.

"Jake is a determined man." I thought back to the way he'd insisted I sign his contract. "I've gathered that much."

Lance refocused on me. "There's a VIP who frequents the club. There's a secret floor set aside at Pendulum just for him. I want his name. I need to get to him first."

"Why?"

"Knowledge is power, or did no one ever tell you that?"

A man allowed to have his own floor would probably have influence. Someone who might step in and stop the takeover, or perhaps allow it. Sounded like someone wanted an alliance.

"How does this involve me?" I asked.

"Because I told you it does."

"If you can't find out his identity, how the hell am I meant to?"

"Submissives can get into all sorts of places."

"Ask Jewel."

"Keep her out of this."

"Why did you want me to meet her?"

"She insisted on signing off on you. I obliged."

"This isn't what we agreed." I stepped closer to him. "You asked me to seduce Jake Carrington. I've done that."

"You've given me nothing I can use."

"I need more time." I regretted saying it.

"Until you find something of use, the situation remains fluid."

"What does that mean?"

"Do whatever is necessary to get me this intel."

What if I say no? But I knew the answer.

"What if I can't find out the name of this VIP?"

"You will if you're resourceful."

Dread crawled up my spine. Lance was using me as his spy, asking me to move amongst dangerous men. If there were consequences, if I was found out, he'd not care what happened to me.

"If Jake discovers you're working for me it will end badly for both you and your brother. Understand?"

My throat tightened. "Yes."

"Would you like to add to that response?"

"Sir."

"You really are very pretty, Stella." He gave me a smile that didn't reach his eyes.

My expression revealed just what I thought about him. "You'd be better off hiring someone who is experienced in all of this."

He shook his head. "Do your homework. Be convincing."

Hate has a way of coming out of you when you least expect it. As though it finds its own way, burning out the truth with a scorching heat.

This man was the evilest person I'd ever met.

Lance turned to go.

"Fuck you!" I stood there trembling, confused by my outburst. "And fuck your club."

Lance stormed back toward me. "There will come a time when you consider betraying me. It's inevitable. But know this—if you do, you'll regret it."

"Please, don't make me do this anymore," I pleaded.

"No one is coming to save you, Stella." He pivoted and strolled back towards the car.

Shaking, I watched him go.

After his car pulled away, I was left standing where he'd berated me, feeling shaken and bruised.

I felt desperately scared for my brother—and unable to see a way out for either of us.

CHAPTER FIFTEEN

Jake

I T WASN'T UNUSUAL FOR RYLEE TO BE LATE.

While I waited for her, I strolled through the endless show-rooms of The Getty, pausing briefly to admire the pretty blues and greens of *Irises* by Van Gogh. His art reflected a pain that was soul-deep. But what did I know about art? That was more Cameron Cole's thing—his family had a wing here.

Perched above a canyon, this museum proudly boasted a vast collection of illuminated manuscripts, drawings, sculptures, photo-graphs, and, of course, paintings.

Years ago, I'd been invited to a cocktail party here by Atticus—an evening of drinking fine wine and enjoying modern art.

Atticus had exposed me to so much more than art that night. He had reintroduced me to the one and only Cameron Cole. I'd known Cameron back at Harvard. I'd studied business there while playing football for the university. But we'd rarely talked back then. We were into the same lifestyle, but we moved in different circles.

The Coles' wing showcased their collection of paintings, such as rare pieces by Picasso and Rembrandt and Botticelli—the Cole tea empire proving the worth of generational wealth.

I stepped outside onto the familiar landscape, walking to the place Rylee and I had agreed to meet.

While strolling through these very gardens, after enjoying a viewing of his impressive collection of priceless paintings, Cameron had invited me to join Enthrall and then Chrysalis, his discreet club secretly nestled amongst rolling canyons.

Later, after my accident, it had been Cameron who'd navigated my transfer to Switzerland. He'd literally saved my life. But it was after my time abroad that Cole had come through for me—those years where I'd literally lost my identity.

I owed him everything.

Chrysalis was also where I'd met Rylee. Even now, as I approached her, Rylee's beauty took my breath away.

She peered up from her phone.

"You're addicted," I joked.

"One of my safer addictions." She patted the seat beside her.

"Want to walk?" I gestured to the flourishing landscape.

"In a minute."

I sat close beside her. "What's up?"

"I wanted to come somewhere we could talk comfortably."

Understandable, considering the last time I saw her I'd kicked her out of my house. We'd have privacy here. If we argued no one would hear us screaming.

That thought made me smirk—she was the screamer.

"You look good," I said, making polite conversation.

I meant it. Her eyes shone brightly, and her casual jeans and sheer blouse reflected the sophistication I adored about her.

She stared at my left hand, noticing my wedding ring was gone. "You look like crap. That sub's testing your stamina, Carrington."

Stella was being handled. Nothing more. Nothing less. "We're watching over her. Making sure she navigates the scene safely."

"What's she like?"

"We haven't fucked. If that makes you feel better."

"Doesn't sound like you."

"What do you want, Rylee?"

"Still angry?"

I met her gaze. "You mean about Lance?"

She looked away. "You chose Lotte over me."

"Tell me you didn't sleep with him because we asked Lotte to run Pendulum?" I said, shaking my head.

"No, of course not. I was hurt, though. That you thought she was a better fit."

"It wasn't just my decision," I explained. "Atticus and Greyson wanted her, too."

"Why?"

"Lotte's been at this longer than you."

"Bullshit."

I glanced at her wrist. "I see you're wearing the watch I gave Lotte."

Rylee ran her fingertips over the strap. "She didn't want me thinking you were fucking."

"You could have just asked me."

Rylee would soon be working for Pendulum—the old boys' network. The last holdout until we took over.

"Rylee, you'll be on the Board for a few weeks. Then we'll disband it. Is it worth it?"

Her joining their powerbase felt like a move. If I failed, she'd be sitting in a Board seat where she'd rule supreme.

"Lance was just a fuck," she said.

"We should have talked," I admitted. "Making rash decisions, especially one like that will get you in trouble."

"Are you still pissed off because I brought him home?"

"*My* home. You don't live there anymore. You visit. You eat my food. Drink my wine. Leave long hairs in my fucking shower." On her look of surprise I added, "You left me, remember? You sent me divorce papers."

"Well, it's done now."

"Leaving me or fucking him?" I asked.

"You're more interesting when you're angry."

"Sounds healthy."

She gave a shrug as though not caring about any of it.

I nudged her ribs. "You and I can be toxic for each other. We know this."

"Yes, but the poison is so damn sweet."

I shook my head. "You need to return to therapy."

"Maybe."

"You could have at least fucked his brains out. But they're still there." The thought of that man touching her infused my blood with loathing.

"I thought you were going to kill him."

"I still might."

She stared at me. "Not funny."

"I didn't think we could hurt each other anymore. Thought we'd pushed our limits, Ryls." I hadn't called her that in months.

She'd sabotaged us. Burned the bridge down. Some part of me knew it was the right decision to separate, but it hurt.

"I thought you were going to whip him to death, but you just let him leave."

"Lance? Tempting."

"You've come a long way."

"Cenobites come get your box. Some idiot's opened it and unleashed Lance."

She scoffed at my reference to Hellraiser.

"Tell me you're not spiraling because of me," I said softly.

"I'm fine." She forced a brave smile.

In that dark dungeon, with Lance standing there and spouting cruel barbs, I'd questioned whether I could let him go without any consequences.

I'd spent my career edging rage. I could keep a handle on my emotions. Long enough to make the right decision. But there was always the chance I'd be pushed too far.

Lance had strengthened my resolve to own Pendulum outright. That's what he'd done.

"I heard Stella is stunning," said Rylee.

"Did you really believe I'd fuck a sub without introducing you first?" I studied her. "After what we agreed?"

"Lance told me he saw you leave with her."

"My intention was pure."

"Pure thoughts that led to fingerfucking."

I blew out a sigh of frustration because if anyone was going to ruin our friendship, Lance would be that man. "Why couldn't you just cut up my clothes like any normal woman? That would have been less catastrophic."

"You know me—never understated."

"I should be furious."

"Lance promised me a place on the Board at Pendulum." She faced me. "I can help transform the club from the inside."

"Did you know Lance told them I hit him?"

She stared. "Well, you did."

"A slight brush to his jaw, nothing more."

"Sounds like you need my help."

I didn't feel comfortable talking with her about our plans. Whatever relationship she had with Lance and his peers made her useful to him.

And a hazard to us.

"I don't want you going back to Pendulum."

She stood up. "I've accepted the offer."

"Un-accept it."

"You don't get to order me around anymore."

"You and I have a good history," I said. "Don't ruin that."

She gestured at the pathway. "I need that walk now."

"You need more than that," I quipped.

Together, we continued down the path, taking in the well-tended gardens. At this time the place was deserted. We needed this, needed to keep the lines of communication open because if not, Rylee could become a liability.

"There's something that intrigues me," she said.

"Go on."

"Who is your silent partner?"

I delivered an expression to convey that was a sloppy move.

"Look at that," she said, pointing. "The view from up here is quite something."

I shook my head at her indiscreet probing. Rylee was a complication I'd not seen coming.

The Getty offered breathtaking views, especially at night. For some reason, my mind flirted with the idea of bringing Stella here. Thoughts of her soothed my soul.

You don't even know her.

But I was good at reading people. Stella was hiding a secret, and my gut said it pertained to me.

"You still love me," Rylee piped up. "I can see it in your eyes." She smiled and walked on ahead, turning slightly with her arms wide to lure me into accompanying her.

Reluctantly, I followed, musing that protecting someone from themselves is an art within itself.

CHAPTER SIXTEEN

Stella

H OW LONG HAD I BEEN STANDING HERE STARING AT THIS terrible mess, trying to come to terms with the fact it had once been my home?

My mind sought refuge from the sight of our ransacked house.

Three days ago, Jake Carrington had entered the penthouse and had me kneeling before him.

It had been a high like no other.

And now, standing here in my childhood home, my life had once more returned to heart-wrenching chaos.

Glass crunched beneath my feet as I stepped carefully, hoping a shard didn't cut through my sole. My stomach was twisted in knots at seeing the place destroyed.

My hatred for Lance fucking Merrill kept increasing.

He had done this—or had at least given the order to wreck our home.

The couch had been ripped to shreds. I'd fallen asleep on it too many times to count, back when it was unthinkable that something like this could happen to us.

The house we grew up in was overflowing with memories of a time when we lived a simple existence, filled with contentment.

Yes, I'd lived a somewhat reclusive life. But it had been mine.

My throat tightened at seeing stuffing spilling out of pillows and all the furniture overturned. I found the dining room table on its side, the meals we once enjoyed there now discarded to history. It was sheer chaos. China plates had been pulled out of the antique dresser and smashed into tiny pieces.

Bolting upstairs, I hurried toward my bedroom, feeling violated before I even reached it. They'd knocked my romance paperbacks off the bookshelf. Mom's Harlequin collection had been torn up and thrown onto the carpet. I'd inherited her love of reading. During her cancer treatments, she'd devoured so many books, disassociating from life by disappearing inside these novels. I'd learned to do that, too.

Because sometimes life was too much.

Now, though, it was intolerable.

The dresser drawers had been pulled out and the clothes dumped on the floor. Nausea welled up inside me at the thought of someone touching my underwear. Within the small wardrobe, a stack of clothes had been left in piles.

I went into my brother's bedroom.

His desktop computer was gone, a square of dust to mark its theft. His childhood comics had been ripped apart. *No.* I drew in a sob, seeing his boyhood treasures destroyed—kept because they hailed back to when Mom and Dad were alive.

I wondered if they'd found what they were looking for.

AJ had never been one for secrets.

Unless…

Those comics gave me an idea, reminding me of a childhood thing he liked to do, back when we'd both play at Mom's feet while she puttered around the kitchen.

Heading back down to that very room, I knelt before the rug covering the floorboards. If they'd pulled this up, there was no sign of it.

I glanced toward the window to make sure I wasn't being watched, and then rolled the rug back to reveal the boards. They were shinier than the others from being protected over the years.

I reached into the open cutlery drawer for a blunt case knife, using it to pry the board loose, my heart pounding in my ears. I hoped to discover something that would explain why our lives had been turned upside down.

I'd not thought about this in years. Back during our childhood, AJ had discovered this little gem of a hiding place one day when Mom had been washing the floor, a trickle of water between the slats giving it away. She had tolerated him hiding all sorts of things down in the square compartment.

Dust scattered as I pried open the floorboard.

Mom had rolled her eyes when my brother had hidden his toys here. Memories of her filled my mind as I prayed for her to help us. AJ and I both missed her, and that had brought us closer.

At least she had been spared this ordeal. Mom would never see what they'd done to her home, the house we'd inherited too soon.

A tin box was nestled inside the square compartment. I lifted it out and set it on the floor, using the knife to pry open the lid.

Inside was a business card:

Dean Hersey
Senior Reporter at the Los Angeles Times

A phone number was listed beneath his name.

Had AJ reached out to Hersey about something he'd discovered on Lance's yacht? It was out of character; AJ had always shown loyalty. Yet him hiding this card made me believe he'd found something important enough to risk blowing up his career—blowing up our lives.

I lowered the floorboard and brushed away the excess dust, rolling back the carpet to cover the secret hiding place before tucking the business card into the back pocket of my jeans.

I stepped carefully over the broken glass, aching to go back in time.

It was me who felt the guilt for our current situation. As though something I'd done or not done had caused our lives to go off track. I'd promised Mom I'd protect my younger brother and I'd failed miserably.

I considered taking something with me, perhaps a few items of clothes, but then thought better of it in case Lance would see it as evidence I'd defied him. I did find my purse and grabbed the cash out of it. It wasn't a lot, but enough to get me back to Marina Del Rey.

Getting back to Dorchester House would take forever. But at least there'd be no way they could track me by phone.

Guilt and anger still raged inside me. Leaving our home looking destroyed made me feel like I was betraying it in some way. This house had once been alive with laughter and love and arguments and milestones.

I was scared I'd never get to see it again.

At least the business card I'd found might offer a clue as to why Lance had kidnapped my brother.

I headed out for the bus stop, taking the route along familiar streets, hoping not to see any neighbors who might ask me why I'd not been around for a while.

Even though I desperately wanted to, I never glanced back.

CHAPTER SEVENTEEN

Stella

STANDING BENEATH THE SHOWER WITH HOT WATER cascading over me, I tried to wash off the feeling of being dirty. The traces of regret I felt for boarding *The Hades* led to more guilt, knowing what defying Merrill would have meant for my brother.

I'd returned to Marina Del Rey in a daze, staring out the bus window and taking in the scenery. I tried to suppress the dread and fear that even more was about to be asked of me. Lance wanted the name of a secret partner and had demanded I discover the truth about a secret floor. I was now to spy for him at Pendulum—and he'd set me up to fail.

I wasn't sure how much longer I could follow his commands.

Turning off the shower, I stepped out and grabbed my towel, wrapping it around my body. I padded barefoot into the kitchen, hungry and desperate for something to eat.

I jolted to a stop upon entering the room.

The kitchen drawer was open.

I'd closed it before taking my shower. Or had I? I'd hidden the business card in there. Even as I moved toward it, I knew what I'd find.

The business card was gone.

Stolen.

Oh, God, what if they got to Dean Hersey before I did? How would I know if I could trust him?

There had to be a camera in the kitchen. Or maybe they were watching me from afar with a telescopic lens. Instinctively, I dragged down the blinds and then scoured the kitchen for areas where a camera might be hidden. It could even be camouflaged by a light fixture.

Regardless, I was certain someone had been here.

Overtaken with fury, and not caring that I was only wearing a towel, I rushed toward the front door and opened it, bolting down the hallway. I expected to see Lance or one of his men, and I was ready to yell at them for violating my privacy. I wasn't so broken I couldn't defend myself against that kind of arrogance.

The elevator pinged. They were coming back.

I braced myself to face off with them.

A tall man stepped out.

"Jake?"

He came closer. "Expecting me?"

"Did you see anyone?"

"What happened, Stella?" His brow furrowed with concern.

"I heard something."

"And you thought leaving the safety of your apartment was a good idea?" He lifted me up into his arms. "What were you thinking?"

He carried me back to the apartment, holding me as though I were as light as a feather. His strong body felt firm against mine, his familiar cologne enveloping me. Or was it just his natural scent? His masculine aura had me burying my face in the nook of his neck and breathing in the arousing smell of his skin.

He entered the apartment and kicked the door closed behind him. Then he carried me into the sitting room and gently lowered me into an armchair.

I sat still, even as the adrenaline continued to rush through me.

The towel slipped, revealing my breast. He covered me without even reacting to that embarrassing slip.

"Wait here." He hurried off.

I assumed he was checking the rest of the penthouse.

Slumping back, I let out a panicked breath.

They'd found Dean Hersey's card. AJ had gone to all that trouble to hide his contact and I'd literally handed it over to them. I buried my face in my hands, ashamed for being so stupid and recklessly behaving like I knew what I was doing. Like I could outsmart them.

Jake came back in. "Gonna tell me what's going on?"

I wanted to sob. Wanted to share that someone had broken into my home. But it wasn't true because this was their place. I was merely their puppet. I wanted to tell him that my life was falling apart. That I'd seduced him because I'd been told to.

Instead, I went with, "I sleepwalk."

"Weren't you just taking a shower?"

I scanned the room as excuses flew around my brain, but none of them made sense.

He gave a nod as though mulling over my poor excuse.

"Why are you here?" I asked.

"You're not pleased to see me?" He knelt before me and brushed a strand of hair out of my face.

I found solace in his dreamy eyes. "Thank you for being here."

"I have great timing, apparently."

His scrutinizing gaze reflected that he didn't believe me. I'd been too shaken to be convincing, and I'd given too ridiculous an answer. I didn't just look like an anxious woman; I appeared like I had something to hide.

I forced a smile, trying to push the awkwardness away. "I'll make us tea."

He pushed up. "Let me."

Jake strolled toward the kitchen.

It's just a kitchen drawer, I reassured myself. Shouldn't raise any suspicion. Shouldn't give away that I'd made another mistake.

I followed Jake into the kitchen.

He was opening cupboards and searching them, making himself at home, trying to comfort me. It made me feel dreadful about my continued deceit.

He turned to look back. "Mugs?"

I thought quickly. "That one."

As he moved toward it, he nonchalantly slid that same kitchen drawer closed. "Where do you keep your tea?"

I walked over and opened a cupboard, seeing plates. I didn't even know if this place had tea. I'd been ordered to familiarize myself with the penthouse, but honestly, I'd had a mental block since arriving. I'd found the coffee right away. Because that's what I drank.

Jake watched me carefully.

It was a good guess; the tea was stored in the same place as the coffee. How nice of them, I mused darkly, to provide little luxuries during my confinement. I brought out the gold embossed Cole Tea tin and set it on the counter, staring at it and hoping it wasn't empty.

Jake stared at it with a troubled expression.

"You don't like this brand?" I asked.

He shook off a thought and pried open the lid. "It's actually preferable." He fished out two teabags and then fixed his gaze on me.

"Something wrong?"

He knows. He can see this isn't my place.

"You weren't sleepwalking, were you?" he said softly.

Swallowing hard, I tried to think up another reasonable excuse.

"Problem with an ex-boyfriend?" he asked.

"No."

Jake came closer, towering over me with a masterful pose. "I don't share my subs."

"You already have me."

He grabbed my waist and lifted me up, sitting me on the end of the central marble island. We were now the same height. He stepped between my thighs and rested his large hands on my knees.

"This is nice," I said.

"Stella."

I was speechless and nervous that a camera was hidden here, hating the idea anyone would watch our intimacy.

A glimmer appeared in his eyes. "What aren't you telling me?"

"Nothing." I peeled open the towel to reveal my breasts in a seductive tease, hoping that would distract him.

He leaned in and his mouth kissed the shell of my ear. The tender sensation and the warmth of his breath were a heady combination, causing a fluttering in my chest. It was the way he went quiet, the way he stayed poised as though time had no power over him.

Finally, he breathed, "When you're ready."

"Thank you for being patient," I said.

His lip curled upward. "I need you to trust me."

With his guiding hand, I eased back so that I was lying on the countertop staring up at the ornate molded ceiling. He peeled open my towel, completely exposing me. Gripping my thighs, he spread them wider—and then he ducked between them.

His tongue traced my clit, circling, sending a shockwave of pleasure through my body. He drew my clit into his mouth, expertly suckling it. His palms glided upward over my body, cupping my breasts and pinching my nipples as his tongue continued to flicker strokes upward.

I wrapped my legs around him, pulling him closer, free falling into oblivion.

If I could find my way to hating him, maybe it would make this easier. If I could witness his dark side, maybe I'd feel no remorse, seeing that he deserved all the wrath that came his way.

"I thought I had to earn pleasure," I said breathlessly.

"As your Dom, I decide." He glanced up at me from between my thighs, lips shiny from my arousal. "You needed comforting."

"I thought you didn't do gentle," I said.

"I don't, Stella. But I'll make an exception."

"I'm flattered."

He was using the tip of his tongue to flick me fast, causing me to rise closer and closer to climax.

I'd committed the cardinal sin—talking without asking

permission. But I felt unsure of where the game began. Was this us acting like lovers? Or were we diving into being sub/Dom? A gray area shimmied and shined as I danced along its edges.

He raised his head again. "How long have you lived here?"

"What? Oh, a year."

Again, his tongue working its magic made it hard to think.

"Did you buy this place?" He watched me.

"Yes," I said, feeling extra vulnerable with my legs spread.

"I was just wondering if a parent bought it for you."

"No." I squeezed my eyes shut so I wouldn't have to look at him.

"It's just that you seem forgetful of where you've put things." He stood straight and switched out his tongue for playful fingers, strumming me with an expertness I'd never thought existed, conjuring magical strokes that brought confusion.

Being touched like this felt a lot like being loved. Ridiculous, because we were strangers, enemies really. Even though we acted like we were more.

"I moved things around."

"Is that so?"

"Yes."

"That explains it."

"Master," I said, my voice husky. "Permission to come."

Holding my breath, I begged him with my eyes to let me release. After the last time when I'd been ordered to kneel, denied further pleasure, I knew I'd cry if he walked away again.

"Granted."

His voice was deep and alluring, drawing me into the centrifuge of pleasure, head swirling, flesh alight as I sunk into the intense pleasure.

His fingers glided in and out of my pussy with masterful strokes as he dived back between my thighs, his tongue dancing on my clit and driving me wild.

Arching my back, I surrendered to his brilliance, thighs shuddering, hips pumping against him as I rode out my climax, my soft cries pleading for more. Until finally he'd wrung me out with too many strokes and his hand slowed its delicious torment.

Afterwards, I lay there panting like I'd just run a mile and not just climaxed, but that was his gift. I stared at him like he was the only man who could save me.

"What about you?" I pushed myself up. "I have to pleasure you." A good submissive serves her master.

Jake straightened. "Get dressed. We're going out."

"Where?"

He helped me slide off the island. "You'll see."

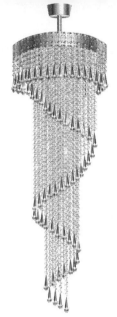

CHAPTER EIGHTEEN

Stella

I F I'D TRIED TO GUESS WHERE JAKE WAS GOING TO TAKE ME, I wouldn't have even been close.

We sat side by side in a luxury booth at SoFi Stadium. It was just us two in here, giving us time to talk, I suppose.

Down on the field the Rams were playing the Chiefs. People in the stands below were cheering. At times the roar was deafening.

Being here was good, since I'd wanted to spend more time with him. I needed to know this man so much better.

Jake leaned forward, resting his elbows on his thighs, engrossed in the game.

A few hours ago, he'd appeared at the penthouse in a surprise visit, his timing eerie. My body still felt aglow from the way he'd laid me back on the kitchen counter and made me forget my problems.

He'd almost made me forget the trauma of seeing my home trashed by those monsters. No doubt Lance had given the order. If he could do that to a property, he could do worse to a person.

Fighting back tears, I bit down on my lip and tried to disguise my feelings.

"What do you think?" Jake winked at me.

"We have the best seats."

"It's wild from down there," he said. "You should see it from the sidelines."

"I can imagine."

I was more comfortable with him now because of the intimacy we'd shared. Still guarded, yes, but I was beginning to see the real man. He was fun to be around, even if he was intimidating at times.

"That was you, once," I said it kindly.

He let out a sigh.

"Miss it?"

"I left too soon."

I watched his reaction. "Because of your injury."

He shot me a look.

I inwardly cringed at my insensitivity and the fact he was now aware I'd googled him.

He returned his focus to the game.

"You should be proud of yourself. Coming back from that."

"Change the subject," he said, his tone sour.

I elbowed him playfully. "This a date?"

"Want it to be?" He leaned back and stretched his arm behind my chair.

"As far as dates go, this is pretty fantastic."

"Rams fan?"

"Am now."

Through the window I could see the guests to our left in an equally luxurious box. We were literally sitting on the same level as actress Arielle Sage and bad boy musician Beau Glazier. Arielle glanced my way and gave a knowing smile.

I stopped staring so as not to weird her out like a crazed fan, refocusing on the field below. "How much does one of these cost?"

"A private booth? I share it with friends." He raised his fist in celebration.

A quarterback's throw was caught by a receiver. The guy had leapt into the air with an extraordinary stride to land a touchdown.

It was thrilling to see Jake in this environment, passionate for that testosterone- fueled aggression and sharing his love of football with me.

I pointed to the field. "Do you know any of the players?"

"One or two."

"You still hang out with your old teammates?"

"We stay in touch. We won a lot of games together. That bonds you like nothing else."

"An incredible feeling."

"The kind of high money can't buy."

"Maybe that's why you're into Pendulum?"

"You have no idea."

"I have a pretty good idea."

"If we're going back there together, I need to know we can trust each other, Stella."

"I'm already a member."

"I'll soon be granted access to the data containing every name." He straightened. "What you don't tell me will be in your file."

Some part of me wanted to be found out.

But then again, that wasn't the plan.

Jake stretched his arms wide across the back of our seats. "I thought we'd get to know each other. Before we deep dive into the scene."

"Great idea."

"I'd like to preface the discussion," he said, "by saying you must tell me every secret. This is essential for any relationship."

"I know."

"Tell me about your dating history."

"I thought it was bad form to discuss exes on the first date."

"That's not what this is."

Hit with a stab of embarrassment, I tried to read his stalwart expression, tried to understand what we were to each other. Lovers?

"Tell me about your ex?" he said.

"Nothing to tell."

"Tell me about the other men or women in your life," he said, continuing to push.

"Women?"

"Yes."

"That would make me bi."

His brow furrowed. "I'm bi."

"Oh, okay."

He fixed his gaze on me.

Dragging my teeth over my lip, I tried not to think about Jake making love to some guy, tried to keep my imagination respectful.

"Did someone hurt you?" he asked.

I focused on the game, hating to bring up that disaster back at college. But something told me Jake would understand how much it had ruined me for all other men.

"I don't date much," I admitted.

Didn't date at all.

"Go on."

"I went to Glendale College. Met this jock,"—I gave Jake the side-eye—"he made me believe he was into me. He wasn't. It was just a bet."

Jake's reaction was serene. "What was his name?"

"Does it matter?"

"It matters."

"Why?"

"I'm going to find out where he works. Buy the place. Then fire him."

That made me chuckle. "Karl Smith."

"Noted." Jake winked.

And right there I melted into my seat, feeling a tingle in my chest. For the first time I believed in a frisson's significance.

"After that I didn't date," I said softly.

"That would make you wary. Asshole."

"Yes."

"What made you feel drawn to our lifestyle?"

"No strings attached." It sounded reasonable.

I felt a twinge of regret for sharing a personal moment. I was meant to be manipulating this man, not the other way around. He'd gotten me to open up about one of the most harrowing times in my life.

"Would you consider yourself a brat?"

"I've been cooperative."

"In the scene."

He was testing my knowledge. "Want me brattier?"

"How much edge play?"

I'd read about this somewhere—where the Dom mindfucks the sub before anything happens. Saying or doing something to scare them and delivering the thrill of fear.

I hated the idea. Hated the feeling of losing control during a scene or in life in general. But that was my life lately—spinning off its axis as I tried to hold on to a semblance of my past.

More than this, the idea of enduring a terrifying incident I'd stupidly consented to felt insane. "Do you like to do that to your subs?"

"Yes. And you won't be able to predict when. I also dabble in dangerous play, with an assortment of…nuanced techniques. But I'll leave those for a later surprise."

I gambled, and said, "Sounds good."

He shouted with joy as the Rams scored a touchdown.

The display of aggression caused the hairs on my arms to prickle. I was turned on, but at the same time I felt I needed to be cautious about these unfolding moments. One wrong word and I'd be ousted.

I waited for the crowd to quiet down. "You want to share me?"

He didn't look at me.

I watched him carefully. "At Pendulum?"

"I'm not sure you're ready. Let's reserve that for later."

I tensed up, afraid I was sowing doubt in him. "You'd be surprised what I like."

He glanced my way.

"I like to keep things interesting," I said.

"Tell me more about what you do?" He smiled. "Makeup artist, right?"

I'd wanted to get into special effects makeup, and someone living in that penthouse would be able to make that happen. I'd put myself through cosmetology school—something I was proud of. I'd worked during the week and studied on the weekends, made it happen. I'd brought in enough money to keep the house.

I smiled back at him. "I love making women feel good about themselves."

"That's a gift." He grinned. "I always think your makeup is pretty."

"No, I just—"

"Shut the fuck up, Stella. You're beautiful. Own it. Enjoy it. And next time I give you a compliment, just say, 'thank you.'"

"Thank you."

"That your only form of income?" he asked.

I went with, "I have rich clients."

I mean, I had a few regulars who tipped me. But not enough to own a place on the water.

I glanced toward Arielle Sage and her boyfriend.

Jake followed my gaze, looking unimpressed.

"Maybe we should concentrate on the game?" I teased.

He watched as the football spiraled high in the air only to miss the receiver. After a grimace, he returned his attention to me. "Any brothers or sisters?"

His words hit a nerve, but I tried to hide it. "Brother."

I couldn't deny his existence.

"What's his name?"

"AJ."

"And where is AJ now?"

"On a yacht. He's a skipper."

"Nice."

"He loves it."

"Whose yacht?"

"AJ signed a non-disclosure so he can't share much."

Jake leaned back. "Do I know them?"

"No."

"Maybe I do."

I tried to read Jake's expression. Did he suspect I was working for Lance?

He changed the subject. "Are you and AJ close?"

"Yes, very."

His gaze stayed on me for a beat too long.

Don't give yourself away. Don't burst into tears. Don't beg him to help you. No matter how much you want to.

Don't.

My throat felt tight, as though I'd already lost him.

"How about you?" I asked.

"Oldest of five."

"That must be fun at Thanksgiving."

"It's rowdy." He glanced my way.

I swallowed hard at his scrutiny. "Where do they live?"

"Kentucky."

"You don't have much of an accent."

"I went to Harvard. That's probably the reason."

"A Kentucky gentleman."

He smirked. "Rarely gentle."

"Oh, I don't know. I've seen your other side."

He ignored that. "Where does your brother live?"

"With me. When he's in town."

"In the penthouse?" He shook his head. "I didn't see anything pertaining to him."

A jolt of fear raced through me. "He travels light."

"You're the older sister?"

"Yes."

"He relies on you."

"AJ's independent, but yes, I do what I can for him."

"Have you told him about me?"

"Not yet."

"Football fan?"

"Of course."

"Tell him he's welcome to join us next time we're at a game."

"Thank you." It felt good to hear that he wanted to invite me back here.

"That's what we do, Stella. We make people's lives more interesting."

"Interesting for me is Pendulum." I held my breath after saying it.

"Why?"

"I want to push my limits," I said it too quickly, setting myself up for the kind of questions I might not be able to answer.

"Your limits are vague." He looked at the field as the Rams' offense continued the drive. "Want to know mine?"

"Yes."

"Sure?"

"We could see how compatible we are." I rested my hand on his knee.

"Don't."

I pulled my hand away.

"I like to have my submissives in and out of the lifestyle. Know what that means?"

I drew in a nervous breath; he'd sensed my reticence.

"The moment I agree to have you as my sub, you tell me every secret."

"Okay," I said, my voice wavering.

"It also means, no matter where we are or what we do, I own you. You're essentially my plaything."

I kept my eyes on the field.

He kept his gaze on me. "What else are you into?"

"Pleasing my master," I said softly. "You?"

I held my breath waiting for his answer.

His expression was serene, his dark eyes still locked on mine as he said, "You won't be judged for walking away from this. After I tell you what is needed to remain in my orbit."

"I'm excited to serve you," I whispered.

The crowd below us roared.

He leaned forward again, resting his elbows on his thighs, watching the Rams' defense moving swiftly to intercept the ball.

Finally, Jake's gaze returned to my face. "I'm into explicit dangerous scenes. Particularly dub con. Does that sound like something you'd like to explore?"

I should say *no*.

Instead, the right words flowed out of me, sounding sincere. "Yes, sir. Very much."

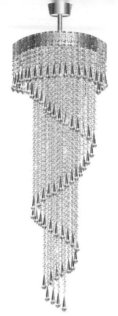

CHAPTER NINETEEN

Stella

I'D CONSENTED TO PRETTY MUCH ANYTHING IN THE CONTRACT Jake had me sign. I was unsure what he'd do if I refused him anything. Dump me, probably.

Yesterday, at SoFi stadium, I'd also consented to explore his fetishes.

He'd picked me up from the penthouse in his Lamborghini just after 8:00 P.M. and had driven us down Mulholland Drive.

I'd worn a bodice beneath my coat—as instructed by him. Jake wore one of his suave suits like it was a formal event we were attending.

A sign for Bel Air revealed we were heading that way. I admired the lush trees along the winding roads and those multi-million-dollar properties that rose tall on either side of us, proving this was an exclusive neighborhood.

Jake pulled a strip of material out of his jacket pocket. "Put this on." He handed me a blindfold.

I secured it around my eyes, not questioning him as we drove closer to our destination. This was another thing his kinky friends were into: Not allowing their sub to see where they were going. The secrecy, the games and the ever-present dangers were all part of the charade.

And just to up the tension, he held his silence.

I'd already guessed we weren't going to Pendulum, even with him driving his Lamborghini at top speed.

Was this the place where his friends would share me?

Or worse.

Once out of the car, Jake guided me inside the place.

After several minutes, I was permitted to ease off my blindfold, blinking as my eyes adjusted to the light. I saw a sweeping staircase ahead, and I was surrounded by exquisite furnishings.

Beneath my heels lay a marble floor. I gazed up at the ceiling and gawped at the mesmerizing crystal chandelier that hung low, bathing everything in shards of twinkly light.

I began to feel less self-conscious in this tight bodice and thong because it seemed all the other subs were wearing the same. They scurried through what appeared to be a foyer, respectfully not looking our way.

I posed with my arms behind me, ordered by Jake to remain like this.

Waiting.

Listening.

My body felt alive with untamed sensations that made me shiver, my breasts sensitive from the rush.

I heard footsteps behind me.

"You should feel honored to be here." Jake's fingers eased strands of hair away from my nape. "The people who own this place are selective on who enters."

"Permission to speak."

"Granted."

"Thank you, sir. For inviting me."

"You don't know where you are."

It was a different atmosphere to Pendulum, with more

sophisticated décor. Pendulum's furnishings favored heavy dark wood, but here the style had a distinguished elegance.

Jake's fingers brushed my nape. "Lift your hair."

I did as he asked, curious as to why. Then I felt the pressure of a collar being placed around my throat. I wanted to reach up and brush my fingers over what felt like a strip of leather. Instead, I kept my hands by my sides.

"You could get to wear one with diamonds," he said. "If you earn it."

I doubted I'd ever graduate to that level.

I felt a rush of relief that it was him placing it around my neck, my nipples beading when his hands traced over my shoulder as though promising he'd keep me safe.

He stood in front of me. "On your knees."

As ordered, I lowered myself to the floor and waited, tracking the golden veins in the marble. *God*, this place was like a palace.

"Follow," he said.

With him walking beside me, I crawled across the pristine floor with my knees feeling bruised from the hardness. It made me wonder how anyone tolerated this for long. When subs reached their destination, I guessed what came next made this ordeal worth it.

I'd never once imagined I'd be doing something as risqué. Not me, the girl who went to work, then to Target, and sometimes shopped at Walmart. I was the college square who didn't draw attention for fear of ridicule. I'd given up on ever having excitement in my life.

Thankfully, I was permitted to walk down the winding staircase, under lighting that morphed into a red hue.

I sank back on my knees at the bottom of the steps, crawling once more along marble flooring past door after door. When we reached the last one, I continued inside the room when Jake opened the door for me.

When I reached the center, I returned to the kneeling position and rested my palms upward on my thighs, obedient and ready, my heart thundering. My face felt flushed from the exertion of trying to keep up with his strides. I was too nervous to look around me, because in my peripheral vision, I could tell where we were.

"Stand," he said, his voice stern.

I followed him over to an oak desk at the back of the room and peered down at the line of instruments along the edge. It reminded me of a collection to be used by a surgeon. Or worse, a medieval torturer.

I tried to read his expression, read his demeanor to see if he was going to use any of these on me.

"Welcome to your exam," he said.

"Exam?"

"To move on to the next level." He smiled. "I need to know you're familiar with these."

Oh, God, he doubted my place in his world. Scanning each one, I tried to push away my terror and focus on what I could remember from that book.

He pointed. "What's this?"

"Pinwheel," I said, guessing he was starting with an easy one.

"And this?" He rested his fingers on an electric device.

"Wand." Again, I checked his reaction.

He led me over to the corner. "And this?"

It was an eight-foot-high contraption, the hunk of metal very much like an Egyptian coffin stood up on its end.

What the fuck.

"A cage," I realized.

"Iron Maiden. Very much like the one from the Carthaginian execution of Marcus Atilius Regulus."

The victim would walk into it and the door would be closed on them. The medieval torture device was beyond menacing—spikes lined the inside, which could easily impale the victim. Any movement meant they'd be stuck with those sharp barbs piercing their flesh. Once the door shut, they'd be imprisoned to suffer a slow death.

"It speaks for itself." He gestured for me to enter the structure.

I pleaded with my eyes.

If this was the final test, I'd fail. I'd scream so loud everyone in this place would hear me. Or more frightening still, maybe they wouldn't.

Anyone locked in there would not only need a tetanus shot, but also a lifetime of therapy.

"Only kidding," he joked. "It's from a collection. It's priceless."

"Pity," I said, pretending I wasn't shaken. "I was looking forward to it."

"Well, we have this." Jake walked me over to the other side.

There, hanging from the ceiling, was a modern cage.

"That's more me," I lied.

"What's your endurance time?"

I swallowed hard before I could help it. "You mean being locked in that thing?"

"That's not what I meant, no."

"Can't recall."

His critical gaze stayed on me. "How many orgasms in a session can you endure?"

"Oh, a lot, actually." I moved over to the St. Andrew's Cross. "I like this one."

Because out of all the devices, it seemed the least painful.

Jake followed me over. "Then we'll begin."

"With?"

"The session."

"About time, Master De Sade."

"You really are a brat."

"I am," I said softly.

I tried not to flinch when he secured my left wrist into the structure. He did the same with my right, capturing me in handcuffs, my arms stretched wide. My breathing became shallow, but perhaps he'd think it was arousal. A sudden terror had caught me in its wake, my expression close to showing fear.

"By the end of this session," he said, "you will belong to me."

"I want that," I said breathlessly.

"I'm going to make you feel so much."

"Pain?"

"We'll see."

Glancing left at the Iron Maiden, I felt glad I'd not had to enter that one, at least. What kind of men liked to collect pieces like this? What if they did terrible things here? Ended lives in some dreadful fetish?

I'd not thought this through. I'd put myself last in all of this because I'd valued my brother's life above mine.

The rest of my motivation dwindled as I recalled his words.

"I'm into dark play."

What did that mean exactly? I was alone with a man who had a kink for doing bad things to people.

Jake stepped closer and yanked down my bodice. My breasts sprang free, nipples pert and beading, trembling against his hand as he played with them like he hungered for me.

His voice low and gruff, he said, "Your body drives me crazy, Stella. Everything about you is seductive." His fingers wrapped around my hair and tugged on my scalp, causing a delicious stinging sensation.

"I've already told you I'm into danger," he said. "And I am that danger."

"You?"

His eyes flashed with a spark that suggested he knew about my ruse. Or so it seemed. But I was already bound and under his control, completely vulnerable. He could do anything he wanted to do.

My heart was pounding hard—I was sure he'd see my doubt.

His mouth clamped around my areola, and he tongued my nipple as he tweaked the other breast, bringing rough discomfort that morphed into pleasure.

With strong hands he ripped the rest of the bodice off.

"I thought this was an exam?" I said softly.

"It is."

"What kind?"

"You were vague when it came to your endurance. I'm going to explore that for myself." He ambled over to the line of instruments and perused them, finally setting his fingers on a long device.

He moved around me, stalking the St. Andrew's Cross as though deciding where to hit me with it, like a predator circling his prey.

He pointed the device toward my thigh and a jolt of electricity zapped through my flesh; pain morphed into heat, which dissolved into a thrilling spark.

I wanted to ask more questions, but I knew silence was expected so I bit my lip. I'd merely have to endure anything he did to me. I told myself it was worth it. What price can be placed on a life?

Even if I was to lose mine trying to save another.

"Relax your mouth." He tipped up my chin. "I don't want you biting your tongue."

Slacking my jaw, I obeyed.

He shocked me repeatedly and it was just about bearable. Yet, as he continued to spark discomfort, a warmth saturated my body, soothed and calmed me, as though that flood of dopamine he'd mentioned at SoFi Stadium was happening to me.

Me, the girl scared of her own shadow.

De Sade brought over a cat-o-nine tails, using it to strike my skin all over, until my flesh flushed red. He also used it to whip my pussy, causing me to flinch at the spike in my arousal each time he brushed it over my sex, nearly causing me to climax. The dampness between my thighs was proof my body yearned for more.

Jealousy surged as I watched him wield that thing with masterful strokes, pining to have that leather handle within my own grasp, as though drawn to control the moment as it unfolded with him as my Dom.

Spacing out, I tried to gauge how long we'd been in here.

Time dissolved as my mind wandered off.

Metal pincers were placed on my nipples, sending a rush through me as he methodically tightened them. Blood flooded into them, bringing a delicious pang of need surging down my belly and between my thighs.

What appeared to be strands of diamond chains were secured around my waist and clipped either side of my labia to expose my clit. This was the kind of bewitching treatment a goddess would receive. The constant attention of a man worshipping her, dressing her in dazzling jewelry. His strokes, pats and caresses something I'd longed for.

De Sade stood back as though admiring his handiwork.

To me, he'd earned that title already—the name given to him by friends in the scene.

"Your exam is, in fact, pleasure," he said, his voice seemingly far away.

"Pleasure?" I felt relief as his words sank into my psyche.

"Pleasure on my terms."

Blinking, I tried to fathom what that meant. It was hard to focus with those pincers causing my breasts to pang as though his mouth still captured them between his teeth, scraping bliss into the sensitive tissue.

De Sade brought over a vibrating wand and rested it against my nipple and then turned it on.

Jaw slack and mouth wide, I tried to endure the radiating pleasure sustained on my breasts as he glided it from one nipple over to the other and back. I couldn't focus, couldn't think straight. Couldn't fathom how something so scary could feel like a drug being released within my veins.

A rush of bliss had me soaring to new heights—he'd pressed it against my clit.

Oh, God, let me stay here forever.

I sank deeper into euphoria and then jolted like I'd been struck by lightning.

Coming hard, and harder still, as some part of me reminded myself that a master must give permission for a sub to climax. But no woman could have that thing pressed against her sex and not go as wild as I was now, squirming and writhing, my deep throaty moans filling the chamber.

I rode the blinding orgasm to its end, chasing after it, desiring more of the intense sensation.

De Sade eased the device away.

"Permission to come," I said too late.

With a nod of approval and surprisingly no chastisement, he eased it between my thighs and this time it rested along my folds, the tip of it at my anus, like I was riding the thing only he held it there.

The powerful vibrations shocked me into an immediate climax as though my entire body was experiencing an orgasm.

Someone screamed—me. I'd been taken to the heights of pleasure too high, too fast, too fiercely.

My scream dissolved into throaty groaning as I roiled against the hard structure behind my back, trying to drag my wrists out of the cuffs to free myself, fighting against this, trying not to surrender to this insanity that was mindlessness. Trying not to surrender *to him*, but that dreadful ache owned me completely.

He owned me.

Seconds passed as he waited with the wand in hand, watching, judging, gauging.

Then, when my trembling ended and I rallied myself, he repeated the action, again resting the wand directly on my clit, directing more of the thundering vibrations deep within me. Again, I was catapulted into the stratosphere, my eyes squeezed shut as though that would help.

Somewhere in the recesses of my mind I'd read this was forced orgasms. The restrained submissive would be powerless to object. Or refuse. Or deny her Dom's desires to see her come again and again and again.

An obedient sub would endure her master's desire to see her wrecked this way, her pussy savaged with pleasure, hear her continuous orgasmic screams, and submit to the unending bliss that raged on.

Sinking deeper, surprised by my recovery rate, I went within, spacing out and rising each time to the challenge he demanded from me. Gritting my teeth, forging new thoughts, new memories, receiving my punishment, my torture as though being born anew.

Free.

I discovered that I wasn't willing to settle for one climax but fiercely hunted after another and another and another. Demanding more, my thighs soaking wet from arousal, my body violently shuddering as I tried to remain standing while De Sade continued to attack my sex with his fierce craving for my orgasms—tearing them out of me.

He was a savage master who refused to relent.

De Sade finally stood back, seemingly impressed. "Again?"

"If you deem me worthy, sir," I said, my own voice sounding far away.

This seemed to please him. "Again, it is."

In a daze, I became aware of him walking behind me. Seconds passed but maybe it was minutes. I felt a pressure near my ass, a finger probing there.

Oh, God, he was playing with my rim, the sensations raw and real as he examined me there. Applying lube from that touch of cold. A push, a shove, and something was inserted into my anus. Then, as he faced me again, he inserted a small dildo into my pussy. I clenched it tightly so that gravity didn't steal it away.

"See how your cunt responds to me?" he said huskily.

"Yes, sir!"

"As I get to know your pussy intimately, I'll know what makes you transcendent."

"I want that." How could I not?

"You're an extension of the Goddess energy, stars bow at your feet. Because you are a woman."

"What?" His words faded into the ether.

"Ready to be exulted?" He lifted a small device that controlled them both and pressed a button.

The vibrations rose from deep within my ass, my entire body wracked with a violent pleasure, causing me to quiver as I rose higher still.

In shock, I watched him turn up the speed.

"Come," he demanded. "This one is for me."

Holding his gaze, I gritted my teeth because it was impossible to relax my jaw this time as I endured the devious pleasure. This filthy craving had me feeling as one with the butt plug, and owned by the dildo. Melting into this moment, I strained to keep my gaze on his as I offered my climax and all that came with it—my body, soul, and my past and future. My entire existence was *his*.

Until finally the shaking became too much, felt too cruel, too impossible to endure.

"Mercy!" I yelled.

"That's not your safe word," he said.

The delay seemed excruciatingly long as I tried to recall my safe word.

"Diamond," he offered softly.

"Diamond!" I pleaded.

The vibrations ceased immediately and yet I stood leaning forward, hanging by my arms like I'd been given a sedative.

"Stand straight," he said.

Pushing up, I tried to straighten, tried to clear my vision as tears streamed down my face. My soft smile proved this glorious abuse of power was something I had always yearned for. The part of me that had been suppressed had found a way out.

I didn't know it could be like this.

Then, as my vision cleared, I noticed him standing there—a man wearing a bone white mask, his chestnut eyes glaring at me as he came forward into the light. He had broad shoulders and perfectly ruffled dark hair. His suit had been tailored around his tall frame.

De Sade had respect for him. That much was obvious. I could see it from the way he gestured toward me.

Was he offering me to him?

I was suddenly aware of the jewelry draped around my waist, exposing me. The thought that this man might have been watching me from the shadows had me blushing wildly.

"What is your biggest fear?" asked the mysterious man.

"What?" It was hard to think straight.

"Answer him," said De Sade sternly.

"Failing," I said, my thoughts gliding over to Jake.

"And?" the man asked.

"That I'd hurt him," I said, my voice trembling.

"You mean me?" asked De Sade.

Tears stung my eyes.

I yearned for him to wrap his arms around me, to give me his warmth, his comfort. I wanted his reassurance that he could pull my life back from the brink.

"I see." The man's gaze grew intense. "Do you consider yourself a good person?"

"Yes." My lips quivered with emotion. "Before, as well."

Before…

Again, I closed my eyes as the truth echoed around us. Had I spoken those words out loud? I felt boneless, with nothing left to give.

"Have you enjoyed this session with De Sade?"

I let out a sigh of relief at his hint that it was over. "Very much, sir."

The man gave a nod. "We look forward to getting to know you, Stella."

He strolled out of the room with a confident swagger.

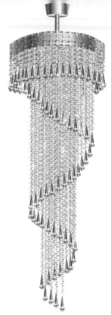

CHAPTER TWENTY

Stella

J AKE HAD DEEMED ME READY TO RETURN TO PENDULUM.
Or maybe it had been the mysterious man who'd visited me yesterday evening in that dark chamber, giving his opinion on the matter of me being De Sade's sub.

I wondered if the Iron Maiden belonged to him. If so, God knows what other things that man liked to get up to.

His strange questions had left me baffled.

But all that mattered was that I'd impressed Jake. Maybe because he'd assumed anything he threw at me would be too much. I'd been just as surprised to find I had a remarkable endurance for unending pleasure.

Those games could become addictive.

I craved a repeat of what he'd done to me in that room. This wasn't my world, but I was drawn to it like a moth to a flame.

I'd looked at him differently, with respect and with a kind of love, I suppose. As though this man had glimpsed inside my soul, even though I was still his enemy.

And now, here, I'd been told to wait.

De Sade had ordered me and another submissive to remain in this room until he returned. Elle and I had already met the first day when Lance had brought me here. She'd been the one to get me ready for my showcasing. Elle seemed more relaxed now. Less jittery than she had before.

"I have to meet with someone," Jake had told us. "Stay here."

From our kneeling position, Elle and I gave a nod of obedience.

"Elle, you have one hour to share everything you can about being a good submissive."

"Yes, sir," she agreed.

He'd revealed why he'd wanted us to talk. He'd also tipped his hand that I knew so little.

The only things in here were a stripper's pole and some leather chairs along the back wall.

Both of us shared glances of mischief. Elle and I mirrored each other in our bodices and thongs. I'd wanted to wear high-heeled boots but was informed those were reserved for dominatrices.

I might have been shy, but I'd never be truly subservient. So, this felt like a game. A game I'd never been destined to play before.

Until now.

"What do you want to know?" she asked.

I mulled over what I might learn from her. "Anything you think I need to know."

"Where did you train?"

"San Francisco." It was the lie I'd been told to tell. "You?"

"Here."

I glanced at the door. "I'm glad to see you again."

She brightened. "I see you ditched Master Merrill."

"He's an asshole," I said.

"No one likes him."

"Why is he like that?" I shook my head trying to figure out what made a man so cruel.

"You don't know?"

"No."

She glanced at the door like he might stroll in at any second. "He's a psychopath."

A chill washed over me, the feeling of danger ever higher. Psychopaths killed without remorse. Jake had warned me to stay away from him but had held onto that detail.

And my brother was being held captive on that monster's yacht.

"Are you okay?" she asked.

"Of course."

I couldn't give myself away by asking rudimentary questions that I should know.

"Tell me about yourself?" I said, shoving down the panic.

Elle looked horrified. "We don't do that here."

"Why?"

She stared off, eyes wide with worry. Then she snapped back into her usual bright mood. "We should get a drink."

"Let's ask for one when he gets back," I said.

Elle got up and lunged toward me, grabbing my wrist and dragging me to my feet.

"We can't leave," I said.

"He'll never know. We'll be back before he is."

She headed out the door, pulling me with her.

This gave me the excuse to explore. We walked along a hallway and took a sharp left. I followed her into an empty bar filled with the lingering smell of cigars. Round tables hinted at boring conversations.

Elle scurried around to the back of the bar. I sat on one of the barstools with my elbows on the counter watching her. She poured two shots of tequila. Then slid one over to me.

Why not, I thought. Bonding with Elle might prove useful. She'd been here a while from what I could tell.

I threw back my drink, tasting bitterness and enduring the burn as I swallowed. The buzz of the hard liquor hit me hard.

"Do you have a Dom?" I asked.

She looked uncomfortable. "You work for them?"

"Who?"

"De Sade and the others?"

"I don't work for anyone. De Sade is my Dom."

"No, he's not."

"Why do you say that?"

"You're not close to being in his league." She raised her hand. "That's not an accusation or insult. That's me being honest. He's primetime pain. From what I can tell you're a newbie."

A nagging twinge of fear. If me being with him didn't make sense, what were the reasons he kept me around? My thoughts swirled in an ocean of doubt.

"Sure you're okay?" she said.

"Who's your Master?"

She lowered her voice. "You can't share this with anyone."

"Of course."

Elle raised a finger. "A few of us are brought here…" She paused as she listened to see if someone might interrupt us.

"What?"

"We're sworn to secrecy about Le Chambre." She shook her head. "The room."

"What room?"

She pointed a finger. "Don't tell De Sade. It wouldn't be good for him if you do."

"Won't he find out?"

"He thinks he's taking over Pendulum. That's never going to happen. No one can stop them."

"Stop who?" I leaned forward. "Lance?"

She whispered. "Someone else."

And that someone else was who Lance was interested in. I was sure of it.

"What happens in Le Chambre?" I asked.

"We perform."

"Perform what?"

"Think *Eyes Wide Shut.*"

This was why Jake wanted me to talk with Elle, so that she'd share this with me. He already knew she was part of the secretive side of Pendulum. He'd probably ask me to betray her trust.

Sensing something sinister was going on, I struggled to subdue my fear. "Another," I said raising my shot glass.

Elle's eyes widened at hearing voices from behind the door.

"We're not meant to be in here?" I said, realizing the truth.

"Hide."

"What?" I scurried over to a slatted door and yanked it open. It led to a staircase. Elle shooed me to go in and then she ducked behind the bar.

I pulled the door closed and crouched behind it.

I heard a scuffling noise.

Cupping my hand over my mouth, I froze, heart pounding so fast it hurt my chest.

I could hear Elle protesting and a chair being knocked over. As I peered through the slats of my hiding place, I witnessed Elle being lifted and flung over a man's shoulder.

Quickly, I stood, ready to spring forward and plead for them to not hurt her. Tell them we hadn't realized this area was out of bounds.

When I tried to push the door open, I was sent tumbling to my knees. The bar door slammed shut.

Leaping up, I flung myself forward and twisted the handle. It was locked. Panic surged within me for Elle's safety.

Jake would be furious.

I searched for another way out.

Around the corner I found another door, this one unlocked. I'd find my way back and tell Jake what had happened. He'd find Elle and rescue her from those men.

A hallway stretched on forever and was eerily quiet. This club looked smaller on the outside than it appeared within.

I walked the dimly lit hallway hoping I'd be able to remember how to get back to the room Jake had left us in.

I jolted to a stop as a man suddenly appeared. Staring back at me was a familiar face.

"There you are." Jake's friend Atticus seemed surprised to see me. His eyes narrowed with disapproval. Lifting his fingertip to his mouth, he warned me to be silent. It was a sinister gesture that set my flesh alight with dread.

"I'm lost," I whispered.

"Jake's looking for you," he hissed under his breath.

"Can you help me get back to him?"

Atticus reached for a door handle and shoved me inside a small room—a closet or something. Again, he raised his finger and rested it on his mouth, ordering my silence.

Male voices trailed past outside. They were looking for me. I just knew it.

Atticus rested a hand on my shoulder. I glanced at his tattoos. One, a snake curling out of his cuff. The ink was beautiful but terrifying.

I'd willingly stepped in here with him.

Atticus seemed equally intrigued with the intimate room as he looked around it. It was small for a cupboard and still out of place.

He gripped me. "What are you doing at this end of the club?"

"I went to the bar to get a drink."

He looked in that direction. "You shouldn't be wandering around alone. We can't protect you if you're out of sight."

"I don't need protecting."

I heard more voices outside—then my name was mentioned. They were after me. I'd made a terrible mistake by leaving that room. But really, now the danger had been elevated by learning more about how sick Lance was, but I'd had no choice.

Atticus' hand swept up and he covered my mouth to stop me from speaking. I reached for his wrist but couldn't budge his hand.

He eased it away. "Talk," he said.

"I told you the truth."

"Don't make me hurt you, Stella."

I stuttered out, "I'm searching for a friend."

Atticus rested his warm palm between my breasts. "Elle?"

"Yes."

His touch felt like a warning that morphed into a gesture of re-assurance. "Where did Elle go?"

"They came for her."

He squeezed his eyes shut in frustration.

"Will they hurt her?"

He ignored that. "Tell me what happened."

"We went to a private bar. Men came and we hid, but they found her. I tried to run after her, but they locked the door. Please help me find her."

He shook his head and his expression turned dire.

"Atticus." I grabbed his sleeve. "Are we moving?"

He'd already sensed it, too, from the way he reacted. His expression turned dark as he rested his hand against the wall.

Perhaps the tequila was making me feel dizzy.

Then I realized where we were. "Is this an elevator?"

Atticus stared at me accusingly. "What did you touch?"

CHAPTER TWENTY-ONE

Stella

THE SECRET ELEVATOR DOORS SLID OPEN, REVEALING A LONG, red-carpeted corridor.

Atticus frowned, his expression one of curiosity mixed with concern.

Slender pillars lined the way with mirrors on either side—the décor a contrast to the rest of Pendulum. It was like stepping into another era.

Atticus frantically searched for a button to push inside the elevator, as though he knew we shouldn't stay on this floor.

Movement down the hallway had us both staring in the same direction.

With reticence, he stepped out of the elevator and peered over his shoulder at me. "Keep your mouth shut."

A tall, elegant woman glided down the hallway towards us. She looked stunning in a diamond-studded bodice that hugged her curves. Her face was completely covered with an ornate mask, and she wore a headpiece with a spray of feathers.

When she reached us, I sensed her concern.

Atticus assessed the striking figure as though he'd been mesmerized by her presence. I hardly knew him, but this man appeared shaken.

This had to be the secret floor.

"What is this place?" Atticus asked her, his voice sounding gravelly.

The woman turned her head sharply as though she'd heard something. "Not here."

Atticus stepped back into the elevator and punched a button on the wall.

I waited for him to join me.

Instead, he stepped out again and faced the glamorous brunette.

The elevator doors closed, separating us. Frantically, I searched for the camouflaged button he had pressed.

The elevator began to descend. I was leaving him behind—leaving that secret floor. The one I needed to explore.

Despite everything, that was the real reason I was here. I'd gotten distracted by De Sade's aura. I'd started to feel like I belonged.

My thoughts scattered as I rallied my courage to find my way back to him.

The elevator doors opened to reveal a masked man wearing the same tailcoats I'd seen the other staff wear. He looked just as surprised to see me.

I'd made it back to the ground floor. But I wasn't out of danger.

"What are you doing?" he said sourly.

I scurried out and tried to pass him.

He studied the space behind me as though he knew it was an elevator. "Where did you come from?"

"I got turned around," I told him.

He seemed to believe me.

I hated leaving Atticus behind. Especially after seeing the fear in that woman's eyes. Maybe it was because we'd discovered *their* secret. My heart was still racing from my close call. Atticus had made sure I got to safety. Or at least he'd tried.

I felt a pinch at my nape.

The man's grip felt so tight it made me squirm in pain. He pushed me forward down a long hallway before opening a door and shoving me inside.

Drenched in panic, I tried not to hyperventilate.

A crowd of men filled the room, some standing in groups and others sitting in leather chairs. They'd discarded their masks. The scent of cigars hung thick in the air. Conversations ceased as they all turned to look at me.

The man's grip still held me in place.

I took a deep breath, trying to calm my nerves and not show any emotion. I stood still, hoping they'd soon turn their dead eyes away.

Then I saw him. Lance Merrill was sitting with three men. A smirk stretched across his arrogant mouth and a psychopathic glint shone in his eyes. I could see it now. Before, I'd not wanted to accept that he was the kind of man who'd kill without question.

It was obvious from his amused expression that he gleaned pleasure from my distress. Even so, I needed to get him alone, needed to tell him I'd found the secret floor he'd wanted me to discover. I'd get him to release my brother now. That had been the agreement.

He stood up and strolled toward me with that familiar swagger. Then he suddenly paused.

I noticed that the men were all staring past me.

"Get your hands off her," said a familiar voice.

I felt relief as the man holding on to me loosened his grip and stepped away.

A strong arm wrapped around my waist. "I've got you."

Jake lifted me into his arms, hugging me against his chest. He carried me out of the room with ease.

I exhaled slowly, my panic ebbing. I wanted to leave, but at the same time, I finally had something to offer Lance.

I nestled against Jake's neck. "I got lost."

His body stiffened. "The dragon's lair is not the best place to get lost."

"I was forced to go in there."

When we made it to the club's foyer, I realized he was carrying me out of the building.

"They took Elle," I blurted out. "I can't go until we find her."

"Leave that to us."

"Atticus," I said. "He's still up there."

Once we were outside, Jake set me down and took my hand in his, leading me over to the passenger door of his Lamborghini. "Get in."

In a shaky voice, I said, "We found a secret floor. Atticus got out of the elevator. He sent me back down."

Jake's brows rose. "I told you to get in."

"Please, I can't leave knowing Elle might be in trouble."

"Get in the fucking car, Stella."

I slid inside and felt the woosh as my door was slammed shut. Jake came around the front of the car and climbed in beside me.

"Aren't you going to do anything?" I asked.

He gripped the steering wheel. "I told you to stay in that room."

A shiver of uncertainty washed over me. "You don't think it's strange that floor is kept hidden?"

"Who told you that?"

I bit my lip. "Did you already know about it?"

He shook his head. "I'm more curious about who told you."

"A rumor, but it turned out to be true. We found it." Keeping secrets wasn't going to help my friend. "Elle told me she's a part of it and that she doesn't have a Dom. I don't think it's a good place up there."

He reached for his phone and angrily texted someone. I tried to read what he was typing but he tilted the phone away. "Forget what you saw." He shoved his phone into his pocket.

"I won't." Because asking me to abandon Elle was monstrous.

De Sade shook his head in frustration.

With a press of a button, he started the engine and zoomed us away from the curb. In my side mirror, I watched Pendulum growing smaller.

"What about your friend?" I asked bitterly.

"Atticus is more than capable of looking after himself. Trust me on this, he's someone who elicits fear."

Yes, I'd figured that out all on my own, having been trapped inside the elevator with him.

"Are you taking me home?" I asked softly.

"It's time for the conversation we should have had back at Chrysalis."

Chrysalis. I mulled over the name, that mystical palace with the grandest of chandeliers.

"What just happened back there?" I glanced over at him. "Is it bad?"

CHAPTER TWENTY-TWO

Stella

JUST AFTER MIDNIGHT, WE DROVE THROUGH A TALL GATE.
Jake's place?

The driveway was overshadowed by towering thick trees. Lush foliage surrounded the property—one of Mulholland's treasures, from what I could tell. His home was a mesmerizing structure. Moonlight glinted off its impressive glass walls.

This guy was rich as hell.

During the ride here, he'd made a call, warning his friend Greyson that I was in the car with him.

At least now I had intel to give Lance, something to placate him.

Also, I could find that floor again and show Lance where it was located. He could get his sick ass up there and discover the rest of what he needed to know.

As for Jake's secret business partner, I doubted I'd ever discover his or her identity. One thing was certain—these men were loyal to each other.

Jake opened my car door and helped me out, gesturing for me to walk ahead of him to the house's front entrance.

Once inside, I fell to my knees and crawled along the hardwood floor into the kitchen, stealing glimpses of Jake's home.

I might have failed to explore Pendulum's sixth floor, but I could look around here. That counted for something, surely.

Car headlights lit up the foyer.

"Pour us a drink," said Jake gruffly.

I stood up as he walked out of the room. I heard him exit through the front door.

Oh God, what if it was his ex? Weren't they still together? She'd throw a fit if she saw me pouring drinks at his bar, making myself at home. I didn't want to complicate things any more than they already were.

I scurried off to hide until it was safe to reappear. Leaning over the stairwell, I peered upward to the top floor and then down to the floors below. This place was huge.

Walking along the main floor's hallway, I found Jake's office.

I scanned his desk for anything that might be of interest to Lance, anything I could use as leverage.

Seeing a file with the word "Pendulum" stamped on the cover, I reached for it and opened to the first page. There were handwritten notes taken from a meeting.

And then I saw it.

My heart jumped into my throat. Journalist Dean Hersey's business card was attached to the page, one corner of it damaged. This proved it had been the one I'd rescued from my home and stashed in the kitchen drawer.

Lance hadn't stolen it.

The thief had been Jake. Then he'd made a show of coming back to the penthouse as though he had just arrived.

I sucked in a panicked breath.

Jake had acted surprised when he had seen me wrapped in a towel in the hallway. But it had been him in my kitchen while I'd showered, him stealing that piece of the puzzle I'd needed to help solve this dilemma. He'd memorized my door code from a previous visit and then had used it against me.

"Stella!"

I heard Jake's footsteps coming down the hall.

A shudder went through me as I shoved the card back into the folder.

"I'm in here," I managed to say.

Slipping out of my thong, I placed it beside the ornate letter opener and leaned over the desk with my palms face down on the wood, my butt stuck out.

I tried to hold back my anger while I held the perfect seductive pose of a sub.

Scanning the room quickly, I noticed that his office was empty of anything personal, with not one item reflecting the man. The only decor on the wall was an intricate gold mask. I guessed it was a collector's item from the way it was showcased.

A warm hand on my butt made me jolt.

"I thought it best to hide," I explained. "In case you didn't want anyone knowing I'm here."

I watched him walk over to a wall safe. He twisted the dial and opened the door, sliding a blue file inside before closing it.

He pivoted toward me with a steely expression. "Stella."

He said my name like a warning, as if he had discovered my secret.

With a tilt of his head, Jake continued to study me carefully. Then he came over to me and brushed my locks aside, causing my scalp to tingle. He caressed my arm, setting my flesh alight. "Did I give you permission to come in here?"

"Oh, can I?" I retorted, as though I'd misunderstood.

"You know what I mean."

"I thought Rylee had shown up," I said. "That's why I hid."

"It was Greyson," he said flatly.

"Oh?"

Which meant that while he was talking on the phone with him, Greyson wasn't that far behind us.

"What did he want?"

He let out an annoyed sigh. "We had business to discuss."

I glanced at him to see if the business might pertain to me.

"Greyson had an interesting update," he said.

"Is Elle safe?"

"Stand straight," he ordered.

"Is Greyson still here?"

"No."

I felt relief that they wouldn't be sharing me tonight—or ever, if I had my way.

I glanced over at the Pendulum file. Jake seemed to notice.

My throat tightened.

He leaned forward and pressed his lips to my throat, his mouth sliding along my collar bone and downward, leaving a dreamy trail of kisses on my skin that soothed and calmed me, making me feel as though he cared about me.

Or maybe this was him lulling me.

Leaning farther down, his tongue teased one of my nipples, then he switched to the other, going back and forth, suckling their pertness and sending ripples of desire through me.

He knelt before me, continuing his show of affection, kissing my belly, and then moving downward.

His fingers gently parted my labia. "Look at this gorgeous clit," he teased.

Flicking it slowly at first, and then increasing speed, he brought bliss to that delicate nub, causing me to lean forward, my toes curling.

"Master," I sighed. "The things you do to me."

"It's a pity this pussy will never be mine."

"But it is," I whispered.

"No, Stella." He peered up at me. "My tastes run different to yours. We're an impossible match. You are exquisite in every way, but I'm not the Dom for you."

His words shouldn't have hurt me, but they did. I was a liar and should know better. Maybe he sensed that, too.

These were games of intimacy interwoven with inner truths, despite all the secrets.

"Is this because I strayed at Pendulum?"

"No, it's a fact. You deserve to know so you don't have expectations about me."

Elle had warned me of this. So had Lance, in a way. This man was way out of my league in so many ways. Yet Lance had nudged me toward him, knowing this very fact.

"Why are you telling me this now?" I asked.

"You've fallen in love with me."

I shook my head vigorously, but it was impossible to deny. I wanted to step away, pull back, but he'd already possessed my sex with a frenzied kiss, his mouth lavishing affection as though his words of denial had never been spoken.

How could he do this? He'd exposed my heart to passion with a raw promise of what could have been, only to let hope fade like a dying flower.

I felt a rush of pleasure, the need for his tongue's fevered thrumming down there to never end. I swayed as strong hands held me in place—a delicious punishment.

Are you breaking up with me?

But we'd never been together. Not really—not in the way my heart needed us to be. Now that I'd finally let down my walls.

My frazzled thoughts reminded me why: I was his enemy, betraying his trust in the worst way. It was delusional of me to think we could ever get past this truth. After it was revealed, he'd never want to see me again.

His tongue continued beating a frenzied pace on my clit, as though he, too, were lying about how he felt about me.

Finally, he broke away and looked up. "You taste like sin and forgiveness."

"I don't know what that means."

"I want to see you rope drunk," he said with conviction.

Jake stood and strolled over to a cupboard, lifting out strands of red rope. He carried them over to the desk and laid them down, pausing briefly to glance at the Pendulum folder.

He turned and stared at me.

He knows I know about the business card.

I scrambled to find words that would prevent me from being bound with the rope.

If he knew I was a spy, I'd be powerless to run.

I'd researched shibari. The submissive would be restrained as her master wrapped lengths of rope around her—an extraordinary kind of immobilization.

De Sade had been granted full power over me.

I'd stopped calling him Jake when he was like this.

Because when he became fiery and controlling, he showed he could rule me his own way each passing second.

"You don't want me to leave?" My throat hurt as I said it. "Instead of this?"

"There's still lessons to be learned."

"What kind?"

"One final session."

Confused and unsure, I remained still, letting him bind me in silky red rope that dug into my flesh, completely restricting my movement. I fell into the rhythm of each tug, each tightening, each pat on my pussy, a sign of his approval. The pleasure surged and then dissipated in a perfect cycle.

Minutes dissolved into what felt like an hour.

He stepped back and studied me. "How does that feel?"

I was left speechless, unsure whether I hated or loved it as I tried to deal with the sensations of this full body tightness.

Maybe if we'd committed to love each other I'd feel more comfortable with my vulnerability. But we hadn't, I'd merely consented to one last session with him.

A long goodbye.

Succumbing to his seduction, I'd willingly remained still even though I knew he'd stolen that business card, even as I'd sensed the danger.

Or maybe that was just doubt creeping in. Because, deep down, I liked this in the way you liked that first taste of something sweet, before it becomes too much.

I'd made a pact with myself to do anything that I needed to do, to push myself beyond what I believed I was capable of—to die if necessary.

Jake tilted his head thoughtfully. "Completely immobile."

"Can you take it off now," I asked. "Sir?"

"We're almost there," he coaxed.

"What happens now?"

He stepped forward and lifted me into his arms, carrying me through the house like I was a bound doll. I was powerless to stop him.

He took me out through the back door and walked along the edge of the pool. It was even impossible for me to wriggle. I was his willing prisoner. The rush I felt made me lightheaded and I could feel the perspiration on my brow. My legs were uncomfortably taut.

When he reached the deep side of the pool, Jake paused there and repositioned me so that I lay across his chest.

I was able to look down at the sparkling blue water.

A jolt of terror slithered up my spine.

"Diamond," I cried out, burying my face against his chest.

"Doesn't count when it comes to edge play."

"What?"

"Want this to end?"

"Yes!" I said, my chest tight with dread. "I won't be able to swim."

"That's the point."

Somewhere in the far reaches of my mind I recalled consenting to his lust for *this*. His obsession with edge play, the art of scaring a submissive.

"Jake, please."

"You're keeping a secret from me. Tell me what it is."

"Don't!"

His grip loosened. "You're only delaying the inevitable."

CHAPTER TWENTY-THREE

Jake

S TELLA SAT ON A BARSTOOL AT THE KITCHEN COUNTER WITH her hands wrapped around a piping hot mug of coffee.

I'd removed the shibari ropes from her body.

She wore a sheepish expression, refusing to make eye contact with me. I'd given her one of my shirts to put on and she had a blanket thrown over her shoulders to keep her warm.

It was 2:00 A.M. and we were both tired—but I could use that against her.

"Would you have dropped me in?" She didn't look like she'd trust the answer either way. Her gaze met mine and I saw confusion and something else there, too. It looked a lot like guilt.

No, obviously I wouldn't have tossed her in the pool. But I still had it in me—that was for fucking sure. I'd warned her about my dark edge of madness that very few are able to accept.

I stood on the other side of the counter watching her closely, my hands gripping the marble with the tension this moment warranted.

The things I could have done to her, had we become lovers. An interesting concept—me taking on such a pretty newbie.

While she'd waited for me in my office, Greyson had delivered a folder. Within it, I found the devastating confirmation of who Stella worked for.

I'd sensed it—we all had.

But some part of me had remained in denial because I'd wanted more time with the beautiful siren.

But this was over now.

My gaze swept over her stunning features and I wanted to run my fingers through her long black hair, brush my hand over her cheek. I wanted a tender moment to lull her into being seduced.

Instead, I resisted.

Stella sat there looking as vulnerable as a frightened bird.

The solemn news Greyson had shared made me sick to my stomach. Stella was working for Lance Merrill.

It made me wonder how much he was paying her.

"You did great," I said. "Did you enjoy the rush?"

She glowered. "Scaring someone into thinking they might drown? You think that's fun?"

I gave a casual shrug.

"You're messed up," she said bitterly.

I ignored her gibe.

After all, she was working for the worst human on the planet. It wasn't enough for Lance to have fucked my ex. He'd planted Stella into my life as a spy. Because everyone knew we took on subs to protect them. Then things often became complicated, like throwing love into the mix. Which, in all honesty, I'd felt the stirrings of with her.

But I had to shut those feelings down, keep my heart safely behind the vault.

"Tell me more about yourself," I said.

"You go first," she said, rallying.

"Sure. As I mentioned before, I grew up in an old-fashioned family. Experienced a well-adjusted childhood. Excelled at Harvard." I raised my index finger to make a point. "Football scholarship. Put myself through college. Was the number ten pick that year. Won a few Super Bowls. I have a taste for the extraordinary."

She pointed to the pool. "You consider that experience extraordinary?"

"That was me warning you not to fuck with me." I broke into a devilish smile to break the tension.

She shook her head as though to say, "What kind of man is into that?"

"I met you at Pendulum, Stella. The most dangerous club in the city."

And now we knew why.

Her lip curled with annoyance and then she eased into a fake smile before taking another sip of her coffee.

"You're able to cycle through orgasms at an impressive pace. You've been suppressed. It's time to enjoy your body. Be who you were meant to be."

And it was time she stopped working for the devil.

"Change the way you see things," I continued. "The way you move through the world. Then you'll find the kind of satisfaction you seek."

"I liked the rope," she said, digging down deep for another lie.

"No, you didn't."

She watched me, her expression riveted. "If you knew I didn't like it—"

"You didn't like it because you've not learned to trust me."

She sniffed. "When did you get into it?"

"The scene?" On her nod I added, "At Harvard. Then I left the lifestyle for a while to focus on football. A friend invited me back in."

"Atticus?" Her eyes widened with interest. "You're good friends?"

"The best."

"How did you meet him?"

"Atticus was in the ER at Cedars when they brought me in after my injury."

"He was your doctor?"

"One of them, yes."

"He scares me."

I wanted to say I approved. "Atticus reintroduced me to..." I stopped myself from saying Cameron Cole. "To other friends."

Back at Harvard, I'd kept my distance from Cole. His brilliance had made him an eccentric. Or maybe it was his intelligence that threatened his peers. His photographic memory. His ability to read everyone in the room and somehow expose their most private thoughts. I'd not been mature enough back then to comprehend that kind of genius. Or maybe some part of me felt shame for my yet to be explored kinks.

Turned out, Cameron Cole was the master of the dark arts himself.

"And Greyson?" Stella asked.

If I told her he'd designed a building in downtown L.A. for the Cole family, she might piece together more details.

I went with, "He designed my home."

She looked around the kitchen as though seeing it for the first time. Her gazed fixed on a photo I'd kept on the fridge—me and Rylee smiling back at the camera. We were standing on Santa Monica Pier together. It was a fond memory of when things were good between us.

I'd kept it there because not having Rylee in my life wasn't considered possible. I'd not wanted to face that pain, and I hated the idea it was inevitable.

When Stella glanced over at me with a pointed look, I gave a nod to confirm it was my ex, Rylee, in the photo. Even though I didn't say her name.

"After my injury, I believed my life was over. But it had just begun. I met *my* people. Discovered a place where my kinks were welcome. I may have lost a major part of my life, but I found the best kind of friends. Together, we do good work. We have the privilege of investing in charities that make the world a better place."

"You're a decent guy." She shrugged a shoulder. "Other than threatening to drown me."

I leaned forward on the countertop. "Talk to me."

"About?"

"How did you find yourself at Pendulum the night we met? Did someone set you up with me?"

She flushed brightly.

"This is me protecting you." I straightened. "We're the good guys."

"Why do you want to own Pendulum?" she asked, confusion showing on her flushed face.

Telling her anything about our plan would be a bad idea.

Even with her intentions to betray us, I wanted to save her. But the only way to do that was to get her to open up to me and confess.

"We want to own Pendulum so we can tip the balance to favor the subs."

"Aren't all clubs like that?"

"No."

"I don't need protecting," she said softly.

"Come on. Bring your coffee."

I led her into the sitting room and gestured for her to sit on the large sofa. I remained standing. Once she was seated, I picked up the remote and turned on the TV.

Stella, still wrapped in the throw, looked intrigued as she clutched her mug with both hands. Even now, I couldn't hate her for the lies. Because I knew the danger she'd stepped into.

I brought up the footage of me on the field that fateful day.

At first, it had been impossible to watch. I'd been encouraged to see it by my therapist in order to desensitize myself from the event. Now, there was distance between me and the man lying immobilized on the field. My teammates were gathered around me, the camera catching their expressions of abject horror.

They knew it was bad.

It was worse than they'd imagined.

I wasn't moving. Couldn't. My neck had been broken, but I wouldn't find that out until later. After the barrage of tests at Cedars-Sinai Hospital, endless examinations, and those noisy MRI's, I'd been told what I had already sensed—walking again was impossible.

During those first hours, I'd cycled through so many emotions, and in the end, they'd had to sedate me. Dr. Atticus Sinclair had called in Cole, because Atticus knew the road back for me would be long and complicated.

Hope came in the form of a brilliant psychiatrist. Cole and I were reunited. This time, unlike those years at Harvard, I didn't turn away from him.

He was the reason I was able to stand and walk. He refused to give up on me.

A blur of movement showed onscreen as the camera swung away from my still body. I wanted to go back in time and kneel beside myself to say it would all work out. That no matter what I would be told, I would find a way to walk again.

Stella looked desperately sad. "Why are you showing me this?"

A flick of a button and there was me again on the screen. Only this time I was trying to walk for that first time during rehab, a neck collar secured tight, taking my first steps with two physiotherapists on either side, rallying me on. They were the best medical professionals that Switzerland could offer.

"It was a long road back," I said, recalling Cameron Cole's words.

"You're very brave, Jake."

"Friends got me through it."

"Why are you showing me this?"

"I lost something precious to me. My career was everything. My identity. My passion. My first love. It was all torn from me. But I found my way back."

Her eyes watered with empathy.

I needed to hear her say it. To see her come around to honesty, be the better person and confess she'd used me.

I needed to know I wasn't wrong about her.

Maybe some part of me wanted to give her the second chance I'd been given. As though karma had paid it forward. My heart told me she was worth it. My mind was warning me that I should push her out of my life and never see her again.

Yet her enduring sweetness, her continued aura of innocence, kept me trying to achieve some semblance of understanding.

"I sense you've lost something, too," I said.

Her gaze shot to the TV—at the image of me forcing a smile as I took that fourth step with a look of determination, my career over. Greatness had been snatched from me—or so it had felt.

Pain therapy brought me back. Those first sensations were something I had clung to, and they had defined who I'd become. I wasn't afraid of it. I chased after it like a diver coming up for air. Desperate for the raw sense of aliveness.

I'd given up the lifestyle in my twenties. And found it again just in time.

With me, it was that first strike of a whip against my flesh that brought intense pleasure, proving my brain had been rewired.

"I've not lost anything," she said softly.

"How about this time you be honest with me?"

"I think I'll go home now." She studied me to see my reaction.

"It's late. Stay here and I'll drive you home first thing." I was lying.

Within minutes, she'd gotten dressed in Rylee's PJs. They were about the same height and size. I made a mental note to pack up the rest of my ex's stuff and send it to her.

Even though that would make it final.

I escorted Stella to one of the guest bedrooms.

"Thank you for sharing that with me," she said, taking my hand and bringing it to her mouth to kiss.

It was a tender show of affection, seemingly authentic. Proving she had a heart despite what she was willing to do to me. Or maybe I just wanted to believe that.

Betrayal can leave a bad taste in one's mouth.

Her tenderness—real or fake—almost made me forget the truth that lay within that blue file.

"If you don't tell me what's going on," I warned her. "I can't help you."

"Jake, what brought this on?"

I walked over to the bed and pulled back the duvet. "In."

"Are we really over?" she asked softly, as she snuggled beneath the covers. "That would be a shame. I really like you."

My heart ached at the thought of letting her go.

"Get some sleep. I'll be down the hall."

"We're not sleeping together?"

"No, Stella," I said. "Not tonight."

Even though I longed to climb in beside her. Claim her.

Never gonna happen.

Because if I let myself truly fall for her, only to find out everything between us was a lie, I'd be destroyed all over again.

Learning to walk again had been virtually impossible, but trusting someone enough to love again? That would probably never happen again in my lifetime.

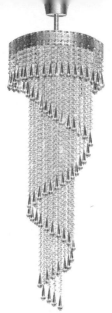

CHAPTER TWENTY-FOUR

Stella

J AKE LEANED ON THE BALUSTRADE OVERLOOKING THE HARBOR. He'd brought us back to the yacht club instead of taking me back to Dorchester House. I peered up at him quizzically. Maybe there was a thin thread of a romantic connection between us that would enable me to continue this ruse.

Before we set out, Jake had found me a pair of jeans and a T-shirt and jacket that belonged to Rylee. Wearing her clothes felt odd. I imagined she'd hate seeing me in her stuff. It'd be awkward as hell, really. Jake hadn't gotten to the point of being able to let go of her belongings, which screamed volumes.

Clearly, some part of him hoped for a reunion.

He'd dressed casually, too. Looking fine in his Levi's, Polo shirt, and bomber jacket.

If he'd thought it strange that I'd not gone to work on a Tuesday, he didn't say it. But then again, I'd given him the impression I was independently wealthy.

I stood beside him, grateful to at least still be in his presence. Last night, he'd shown me that devastating footage of his accident during a game. That meant something. Him sharing that moment made me feel like he wanted to get closer.

Again, guilt wedged itself into my heart.

He almost drowned you, I reminded myself. That's who he is. That sports accident had fucked with his head.

He'd tried to dig deeper into my life—so far, I'd managed to put him off the trail.

From the way he remained calm and seemingly centered, I'd placated him. For now, anyway. Him wanting to spend more time with me was a good thing.

It was hard to tell where his suspicions began. The business card was a vague clue. Jake wouldn't be able to connect the dots with it—a seemingly innocent contact I might have picked up at an event.

My hands wrapped around the rail next to his. "Are we here for brunch?"

He glanced back at the yacht club. "Place isn't open yet."

It was 10:00 A.M. I'd lost track of time.

Having been invited to sleep in his spare bedroom, I'd fretted all night that I'd messed this up. Now I hoped to get back in his favor.

I gazed out at the harbor. "Do you regret throwing your ring in there?"

"Hadn't thought about it."

I wasn't sure I believed him. "Why are we here?"

"See that?" He pointed to a superyacht.

"Hard to miss."

"That's where we're heading."

My intuition told me he knew more about me than he was letting on. The fact AJ worked on a yacht made me wonder. Though these were millionaires. Everything they owned was excessive.

I reassured myself of that as I followed Jake along the boardwalk.

Less than two weeks ago, Lance had flown me out to visit *The Hades* and then had shown me what was at stake. Being close to another yacht brought those memories back.

Jake frowned as he turned to look at me. "Come on."

I felt a jolt of uncertainty.

I wasn't ready to shed this fake persona. Couldn't, even if I wanted to. "Is this yours?"

"Belongs to a good friend."

I hoped he'd not found cracks in my story, or discovered I was connected to Lance. I wasn't sure what he'd do. If Jake knew anything, he was hiding it well.

We soon reached *The Mrs.*

Jake stepped aboard the walkway.

I held back. Once on there, I'd be vulnerable around him or his friends—with a spotty Internet connection, probably.

Jake strolled down the starboard side of the yacht.

After the rope play, after he'd threatened to drop me in his pool, he'd lost my trust. But what choice did I have? I had to push this ruse as far as possible.

I followed him along the polished deck, my stomach clenched with uncertainty. If he discovered the truth, he might harm me in ways I'd not imagined. I feared Lance, too. Feared what he'd do to my brother, but Jake was an unknown risk. He was into dark shit and maybe that bled into real life.

That was why they called him De Sade.

I'd managed to keep up this charade. Surely, I could persuade Jake to trust me again, assuage his doubts. My being able to do this was literally a matter of life or death for the most important person in my life.

I had to pretend I wanted to be a part of Jake's mysterious life-style. That I wanted everything he threw my way. That I was into whatever he got up to. Even though I'd shown annoyance back at his place.

I followed him down a well-lit hallway and into a conference room. I closed the door behind me. With no windows, the room felt suffocating.

"Let me guess?" I tried to hide my nervousness. "Sex on the table?"

Jake kept his distance as though knowing I needed that. "Not exactly."

I gave a seductive smile. "Then?"

"You've entered a high stakes game." He reached for my handbag and fished out my phone, sliding it into his jacket pocket.

My gut told me running should be my next move—getting off this yacht as fast as possible.

He folded his arms across his chest. "Tell me everything."

I stared at him. "About what?"

"He is going to destroy your life."

My throat tightened. "Who?"

Jake rounded the large oak table and stalked towards me.

"Master—"

He towered over me. "Cut the bullshit, Stella. After they've used you, they'll kill you."

My eyes widened.

"That got your fucking attention." He backed me against the wall, his arms placed on either side of my head, caging me in with his tall frame. "I want to help you. But until you're honest, I can't."

His chest felt hard against mine, his familiar cologne setting my senses alight.

I peered up at him from beneath long lashes. "I don't know what you're talking about."

"That penthouse isn't yours."

Fear slithered down my spine. "Why do you say that?"

"I've watched you."

"I don't spend much time there—"

"And whatever you learned about our lifestyle came from a fucking book."

"I'm doing my best."

"Your best is fraudulent."

"That's unfair."

"You targeted me specifically. Why?"

"I'm leaving." I pushed against him.

He didn't budge. He was all hard muscle, using his strength like a weapon of control.

"Who do you work for?" he snapped.

"Jake, what's going on?" I smiled. "Is this role playing?"

"How do you know that journalist?"

My smile faltered.

Jake was admitting he'd stolen the business card.

"They've been known to kill, Stella. Still believe holding out on me is a good idea?"

"You're the enemy," I snapped. "You threatened to drown me."

"To get you to talk. To see sense. Look, you seem like a good person. I'm a pretty good judge of character. But I know someone got to you. They have something on you. They're using it as leverage to make you do things you'll regret. After you've served your purpose, they'll dispose of you."

"You're wrong," I whispered.

"You are the evidence that leads back to them. You'll have to go."

"I still don't know what you're talking about." I peered up to him. "Please, I need air."

"How much is he paying you to destroy me?"

I flinched. "I'd never do this for money."

I've just given myself away.

"We can't help you unless you're honest with us."

Blood drained from my face. "We?"

"I'm the only one willing to give you this chance. The others, they have no patience for fuckery. If you refuse this opportunity, I'll have no choice but to back out of your life."

Tears stung my eyes. "I don't want that."

"And why is that, exactly?"

I broke his gaze.

"Don't disappoint me, Stella."

"You're the one buying *that* place."

He glared. "We're purging evil. That's why we're there. The question is, why are you?"

"Give me something," he said. "Something to prove we can move forward together. That you're worth protecting."

A sob broke from me.

He pulled back, allowing me a chance to run for the door. But I didn't. I don't know why—maybe it was because deep down I sensed there was truth in his words. That he was my only chance of surviving this ordeal. That for AJ, he was a savior.

He moved over to the table and rested his hand atop a blue folder. It was like the one I'd witnessed him securing in the safe at his office. Right before he'd bound me in red rope, performing shibari.

Before he'd almost drowned me.

He tapped his fingertips on the folder. "This is a photo of a submissive at Pendulum who's not going to make it out alive."

"Who is she?"

"Someone we're very concerned for."

"Maybe she doesn't need your help."

"Trusting me is the leap of faith she must take."

"Who is she?"

He slid the folder toward me. "Time is running out."

"For what?"

Jake studied me carefully. "Whoever hired you wants your help sabotaging us."

I shook my head. "I wasn't hired."

"Blackmailed?"

I drew in a shaky breath. "I'm sorry. I don't know what this is."

"We know."

The room fell silent.

I heard the cries of a seagull not that far away.

Again, I shook my head to deny it, trying to figure out how much they knew. Maybe Jake was bluffing so my response was crucial.

"I'm the only man standing between you and danger, Stella."

Agony settled in my chest. If I was wrong about Jake, then my brother would die.

This could be the ultimate test of my loyalty to Lance.

Who do I trust?

Jake pulled out a chair for me. "Think about what I've told you."
I refused to sit.

"You're under duress." His expression was calm. "That's why I never took you all the way, Stella. That's why we never fucked."

Because deep down, despite his dark kinks, Jake was still a gentleman.

"But you touched me," I said.

"And you liked it. I may have played with you a little. But you never saw what I'm capable of."

"I want this," I said, pleading with my eyes. "I want you."

"You revealed everything we needed to know at Chrysalis."

Wait, that man who came into the room? "The masked Dom?" Confused, I added, "He didn't really say anything. Who is he?"

"The fact you don't know gave you away, Stella."

"I don't understand."

"Did they threaten to kill you or someone you love?"

I trembled, not being able to hide my panic, as though fear oozed out of my pores.

"Someone you love," he said, realizing the truth.

I couldn't bring myself to admit it.

"Make something good come from this," he said.

"You're wrong."

"This yacht will take you to a safe place." He strolled over to the door and opened it, glancing back at me. "You can thank me later."

He closed the door behind him.

I ran forward and flung myself at the door, twisting the handle. It was locked. Drenched in perspiration, I tried to think clearly, even though my mind was spinning.

Then I felt it—that shifting movement beneath my feet. The yacht was moving. We were sailing out of the harbor.

"Jake! Let me out!" Frantically, I banged on the door, bruising my fists.

I tried to figure out where I'd gone wrong, tried to comprehend all the mistakes I'd made.

No one responded to my pleas.

Several minutes passed and still no one came.

Fighting back tears of frustration, I walked over to the blue folder on the table and flipped open the first page.

I stared down in horror at a photo taken from a wide-angle lens. *Oh, God.*

It was me at Venice Beach. It had been taken on the day Lance Merrill had visited me during my morning run.

Jake knew.

I sprinted back to the door and banged on it again. "Please, don't do this! Jake, they'll kill him!"

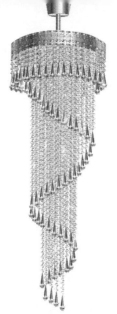

CHAPTER TWENTY-FIVE

Stella

HALF AN HOUR PASSED, MAYBE LONGER.

There was no way of telling the time. No windows to gauge how far we'd sailed out, which was probably why I'd been imprisoned in here. I wouldn't be able to signal for help—and I couldn't make a call because Jake had confiscated my phone.

Finally, I tried the door handle again.

It turned.

I blinked in surprise, opening the door and cautiously peering out.

I headed down the hallway passing cabin after cabin before hurrying through an outer door. I'd dive into the water and swim if I had to—even though I knew the danger of the tides.

I jolted to a stop, seeing the familiar view of anchored yachts, proving we were still in the harbor. They'd wanted me to believe we were leaving.

Hearing voices, and wary of being seen, I made my way toward the bow.

Jake sat at a round table. Beside him was a blonde, middle-aged woman I didn't recognize. She was around fifty, maybe.

This moment reminded me of the second I'd turned the corner on *The Hades* and had seen Lance for the first time.

Always follow your intuition, I mused darkly.

The woman's gaze met mine, her expression kind. I stared at her and realized she looked familiar, but I couldn't place her.

Jake's brows rose when he saw me. When I approached the table, he reached for a tall glass of water and slid it across to me.

I stood there trembling, my heart pounding, fighting the urge to run. Because if Jake went to Lance with any of this…

"Stella," he said. "Meet Mrs. Jenner."

I ignored her. "You locked me in there."

The woman pushed up. "It's nice to meet you, Stella."

"What is this?" I blurted out.

"Jake wanted us to talk." She emanated warmth. "Our situation might help you see you can trust him."

"I don't trust anyone." *Not anymore.*

Jake appeared serene. "Your mind is your only prison."

"Fuck you," I bit out.

The woman nodded with understanding. "You've been through so much."

"You don't know anything about me," I told her.

"You met my daughter, who's close to your age," she said. "She liked you."

"I don't know who you're talking about." I glanced behind me, close to running.

It still wasn't out of the question.

"Elle," she said, sensing my reticence.

The deck beneath my feet felt unsteady. "Elle?"

"Thank you for being part of the plan to get her out of there."

No, that wasn't how it went. I'd made things worse. When Elle had wanted to leave that room, I should have refused to go and clung to her.

Jake nudged the glass of water toward me again. "We have a lot to discuss."

I'd lost Elle and hadn't seen her since the day those men had taken her. "I didn't help." I cringed. "I made things worse."

"Because of you," said Jake, "we intercepted them."

"What happened to her?" I drew in a sharp breath waiting to hear, haunted by the memory of her being carried off by those hulking men.

Jake gave me a smile. "We found her and got her out of there."

Out of Pendulum.

Away from that secret floor.

"Elle wanted me to talk with you." Mrs. Jenner's expression was sympathetic. "She's left California, or she'd be here."

"I went after her," I whispered. "Tell her that."

"She knows." She glanced at Jake with a warm smile.

"Where is she?" I asked.

I met her gaze and saw that she couldn't share that information. *She's safe, at least.*

"I thought Elle wanted to be there," I admitted, knowing well enough not to say Pendulum. "She didn't say anything about being there against her will."

"Self-preservation," said Jake.

Elle's mom turned to face Jake. "Promise you'll get the others out."

His expression softened and then he looked at me. "We will do everything we can."

In a daze, I watched the woman say goodbye to Jake. She gave me a warm smile before walking away, headed for the ramp and to the harbor.

Stepping forward, I lifted the glass of water and quenched my thirst. Jake waited for me to set the glass down and then gestured for me to have a seat.

I shook my head, unable to relax.

"Talk to me," he said.

"Did you ransack my house?" I asked bitterly.

Jake pushed back from the table and stood. "You mean the place you really live?"

"Yes."

He walked over and captured me in an embrace. "Wasn't us."

"Did you come into the penthouse and steal that business card?"

"Yes."

"You made it seem…"

"We have both deceived each other."

"How did you know the card had value?"

"You'd stashed it in a cutlery drawer. Looked out of place. I took it on a hunch."

"Do you know who Dean Hersey is?"

"An investigative journalist." He stepped back and gazed down at me. "We want to reach out to him, but we're obviously guarded. Who is he?"

A sob broke free. "I can't say it."

"Take a breath."

"I don't know what to do."

"You must tell me why you were at Pendulum. Why you targeted me."

"I didn't know what else to do. I had no choice."

"Ah," said Jake quietly, "he has your brother."

My hand flew to my mouth to prevent a scream from escaping, one I'd held in all this time—suppressed from the moment I'd first stepped onto a yacht like this one. Somehow, I'd been brought full circle.

"Can you help us?" I whispered.

CHAPTER TWENTY-SIX

Stella

JAKE PARKED HIS LAMBORGHINI OUTSIDE DORCHESTER HOUSE.
He turned off the engine. "I don't like the idea of bringing you back here."

"I have no choice," I said, not wanting to go inside.

"You have a choice."

I unclipped my seatbelt. "My gut's telling me it's the right thing to do."

Until I knew AJ was safe, I'd keep up the appearance that nothing had changed. Lance was still wielding his evil control over everyone.

Jake's jaw tensed. "If you sense danger, you get the fuck out of there, understand?"

"If I take off, away from here, he'll hurt my brother."

"We won't let that happen."

"How?"

"A friend of mine is a retired SEAL. He'll help us rescue AJ."

"You promise?"

"Every resource is at our disposal." He unclipped his seatbelt and turned to face me. "How are you holding up?"

"I'm scared of making the wrong decision," I said, my words coming out in a rush.

And I was still afraid to trust anyone.

He reached out and brushed a strand of hair away from my face. It felt comforting. Tilting my head, I rested my cheek against the warmth of his palm, wanting to stay like this until the ordeal was over.

I had to be strong for a little while longer. "When you found the business card, why didn't you say something then?"

"We were gathering intel on you, Stella."

At least he was honest about it.

"Have you personally reached out to Dean Hersey?" he asked.

"Not yet. I think he's my brother's contact in all this. Maybe the reason they have him." I paused, thinking. "I'm not certain, but I think AJ saw something illegal on *The Hades* and was going to give that journalist the evidence."

"Move forward with caution."

I drew in a sharp breath. "How long have you known about me?"

"Pretty early on."

Air rushed from my lungs as I let that sink in. "You played with me?"

"Gently." He gave me a devilish wink.

"Thank you for being patient enough to find out the truth."

"We get it. You feared making one wrong move would lead to Lance's threat coming true. Which is the only reason I'm letting you come back here." He raised a finger. "On my terms."

"I didn't know what else to do."

"I'm glad you finally told me."

"We're not going to the police?"

"We have a contact at the D.A.'s office."

"Please, Jake, my brother is everything to me. I'd die if anything happens to AJ." Panic swirled inside me, but I tried to stay calm.

"We've got this, Stella." Jake shook his head. "Lance just couldn't help it. He had to make an appearance at the point you and I met for the first time."

I recalled the exact moment when Lance strolled through the great hall with a submissive on a leash, his dull eyes on me and Jake during our first meeting.

Thinking of all the times I'd lied to Jake had me cringing. "When did you first know the truth about me?"

"Honestly, the first time I made you come. The look in your eyes as you gazed at me let me know that you'd never experienced that level of pleasure—a simple orgasm."

I swallowed hard. "I never meant to hurt you."

"Forget about that."

"I hated lying to you."

"I'll protect you, Stella. You'll become nothing but a memory to these people. Untouchable."

I wanted to say *I believe you.* The stress I was under had caused me to feel like I was having an out of body experience at times. Dissociating had become my refuge.

"AJ," I whispered his name as though by some miracle he'd know we were close to finding him.

Closing my eyes, I prayed I'd made the right choice.

Jake stared into the distance for a few seconds as though he, too, felt the weight of this nightmare.

Finally, he broke the silence. "I can't leave you here."

"I'm staying."

"You're not going back to Pendulum."

I shook my head. "You don't own Pendulum yet."

His jaw tightened with frustration.

"If Lance wants me to, I'll go. What choice do I have?"

"We'll get you a phone so you can keep in touch with me. I'll have it hand delivered this afternoon."

"What if he sees you doing that?"

"I'll put it in a box of chocolates." He smirked. "Very covert."

"We need to keep up the charade," I said. "You and me."

"We can have dinner again."

"That's not enough. I need to convince him I've seduced you."

"You did seduce me." He gave me a wicked grin.

It made me smile.

"Let us handle it from here," he said.

"If Lance sees me at Pendulum with you, it will placate him."

"What are you asking?"

"I need to convince him I've become your submissive."

"Absolutely not."

I studied his expression to see if he'd change his mind. "Please."

"It wouldn't work, Stella."

"Why?"

"A submissive on that level surrenders her heart, mind, and soul to her Dom. You're not capable of being that convincing."

"I can pretend."

"You can't fake subspace."

"Then teach me!"

"If you can't cope with fucking in public, you'll give yourself away at the first event."

I felt a terrible rush of desire, the heat of arousal.

It was the way he'd spoken those words with an erotic flourish as though he had no idea of how seductive he came across.

And I'd been the one meant to seduce him.

He got out of the car and strolled around to the passenger side to open my door. "That's not where I saw the conversation going, Ms. Adair," he said, offering me his hand.

"I think you like me."

He pulled me up and into a hug, wrapping his arms around me. "Tell me if you're heading back to Pendulum, okay?"

"Kiss me goodbye," I said, wanting to make this convincing.

Not a lie, a need for closeness.

His lips were already on mine.

I needed this, needed him more than I could remember ever needing anyone. His tongue slid into my mouth, caressing mine, searching, sharing something profoundly tangible.

I never wanted the kiss to end. I wanted us to have met under

---

different circumstances, at another time. Not like this, when the walls were too high to scale, and the heartache ready to be unleashed seemed inevitable.

Jake pulled away. "As far as goodbyes go, that was pretty decent."

I turned my attention toward the penthouse. "If Lance finds out I've failed…" I couldn't imagine what he'd do.

"Say the word and I'll come for you."

Maybe, just maybe, Jake Carrington was the knight in shining armor I didn't deserve.

I watched him drive away, already missing the warmth of his embrace.

CHAPTER TWENTY-SEVEN

Jake

THE WARM BREEZE COMING OFF THE MOUNTAINS HIT ME just right.

A lazy Saturday at home had morphed into a fun evening. I'd taken a breather from the party inside, preferring a different kind of company—*his*.

The ingenious psychiatrist Cameron Cole. We stood shoulder to shoulder, both of us admiring my cultivated landscaping, and of course, indulging in people watching. He was scary good at reading a person. Cole didn't offer to comment, because he was also discreet as hell.

I'd wanted to cancel this party, even though I'd planned it months ago. It was another one of my infamous soirées where the booze flowed and the guests roamed around freely. Mostly, I'd invited my closest friends from Chrysalis.

It was hard to relax knowing Stella was still in that penthouse. Lance, or his men, could wander in at any time. It made it hard for me to focus on anything but her.

"I wished we'd spent more time together at Harvard," said Cameron, interrupting my daydreaming.

"I needed that time to refine myself," I joked.

"We all did, I suppose." He sighed.

We mulled over how those years had flown.

"I know why Lance did it," I said finally, comforted by the fact I was having this conversation with a person who'd validate my suspicion.

Cameron glanced at me. "Lance's motivation?"

"Yes."

Cameron appeared fixated on the skyline in the distance and the impressive skyscrapers of downtown L.A. Amongst them, reigning supreme over all the others, rose Cole Tower. His brother Henry ran their tea empire now. But Cameron gave just as much time to their company.

"What's your theory?" He turned to face me.

"Lance is trying to distract us, right? If he puts a sub between myself and Rylee, that blows up my life, leaves me emotionally wounded and incapacitated." Because everyone assumed we were still inseparable.

"Only Lance doesn't know you were already done with your relationship," he said. "His aim is a misfire."

"Makes me even more determined to bring him down," I said.

"We'll prevail," he said.

Despite recent events, Cameron remained seemingly calm. With his hands tucked inside his jacket pockets, he appeared to be more interested in how I was holding up.

"Spill the tea," he joked.

"Stella means nothing to me." I was taking a gamble that he'd believe the lie.

He watched me carefully.

There was no deceiving this man.

I changed the subject. "How's the family?"

Cameron lit up as he often did when sharing that aspect of his life. The world still hadn't recovered from this ultimate bachelor being off the market.

"Everyone's doing great," he said. "Mia is Mia, fun and easy going."

They were cute together, too—balancing out each other in all the best kinds of ways.

Our attention was pulled to the other side of the lawn.

Atticus and Greyson were arguing next to my pool. I stared at them, throwing daggers their way.

We'd decided not to change anything in our routines so as not to arouse suspicion. Yet here they were, drawing attention.

Cameron and I didn't want Lance to realize we knew about AJ. We'd agreed to keep it between the two of us, along with our mutual friend Shay Gardner. With Shay's extraordinary military skills in covert operations, AJ stood a reasonable chance.

We threw money at the problem, as we always did, ready to hire the best team.

"What is it with those two?" said Cameron, looking over at Atticus and Greyson.

The music wasn't loud enough to drain out their heated discussion.

Stalking across the lawn, I quickly reached them. "Don't put it past me to throw you both out," I said, with a dark edge of humor.

Atticus shrugged my hand off his shoulder. He was fired up as fuck, your usual moody surgeon.

"Wanna tell me what's going on?" I asked him.

"Nothing," he said.

Greyson seemed just as pissed off. "Atticus won't tell me what happened with the woman he met on the sixth floor."

Atticus and I swapped a wary glance.

"You didn't tell me you met someone," I said.

Atticus looked me right in the eyes, conveying a warning. We were close to taking over that place, but there were even more secrets to uncover. I wanted the name of that mysterious woman, too. I needed to make sure we were gathering all the intel.

Why in God's name would Atticus keep anything from us?

Cameron joined us. "Not here, gentlemen." He gestured for us to go indoors.

"Should we be worried?" asked Greyson.

"She wore a mask." Atticus appeared uncomfortable.

"Can we meet her?" I asked.

"No." He was adamant, clearly protecting her.

But why?

"I'm not letting it go," Greyson said, pushing back.

Finally, Atticus relented and ambled across the lawn toward the house. We followed him.

I was cut off by Rylee appearing at the kitchen door. With a wave, I gestured to the others to go on ahead. I'd join them in a second.

Cole strolled away from us as though he wasn't part of our group.

I could always count on my ex-wife to wear something revealing to one of my infamous parties. Her low-cut top and tight jeans were sexy, though. I hadn't even invited her, but she'd turned up anyway. We were going to have to be careful about her overhearing conversations.

Holding up her plate, Rylee offered me one of her hors d'oeuvres. "What were you boys discussing?"

I tried to change the subject. "How's the food?" I asked, taking a bite of the mouthwatering morsel of caviar and salmon. One thing was for sure, I always hired the best caterers.

Rylee brightened. "I've eaten my weight in these."

"Good. We need to fatten you up."

She smiled, and that cute dimple I'd kissed a million times appeared. Then I felt a stab of pain, remembering her betrayal.

I gestured toward the pool. "That's where you'll die today if you invited Lance."

"He wouldn't get within fifty feet of Cameron." She beamed toward Cole as though challenging him was a good idea—even from a distance.

Cole stared back until she shrank beneath his scrutiny.

"Anyway," she said, turning back to me, "you're a fine one to talk."

Through the window, I watched Greyson and Atticus head toward my office.

"You told me you weren't going to see Stella again." Rylee's expression was a mixture of jealousy and satisfaction.

"She wasn't invited."

Triumph shimmied over her. "Then why is Stella secured to your St. Andrew's Cross, stripped down to nothing but a thong?"

The air left my lungs. "What are you talking about?"

"She's stunning. I can see the appeal. She's very edible."

No, she had to be wrong. It was another mind-fuck delivered with panache.

"You didn't know," she said, amused.

Realizing she wasn't messing with me, I found myself teetering on the edge of a precipice, feeling like I'd slip off any second.

"I'll talk to you later." I hurried inside. Navigating through the crowded kitchen, I feared what kind of encounters Stella might fall prey to, should a wayward guest wander into the dungeon.

She'd be powerless to refuse their touch.

I flew down the stairs toward my private dungeon, my heart pounding, feeling anger towards Rylee for not rescuing her.

Another revelation hit me. It had probably been Rylee who'd escorted Stella in there and manipulated her into being handcuffed to my bespoke device.

Jealousy.

That's what she'd shown.

We'd moved beyond toxic. My ex was now a dangerous woman to be around. I'd been too distracted by Stella to experience that gut punch over the decision to expel Rylee from my life—which was imminent.

Filled with dread and regret for not protecting Stella, I burst into the dungeon, catching my breath when I saw her.

CHAPTER TWENTY-EIGHT

Stella

I'D SEEN A PHOTO OF RYLEE ON JAKE'S FRIDGE DOOR, SO I KNEW she was his infamous ex.

"I'll go get him," Rylee had told me.

She'd answered his door upon my arrival at his Mulholland home. After inviting me in, she had escorted me down to Jake's bespoke dungeon.

She'd not shown any signs of jealousy—just extreme interest. But women like her were good at hiding their feelings. They'd learned to poker-face the shit out of stuff.

Thank goodness they were already divorced, or I'd have had even more guilt to carry over.

I braced myself for the possibility that a stranger might see me like this—anyone could wander in here.

I'd taken off my dress and thrown it over the corner chest. Now I was left standing in a thong with pasties over my nipples, looking super sexy and ready to talk with him. I would try to get him to see me differently, not as the vulnerable submissive he'd come to know but a young woman capable of so much love.

I'd found the nipple coverings in the underwear drawer. I wanted to impress Jake with the raunchiest outfit that was guaranteed to arouse him—maybe even persuade him to take me back.

I'd not expected anyone else to be here.

On the way in, I'd been met by loud music and realized there was a party in progress. I'd been met by the fire dragon.

I'd considered leaving and going back to Marina Del Rey, but the need to see Jake had been too great to turn away.

The door to the dungeon was suddenly flung open and Jake burst in.

I felt that familiar rush from standing in his presence, my flesh alight already from merely the sight of him.

He glared at me with a quiet fury, breathing hard, his brows furrowed and hair ruffled—and looking incredible in designer jeans and a casual T-shirt.

Music from Harry Styles flooded through the open door—until he closed it.

His attention shot to the St. Andrew's Cross, then back to me. "Rylee told me you were secured to the Cross. But you're untouched?"

"Yes," I said.

"Did something happen with Lance?"

"No."

"A problem at the penthouse?"

"No."

"Why are you here?" He stepped closer.

"I wanted to see you."

"Who told you to wait here?"

My mouth twisted in embarrassment. I might have messed up by being seen.

"Rylee?" he confirmed.

"She seems nice. Told me she'd met all your subs, of which there have been many." A dig at me, I imagined. "She seems to approve."

"I don't need her approval."

"It was good to hear it from her."

"Only you're not my fucking sub, Stella," he bit out, reminding me of that fact with the ease of a verbal sledgehammer.

He stalked over to me and cupped my cheeks with his palms, leaning down as though to kiss me, his breath warm on my lips, his presence clouding my doubt.

Seconds passed as we stared into each other's eyes. I surrendered to the fiery sensation of want, lust causing my breasts to swell, my nipples to harden.

There were speckles of hazel in his brown irises. I'd never noticed them before. I'd never been brave enough to hold his gaze this long until now. His power endured, yes, but it was as though during these unfolding moments, he had become my equal.

His lips brushed mine. "This isn't going to happen."

His words cut deep because I could see he wanted me as much I did him.

His fingers roamed over the pasties, causing my nipples to bead. "Why are you wearing these?"

My cheeks flushed. "I didn't know you were having a party."

"That's because you weren't invited." He stepped back.

The loss of his heat made me shiver. I could feel his affection dissipating.

"Disobedience won't be tolerated."

"It's me," I stuttered. "Please."

I wanted to tell him to throw these games away and love me for me, as a normal girl and not one of his subs.

"Stella, I have guests."

"I saw that."

"Why are you here?"

"You told me you weren't seeing her anymore."

He sighed. "Rylee wasn't invited either. The women in my life keep turning up uninvited." He paused, shaking his head. "We agreed you were going to keep a low profile."

"I didn't say that."

"Did you drive yourself?"

"Came in an Uber."

He looked surprised. "I'll arrange a car to take you home. I use the word 'home' lightly, obviously."

"I've been thinking—"

"That's never good."

I ignored his quip. "I want to discuss something."

His mouth curled into an annoyed smile. "A phone call would have sufficed."

"Thank you for the iPhone."

"I hope you're keeping it hidden in a reasonable place."

That dig was referencing the business card he'd been able to steal.

"I just thought that…"

He stared at me. "This was a dangerous decision."

"These are your friends."

"I'm referring to me."

His hungry gaze roamed over me, his eyelids heavy, wanton with all the things he wanted to do to me. My body responded as though that look was an extension of his touch, heated and eliciting endless thrills.

He moved closer and traced his fingers down my arm, stopping before he reached my hand. "Go home."

"I'm not leaving," I said. "Not until you agree to let me be your submissive. It's what Lance needs to see."

"You're under duress, Stella. This isn't going to happen. I may be a monster, but I'm not unethical."

"You would be helping me," I said, trying to reason with him.

"I know you don't want to hear this," he said. "But you and I will never be lovers."

Tears stung my eyes even as I fought to hold them back.

"You're beautiful. But I'm a southern gentleman. So, there you are. Go home."

"Why not me?" I finally said it.

"It's complicated." He turned to leave.

"I deserve the truth," I said.

"You don't want to hear it."

"I'm here, aren't I?" I shot back.

He looked back at me. "The way I get into the mood to fuck is through excessive pain."

The silence between us brought with it a sense of loneliness. The room expanded around me as though I were seeing it for the first time. The instruments and contraptions all pointed towards agony. This place wasn't where he came to dominate. This dungeon was a form of pain therapy for *him*.

Suggesting he *needed* violence to…

"That's…" my voice trailed off.

I wanted to say something comforting or reassuring, or at least let him see I was open to his needs.

He watched my reaction, searching for proof that his secret was something I could endure, or even be capable of accepting. If I could just behave like he hadn't shaken me to my core.

"Get dressed." His shoulders slumped in resignation. "I'll have Greyson's chauffeur take you home."

"He won't mind driving all that way?" I asked softly.

But Jake had already left the room.

I took a deep breath, and then another.

The assortment of equipment around me offered way too many restraints. I saw that now. The accoutrements were designed for agony. And he'd been married to a prestigious dominatrix.

Yet my body craved all this. The thought of tying Jake up flashed into my mind and sent a shiver of arousal through my body.

It was a strange thought, doing that to someone. Yet it was arousing to think of myself wielding that kind of power.

Me in control.

As it always should have been.

Maybe Jake would come back after realizing I was open to all of this. He just needed to cool down.

Even outside of these circumstances, I still would want this man. I felt this certainty deep in my soul.

Because he was right about one thing: I'd fallen for him.

Reaching low, I slipped my hand beneath my thong and stroked

along my wetness, then examined my fingers for the evidence of what
Jake did to me.

This.

One stroke was all I needed to tremor with desire, yearning for it
to be him touching me. I had become addicted to the only man who'd
ever made me comfortable exploring my sensuality.

I was losing my fear of leaving my house—as though I'd learn
to thrive despite being thrown into the cruelest corner of the world.

And it was all because of Jake Carrington.

I should have told him that.

And I would—all I had to do was find him.

I exited his private chamber, determined to prove I was ready
for this. *For him.*

I could be anything I wanted.

I'd been lonely in that penthouse and now I questioned whether
to ever go back there. Not that I had a choice. I was a prisoner who
could come and go.

And I'd chosen to come here.

But I still pined for my old life. The one where I spent time with
my clients, made them feel good about themselves with their makeup
transformation, seeing their eyes light up with the realization they
felt pretty.

My clients probably felt let down that I'd not returned their calls
or messages. Who does that? Only people who don't care. My job had
given me purpose. But now my career was in tatters.

I'd lost a part of myself during this ordeal. I had doubts that I
could ever get back to that life.

But at least I'd found Jake.

Only now I might lose him, too.

I followed the winding stairway upward until I reached the
ground floor, passing others who were dressed casually. They didn't
bat an eyelid at what I was wearing—presumably because this crowd
came from the same lifestyle.

I strolled through the living room, trying not to stare at the
woman lying on her stomach. Fine needles were being inserted all

over her back by the man sitting beside her. This was needle play, something I'd never want to try. Onlookers observed the tranced-out submissive and her master as he inserted fine pinpricks of pain into her reddened flesh.

I went in search of Jake, passing more guests as I strolled along the main floor.

There, at the end of the hallway, stood Atticus. He was staring down at his phone and texting. I recognized his tattooed hands.

The last time I saw him we'd ridden that elevator together at Pendulum. Then he'd sent me back down to the ground level, either to protect me or because he'd found me annoying.

Atticus seemed to sense me behind him. Tucking his phone away, he turned sharply to face me. "Where the fuck did you come from?"

"Good to see you, too," I said.

He gave me a thin smile. "Glad you're okay."

"Can I ask you something?" I moved closer to him. "Was that the sixth floor we ended up on?"

He frowned down at me. "Jake didn't invite you."

I ignored the comment. "Did you see anyone else there?"

He exhaled sharply. "Forget you saw anything."

"Why?"

"Having fun stalking people?"

"I'm looking for Jake."

"I don't trust you, Stella." He stepped back. "You shouldn't be here."

"What has Jake told you?"

Anger flashed in his eyes. "You're not his sub. You need to get that into your pretty head."

"Rylee told me I'm his type."

"When?"

"On the way in."

"Jake and Rylee are out of your league," he huffed. "Anyway, Jake's a masochist who loves to dabble in sadism. Something tells me you're not into any of that."

I flinched.

Atticus reacted with triumph. "You didn't know."

"He told me, but…"

"You have no idea what level he's on. We're talking exalted grade torture."

"We've not tried it."

"Of course not. And you never will."

"You're not much of a friend to him."

"Why do you say that?"

"You should want the best for him."

"And that's you?"

"You share your subs," I said. "What does that make you?"

"Now you're boring me."

"Fuck off."

"The last time someone said that to me I injected insulin between their toes. The coroner didn't find it."

"That's a lie!"

He had to be bluffing.

His volatile reaction toward me made me realize Jake hadn't told him about my brother—even though Atticus was his best friend. Which made me question Jake's taste in buddies.

"You're still standing there," he snapped.

"You're gatekeeping whatever they do on the sixth floor. Not just one sub, but many at the same time."

I watched his reaction.

Now that Elle was out of there, I was able to weaponize that knowledge.

He arched a brow. "For you, I'll imagine a more interesting way to die."

I was left speechless.

Happy with that result, he walked off.

I was unsure if he simply had a dark sense of humor or if he was a sicko. I swore to myself I'd never be alone with that man.

Anyway, until AJ was safe, I needed to placate Lance if he turned up out of nowhere asking what I'd learned so far. Atticus knew something. I needed more of what he knew.

I followed Atticus and saw him enter Jake's office and close the door.

I hurried over and pressed my ear to the door, overhearing voices within.

"What the hell is going on with this office? You have nothing in here still!"

"I'm in the process of decorating it." That was Jake's voice.

I, too, had wondered about that. A man with such a rich history should have more to display in celebration around him. But Jake kept his office sparse.

"How did you find the sixth floor?" asked that first deep gravelly voice.

"There's a secret elevator," said Atticus.

"We need to see it," said Jake.

"Greyson, no one else goes up there until we know more," snapped Atticus.

"Why?" asked that familiar voice with a sophisticated lilt, who must have been Greyson.

"For fuck's sake," said Jake. "Give us more to work with, Atticus."

Atticus cleared his throat. "No one goes to the sixth floor without an invitation."

"Atticus, you walked in on their seat of power," said a man with a worldly cadence. I recalled where I'd heard his voice before—it was at Chrysalis. He was the masked man who had given me that brief interview.

Jake's voice piped up. "Cole, do you really believe that? It's not Lance that's the real problem here? All this time we've been misled."

Cole? I had a name to go with the masked face.

"Atticus, this woman you met on the sixth floor," said Cole. "Did she tell you anything?"

I recalled the tall and elegantly dressed woman wearing a bodice with a plume of feathers sprouting out of her headdress. She had a supermodel's figure and a diamond the size of a house on her left hand—a wedding ring, too. Atticus was clearly enamored with her, so much so, he'd refused to leave the sixth floor when I was there.

He'd sent me downstairs so he could have his fun.

Atticus' gruff voice held a warning. "Look, she told me that whoever enters the sixth floor uninvited doesn't make it out alive."

I drew in a sharp breath.

Shit.

I turned and a floorboard creaked beneath my foot.

The door flung open.

Atticus stood there looking annoyed. "Why am I not surprised?"

Jake squeezed his eyes shut. "I sent you home."

Atticus glanced over his shoulder at Jake. "What do you want to do with her?"

CHAPTER TWENTY-NINE

Jake

"GET IN HERE," I ORDERED.

Cautiously, Stella stepped inside my office. Atticus slammed the door shut, making her jolt.

That was unnecessary.

But they all had a right to be pissed off.

I'd made the mistake of not escorting her to the limo myself, ensuring she went home. Sarabeth, Greyson's chauffer, was probably still searching for her all over the house. I'd tasked her with driving Stella back to Dorchester House. A massive failure on my part.

As hard as it had been for me to tell Stella to leave, it was more about protecting her from myself than anything else. Because when Stella stood before me dressed like this, all I wanted to do was run my hands through her silky locks, drag her in for a kiss and then fuck her like crazy.

Maybe even make love…

I shook that ridiculous thought away.

When Cameron had suspected someone was at the door, he'd

grabbed my gold masquerade mask off the wall and put it on. Now, his hard gaze held mine behind that disguise—my first mask worn at Chrysalis and kept for posterity. We'd found another use for it: protecting our fourth partner.

"Looks good on you," I jested, trying to make it seem as though Cole rarely wore a mask.

Cole was observing both me and Stella now that we were in the same vicinity. He no doubt saw the chemistry between us, the undeniable need for her that I tried to hide. There was no escaping his scrutiny.

Cameron Cole was a mirror reflecting all our truths and secrets.

I'm sure my craving for Stella was glaring. Her beauty and her confidence grew more intense by the day. I wanted to believe I'd had something to do with it.

Stella's focus was locked on Cameron, as though the mask looked out of place. Four men meeting in my office and only one of them in disguise? It brought more attention to our fourth partner. But I got it. Cole had a family to protect as well as an empire that stood to lose billions.

I could tell he'd already summed her up with that uncanny ability of his to read a person, to leapfrog ahead of them and cut the individual off at the pass.

To Stella, he no doubt appeared intimidating.

From the way Stella was staring at Cameron, she might have recognized him from Chrysalis. That time he'd visited us during a session was memorable.

Cameron walked over and sat in the corner high-backed chair, crossing one long leg over the other and zeroing in on her with a laser focus. He glanced at his watch as though realizing she'd just recognized it.

Still, she'd not see his face.

Smart girl, not everyone caught the smallest details.

"It's rude to stare, Stella," I snapped.

She refocused on Atticus and Greyson.

"I caught her spying earlier," said Atticus.

"You should have told me," I said quietly.

"I was looking for you, Jake," said Stella.

"Our conversation had ended," I bit out harshly. "Nothing more to discuss."

Atticus glanced at Stella and then at me.

She pointed at him. "They don't know."

"Know what?" asked Atticus.

Stella hugged herself. "You really think I'm a spy, Atticus?"

"Now, now," said Cameron, his tone soothing. "I think it's time we told them, don't you?"

"Told us what?" said Greyson.

"How are we meant to believe her?" said Atticus. "She's working for Merrill. The photos prove that."

"I'm not," she burst out. "Well, not in the way you think."

I stepped closer to her. "It's safe to share what's really happening."

Her eyes strayed from my face to Cameron's mask.

Atticus shrugged out of his jacket and rested it around Stella's shoulders in a show of reassurance. Unusual for him, but he could see she was distraught.

Finally, the tension lifted enough for her to talk freely.

They listened, hearing how two weeks ago, she'd been summoned by Lance Merrill to board his yacht *The Hades*, sharing in her horror at seeing her brother held captive.

"I understand," said Cameron. "You don't want to be passive in your brother's rescue."

"No," Stella said, shaking her head. "Tell me what to do. I'll do anything."

"Avoid Lance," I said. "We'll do the rest."

She looked nervous. "If Lance finds out you know about AJ—"

"He won't," said Greyson. "As long as you don't tell him."

"I wouldn't."

"What have you told him about us already?" asked Cameron.

"Nothing really, because I haven't seen him since that last time at Pendulum."

She was referring to the time I'd rescued her from the lion's den.

"Don't tell Merrill about the sixth floor," snapped Atticus.

"I won't," she said. "But Lance wants to know the name of your fourth partner."

None of us reacted.

She turned to me with a sheepish expression. "He ordered me to seduce you so that I could hear what the plan is with Pendulum's takeover."

"Thank you for sharing that," said Cameron.

I was feeling the brunt of her words. The cruel truth meant that we'd never been destined to be anything but enemies.

"You will not return to Pendulum under any circumstances," I said. "Do you understand?"

"I promise," she said softly. "Have you reached out to Dean Hersey?"

We all swapped wary glances, not wanting to discuss that train wreck.

I closed the space between us. "Stella, I'm taking you back to the penthouse. I need you to wait there. I'll come get you tomorrow night."

"So, you know where AJ is?" She reached for my sleeve and clung to me.

"The less you know the better it is for everyone concerned," said Cameron.

"Your work is done," I told her.

To protect her and restore her faith in men, I had to remove Stella from the scene and expel her from my life.

It didn't mean it wouldn't hurt. It wouldn't be easy to let this extraordinary woman go. I'd developed feelings for her, but it was the right thing to do.

And all I had to guide me was my inner compass.

CHAPTER THIRTY

Stella

J AKE DROVE ME BACK TO DORCHESTER HOUSE IN HIS Lamborghini.

I'd returned to his dungeon first to retrieve my dress and put it on.

In his office back on Mulholland, I'd felt the burn of *their* power. Atticus, Greyson, Jake, and their secret friend were all intimidating in their own way. If anyone could take on Lance Merrill, they could. Or at least they seemed to have the courage and means to bring this ordeal to an end.

Jake escorted me inside the penthouse. I waited in the living room as he searched the entire place to make sure we were alone.

I was glad for the company. Being isolated hadn't been easy. The unrelenting dread never let up. But he was here, which meant something.

I'd paced the living room more times than I could count, trying to see my way through this situation. Maybe now, there was some real hope.

I dreaded watching Jake leave. Each interaction threatened to be our last.

He reappeared and gave me a nod to indicate all was well.

"Want a drink?" I asked.

"No, I'm fine."

"I pulled you away from your party."

He came closer, reaching out and cupping my face like he'd done so many times before. Only this time there was no kiss. Our gazes locked, our expressions showing we both knew our time together was growing to a close.

"Will you miss this place?" he whispered.

"Hardly." The only memories I'd hold onto were of us.

He stepped back and brought out his phone, sweeping his finger along the screen. Jake held up the phone to show me AJ's Instagram page.

I peered at his screen and gave a nod.

"You'd tell me, right?" I asked, hopeful that he'd tell me when the rescue would take place.

"Go to bed," he said. "It's late."

AJ, hold on. Help is coming.

Catching up on sleep would be easier if Jake stayed and watched over me, guarding me from the evil men who circled this place.

"No more turning up at my place unannounced," Jake added.

I hung my head. "I don't blame you for not trusting me."

He pulled me into a hug, my cheek resting against his chest. His subtle cologne brought with it the memories of all those times he'd brought me to my knees. Realizing my makeup had smudged his T-shirt, I nudged him away, feeling like it was the greatest mistake I'd ever make.

He looked down at his shirt. "Oh, no, if only someone had invented washing machines."

For me they were words of comfort. Because this was his playful side and it soothed me.

Jake pulled me toward the bathroom. "Get ready for bed."

He waited for me in the bedroom.

After brushing my teeth and washing off my makeup, I entered the bedroom and saw him standing by the window, peering out. "It is a great view."

"It is, but it could never replace home."

"You're going to be out of here very soon. If there is anything you want to take, have it ready."

He had me turn around so he could help me out of my bodice. Naked and tired, I slipped beneath the covers and felt grateful for the warmth of the duvet.

Jake sat on the edge of the bed. "I'll stay until you fall asleep."

"I'll never sleep."

"I'll watch over you."

"You're never going to trust me again, are you?"

"I'm still here, aren't I?"

"I regret going aboard *The Hades*, but if I hadn't…"

"I'm proud of you, Stella."

"Why? I feel like I've failed at every level."

"You haven't crumbled beneath the pressure Lance has put on you. That reveals character."

We were silent for a few moments, and then I asked softly, "Do you think you'll get back with Rylee?"

He shook his head. "No."

"You're still single, then?"

"Yes."

"I'm single, too."

"What's your point?"

I pushed down the covers to reveal my breasts to him. He started to lift the blanket up again.

"No," I said. "I'm hot. I'm going to sleep like this."

He stood and walked over to the chair in the corner. "I'm going to sit here."

"Can you help me take these pasties off?" I cupped my left breast.

"You can peel it off. Gently."

"Show me."

He gave a knowing smirk and came over to me. His hand felt

warm on my breast as he touched the edge of the pasty, peeling it back and lifting it off my nipple. My jaw went slack at the sting it caused. Jake's thumb brushed my areola to soothe the soreness. Then, he turned his attention to my right breast, easing off the sticky pasty, peeling it back to reveal my pert nipple.

"I want you to do it to me," I said.

"Do what?"

"You know. Bring me pain."

He flinched and rose quickly.

I sighed. "Why not?"

"Because you've been through too much."

I pushed myself up. "Don't look at me like that, like I'm someone who's weak. I'm not that person."

"I should go."

"Fuck you!"

"That's unnecessary."

"Is it?" I rose onto my knees. "We lied to each other. You didn't tell me you knew why I was trying to seduce you. We're both guilty."

"You're tired."

"You don't come into someone's life and show them pleasure on that level and then say, 'Well, see you. I must be going.'"

"I should've had someone else bring you home."

"Don't make me say something to trigger you."

He stepped forward and grabbed my throat. "You think a little girl like you is of any interest to me?" His grip tightened.

Eyes wide, I slipped into subspace, down and down and down I went, body alight with arousal, fire in my belly.

"Master," I managed.

"The things I would do to you," he said gruffly.

"You're not man enough," I retorted.

He smirked. "That insult doesn't work. Because I know my worth. I'm more of a man than you'll ever meet. If it's pussy annihilation from a hard night of fucking you're after, I can give you that—ravage your cunt until you're rung out from too much pleasure, until you beg me to stop. But I'd just keep storming the castle, keep grinding into you, wringing you out until there is no part of you left unravaged."

Oh, God.

His pupils dilated in a wild way, proving I'd unleashed the fury within him that had lain dormant.

"I'm ready for the agony," I whispered. "De Sade, sir."

"It's all the same, baby. Pain comes from the same circuits in the brain that deliver pleasure."

Shuddering, I braced for the beast within him, readied myself for whatever came next because I'd begged for it. He could never be blamed for what he did to me now.

Resting his palm on my head, he soothed me as only a master can. "You please me."

He pushed me back onto the bed.

"I offer my cunt to you." I squeezed my eyes shut. "If you'll accept it."

He leaned down and suckled my nipple, pinching my other breast as he mouthed the pertness, causing that familiar pleasure to radiate between my thighs.

Seconds later, he dragged his T-shirt off, revealing toned abs, and quickly discarded the rest of his clothes after kicking off his shoes, not caring where anything landed. Naked now, he climbed on top of me, his mouth capturing mine in a leisurely kiss.

"This is the best goodbye I can offer," he whispered. "Is it enough for you?"

I knew it had to be. I nodded gratefully.

His mouth grazed my breasts again, then moved down along my belly, finally settling between my thighs. He possessed me there with a frenzied kiss, delivering genius strokes of his tongue that sent me skyrocketing into oblivion.

His hardness grew against my thigh into a shocking size. He reached down and stroked himself as though fascinated with his growing erection.

"I want you inside," I purred.

He lifted my arms up and over my head as I lay powerless beneath him, gripping the headboard.

Using his elbows to keep his weight off, he lay on top of me.

That first thrust stretched my pussy wide as he waited for me to adjust, his patience proving his affection. He thrust deeper, causing my back to arch as I wrapped my legs around his waist.

"Tell me when you're ready," he said gruffly into my ear.

"I'm ready," I said, squeezing my eyes shut.

Instead of discomfort, I felt the twisting of his hips as he moved in a circle, slow at first and then a little faster, all the while watching my reaction.

Being subjugated by this gorgeous man made me go limp as I surrendered to this moment. He'd warned me these passing seconds were our last together. I needed this memory of him, these precious moments to hold onto when we parted, and the nights became lonely.

Soon, I would be relegated to a fleeting moment of his existence—a girl he'd wasted time on along his pathway to own one of the most dangerous clubs in the world. I'd almost sabotaged his plans.

Still, I deserved this goodbye. When he left, I'd imbibe that sorrowful poison from the cup of agony once more and it would define the rest of my life.

Like a ragdoll, I was lifted and pulled into his arms.

Turning me around so that I sat in his lap, he slid his cock into me, stretching me again. I faced forward, my back to his chest, the discomfort of the stretching morphing into pleasure.

Jake reached around and found my clit, flicking it, setting a brilliant pace as I rose and fell, sinking deeper onto his length. I rode him wildly, bucking as I reached a blinding climax.

There was no more me. It felt like I was gone from this place, this heady bliss shaking off all ties with reality, expelling fears and cleansing thoughts. This intense pleasure stole me away, making my thighs tremble as our soft moans mingled, his heady cologne lulling me into oblivion.

And then, all at once, I was back in his arms, and he was on top of me.

My breaths came in short, sharp gasps as I tried to recover from these dizzying sensations.

I felt his strong hands on my hips now as he pummeled me, drawing his pleasure from the way he controlled my body, thrusting hard and fast, a raw pounding that proved he needed this as much as me.

We'd held back, resisted, and yet this chemistry had pulled us together time and time again. Feeling boneless, sore, and yet invigorated, I came again with a full body orgasm, groaning my pleasure.

We grew still.

Jake's strong arms brought me back against him in a hug.

This was goodbye—a sacred way of letting each other go. And if this was all that was left of us, I would accept it.

Until the reality hit that it meant I'd never see him again, and then every cell of my being would want to fight for an *us*.

Trembling, I lay against his muscular chest, already fighting the agony of his loss.

CHAPTER THIRTY-ONE

Jake

THE VENICE BEACH CANALS WERE QUIET FOR THIS TIME OF night. Usually, the famous interconnected waterways were bustling with kayakers, joggers, and tourists.

But now, all it offered was silence.

Within an hour, this would be over.

I'd left my beauty sleeping for now. Soon, I'd drive back to Dorchester House and get Stella out of the penthouse. There was no reason for her to stay there.

Getting her away from Lance was imperative.

Leaving her had now become a thing, my mind spinning with thoughts of her as I mulled over what we had now. Perhaps it wasn't much, and yet it felt like everything.

Fucking her a few hours ago had felt like fate. The way she moved against me, with me, causing me to have a growing sense of desire for one woman.

I always came back to the realization that having her in my world would always be a hazard for her. Maybe if I'd not made the decision to pursue Pendulum, but what was done was done. There was no going back. We had to see the bigger picture.

I check my watch for the hundredth time, and then gripped the steering wheel, waiting impatiently for Shay. He'd given me these co-ordinates and I'd triple checked them, so I knew I was in the right location. Unless he'd sent me here to keep me out of the way.

I'd insisted on being present. Not because I was qualified for covert operations, but because I'd promised Stella.

A few minutes later, a car's headlights came into view.

A Jeep pulled up beside mine. Shay looked over and gave a wave. He climbed out, looking ruggedly handsome dressed like a security guard in jeans and a combat jacket.

He leaned down to look through my window. "Glad you ditched the fucking Lambo," he said.

That made me chuckle, lessening the tension somewhat.

I got out and joined him on the sandy edge of the water. My "Prickster 900," as Stella liked to call it, would have given me away.

All five of Shay's men were dressed just like him. I, too, wore jeans, but he threw a jacket at me. He'd seemingly thought of everything.

Pulling it on, I found it fit perfectly. I gave him a nod of thanks.

"You good?" he said.

"Of course." I stepped closer. "I'm here as back up."

That amused him. "Okay, then."

I cringed at how that sounded.

He was all business. "My team's been briefed."

"Thank you for doing this."

"It's what I do." He looked off toward the canal, giving me a few seconds to take in this version of him. The Navy-era beard was back. I saw contentment where before there had been only sorrow.

What we'd had between us was still a sacred memory—a friendship that endured even now. I'd hated myself for not being able to personally save him from his ghosts. But I'd stood on the sideline, watching and waiting for him to find peace. And he had, with the help of all of us. We were always there for him, like he was for us.

But *this*, this was a big ask.

The realization of what we were going to attempt only now dawned on me. I'd gotten caught up in the details and the logistics we had to execute.

But my faith in these guys was solid.

Shay had once told me about Hell Week, which took place at the end of a SEAL's basic conditioning. It was the most challenging week not only in the military, but in the world. They literally woke the SEAL recruits up on a Sunday and there was no sleep for them until the following Friday. They'd spend the week running over seven marathons to prove they were the best of the best.

And now they were here for me.

Secretly, I sensed Shay missed this type of action, having recently suited up to go work at Cole Tower for Cameron's brother Henry. But deep down, I knew Shay felt this was where he belonged—in the thick of the action.

If this went south, I'd be the one who'd have to tell Stella. And if anything happened to Shay, or his men, that would be my responsibility, too.

My stomach roiled.

Shay glanced back at me, smirking at my expression. "What?"

"Proud of you, that's all," I said.

He shook that off like it was water. "Our intel is good. AJ's transfer is planned for 2:00 A.M."

I was reminded that this kind of work was more than just muscle. It was intel gathering and covert operations at the highest level.

The shoreline was still and quiet.

"We're exposed," I said, concerned.

"That's why we need to be convincing." He was acting calmer than he should be. "We're the transfer team."

"What happened to theirs?"

"We sent them new coordinates after intercepting their coms. One of our guys will keep that ruse going. So, if they check in with *The Hades*, they'll get our guy."

I felt humbled by their professionalism.

Of course, I always knew Shay was a skilled warrior, but seeing him in action was enlightening.

Shay reached into his pocket and pulled out a nightscope, training it across the canal.

"Jose," Shay called over to one of his men. "Give me your cap." He took it from him and gave it to me. "Keep it pulled low. We don't want anyone recognizing you."

I put it on.

Shay called his men into a huddle. He held up his phone and showed each man a photo of what AJ looked like. They each gave a nod to confirm they'd memorized his face.

Next, Shay gave the hand gesture for us to move out.

The men made their way down the bank to the edge of the water. We heard it first, the sound of an outboard motor approaching. A small boat slowed as it passed under a pedestrian bridge.

Squinting, I made out three burly guards. With them, the figure of a smaller man—AJ? Too far away to see, but I imagined this was harrowing for him.

The boat came closer.

This was where the transfer of AJ was set to occur. Their captive was being ushered off to a new location, away from *The Hades* to God knows where if we didn't intercept this transfer.

"Wait." Shay held up his nightscope. "There's another boat." He swapped a wary glance with me.

I held out my hand for the nightscope and he passed it to me. I peered through it, my eyes adjusting.

Shit.

They had an escort boat with two more men on board.

Shay took the nightscope back and again peered through the lens. "AJ's on the first boat."

Getting this wrong would be a disaster. The boats might turn around and he'd be lost to us.

Not that far from the shoreline, I watched as Shay's men ambled along acting bored, as though put out by this late-night job.

The first boat banked on the ridge.

Voices carried as AJ's captors checked in with who they believed were the security team working for the same boss.

I admired Shay's calmness and the way he acted so damn cool despite the fact I saw at least one man with a gun.

AJ remained handcuffed as he stepped off the boat and onto the bank, terror etched on his face. He struggled with those first steps on the uneven ground.

One of Shay's men helped him find his footing. After a few more words were exchanged, AJ was escorted clumsily up the bank, his shoes slipping in the mud.

I kept my head bowed, let the shadows hide my face from anyone who might recognize me.

"Don't say anything," Shay ordered AJ. "Not until we're inside the car."

AJ looked at him, puzzled.

He wouldn't know we were the good guys until the others were out of sight.

We got back into our vehicles as the boats turned around and sped off. Shay had AJ sit in the back of his Jeep with one of his men beside him.

For AJ, the night wasn't over. We had a doctor standing by and then a lawyer would debrief him before the relevant authorities were called.

But at least he was free.

I lowered my window and Shay lowered AJ's so he could talk to me.

AJ was staring at me. "Are you…?"

I gave him a warm smile. "Yeah, I get that a lot."

Shay's car sped off into the night, and I headed back to Dorchester House.

Glad to deliver the good news.

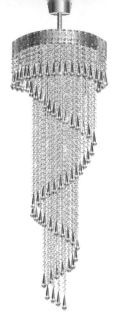

CHAPTER THIRTY-TWO

Stella

SLEEPILY, I REACHED OVER AND FELT THE ABSENCE OF JAKE. Glancing at the clock on the side table, I saw it was just after 2:00 A.M.

I wished he'd stayed, but I understood why he couldn't. We weren't a conventional couple. In fact, we weren't a couple at all.

I wanted my old life back, but also, some part of me needed to be with this man I'd fallen for—create a life that was new and exciting and fulfilling.

Instead, our friendship left me with a heavy heart, knowing I'd betrayed him with each conversation, each kiss.

I'd have walked away, too.

My thoughts once more returned to my brother, and I hoped I'd made the right decision to involve Jake.

I climbed out of bed and pulled on my T-shirt and PJ bottoms and padded out to the kitchen.

I made some toast and brewed some Cole tea. The first bite of toasted bread tasted delicious, probably because I'd slathered it in butter. It dripped onto my fingers, and I licked it off.

I peered down at the PJ bottoms, promising myself I'd burn them after I left here. I'd destroy everything from the tyrant who'd made me stay here. If there was any justice in the world, he'd go to prison.

Maybe I'd keep one pair of the fancy shoes, though. I'd never be able to afford those in real life.

The tea soothed me. I'd made sure it was caffeine-free so maybe I'd be able to go back to sleep. Reaching for the fancy tin on the counter, I turned it around, recalling how Jake had admired it.

Wait.

At Jake's Mulholland home, he'd called the man in the mask Cole. It was a common design. Yet, I felt the urge to follow my hunch. I reached into the microwave and brought out the phone Jake had given me. I'd kept it stashed in there so no one could use it to listen in on me. I couldn't exactly do research on the phone Lance had given me.

I googled Cole Tea.

Thousands of photos came up in the search, referencing the family beverage empire. They sold coffee, too. The head of the company had retired, leaving behind his two sons to run the business—Henry and Cameron Cole.

In the photo, the man standing on the right with his arm around his brother was the exact height and build of the Cole I'd met in Jake's home—the man behind the mask.

The fourth partner?

It made sense. With his impressive empire, he couldn't be caught owning a place like Pendulum. That would cause a scandal. From what Jake had told me, Cameron had frequented that other club, too—the one in Bel Air.

What was it Jake had said? I'd given myself away because I didn't know who Cole was?

A knock at the door startled me.

I put the phone back in the microwave and headed toward the front door. I started to look through the peep hole.

"Hello, Stella," said a voice from behind me.

I spun around.

Klein was already inside the penthouse, wearing a sinister smile. Shadows fell across his face, highlighting his cold eyes.

A slither of terror ran up my spine. "What are you doing here?" I wanted to run into the bathroom and lock myself in there.

"You're out of time, Stella," Klein said, his tone impatient.

"I wasn't aware there was a countdown."

"Mr. Merrill has decided to draw this situation to a close."

"How do you mean?"

"It's hard to know who to trust, isn't it?"

"What?"

"Mr. Merrill has been honest from the beginning. Or maybe you've made the mistake of trusting Jake Carrington."

There was never going to be a time I trusted Merrill more than Jake.

"Mr. Merrill is growing impatient."

"I might have something," I lied. "I'll call him first thing tomorrow."

He gestured toward the bedroom door. "Get dressed. You can share it now."

"It's late."

He gestured at my PJ's. "Or you can see him like that."

"I'm not going anywhere right now."

"He's waiting in the car. Just talk with him."

Within minutes, I'd pulled on my jeans and T-shirt and followed Klein out of the penthouse.

In the elevator, keeping my distance from him, I ran over what I would say. When the doors opened, I saw the limo out front.

We walked outside, and I was hit by the chill of the night air. I should have brought a coat with me.

When we approached the car, the chauffeur opened the door.

I peered in. "It's very late, Mr. Merrill."

On the backseat, Lance nursed a tumbler filled with a dark liquor. This man, or his men, had ransacked my home. I wasn't even sure he knew I'd been back there to see the damage.

"Get in," he said.

"Can we do this tomorrow, please?" I said flatly.

"I imagine Jake tried to persuade you he's the good guy in all this."

My eyes told him that I truly believed that.

"Yet you disregard the fact that Jake and his buddies want to own Pendulum." His tone made this sound reasonable. "You've seen the place. Heard the rumors. At no time did you question why they want full access. It's to make it their playground, Stella."

I leaned into the door. "Where's my brother?"

He lifted his glass and took a drink.

"You've been spending a lot of time with Jake. You must have something by now."

"I do," I said. "But first, prove to me AJ is alive."

"If your intel is good," said Lance. "I'll take you to him and put this behind us."

Right. "How do I know I can trust you?"

"Well, you can't trust Jake."

"Why?"

"Dean Hersey is dead." He held up his phone, watching my reaction.

A jolt of fear made me freeze, my eyes wide as I stared at Lance's phone, reading the news headline that Dean Hersey had fallen from a window.

Pushed?

Jake had admitted to stealing the journalist's business card. I'd naively believed he wasn't going to reach out to him, that he wouldn't harm him.

Who to trust?

"Get in the fucking car," Klein said.

Confusion addling my mind, seeing no other choice, I climbed in and sat down on the leather seat. Immediately, I regretted my decision.

His driver slammed the door shut.

Fear slithered up my arms like insects crawling over me.

"Take me to my brother," I demanded, as the car took off. "And I'll tell you what I know."

Lance finished off the rest of his drink. "I can live with that."

My heart skipped a beat. "Where are we going? To your yacht?"

His silence proved how much he liked to torture me.

Sick bastard.

I let the hatred I felt show. "Are you really taking me to him?"

"You've overstayed your welcome in the penthouse," he said, in a thick Texas drawl.

"Did you ransack my house?" I blurted out.

Lance looked away. "I imagine you've developed feelings for Jake?"

He'd not denied entering my home, which to me was an admission of guilt.

"You get off on hurting people," I said.

Sick fuck.

"Very perceptive of you, Stella."

As the limo drove along the freeway, I counted the seconds until I saw AJ again. Getting him to safety was everything.

Jake was taking too long. I had to deal with this myself. I'd always been independent, not relying on anyone but me, and that wouldn't change. Still, I prayed I'd made the right decision.

Lance made several phone calls. Business as usual, despite dealing with kidnap victims, apparently—his tone not giving anything away to the person on the other end.

I could scream, call out for help. But Lance would no doubt hang up and turn the car around, forbid me to see AJ.

From what I picked up, he was talking on his phone to someone in Dubai. Droning on about a deal involving billions. All I could think about was getting out of this stuffy car. The stale smell of a cigar still lingered.

"Can we open a window?" I asked.

That request was ignored by everyone.

Eventually, I recognized the road to Pendulum.

Lance watched my reaction serenely, as though looking right through the girl having a quiet panic attack. Fearful of passing out, I slowed my breathing, trying to get a grip on my fear.

I'd made a dreaded miscalculation. Because they'd never bring AJ here. Or would they?

The car pulled up in front of Pendulum and stopped.

"Why are we here?" I asked, trying to sound calm.

"Have something you want to share?" he said flatly.

"My brother first," I said. "I need to see—"

"Get her out," snapped Lance to his driver.

I tried the door handle, ready to run.

Lance continued. "The agreement was you'd get Jake to talk."

"Which I did!"

He gestured for his driver to wait. "Stella, what do you have for me?"

I shook my head. "Brother first."

"Get her inside." Lance slid out of the limo and slammed the door behind him.

He went on ahead as his driver pulled me out of the car. I struggled to escape, but his grip was too strong. He pushed me up the steps and into Pendulum.

I was forced down familiar corridors, through the main ballroom, passing the room where I'd met Jake. Where he'd barely saved me from being auctioned off. I wondered if Lance would have let that happen if Jake hadn't found me.

We passed through another chamber where a session was in full swing, with several guests enjoying a submissive being whipped in front of them—my heart wrenching over the thought that she might be one of the submissives here against their will.

No one reacted to me being forcibly hurried through a room because that's what they did here, even with me wearing ordinary clothes.

Halfway through another room, I recognized Rylee sitting at a bar.

She saw me, too, then looked away, as though disinterested. She didn't even react to Lance's driver shoving me into an elevator.

The doors closed and we descended. It seemed like it took forever for the doors to glide open.

Ahead lay a long line of doors. I was blindly maneuvered onward, panic surging, angry at myself for not trying to escape like Jake had told me to do.

The rest was a blur.

I was dragged across the room violently by Lance's driver, the man vicious and cruel, striking me several times until I did what he asked and undressed down to my underwear. My face burned like fire, my flesh bruised, my limbs twisted uncomfortably. I became too subjugated to fight back.

This place, it was beyond saving.

Jake should know that.

If I had my way, I'd burn Pendulum to the ground. Only there were women here who needed saving. That, I knew, was the only reason anyone would spend another second in this hellhole.

I was haunted by Lance's words. *"You've seen the place. Heard the rumors. At no time did you question why they want full access. It's to make it their playground, Stella."*

Had I been wrong about everything?

Wrong about how far Lance would go? Wrong about trusting Jake? Because if they really wanted to rescue my brother, they'd have done that already. I'd given them the location of where to find him. They had the money and resources.

Had I sealed my brother's death?

A bodice was thrown at me. I was told to put it on. I removed my bra, and when it came to securing the bodice's straps along my back, the man did it roughly.

Don't cry.

Don't let them know they've won.

Their lies. Their deceit. Their evil was something I would never forget. One day I would take my revenge on them.

When the man tried to secure me to the St. Andrew's Cross, I broke free and bolted toward the door.

I almost made it.

CHAPTER THIRTY-THREE

Stella

WITHIN THIS DARKLY LIT CHAMBER, I WAS SECURED TO a St. Andrew's Cross with my arms outstretched. Completely immobilized, I felt the sting of the red contusions on my arms, the result of being manhandled.

I tried not to hyperventilate.

Please, Jake, find me…

But he wasn't coming.

Jake didn't know I was here. Rylee had pretended not to see me—probably because she was scared for herself. My mind railed against the reasons she'd turned her eyes away.

Lance strolled in and slipped off his jacket as though this was a session—as though he did this kind of thing all the time.

I felt sick to my stomach.

Money had protected him up until now. And power, too. The kind that comes from international influence.

"Out." He dismissed his driver.

The man scurried out proving he was a lackey and nothing more.

"You told me you'd take me to my brother," I said, wrists smarting from the metal cuffs.

It was sinister, the way he rolled up his sleeves. "You've refused to give me anything substantial."

"Let me go."

"I'm intrigued to see how well De Sade trained you."

"He never did."

"I heard a rumor he took you to Chrysalis?"

"I don't know where that is."

"Bel Air." He watched my expression.

The place with the vast chandelier had felt like a dream world, welcoming me with a sensual tenderness this man would never comprehend.

A shiver of uncertainty raced up my spine.

I was breathing so fast it made me dizzy. I watched as he strolled around the structure, playing with me to get his sinister fix.

"You've been trained to extract pleasure from pain by the ultimate sadist. Let's see how well you do."

"That never happened," I said breathlessly.

Squeezing my eyes shut, I braced myself for what was coming.

The door flew open.

"Lance!" Rylee stood in the doorway with a horrified expression. He turned to face her.

"What is this?" She walked into the room.

Lance wielded a whip in the air, threatening to use it on me. "This is a private session."

"Darling," Rylee said, her tone soothing. "If you want to play hard you need to find someone your equal."

"Where's your ex?" he asked bitterly.

"Actually, I phoned him. Told him I saw you here with Stella." She threw me a reassuring glance. "Jake is on his way."

Her words were a beacon of light in this dimly lit chamber.

"Good." Lance smirked. "He can do her aftercare."

"Stella hasn't given her consent," said Rylee. "So, stop."

Lance lifted my chin with the tip of his finger. "Stella has something to tell me, don't you?"

"Step away from her," said Rylee. "She's not enjoying this."

"That's what pain is about." He glanced her way. "Or have you forgotten?"

"You won't be allowed back," she said. "Not after this."

"You're wrong."

"Jewel will not allow this violence."

He looked triumphant. "Then you don't know Jewel."

Fury flashed in Rylee's eyes. "If you touch Stella again, I will—"

"If you don't leave," he said. "I'll make your life hell."

"You and I," she said softly. "We had something."

"I fucked you to piss off Jake."

She hurried forward and grabbed the whip, struggling to get it away from him. He slapped her hard across the face and she fell.

"Leave her alone!" I yelled, feeling guilty that she'd been hurt because of me.

Rylee sprang to her feet and started to rush at Lance again.

He held up his hand. "You're off the board, Rylee."

"Give me the key." She looked around for the key to the handcuffs.

"Step away from her," he snarled.

She glared at him. "They will ruin you."

"Try to take me down?" he said. "I have enough dirt on everyone to take you all down with me. I'll burn this entire league to the ground."

"Why are you doing this?" She took a cautious step forward.

Lance ignored her. "Stella, tell me what you know?"

"I know the name of their silent partner," I said, shivering.

Cold air seemed to seep in through the brick walls.

Lance's left eye twitched, proving he wanted to hurt me to get the information.

How many people had he destroyed? How many lives had he ruined? And because of his power, no one had dared to cross him.

"Who's the silent partner, Stella?" Lance grabbed a fistful of my hair and yanked my head back.

"It's…" I paused, pleading with my eyes.

I hated the thought of giving him Cameron's name after he'd promised to rescue my brother. A man's family would be at risk, his personal life held in the balance. An empire might fall.

From the way Rylee's eyes watered she knew it was him, too. Or maybe I was just reading that into her fraught expression.

"Listen to me, Stella," said Rylee. "Jake's on his way. He wants you to know AJ is safe."

I sucked in a breath of relief—wanting to believe her.

AJ was rescued?

Lance turned and flashed her an angry look. "Fuck off."

Lightheaded, but calmer now, I tried to read the truth in her words.

AJ's safe.

"You don't need to tell Lance anything," said Rylee.

"You don't believe her, do you, Stella?" asked Lance.

"I'll tell you the name," I said. "But she has to leave."

"Don't," said Rylee. "If it comes out you revealed it—"

"Get out!" snapped Lance.

"I'm not leaving," she said, shaking her head. "Not without Stella."

Lance's driver appeared in the doorway. He rushed toward Rylee and took hold of her arm, dragging her out of the room and down the hall, despite her protests.

I hoped she hadn't been bluffing about AJ being safe.

Wanting to cry, but refusing to break down, I rallied my strength, biting my lip to stay focused, stay brave.

Lance stared at me, looking as smug and cruel as the day I'd first met him on *The Hades*. "Who is the secret partner?"

"Let me see my brother first," I whispered. "Or you'll never know."

He'd never know regardless, because I'd never share that information.

He grinned, and then slapped me hard across the face, causing my head to strike the wood.

Dazed, tears stinging my eyes, I managed to speak. "I found it."

"Found what?"

"The sixth floor." My throat tightened, knowing what might happen to him.

I assumed it was the same rule for anyone who trespassed on that floor, having eavesdropped on Atticus when he'd shared the details. *"Whoever enters the sixth floor uninvited doesn't make it out alive."*

A part of me hoped Rylee would find a way to bring help.

Too late for that.

"Show me," he said.

With the same violence with which I was restrained, I was released from the St. Andrew's Cross. My jaw was bruised and aching, my wrists weak and numb from the metal handcuffs.

But I held on to my resilience.

We headed out of the chamber together, me wary of him following close behind as we walked along the hallway. I could sense his intrigue.

I retraced my steps through the empty bar and onward toward the familiar doorway, holding it open for him. *Yes, come this way, asshole.* All the way down to the last door on the left.

We made it to the secret elevator.

"This is how we get there," I told him.

Doubt clouded his expression.

Stepping inside ahead of him, my flesh chilled when I tried to recall where Atticus had pressed the UP button on the decorative wallpaper.

Lance followed me in. "Sure about this?"

"It takes you to the sixth floor."

He flashed a sinister smile.

There was only one way to see this through. I was going to have to ascend with him.

Fingering the wall in the area I thought was correct, I pressed my hand against the wallpaper, felt a bump, and pushed.

Lance peered down at his feet when the elevator began to move. The quick smooth ride seemed to impress him.

Strange, how a handsome man can appear ordinary. That business suit was cloaking the devil himself.

The doors opened.

Lance had a thing for Hades. Hades was what I hoped to deliver.

He stepped onto the sixth floor. "Well done."

I reached for the button, hoping to descend.

Lanced grabbed my wrist and pulled me out. The doors closed and I heard the elevator returning to the ground floor.

My flesh chilled and I tried not to panic.

"Let's take a look around," he said, pulling me down the hallway.

CHAPTER THIRTY-FOUR

Stella

BEFORE LEAVING THE ELEVATOR, I HAD EASED OUT AN earring and dropped it to the floor. At least that way, they might discover what happened to me—unless it was assumed to be a diamond stud lost by a submissive.

"How did you find this place?" Lance asked.

"Another sub told me," I said, again feeling relieved that Elle had escaped. Because if this floor was kept hidden within the most secret club in L.A, there had to be a sinister reason.

Lance pushed me forward ahead of him. "What do they do here?"

"She didn't tell me."

I felt his unpleasant gaze burning my back. Lance probably didn't believe me, but we were here now, and that seemed to placate him.

Atticus had alluded to something terrible happening here. But he'd escaped. So maybe someone with Lance's influence would survive this, too.

My throat tightened at the thought that I carried no such

influence. I recalled the dread in that masked woman's eyes when Atticus and I had first set eyes on this secret floor.

At the end of the hallway, I turned a door handle and peeked beyond. Lance shoved me out of the way. He slid into the room and turned sharply to grab my wrist.

Surely there were signs of bruising beginning to show on my face—signs of what he'd done to me.

If I caused a scene, I'd draw unwanted attention.

Submissives were considered chattel, I knew that much.

We walked into a room with lavish décor. Soft red lighting enhanced the stately art and the hand-crafted furnishings in gold and red. Above us was an inlaid blue pearl ceiling.

Classical music flooded in, providing a welcoming mood for those invited into this dark, luxurious setting. For me, it sounded like a death march.

Tall, beautiful women in gowns slow-danced with men in tuxedos, the scene seemingly tame. Lance appeared disappointed in the lack of debauchery. He grabbed my arm and pulled me along the edge of the room.

I glanced back, recalling the way we'd come.

Lance dragged me through another doorway and into another lavish space. Couples were fucking in every corner.

I turned my eyes away, only to find another scandalous scene. On the couch a naked woman rode a man hard. And over on a table with ornate legs, three muscular men elegantly had sex. In the corner, a woman wore a dildo and was fucking a man. Her male submissive bent over a table as she took him hard from behind, the tell-tale collar proving his submissive status.

We made our way through yet another doorway.

My heart lurched.

In the middle of the room sat a submissive with her head bowed. I didn't want to leave her with this crowd, but I had no choice.

Lance dragged me onward into a vast chamber.

I froze in dread as I took in the vision of three cloaked men wearing terrifying masquerade masks. One mask was a plague doctor with a golden long beak.

About thirty men in suits were here, too, hiding behind a variety of decorative faces.

In the center of the space knelt ten elegant women, dressed in nothing but diamond studded thongs. All wearing identical feathered masks.

The cloaked men turned to look at us.

Lance returned their stares.

"I should go," I whispered.

"Gentlemen," Lance said over the music. "I've brought you a gift."

I pivoted fast to run, but I was cut off by two men wearing plain masquerade masks. They forced me to my knees.

Blood drain from my face. If I hadn't been kneeling, I'd have fallen to the floor in sheer terror.

Atticus' words tore through my mind.

All I wanted was to live. To hug my brother. To go home.

A familiar woman's voice said, "Gentlemen, this one belongs to Le Chambre."

Elle had told me she'd belonged to this chamber, with no master to rule over her.

This was a nightmare I was afraid I'd never wake from.

I peered over my shoulder to glimpse the woman who'd spoken those words. She stared back at me from behind her elaborate mask, kindness in her demeanor. It was the very same woman with the headdress of peacock feathers, who Atticus had remained with before he'd sent me down in the elevator to escape. The impressive bling on her left hand proved she was married to wealth.

"This is most unusual," called out a man wearing a full devil's mask with realistic horns curling upward.

The Queen of Peacock Feathers turned to look at him. "It is done."

The devilish masked man approached me—and then I saw his leather gloves. My gaze rose from his swanky polished shoes up to his dark eyes. I'd stared into those cruel eyes too many times. Even behind that gilded mask I knew it was Atticus. He wore the gloves so as not to give himself away—his tattoos being the one thing that could identify him.

He glared down at me. "You again," he said with an edge of amusement.

My hope slipped away when I remembered overhearing Atticus refusing to share any details about this place with Jake—keeping it all to himself in his own twisted way.

This was the same man who'd told me he'd once murdered someone by injecting insulin between their toes.

Oh, God.

I was as good as dead.

I wanted to plead with him to get me out of here. But instead, he raised a finger to his mouth, warning me to be silent.

"Stand," he demanded.

Trembling and trying to hold back tears, I did as he ordered, pleading with my eyes for him to get me out of here.

"Stella," he said softly, drawing out my name with a disappointed tone. "Don't react to what you see or hear."

"I want to go," I whispered.

"No," he whispered close to my ear, his grip around my throat tightening. "We can't let you leave."

CHAPTER THIRTY-FIVE

Stella

THE ROBED MEN STROLLED TOWARD THE END OF THE ROOM and took their seats on what appeared to be three thrones, proving they were the ones wielding all the power. The chair in the center was raised slightly to show seniority. They ruled this chamber. That much was obvious from the way everyone else deferred to them.

I looked over at Lance with my anger rising, frustrated to think I'd once believed there was justice.

A deep male voice echoed from one of the regal thrones and a cloaked masked man stood, gesturing to the center of the chamber.

Lance Merrill had been welcomed.

He glanced at me, his expression smug, standing there tall and sleek, his silver-gray hair messy from his session with me. He'd had no time to groom himself after his savagery.

Feeling lightheaded, I obeyed Atticus and resisted crying out that I was innocent, that Lance had forced me to be here.

But it would have been a lie. I'd personally shown him the secret floor.

And I had probably sealed my own fate.

On the dais, sitting on the throne to the right, the person who'd been quiet until now stood up and spoke.

"You weren't invited, Mr. Merrill." It was a woman's voice, her cadence familiar.

Lance was peeved. "I've poured millions into this place."

"You've broken the rules, Mr. Merrill," she continued.

He shrugged, but his expression was apologetic. "I'll pay the fine."

The room fell quiet.

"I came here with a gift for you," he reminded them.

That seemed to pique their interest. I could see them swapping glances.

"I've brought someone who knows the identity of the fourth partner. Jake Carrington, and his buddies Atticus and Greyson, have been protecting him. But now, we have a name."

He gestured to me. "This is Stella. She's Jake's submissive."

I felt a chill run through me as the room grew silent again.

Do what is right, not what is easy.

I'd heard that somewhere.

One of the robed men on the dais gestured for me to speak.

Terrified, I took a few steps away from Atticus and faced the rulers of Pendulum. "It's true," I said.

"Don't," hissed Atticus from behind me.

I stepped forward, putting more distance between us so that he couldn't stop me.

If I was to survive this horror, I'd have to make the ultimate sacrifice. I wanted to believe they'd rescued my brother but seeing him was the only way I could be sure. These men, these billionaires, could look after each other. That much was true.

Surviving, now that took the rawest courage.

"Well?" said the female on the dais. "Did you become De Sade's submissive?"

"I don't like pain all that much," I admitted. "So, no. I'd never be good enough for De Sade. No matter how much I wish I were."

I could feel their intense scrutiny from across the room.

I drew in a sharp breath. "But I was with De Sade for a while. Until he got bored with me."

"Go on," said the robed man on the left.

"It's me," I said. "I'm the secret partner."

My shocking revelation was met with silence. But I heard a sigh of annoyance from Atticus.

Clearly, I hadn't thought this through.

Laughter broke out around the room.

The tall, elegant woman who was Atticus' secret friend approached me and nudged me back into the crowd.

"Gentlemen," she chastised them. "Show reverence for Le Chambre."

Atticus suddenly pulled me against him, my back against his chest. He gripped my throat to control me.

I'd been right not to trust him.

I braced for the moment when Lance would pay the fine he'd spoken of. When they welcomed him into their secret society. Maybe Atticus would throw me forward, so that I'd fall at Lance's feet, giving me back to him.

Atticus wrapped his other arm around my waist and hugged me to him, as though sensing I was about to protest the unfairness of it all.

From the far end of the room, a man approached Lance from behind. He was carrying something in his hands.

Atticus' body stiffened against mine, and his gloved palm moved from my throat to my face to cover my eyes, sending me into blackness.

"Don't scream," he whispered into my ear, causing my heart to race.

"Why?"

I heard scuffling from the center of the room, shoes squeaking and sliding on the hardwood floor. Then a deep-throated gurgling noise came from that direction.

The sound of something heavy being dragged along the floor reached my ears. Was that something a body? A door opened and closed. Chatter began emanating from around the room again.

Finally, Atticus removed his hand from my eyes.

Lance was gone.

But I knew what they'd done to him.

I shrank back against Atticus, trying to catch my breath.

CHAPTER THIRTY-SIX

Stella

I STARED TOWARDS THE CENTER OF THE ROOM, MY EYES scouring the floor for evidence of what they'd done to Lance.

The blonde goddess approached me and asked for all to hear, "Do you know who the fourth partner is?"

Again, the room got quiet as all eyes turned to me.

Freedom was promised if I answered her question—as though I could buy my way out of this predicament if I gave them what they wanted.

So easy to do, taking a wild guess and throwing it out there. I could tell them Cole's name.

Instead, I shook my head *no*.

She gave me a thin smile. "Let's not keep the Grand Master waiting."

Atticus applied pressure to my shoulders, forcing me to kneel. "Down."

Dazed, I did as he ordered without struggling.

What I'd thought were the big things in life now seemed so small.

Surviving was my only focus—getting out of here and not being trapped in this place with all those other submissives.

"Crawl beside me," ordered Atticus.

He was leading me toward an enormous double doorway.

Beside Atticus walked the elegant, masked woman who'd befriended him. Straight ahead was a towering entrance, the Egyptian décor carved with intricate details, revealing the impressive imagery of pharaohs.

Guards on either side opened both doors at the same time.

"Do as I say," whispered Atticus.

"We can't leave?"

"They're watching." He placed a hand on my head as though to comfort me, as though to praise and then lure me on.

As though that alone would placate me.

I had no choice but to follow his lead, digging deep for faith that Jake wouldn't have befriended a man like Atticus if he didn't have some good in him.

More Egyptian art decorated the vast golden chamber. Immense pillars were adorned with hieroglyphics, the writings of the ancients. It was as though we'd stepped inside a temple. A four-meter-tall bird was perched high above us.

Stained-glass chandeliers ran along the center of the space. If Chrysalis was a chandelier heaven, this was a nightmare coming alive.

The submissives around us were posed in every fashion—some staying still as they leaned over tables, others tied to St. Andrew's Crosses. Some were lined up along the wall, pulling their ass cheeks apart to pose erotically.

Beside each group of subs stood a masked tuxedo-wearing Dom to wield his power over them, the whip he held threatening to strike.

Atticus helped me to my feet.

"Like this." He nudged me forward to lean over a table face first. "Remain silent for the entire time." He positioned himself behind me and pressed his hips against my butt.

His goddess leaned over to me and whispered, "Don't look him in the eyes."

Who?

I squeezed my eyes shut as a finger slid along my folds. Atticus was touching me intimately.

The room suddenly came alive.

The strains of a classical, foreign-sounding song rose on the air from somewhere. It was hard to place its origin, but it sounded exotic, rising ever louder as the lights dimmed to a soft red hue.

This could have been a ceremony, a sacred worshipping of other gods, everyone knowing their part and playing it with solemn grace.

Raising my head to see more, I glimpsed erotic scenes playing out all around us. Submissives writhed and moaned in pleasure.

An orgy came alive.

Don't look at him.

Only, it was hard to know who they meant.

I felt a surge of dread as I tried to grasp those words. I'd have to turn my eyes away from anyone who approached us.

The sex acts were becoming noisier; loud moans and groans filling the room. As I glanced this way and that I saw the subs were not making eye contact with anyone.

They knew the rule.

"Brace yourself," said a husky voice from behind me.

Wait?

Where did Atticus go?

With no time to protest, reaching out, I gripped the end of the table. I had no choice but to submit now that this orgy had begun, and I was part of the show. Not wanting to draw more attention, I went with the sultry mood and surrendered.

I jolted and let out a gasp when a cock entered me, pushing my body forward.

A hint of pleasure and discomfort surged inside me, but I refused to believe Atticus would take me against my will or leave me at the mercy of a strange man—even if we had to act like everyone else.

The thrusts came faster now, and I could hear slapping sounds as the man's hips struck my ass cheeks, grinding against me as though to grind out my arousal.

The sounds of people having sex echoed around us.

Glancing left, I saw a tall man enter through those grand doors, wearing a silver masquerade mask. He was being escorted around the room by the goddess, who was gesturing to each sexual act as though showing off exhibits in a gallery. He nodded approvingly at each display.

I was suddenly flipped over on the table to face the masked man.

"Don't take your eyes off me," he said, his voice sounding familiar.

My gasp was drowned out by the ruckus. I recognized the eyes staring at me through his mask.

It *was* Jake who'd swapped places with Atticus.

He nudged me back, so that I lay on the table with my legs splayed, and then he slid inside me, his slick cock gliding in and out with a deliberate rhythm. Pleasure soared in me this time, because I knew it was him—my recent lover, my old enemy, the man who'd somehow found me.

I held Jake's gaze, trying to convey the gratitude I felt for him coming to me. He'd placed himself in harm's way to do this, and I hoped my expression was enough to convey my thanks.

He gave a nod of acknowledgement, but his eyes looked wary, as though he was aware of someone watching us.

I sensed the man close by before I saw him, felt his intense observation without even looking his way.

I kept my focus on Jake, allowing myself to be taken, pounded brilliantly as he had his way with me. The pleasure I felt kept rising, the erotic darkness devouring us both as I writhed beneath him.

The only man I'd ever loved.

It came out of nowhere—a sudden rush, a devilish desire to perform for that asshole witness, whoever he was. Feeling empowered and emboldened, I arched my back and moaned at the rising bliss.

Facing off with the danger left me spellbound with a sense of aliveness, and the realization that, finally, we were all free from that terrible man who'd been taken care of in the other chamber.

I'd done that—led Lance here.

I was no different than any of these people who went after what they wanted and took the world by storm; I was like a hurricane ripping through lives, leaving devastation in my wake.

Equal in blame but free at last.

Jake pulled me up into the sitting position and then forward into his arms. I pressed my face against his chest, feeling the hard muscle beneath his shirt as I was enveloped by his familiar cologne, an addictive scent I couldn't get enough of. I wrapped my legs around his waist, shutting out the room.

The goddess sounded as though she was ordering someone to come.

Me.

"Come," Jake repeated.

We were performing for them, under their rule.

Jake entered me in a series of hard, deep thrusts, drawing out my pleasure.

Toes curling, I surrendered, riding out the intense bliss as he pummeled me. I groaned, throwing my head back as my climax swept over me, possessing me. I trusted him, *my Dom*, to see me through this.

I continued to clutch at him as the climax faded, as though he was all I had in the world—all I had to help me find the light.

He slid out of me and tucked himself away.

Then he tipped up my chin and planted a kiss on my mouth. He was gentle at first, but then his kiss became frenzied and possessive, his tongue warring with mine. It was as though he was telling me he was relieved to have found me, but we weren't safe yet, we weren't out of danger.

A blur of movement on the periphery dragged his attention away. It was Atticus, gesturing for us to follow him.

Jake lifted me up and carried me out of the room in his arms. I refused to look back—fearful I'd make eye contact with He Who Should Not Be Seen.

A tuxedo jacket was flung over my shoulders to keep me warm, the material's warmth soaking into my chilled flesh. Judging by the scent of the rich cologne coming from it, it belonged to Atticus.

He'd saved me in his own dark way.

Jake carried me through all the secret rooms and back along the endless corridors. I roused myself enough to realize we were headed toward the clandestine elevator.

Atticus stepped inside with us.

He turned around and spoke to someone outside the elevator doors. "Come with us."

It was his goddess. She'd escorted us out.

"You know I can't," she said.

"I'll protect you," Atticus told her.

"Go," she insisted.

As the doors closed, shutting her out, I saw agony reflected in Atticus' eyes.

"I never told him," I said faintly. "Never told them his name." The fourth partner was to be protected at all costs.

"I know." Jake hugged me tightly in his arms. "I've got you now."

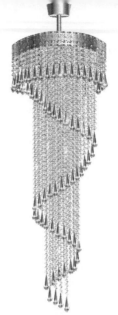

CHAPTER THIRTY-SEVEN

Stella

DAWN GREETED US AS WE HEADED OUT OF HIS MULHOLLAND home. Jake had wanted me to take more time to recover before we left the house.

But I couldn't think of anything else. I'd showered quickly and dressed in a T-shirt and jeans, making sure those light bruises from Lance's roughness wouldn't show. The long sleeves of my shirt covered the ones on my arms, and makeup camouflaged the one on my cheek.

I brushed my fingers over it self-consciously.

As promised, Jake was driving me back to Burbank. We'd be meeting my brother there.

Digging my fingernails into my palms, I willed this to be real— now and again realizing I was holding my breath to press time onward.

I didn't care about the mess at home. It was so trivial compared to this precious reunion.

We navigated off the I-5 Freeway and familiar streets came into view. I tried not to think how my brother would react to seeing our house in that terrible state.

Jake reached out and squeezed my hand. "Sure you don't want to talk with a therapist? I can set it up."

"No—but thank you." Maybe in the future, but right now this wasn't about me. It was about AJ and what he needed.

"We should still talk about it." He'd been showing concern ever since we'd left Pendulum in the early hours.

"Okay," I said. "What happened to Dean Hersey?"

"Lance told you?" He glanced my way. "I didn't want to upset you by telling you he'd died."

"Did Lance kill him?"

Jake watched my reaction. "Dean reached out to Lance for a response to the allegation he was doing business with…an influential character."

"Who?"

"We don't know." Noticing my stare, Jake said, "Anyway, the less you know the better."

"AJ knew who this person was?"

Jake shook his head. "When he's ready to talk about it he will. Don't push him."

"What's the plan?"

"We move forward. Nothing's changed."

"You have to get those women out."

"We will."

"Can you drive faster, please?"

"We're close," said Jake, reassuring me when we stopped at a red light.

Waiting for it to turn green seemed to take a million light years.

It had to be said. "I think…Lance is dead."

"I'm sorry I wasn't there."

"So, he is?" Everything pointed to it being true, but hearing Jake say it brought mixed emotions.

I'd played a major part in his death.

That chamber, that strike of a whip.

What he'd done to my brother.

My guilt started to ease up.

"Rylee called me when she saw you at Pendulum." He tapped his fingers on the wheel when we reached another red light. "She's sorry she couldn't do more."

"She did everything she could." I looked his way, wondering if, now that we were parting, he and Rylee might reunite.

She'll get him back.

As though sensing my thoughts, Jake said, "Rylee and I are over, okay?"

"It's none of my business."

"Look, I want to apologize for what happened on the sixth floor."

"In Le Chambre?" I asked. "Don't." It was Jake who'd fucked me. That's all that counted.

"Forget you saw Atticus there, please." Again, that cautionary glance.

"Has he infiltrated the sixth floor? Is that why he was there?"

Jake exhaled in frustration. "We're going to dismantle everything you saw."

I peered out the window, his words echoing like a nightmare I couldn't wake from.

Hugging myself, all I could do was watch the world fly by.

AJ is free.

But that happy fact also came with a different kind of consequence. My heart ached when I realized this car ride would probably be our last.

Jake again seemed to sense what I was feeling. He reached out and squeezed my hand.

"Thank you for everything, Jake."

"Don't mention it." He winked. "It was fun at times, right?"

"It was...everything."

"Just take care of yourself, okay?"

He parked outside my house.

The last time I'd braved a visit here my world had been shaken beyond repair. But seeing the damage they'd done inside was nothing to what they'd done to my heart.

Only, if this was another ruse...

"They'll be here in a second," said Jake calmly.

I'd been reassured that my brother had been checked thoroughly by a doctor. It made me wonder what kind of residual stress he'd have.

"I want you to know," he said softly, "that you mean a lot to me."

My chest tightened and I found it hard to breathe. I had only mere seconds left with Jake.

"I want you to be happy," he whispered.

I reached over and played with the hair on his nape. "That's what I want for you."

"If I could have this any other way..."

I read the truth in his eyes.

He turned toward the road. "Here they are."

A town car pulled up, and I climbed out of Jake's vehicle, waiting on the curb until the door opened.

Please, be him.

And then it was.

AJ got out of the back of the car, breaking into a wide smile when he saw me. I hurried toward him, and we met halfway, falling into an embrace.

Jake stood back to give us some distance.

"Stella!" AJ squeezed me tightly. "I'm home!"

I cupped my brother's face. "Are you really all right?"

"Yes, I promise." He stepped back from me, his face pale. "You sent them to get me?"

I nodded. "Sorry it took so long."

"I'm the one who's sorry."

"Don't be."

"I messed up."

"Just seeing you safe is all I care about."

He hung his head. "Lance discovered I'd taken photos of a visitor to the yacht."

I wanted to ask why he'd done so but didn't. I sensed it would come out wrong either way. As Jake had advised, it would be better for it to come out naturally.

AJ glanced behind me at Jake and frowned, then refocused on me. "I was going to blow the story wide open."

"With Dean Hersey?" I watched him carefully.

"He's going to run a story on him."

I glanced toward Jake who shook his head *no*. We wouldn't be sharing the news that Dean had been murdered until later.

AJ tapped my shoulder. "Do you have any idea who that is?"

"Yes."

"He was there!"

I looked toward Jake, confused. "You helped rescue him?"

Jake gave a nod.

I squeezed my eyes shut, realizing that after Jake had left the penthouse in the early hours, he'd joined the others to rescue AJ.

"Give me a second, okay?" I left AJ's side and approached Jake.

I took his hands in mine and he peered down at me with compassion. "Hey, all good?" he asked.

"He's home now."

"Yes, are you going to be all right?"

"Of course. Jake, I'm sorry I betrayed you all those times."

He sighed. "I put you through it, too."

"I can't believe this is it."

"Come here." He pulled me into a hug, the warmth of his body saturating mine.

His strength, his power, his everything, would soon be lost to me. The time had come for the man I loved and wanted to leave my life.

I pulled away from him.

"Stella, remember that you're indescribably gorgeous." He broke into a devilish grin. "You deserve the best."

I tapped his arm. "You'll find her. The one who makes your life perfect."

He leaned forward and kissed my cheek tenderly.

"Did you ever think of me like that?" I whispered. "Like someone you could love?"

"The first time I saw you, I knew that loving you would be easy.

You were perfect in my eyes. Always will be." He looked at me longingly, as though to say under any other circumstances I'd be *that* person.

But that had never been our destiny.

"Thank you again for saving my brother," I said softly. "I'm so grateful."

Jake gave a nod and turned away, strolling back toward his car. He pointed to his Lamborghini and laughed, his eyes twinkling with mischief. "I'm going to get into my Prickster now." His grin was adorable.

I burst out laughing, fighting back tears—wishing with all my heart that this wasn't goodbye. Deep down, I knew it was the best way to part. He'd sliced through my hope with his honesty. Jake didn't believe I belonged in his world.

From the front seat of his car, Jake gestured for us to go on inside.

I had to force myself to break his gaze—break the connection between us that held me in its thrall.

CHAPTER THIRTY-EIGHT

Stella

BEFORE I TURNED THE KEY, I RESTED MY HAND ON AJ'S shoulder. "I need you to be prepared."

Sadness showed in his eyes. "Did they do something in there?"

"I'm sorry. But he can't touch us again, AJ. I need you to know that."

"How do you know that?"

"Trust me on this."

I refused to look back and watch Jake's Lamborghini drive away, needing to be strong for my brother. He needed my full attention. But even as I bolstered my confidence, I felt the ache of loss.

Let's do this.

Standing inside the entrance, I blinked at the décor in the living room and then glanced at AJ.

"It looks fine."

"Right," I said, unsure.

The room had been restored. Gone was the ripped couch—a new

one was in its place, a luxuriously cozy sofa. Everything that had been shattered or destroyed had been replaced, giving our home a sense of new-found serenity.

A professional clean-up crew had worked their magic.

"It didn't look like this…" my voice trailed off.

AJ turned to face me. "You didn't know?"

"Jake must have arranged to have the house cleaned up and redecorated."

"Why would he do that for us?"

Not wanting to share too much, I went with, "I think he likes me."

"Jake Carrington wants to date my sister!"

I suppressed a smile. "We're not like that…" I didn't want to let him know I'd never see Jake again. A part of me was not quite ready to say it.

Because that would make it real.

We moved from room to room investigating our home. My heart rejoiced that we didn't need to step over broken glass and ripped pillows or see the dining table flipped on its side.

I hugged AJ. "I'm sorry to tell you this, but they destroyed your comics."

"Who cares!" he said. "You and I survived and that's all that counts."

"True."

"Hungry?"

I was glad to hear he'd not lost his appetite at least. "Starving. Come on, let's see what we can whip up."

We made our way into the kitchen. There, on the table, was a bouquet of flowers in a blue vase. I reached for the card that was attached.

"Are they from him?" AJ grinned. "Oh, my God, Jake Carrington is into my sister!"

I leaned over the bouquet and breathed in the exquisite scent of carnations and roses. Jake's note was probably a kind message of goodbye.

I'd read it later.

AJ opened the fridge and howled with excitement. Inside, I saw that it had been restocked with a variety of food. Jake had thought of everything.

Within twenty minutes, I'd made our favorite breakfast of fresh chopped bananas on waffles soaked in syrup. I smiled to myself when I brewed us some Cole coffee.

Our lives would soon return to normal. Our home, our sacred space, felt safe again—a place where AJ could continue to recuperate. His mental health was my top priority.

"Were you here when they broke in?" he asked, as we sat down at the table to eat.

"No."

His shoulders dropped. "Tell me they didn't hurt you?"

"I'm fine."

"When I saw you on *The Hades*, I was scared for you," he said. "Didn't know what to think."

"Jake protected me." I took a sip of coffee. It tasted of a delicious combination of nuts and toffee, a soothing combo.

"Tell me what they did to you," he said, with sadness in his eyes.

"Lance put me up in a penthouse in Marina Del Ray."

"Why?"

"To keep me under surveillance."

"Why couldn't he do that here?"

I shrugged, not wanting to say how the last few weeks had been for me. And in all honesty, I didn't think I'd ever be ready to share with him what I'd been forced to do.

"What was the penthouse like?"

"Flashy and luxurious. But I hated it."

Our home was here.

AJ's eyes watered. "They told me Dean had reached out to Lance for comment on the story. Didn't take a lot for him to figure out it had been leaked by someone working on the yacht."

"You did what you believed was right," I reassured him. "What was the story?"

"A woman borrowed Lance's yacht. We sailed to Canada where she brought some young women aboard *The Hades*."

"Are you saying she used Lance's yacht for human trafficking?"

"That's what some of the crew suspected. We were kept away from them."

He'd gone to Dean Hersey with that story and not the police.

But why?

AJ added, "The sommelier, our wine steward, asked Lance about the women."

"What happened to him?"

He shook his head. "He was fired, I think. But it was strange. He disappeared before we made land."

"Oh, God."

"I overheard Lance boasting that he was above the law. I figured if we got the story out there, more could be done."

"Makes sense," I reasoned, wanting him to know I understood.

"How did you meet Jake?"

I looked over at the vase of flowers. Pushing up, I leaned into the blooms again to breathe them in. "We kind of found each other."

"Are you going to see him again?"

I sat back down in my chair. "Maybe," I said, not wanting to disappoint AJ. He'd have gotten a kick out of me dating a football star.

"He's been good for you," he said. "It's been years since I've seen that sparkle in your eyes."

"That's because you're here, home safe."

"No." He shook his head. "He's special to you."

I took another bite of my waffle and smiled at the fluffy, maple taste. I mused that at least I had my memories of Jake, and no one could steal those away.

"Open the card," said AJ.

I picked it up off the table and opened the seal. The note said:

May your life be filled with endless love. —Jake

"What does it say?" AJ asked brightly.

"He wants me to know the flowers are from him."

I'd had a glimpse behind an erotic curtain. It would be impossible to find my way back down that surreal rabbit hole. The secret location of Chrysalis was lost to me.

Just as Jake was now lost to me.

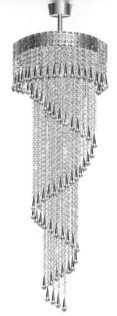

CHAPTER THIRTY-NINE

Stella

A Month Later

I'D SPACED OUT FOR A SECOND.

I shook myself awake in the staff's small coffee room. I'd come in here to grab my handbag, ready to leave and get on the road for home—a ten-minute drive from the mall.

My feet were sore after a long Friday at Save Face. I blamed that on the high heels I was wearing. The Christian Louboutin stilettos were the only item I'd kept from the penthouse. I'd worn these shoes the night I'd met Jake.

Our lives had resumed with a new normal. AJ had been hired aboard a new yacht and had set sail yesterday for the Bahamas, eager to return to the ocean. Once more our house would be quiet with him gone.

I'd have long evenings to myself again, but I didn't mind. I'd always been independent and that would never change.

I glanced at the staff room's corkboard on my way out. An event had been posted for next Friday at a restaurant called Chevy's. I considered joining them this time. It would be good for me.

Also pinned upon the corkboard were *Thank You* notes from happy clients, along with photos of their weddings and movie premieres, etc. All were images of people enjoying their lives.

For me, it would be a weekend of grocery shopping and then Netflix.

Alone.

This was like waking from a strange dream and having to go on with my life as though none of it happened.

A week ago, I'd done the unthinkable and totally embarrassed myself by driving past Jake's Mulholland home—not approaching his gate, obviously. I just needed to see it was real.

I'd imagined what being back at work might be like. It felt good. A part of me missed the excitement of all that had gone before.

Before heading out, I returned to my workstation in the middle of the store to tidy my makeup brushes and put away my tools.

That's when I saw it—leaning up against my mirror. I lifted the postcard and turned it over, seeing nothing written on the back. The photo was an aerial view of a mega mansion in Los Angeles that was perched on the edge of a canyon, an Olympic- sized swimming pool ensconced on the impressive grounds.

I glanced around but didn't see anyone. The shop was empty.

The check-out station was positioned at the back of the store, which meant my co-workers probably wouldn't have seen who'd dropped it off. We had security cameras, but someone like me wouldn't be able to access them.

Again, I examined the postcard—and realized I was looking at Chrysalis. It had to be. Squinting, I read the minute address along the bottom.

I have to know.

Hurrying out to the parking lot, I hugged the photo to my chest like I'd found a clue to get me back through the secret wardrobe. This had to be the same location Jake had taken me.

Maybe it had come from him?

If he had dropped it off like this, it meant there'd be no pressure. I could return on my own terms. If I felt ready. If I wanted this. *And God, did I want it.*

I remembered the chandelier above me refracting light off its crystal teardrops. Me dressed in a bodice beneath that glamorous fixture, right before being escorted to a dungeon.

Me cycling through blinding orgasms.

In a misty haze, I leaped into my Mazda, plugged the address into my GPS and drove in that direction.

Maybe it was the beauty of Chrysalis that had captured my imagination. Or those twinkling crystals that had rained light down on me, making me feel beautiful for the first time.

Maybe it was the promise of falling into Jake's arms again.

I felt a jolt of uncertainty, fearing that I'd be turned away at this location if I'd gotten the message wrong.

But at least I could show them the postcard.

I thought about how far I'd come. How brave I'd been through all of it, recalling how those moments had made my life all the richer.

Now here I was again, driving through Bel Air, only this time I could admire the scenery. The last time I'd gotten close to this place I'd been blindfolded. I passed by numerous mansions, some behind tall iron gates with sweeping lush greenery.

As the blue dot that was me on the GPS screen closed in on the location, the properties thinned out, proving Chrysalis stood on acres of land.

Finally, after making my way up a long driveway, I saw the grand manor rising into view, surrounded by lush landscaping. A peacock pecked at the ground close by.

Then I saw an impressive looking man standing on the steps of the mansion. He was tall with dirty blonde hair and was dressed in a T-shirt and jeans.

Drawing in a deep breath, I climbed out of my car and approached him, ready to explain why I was trespassing. I'd be vague, of course, but at least I had a reason to be here.

"Welcome to Chrysalis, Stella," he said brightly.

I jolted to a stop. "You know who I am?"

"Of course."

"Did you put this card at my workstation?"

"Not me, no."

I joined him on the top step.

"I'm Richard Booth," he said. "The director."

I followed him inside.

I stepped over the threshold and saw the same grand crystal chandelier, proving I was once again at Chrysalis.

"Is Jake here?" I asked.

"No, he's not."

Uncertainty shivered up my spine. "Then why am I?"

"Why do you think you've been summoned?" His hand swept through the air. "Back to our sacred place?"

I looked around, taking in the glorious interior, soaking in the dramatic atmosphere, seeing the sweeping staircase that invited adventure.

"Because I belong."

"Very good, Stella. That's what we believe, too."

"I kept all your secrets," I whispered.

"They are your secrets now."

His words resonated. I'd cherished many of the experiences I'd had, particularly those at this place. Here I'd felt protected in my exploration.

I saw movement halfway up the central staircase.

A tall, dark-haired man was descending the steps with an air of sophistication, his expression serene.

Cameron Cole.

There was a familiar suaveness in the way he moved, his dark tailored suit creating an aura of power.

I glanced over at Richard, and he gave a nod as though to say, "*Yes, it's him.*"

Instinctively, I sank to my knees as though Cameron controlled my mind with merely a thought. He was literally that charismatic. That beautiful. That mysterious.

With my head bowed, I surrendered as an obedient submissive.

"Hello, Stella," Cameron said, his voice deep and alluring. "We've been expecting you."

Peering up, understanding why I was here I said, "I'm ready."

"We know you are."

To my right, I watched Richard walk away without looking back, leaving us alone in the foyer.

"Will it be you?" I whispered. "Sir?"

Wanting what was offered, I exulted in the realization that this was happening.

"Stand, please," said Cameron. "You'll walk the rest of the way." He gestured to his right.

I followed him down a long hallway until he stopped and opened a door for me, gesturing for me to go into the room.

It was an office.

And there before me stood three dominatrices, their expressions warm and inviting.

"They've come here especially for you," said Cameron. "Welcome to Chrysalis."

CHAPTER FORTY

Jake

"LOSING YOUR EDGE, CARRINGTON!"

Cameron's épée struck my chest—the prod felt through my protective vest.

We stepped back from each other, removing our meshed masks and taking a breather from our bout.

I'd been summoned to his Beverly Hills home. More specifically, his fencing studio, where he'd insisted we fence. He'd thrown a suit at me, since I'd not brought mine, and had not given me a choice in the matter.

"Okay," I said, "not that I'm not flattered you invited me, but why?" Time with Cole was always insightful and inevitably thrilling.

"You've not been yourself lately."

I shook my head. "That's not true."

Not really.

I'd just taken my grumpy-ass attitude up a notch.

He saw right through me. "You could have refused."

This brilliant psychiatrist had been compared to Carl Jung. He was renowned for many reasons, not the least of which was his ability to discern the truth before it was spoken. Cameron had an uncanny gift to see into the depths of a soul.

"Refuse you?"

"I wouldn't take it personally." That dashing grin awed everyone on the receiving end of it.

I held my sword by my side. "I never take for granted what you did for me."

"You were a good patient."

"You gave me hope."

Looking back, that had been my darkest blessing. Because during those days and nights of futility, I'd learned so much about myself. Changing paths hadn't been easy, but I'd discovered I had more to offer the world than just what I did on the football field.

"Well, that's Swiss doctors for you," he said. "Their medical innovations are astounding."

"Neuroplasticity," I said thoughtfully. "Having faith in the body to heal."

"We need that same grit when dealing with Pendulum."

"We have that."

"I agree."

Arrogance had a way of finding me. "I will win this bout." I lifted my meshed mask and uncovered my face for a beat. "Just warning you."

He chuckled.

I lowered my mask. "Tell me this isn't about that submissive?"

His expression showed that I'd piqued his interest. "Stella Adair?"

Her face still entered my dreams, her perfume a memory I'd refused to forget. I'd not treated her well at times, and for that I felt a measure of guilt.

"I'm not the man for her," I said softly.

"Not man enough?"

"Not the *right* man." I glared at him.

"Bravo," said Cameron. "Figuring these things out is essential."

I paused. "You think I was no good for her?"

"Ultimately."

"We agreed me getting close to her was important so we could discover who she worked for."

"Yes, but there were unforeseen consequences." He looked serious.

"It ended badly for her."

"Badly for you, Jake."

"How?"

"She made you question your place in our world."

Damn Cole and his mind games. "How do you know that?"

He stared at me.

"Say it."

He shrugged. "She represented something you've been searching for your entire life."

Our conversation was too deep for this time of the morning.

I wasn't in the mood for his mind-fuckery.

"Maybe we should check in on her?" I suggested. "She needs a therapist."

"Why?"

I flinched, wondering why he'd had to ask. "She witnessed Lance…"

"I thought she had her eyes shut."

"Atticus covered her eyes. But she was *in* the room, Cole. It still could have been traumatic."

"Haven't we all been there?"

"I haven't!"

"Squeamish?"

Why was he being obtuse?

"After what Lance did to her, I'm sure she'll get over it." He waved his épée to move along the conversation. "Any updates on Pendulum?"

"We're no closer to signing."

"Let's give the lawyers a nudge."

I gave a nod. "If they shut down Pendulum, it will move elsewhere."

"We've entered the snake pit now," he said. "Slithering bastards."

We'd discussed at length the rituals on the sixth floor. Secrets within secrets yet to be exposed, endless layers to be peeled back. Everything we'd learned about Pendulum just made us more determined. How could Atticus, Greyson, and I give up when we knew submissives were suffering at Pendulum—knew that no one was doing anything to help them. Those elite members might be above the law, but they weren't beyond our reach.

"Atticus is our trustworthy spy," he said. "He's infiltrated the sixth floor. More updates soon, I imagine."

It had been him who'd escorted me up to that floor so I could rescue Stella. But the risk to Atticus had been extraordinary—the repercussions yet to be seen.

"Who is his contact?" Cameron asked. "The mysterious masked lady? Has he shared that with you yet?"

"No," I said. "But the woman in question is close to the guest at Pendulum who appears to have the most influence."

"The guy who hosted the orgy?"

"We need to find out who he is," I agreed. "Atticus is not saying much."

"Protecting his female contact. Interesting."

"Appears that way."

"Sounds like infatuation."

"She's married," I said. "Stella told me she saw her wedding band."

"We're going to have to dismember that secret society," said Cameron. "One floor at a time."

"I'm ready," I said, waving around my épée.

"One more thing," he said. "Before I win this."

"Ha!"

"Your submissive."

"Don't have one."

"Maybe you're looking at all this the wrong way."

He was talking about Stella again. "It's over." I reasoned it had never officially begun.

But it was good to know she walked the earth—a poetic thought that was out of character for me. Comforting, nonetheless.

"She overcame everything meant to destroy her," he said.

"True."

"Takes character."

"She was special."

"Still think of her?"

"Not being with her means she can live her best life."

"What about what she wants?"

"She wants normality, Cole. I'm giving her up for that reason."

"Very romantic of you, Carrington." He emphasized my last name and then put on his meshed mask, covering his face.

I did the same, heartrate already racing with a surge of adrenaline.

"Anyway," I added, "our kinks don't align."

"You'd be surprised what goes on in someone's head." With his mask on, I couldn't read his expression to see what he meant.

Cameron posed flawlessly, ready to attack. "En garde!"

He couldn't see me smiling behind my mask. Because maybe, *just maybe*, I was going to use everything he'd taught me to win this time.

And anyway, this was the distraction I needed not to think of *her*.

The girl with the almond-shaped eyes.

"Come to Chrysalis," said Cameron. "Tomorrow night. We have a thing."

"I'm not sure," I said.

The point of his épée struck my chest through the vest.

I assumed that meant he'd not accept *no* for an answer.

CHAPTER FORTY-ONE

Jake

I LOCKED MY FRONT DOOR AND HEADED FOR THE "PRICKSTER." The nickname Stella had given my car should hurt my ego, but it just made me chuckle.

Tonight's event was going to be a palate cleanser for Pendulum. I'd accepted Cameron's invitation to meet Atticus and Greyson at Chrysalis.

I paused in my driveway, hearing the sound of an approaching car engine. Rylee's silver Hyundai soon pulled up too fucking close to my toes.

I stepped back, annoyed.

She lowered her window. "Going somewhere?"

"Evening stroll."

"In a tuxedo?"

I peered down at my Hawes & Curtis black tuxedo. "Well, look at that."

"We have to talk."

"I have some time." I always had time for Rylee.

She glanced back down the driveway. She'd never been paranoid before, but the way she was acting made it appear that way.

"What's up?" I stepped closer to her car.

"I'm going to be called in for questioning."

"By the police?"

"Yes, by the fucking police," she bit out. "Lance has gone missing. I'm one of the last women to be seen with him." She pointed my way. "And since I'm your ex, they might want to talk with you."

"Me?"

Made sense. As the jealous ex, I might be a suspect in that bastard's death.

Her hands returned to the steering wheel, gripping it tightly. "Have you spoken with Lance?"

"Not lately, no." I looked away from her worried gaze.

Atticus had succinctly described the way Lance had met his end. Just thinking of it made me shiver. As a surgeon, Atticus was used to that kind of thing—death in all its variety of colors.

I might be into dark play, but it was all for show to satisfy my kinks, obviously.

"You *know* something?" Her tone sounded suspicious.

She could still read me, even now. "I'm thinking about my last interaction with Merrill."

"Which was where?"

"At Pendulum." I pretended to vaguely recall it. "He was in a room full of other people. We didn't talk."

My thoughts naturally drifted to Stella. I wondered what she might be doing now. Living her best life, I hoped. Healing from all the trauma she'd experienced. Enjoying her job back at the mall.

I'd strolled by her place of work just once, glancing into the makeup store Save Face. I'd not seen her in there, but it had been good to know she was in Burbank, and not that far away.

Maybe she thought of me from time to time. Or perhaps I was an unwelcome memory.

"Are you still seeing her?" she said, seemingly reading my thoughts.

I feigned ignorance. "Who?"

"Stella."

I gave her a curious look. "Haven't seen her since…" *Since she was reunited with her brother.*

"When did you last see her?" she asked, pushing for an answer.

Three months ago. *Exactly.*

But I wanted to protect Stella. "Can't recall."

"She wasn't your type."

I resisted a retort. "What you did for her, at Pendulum, is commendable. I'm proud of you."

"Should have done more." Her expression softened.

"It was a challenging time." I still missed us—me and Rylee when things were simpler, and our love was sure. Now, I felt an unfillable void where my heart used to be.

Rylee brightened. "But you're addicted to pain."

"Probably why I'm still talking with you."

She almost smiled. "Yeah, you miss her."

"I miss the drama," I bit out.

She stared up at me. "Secretly, I think you wanted to watch me with him?"

Did she really fucking believe that? "Anyone who fucks Lance Merrill is excluded from being my type."

Her pride dissipated. "Will you come with me if I'm questioned?"

I sighed. "Don't take this the wrong way, Rylee, but I imagine Lance was fucking a lot of women while he was seeing you. You're probably way down on the list of suspects."

Her eyes narrowed. "Was?"

"How do you mean?"

"You made it sound like he's dead."

"I meant he's fucking other women." I widened my eyes. "His ex-wife is a crazy bitch. She'll be the prime suspect."

"Helete lives in Paris."

"Look, this is fun, but I have somewhere to be."

"I can see that."

I stepped closer. "You have nothing to worry about. Lance had a lot of enemies."

"I'm on the committee at Pendulum. Or did you forget that?"

"You went ahead with that?"

"Yes, of course."

"Resign."

"Why?"

"We've uncovered some unsavory activity."

"They've offered me a decent salary to be on their committee."

"Don't share this, but their money doesn't have a legal source."

"And you know this how?"

"We promised to look out for each other. Remember?"

She seemed to mull it over. "Won't it appear suspicious if I resign?"

"Extract yourself from that place ASAP."

"Are you going to?"

"We have some loose ends to tie up."

Like taking out the kind of hosts who'd eradicate you if you broke their rules.

Yeah, not good.

"Well, I can tell you this right now—I'm not resigning."

"Give it serious consideration, at least." I reached for Rylee's hand on the steering wheel. "And if you need anything, call me. I'll always pick up for you."

"The De Sade I used to know would never say something like that."

"People change, Rylee. You should try it."

"What is that supposed to mean?"

I turned and strolled toward my Lamborghini, climbing in and slamming the door to all that idiocy.

Rylee's Hyundai shrank in my rearview as I sped down the driveway, turning onto Mulholland.

I wasn't afraid she'd enter the house. I'd changed the access code. Thrown out the sheets and bought new ones. The memory of her with Lance in our bedroom had left me with the urge to burn down the house.

Of course, there were good memories, too, of Rylee and me during our best times.

And there were also memories of Stella.

Had I protected her enough? That question continued to haunt me.

A dull sense of unease settled over me as I replayed my last interaction with Lance. I hated him—we all did. But no one wanted that fate for him. We'd just wanted him gone.

Shit.

His fingerprints were all over my house. I'd have to deep clean and hope that didn't appear suspicious. Detectives trekking through my private dungeon would be a violation. But more so, a CSI team searching for a motive.

Maybe it was time to lawyer up.

Or maybe it was too soon.

I blasted music as I drove the rest of the way to Bel Air, the car hugging the tight curves.

The panel lit up with a text from Atticus asking my ETA. He seemed eager to see me. Atticus and Greyson had insisted they meet me there tonight.

Maybe they had an update.

I arrived within the hour, a little worn from fighting the Friday evening traffic.

Upon entering, a submissive greeted me and offered to escort me to "where the meeting would be held."

"I wasn't aware there was one," I told her, following along and soon entering Richard's empty office.

"Am I the first?" I asked.

She nodded yes and then closed the door on me. I fished out my phone and texted Atticus telling him I'd arrived, this time asking *his* fucking ETA.

I didn't mind being alone in here for a while.

I'd always found refuge in this office.

Sometimes during events, we'd all find each other in here, taking advantage of the serenity, savoring the night. Too many memories to count.

This office had been decorated in an eclectic fashion. Richard had taken it over from Cameron, but much of the artwork and décor had remained. Like the walled portrait of Carl Jung, the therapist Cole was often compared to.

The back bookcase was stacked with first editions, a mint collection. I coveted Richard's ornate carved desk. The picture on display there of him and actress Andrea Buckingham hugging each other in front of the Eiffel Tower looked like a photoshopped image. I mean, Booth had landed one of Hollywood's most beautiful women, and what she saw in him, other than his dashing good looks and endless charm, was anyone's guess.

That thought made me chuckle.

These were my friends and keeping them safe meant everything. The threat of Pendulum might encroach here—a fact we had to be wary of.

The hierarchy at Pendulum, along with Lance, had tried to seduce me with a submissive.

But instead, I'd fallen in love with her and then set her free.

Had I just admitted that to myself? That I'd developed feelings for a woman on an entirely new level?

Now that was worth celebrating. My armor had been breached and I was finally able to let my ex go. I could be free of the past and move on.

A new chapter in my life.

I looked around for something with which to toast my epiphany, strolling over to the liquor cabinet.

I loved this place, but there was nothing to fix at Chrysalis. Richard and Cameron had perfected the manor in every conceivable way.

There was always something new and interesting here to examine, like the silver cork with a quote on the side from Winston Churchill: *If you're going through hell, keep going.*

Timeless advice.

I heard a knock at the door and turned.

Fake smoke billowed around the feet of a fully masked dominatrix. White mist poured in and blanketed the office. Captivated, I fixed my gaze on the view of perfection in the doorway—a silhouette of a curvy female in high-heeled boots.

Swirls of mist curled around her legs, her bodice snug around her small waist. The woman seemed ethereal as light from the hallway danced over her.

She stepped inside the room and closed the door behind her.

Glistening brown eyes fixed on mine through her mask, her dark locks falling straight down her back. *Like hers*, I mused. Her eyeliner was also worn in a similar way, and those long lashes looked familiar. Golden feathers sprayed out from the top of her headdress.

I smiled. "The golden goose lost the fight, I see."

Better to use humor to deflate the tension than let it affect me.

She didn't respond.

The tension in the room was as tight as a band and close to snapping.

She didn't react. No smile, just a pouting of red rouged lips. Under other circumstances, I might have asked to kiss her to shake up her steely demeanor.

But now, that felt like betrayal. I didn't need an hour in Cole's chair to work out why.

"Richard's not here," I said flatly, and turned away.

"I'm here for you."

Her sultry voice sent a shiver through me.

I didn't want to lay my eyes on anyone but *her*—even as this sensual creature came closer, close enough to be captured in my arms if I dared. Kissing her was possible—but I wasn't that man anymore.

Not tonight.

"Jake." Her voice sounded familiar.

My back stiffened. "Stella?"

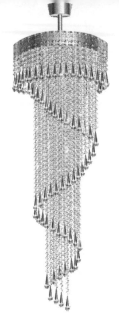

CHAPTER FORTY-TWO

Stella

"STELLA?" THE WAY HE SAID MY NAME MADE MY HEART beat faster.

He didn't recognize me at first, his brows furrowing as his gaze analyzed my appearance.

A sliver of arousal shimmied over me. Jake looked handsome in that tuxedo. It was the same one he'd been wearing the time I'd met him at Pendulum. He had observed me just as intently that evening.

His lip curled in a dry smile. He still seemed unsure of my identity.

This was the only time I'd witnessed him speechless.

I reveled in this moment—we were equals for the first time.

I strolled across the room and took a whip off the wall. "This is a collector's piece, apparently."

"That's right," he said. "Belonged to a French dominant."

"Danton Belfort," I said, the former lover of Scarlet Winters— the impressive dominatrix who'd secretly trained me.

Jake seemed to be processing every second of this encounter, as though seeing me with new eyes. And in many ways, he was.

I caressed the whip with reverence. "When used correctly it elicits a delicious trance."

An obvious statement. He was beyond a master's status. De Sade was a god in this space, and it would take a goddess to capture his heart.

"What are you doing here, like this?" He gestured towards my dominatrix outfit.

I set the whip on the desk.

With my head held high, I closed the gap between us. "Same as you."

"No, Stella." He shook his head. "I'm a member."

"So am I."

"Since?"

"Address me as Mistress."

"Mistress Adair?" He tried it out. "Who let you in?"

"Wrong question."

His lips quirked in a smile.

"Who trained me." I tilted my head. "That would be a good start."

"Booth?" he asked, surprised.

"Grander, De Sade."

He blinked at me. "Cole?"

I eased off my mask, so he'd see the volition in my expression. The confidence. The power I now wielded, and my desire to be in control.

He swallowed hard as he looked me up and down again. "You're stunning."

"I know."

"This is an interesting surprise." Then his expression turned dark. "You can't be around me right now."

"Why?"

I saw regret in his eyes. "We're still working on Pendulum."

Reaching for the whip, I examined it and then used the tip on his thigh. He jolted and then regained his composure.

"I'm calling the shots," I said.

"Is that so?"

"You're not the only one who's mastered the dark arts." I circled him slowly.

"Since when, Stella?'

The whip struck his other thigh. "Mistress."

"Sure, we can do that."

I snapped the whip against his chest. "Obey."

I noticed a change in his demeanor, gradual at first and then I saw a hint of him edging toward subspace—holding on, holding back, as I'd been warned he'd do.

He was resisting me because that's what he liked—a fight.

"Hit me again and see what happens," he chided.

"De Sade, you like your sessions filled with pain."

"Did Cole analyze you?"

Running the tip of the whip along the desk, I gave a nod, gliding it across the shiny mahogany surface, caressing the edge in a tease to suggest that if he was a good boy, that would be his cock soon. He seemed to get that suggestion. Glancing at his pants, I could see his arousal growing in length.

"I was literally fencing with him yesterday," he said, surprised. "How long have you been training?"

"Two months."

As though rising from the trance he edged, eyelids heavy, breathing shallow, he blinked at me. "This is what you want?"

"This is what I am."

"Together we may just burn up."

"Present yourself," I ordered.

"We're not there yet, Mistress."

"I disagree."

"You haven't come to understand what I am, Stella."

"Show me."

He stepped closer and cupped my face with his strong hands. Leaning down, he pressed his lips to mine, and then forced his tongue in my mouth, taking me harder like this than he ever had, dominating me.

I fought back, scolding him with an equally frenzied kiss, both of us finding our way together again, only this time our authentic natures meshed naturally.

Reaching for his bowtie, I pulled him across the room. "Come."

"I'll allow it," he quipped.

We strolled down the hallway, my heels echoing on the marble flooring, crossed the empty foyer with that grand chandelier twinkling above our heads. Both of us looked up for a few seconds to admire the brilliance of it.

That same light had drawn me back.

Passing familiar landmarks within the manor, we reached the stairway and descended, down and down, until we made it to the last chamber on the right, both of us stepping inside.

Jake sucked in a breath at the awe-inspiring spectacle—thirty chandeliers hung above our heads.

"They created this for us," I said.

"Don't take this the wrong way, Mistress Adair," he said, shaking his head, "but why?"

"For all you're doing at Pendulum. They want to show you how much they appreciate what you and the others are aiming to accomplish."

Surprise flashed across his face.

"We call this chamber Chandelier Dream." I watched his reaction.

He squeezed his eyes shut in realization. *One who looks outside, dreams; one who looks inside, awakens.* "Carl Jung."

I gave a nod. "We should look inside and know our hearts' desires."

"To see clearly and observe honestly," he added. "That is how we come to truly know ourselves."

"What do you think of the chamber?"

He spread his arms. "This is the ultimate dream I didn't know I wanted. You and me, in here."

"And dreams are the mind's way of conveying what's important."

"Guiding our way." That made him smile.

"Let's begin your first session with your new mistress." I gestured toward the modern Iron Maiden, not dissimilar from the antique version Jake had shown me the first time I'd visited.

I strolled over and stood beside the door, waiting for him. *In you go.*

He hesitated, second guessing himself, as though wanting to step inside, but still unsure.

"Safe word?" I asked him.

"We should talk first."

"This is our language." I gestured for him to enter.

"Echo." He slipped into subspace, his breathing shallow. "Echo is my safe word."

"I'll remember."

"Dear God," he said huskily.

After quickly removing his clothing, De Sade stepped forward and turned to ease himself back into the tall coffin-sized contraption. We shared a knowing moment, a surrendering to where we now found ourselves. The journey we'd shared had brought us to this moment, this place, this session.

"We only serve one mistress here," I whispered. "And her name is pain."

I closed the door on him.

Those metal spikes would dig into the flesh over his entire body, the pressure flooding him with endorphins—producing a high similar to a freezing cold shower, but more intense as the dopamine flooded his brain.

I could hear his heavy breathing from behind the door.

"Present yourself to me," I ordered, kneeling before the structure, ready to take his high into the stratosphere.

Reaching into one of the holes designed for this very purpose, I helped ease out his erect cock, caressing the stiffness.

He became as hard as iron in my tender hands.

Accepting this gift of his trust, I took him into my wide-open mouth, and he fit tight, his girth substantial. With measured strokes, my head dipping, I took him all the way to the back of my throat, needing this more than I'd believed possible. I delivered pleasure as a delicious torture to worship De Sade.

His moaning turned into groaning. Sharing his experience was a thing of beauty.

I felt his body jerk back, his cock deep in my throat, the heat as he came hard and I swallowed him down, working him intuitively, pleasuring him to the point of bliss—taking us toward everything we were meant to be, had always been.

I was taking this man all the way to nirvana.

But I wouldn't let him out of the iron prison—not yet.

There would be so much more to this session, but first, I gave him as good as he'd given me in this very room, delivering endless orgasms during his confinement in there. I waited patiently for him to recover, then I'd make him come again.

Finally, I opened the door to the iron chamber.

De Sade came at me with force and shoved me backwards towards the St. Andrew's Cross.

He was too strong for me to fight him.

As he strapped me to the device, he said with gruffness, "We are equals, Mistress Adair. Don't fucking forget that."

"We shall see," I chided.

A smirk slid across his handsome face, his hand reaching low between my thighs. He began delivered controlling strokes there, bringing me closer.

I glared at him, ready for the delicious fight of control that lay ahead. Soon I gritted my teeth as the climax came for me, owning me, shattering me into a thousand pieces.

As my pleasure dissipated, I leaned back against the structure, spent and content, having found the fulfillment I'd been chasing after.

Because Jake Carrington was with me again.

CHAPTER FORTY-THREE

Stella

J AKE TOOK US TO COCO'S, AN APOTHECARY-THEMED BAR IN
Culver City with an eclectic vibe and a fun atmosphere.

"Wear your sexiest dress," he'd told me before picking me
up from home.

I'd been more than happy to dress up for this mystery date.
Glancing in the bar mirror, I noted my reflection looked as sexy as
hell. I was wearing an exquisite sheer-paneled black velvet dress with
strappy heels and a studded clutch to round out the glamor.

My looks matched the suaveness of his swanky jacket and black
pants, and his expertly styled dark hair. It was impossible for me to
resist running my fingers through his locks—until he got sick of me
fawning over him and playfully punished me by reaching below my
dress and snapping my thong against my hip.

It made us both laugh.

We must have appeared like two lovers who couldn't keep their
hands off each other, neither of us caring what other people thought.

"Why did you choose this place?" I asked, watching him carefully.

He took a sip of his champagne cocktail. "You always look stunning but, tonight, you're particularly dangerous."

"Are we celebrating?"

He waggled his eyebrows. "We'll save that for later."

The décor around us was lavish, with tall palms in brightly colored vases and a towering bookcase along the back wall. Purple velvet seating was positioned here and there to create an inviting space. The place buzzed with a trendy L.A. crowd.

Jake finished off his drink. "This will be good for you. Closure isn't a thing, but this might help break a circuit."

"What are you talking about?"

"At SoFi stadium, you shared something personal."

I racked my brain trying to remember.

"While at college," he added, trying to jog my memory.

"You've lost me, Jake."

"We create stories about our past," he began solemnly. "Build them up. That's how they keep a hold on us."

"I don't know what you're talking about."

"Karl Smith."

My flesh chilled.

"Until you confront him for what he did to you, you won't be whole."

I reached for my drink. "I don't want to think about him."

"In the stadium, you were with me, and yet your thoughts turned to him."

I sipped my cocktail. "Don't tell me Karl likes this place?"

Jake checked his watch.

I stared at him. "He'd better not be meeting us?"

I started to slide off my barstool, but Jake's strong grip pulled me back. "Not exactly."

"If this is some new kink—"

"Stella, you know me better than that." He looked annoyed. "This is serious."

Then I saw him.

Karl Smith was now standing behind the bar—for his evening shift?

"He's a mixologist," whispered Jake.

The taste in my throat was bitter. This was the man who'd bet he could bed me and had ghosted me afterwards. What he'd done had turned me off all men.

My eyes watered as, in my mind, I walked that college hallway again.

I felt an ache in my belly from shame.

Why would Jake do this?

Even as my mind spiraled, I watched the jock who everyone had admired start his shift.

"Why?" I said softly.

Still, it was impossible not to watch him work. His hairline was receding, and Karl was stockier now with a fuller face, but the same cold eyes.

He didn't recognize me. Probably because of my makeup and this elegant dress—a far cry from my uniform and the girl I'd been who'd crumbled beneath the strain of his cruelty.

Karl recognized Jake, though, like so many people did. He tried to hide his nervousness around him, stealing glances his way.

My trust in men had remained shattered—until Jake had walked into my life. He was my knight in a shining tuxedo.

I was stronger and wiser, able to handle anyone. It wasn't how I'd imagined this moment would be.

Or maybe I'd flowered into the woman I was now because of the love I'd been shown over the last month or so.

I had to trust Jake's intuition on this.

My shoulders relaxed as I observed Karl moving around the bar, pouring drinks and chatting with customers.

Jake looked at me, his expression conveying, *Stella, he's all yours.*

I gave a nod of thanks.

I waved to get Karl's attention. "Remember me?"

He blinked and then peered at Jake as though trying to recall if he should remember both of us.

"Stella Adair," I reminded him.

He froze, panic reflected in his guilt-ridden gaze.

"It's been a while," I said, confidence sharp.

Jake was right. I'd needed to see Karl like this, needed to dismantle what I'd built up in my mind. Because seeing him again proved what I'd not considered before—that Karl's personality was flat and uninteresting and back then he'd been compensating to win points from his friends.

Karl appeared taken aback by my beauty and then turned to my man. "You're Jake Carrington?"

"That's right," said Jake.

Karl set down the glass he was holding. "Cool, man."

"And you're fired," Jake said flatly.

"What?"

"Now get the fuck out of my bar."

"Yes," I concurred. "Get the fuck out of our bar."

Karl hesitated, and then turned his focus to me—reflecting fearful eyes.

Losing a job was no small thing—but the consequences of our actions can come out of nowhere.

Without making eye contact—because he knew he'd been an asshole back then—and without any come back, he left the bar.

Karma had come back around to kick his saggy ass.

Turning to face Jake I asked, "You own this place?"

"Me, Atticus, and Greyson thought it might be fun to own a bar."

"You bought this place because he works here!"

"I told you I'd hunt down anyone who hurt you."

"Didn't think you meant it." I leaned back. "I told you that at SoFi Stadium. We'd only just met. I'm surprised you remembered."

"Oh, I remember everything." His grin slid wide.

"I can see that."

"I'm a gentleman. Always mean what I say." He reached for my wrist and pulled me in for a long, leisurely kiss.

Our tongues fought for control as we matched each other in an impressive battle of wills.

"I...love you," I whispered against his mouth, finally sharing how I felt.

"I'm very lovable," he quipped.

I punched his arm.

Again, he pulled me into a kiss.

Finally, I surrendered to his affection, my lips crushing his, sharing my gratitude for the way he had extinguished that haunting memory from my college days.

Our future would be brighter for me having let it go.

Jake gestured towards the bar. "Champagne."

Only he'd fired the bartender.

We burst out laughing.

"Please tell me you hired a new barman?" I asked.

He winked. "Of course, I always think of everything."

"Thank you." I leaned against my big guy.

"If all it took was for me to buy a bar, then..." He kissed the top of my head. "Let's think grander."

"It's because you listened. You cared enough to do this."

"I haven't even begun to show you what you mean to me, Stella. Buckle up, baby. Things are about to get epic."

CHAPTER FORTY-FOUR

Stella

I PAUSED WITH MY HAND ON THE DOOR HANDLE, HOPING I wasn't making a mistake.

Jake had changed the locks to keep *her* out. Yet here I was about to invite Rylee into his Mulholland home—the place where their relationship ended horribly.

I opened the door.

Rylee almost looked surprised to see me. Or maybe she was taken aback by the gall of the other woman's intrusion into her old home. Until this second, I'd not thought about how it would affect her. I'd been too intent on doing something special for Jake.

Rylee wiped her shoes on the doormat out of habit, or maybe it was me she was imagining beneath her heeled boots. We both were wearing jeans and T-shirts, which didn't bother me, but it seemed to throw her—like I was a younger version of her, only annoyingly happy.

I decided to tone down my enthusiasm as she stepped inside.

Rylee was a little shorter than me, but despite her petite frame she still packed a dynamic punch.

She rested a hand on her hips. "Well?"

I gave her a bright smile. "I hope you and I can be friends."

She looked at me intently. "Jake doesn't know I'm here?"

"We can tell him later."

She strolled by me and walked into the kitchen like she still lived here. "Never did like those cabinets. Jake wouldn't let me change them."

Personally, I loved this room's brightness and its welcoming design, but it was better not to share my opinion.

She glanced over at the fridge. Her photo was gone now, and she must have noticed.

Rylee moved over to the central island and rested her Burberry handbag on the countertop. Then she lifted a freshly baked cookie off a plate and bit into it, smiling at me as she chewed. "Good little housewife."

I guess I deserved that.

It was easy to see what Jake loved about her. Rylee was confident in her beauty. She was wild in a carefree way, and so damn sexy. I found it amusing that we resembled each other.

"Coffee?" I placed another cookie on a plate and set it before her.

"Sure."

I walked over to the coffee pot. "I just brewed some Cole coffee."

"Prefer Intelligentsia." She looked around. "You're living here now?"

"I live with my brother in Burbank." I filled a mug with fresh coffee and carried it over to her, setting it on the counter. "But he's rarely there."

"What does he do?"

"He's a yacht skipper."

"Nice.

A minute passed with neither of us saying anything.

I looked over at her. "Is this awkward?"

"Kind of, yes." She took a sip of the coffee.

I let out a sigh. "Look, I need your help."

She studied my face. "Let's hear it."

Maybe this was a bad idea. "I want to decorate Jake's office. Put his memorabilia on display and make it somewhere he can celebrate his achievements."

Her brows rose. "You should talk to him first."

"I want to surprise him."

"You'll achieve that."

"I think it will be good for him."

"He has an aversion to anything pertaining to his career. Ever since…"

"I know."

"Let him do his thing, Stella. Don't push your man too far. He'll end things."

"But it was such a big part of his life. I want him to recall his career with fondness."

"Trust me, I've tried to change his attitude."

"Maybe it's worth trying again?"

She met my gaze. "You're in love with him."

I didn't deny it.

Rylee looked away. "Has he told you he loves you?"

"He's good to me."

"That's not what I asked."

"He's deeply private."

"We were good together once." She sighed. "It was my fault."

"You had an open relationship," I said, trying to comfort her. "Maybe that complicated things."

"It worked for us."

"Do you regret it?"

Her expression became sad. "We couldn't be together. Couldn't be apart. One of us needed to take a hammer to the thing."

"Jesus," I said, before I could stop myself.

She gave me a thin smile and then a shadow crossed her face. "You don't think Jake did something to Lance, do you?"

"Never," I said quickly.

That made her pause. "I mean, after what Lance did to you and me, I wouldn't be surprised."

Recalling that chamber at Pendulum made me swallow hard.

"You know something, don't you?" she asked.

"I know this—Jake wants you to be happy. Even after what happened with *him*."

"Lance?"

I nodded. Whenever I said his name, it tasted like poison in my mouth.

I couldn't imagine what Rylee had seen in him. "What was the appeal of being with that man?"

Rylee took a deep breath. "It was like edging with Satan."

"And you liked that?" It came out sounding naive.

"I like lots of things." She pointed at me. "So does Jake. He's complex. I hope you're prepared for that."

"I am."

"Is it true you've become a member of Chrysalis?"

I took a long sip of coffee.

"Never took you for a dominatrix," she added.

I picked up her plate and carried it over to the sink.

"Who trained you?"

I turned around to look at her. "Discretion is our code."

"Right. I like you, Stella."

"And I admire you," I admitted.

She closed the space between us and took my hands. "How have you been, since what happened at Pendulum?"

"You tried to rescue me from that room." She'd know I meant that chamber Lance had captured me in. "Thank you."

"I'm sorry I wasn't strong enough to fight off that man who dragged me out." Her expression softened and the way she looked at me seemed different, with kindness and empathy.

Then her demeanor changed.

She let go of my hands. "You were the last person to see Lance."

"No," I said. "He went off and did his thing."

"Are you sure Jake didn't do something?"

"I know for sure," I said. "I was with him the entire evening."

"Maybe Lance is in hiding. He has a lot of enemies."

I decided to change the subject. "What do you think of my idea about Jake's office?"

"Are you sure you're willing to test the beast?"

"Why not?"

"Okay, let's go check out those boxes in the basement."

Within an hour, we'd brought out Jake's sports memorabilia, and with Rylee's design skills, we hung photos, framed posters, and placed other signed items along the shelves, highlighting his awards. His Superbowl rings had their own display case that would remain locked.

We turned his office into a shrine to his favorite sport, which he'd dedicated his life to, creating a space he'd be proud of.

We stood back and admired our work.

"I used to hate coming in here," she said. "The absence of all this screamed louder than if he'd put a few things out."

Jake's wall safe was now covered by a poster of him.

"That mask," I pointed to it. "Why did he have it in here?"

Rylee hesitated. "He wore that the night we first met."

"Oh."

"It's sentimental," she reasoned. "It's probably because it was his first time at Chrysalis, too."

We shared a knowing look—a glance that conveyed the thought that Jake might never get over her. My stomach twisted at that possibility.

We heard the sound of the front door opening and we shared another concerned look.

"Tell him I'm here," she said.

I hurried down the hall to greet Jake in the kitchen.

He brightened when he saw me. "What are you cooking? Smells amazing."

"Lasagna," I said. "Listen, we did something for you."

"We?" He looked puzzled.

Jake was taken back when he saw Rylee come up behind me.

His frown deepened. "Really?"

"I'm not staying," she said.

He glanced at me searching for the reason she was here.

"We were talking about Lance," said Rylee, observing Jake's reaction.

He didn't flinch. "How is he?"

Rylee ignored his question and reached for her Burberry handbag. "She's a keeper, Jake. Hold on to this one." She paused by the door, holding his gaze, sharing a look of affection with him.

I glanced from one to the other, sensing this was a private moment between them. They had a special bond that had been forged over the years, their enduring love seemingly unbreakable.

Rylee finally broke her gaze away from him and gave me a nod before walking out with her head held high.

I couldn't understand how she could have thrown away a relationship with this man. The way they'd looked at each other seemed sacred—a love like no other.

And I'd witnessed it first-hand.

I'd literally put them both in the room with each other.

Jake's jaw twitched. "Care to explain?"

"She was here because I asked for help with something."

He leaned on the counter, anger defused as he zeroed in on me. "What?"

"It's best if I show you." I reached for his hand and led him through the kitchen and down the hall toward his office. "Keep an open mind."

He watched me open the last door on the right.

Jake stepped inside his office and took in the room. "Your idea?"

"Yes."

He blinked as he took everything in, his eyes dancing from the shelf of Superbowl rings to the print of him on the far wall.

He pivoted fast and left the room.

No comment.

No reaction.

He just needed to get away.

I'd wanted this to be a place where he could be reminded of his brilliance. Not somewhere he'd be triggered.

I found him in the kitchen, opening the fridge door and bringing out a beer. "Want one?" he offered.

"No, thank you."

"I need some air." He opened the door to the backyard.

I followed him out, walking across the lawn toward where he'd stopped at the edge of the property. He was staring out at the view.

I couldn't see his expression. "You have to celebrate your life now," I began. "Not in years to come."

He kept his back to me.

"You're one of the greatest quarterbacks of all time."

He took a swig of beer. "And you think it's your place to rearrange my home?"

"One room."

"I don't need to see that shit."

I stepped closer. "I didn't know much about football when I met you. You know that. But I've watched every single game you played."

He pivoted to look at me.

"It was all I had of you," I said quietly. "During the time we were over. The time I believed I'd never see you again. I kept the shoes, too." Silly thing to say.

He downed the rest of his beer.

"You bought that bar, Jake. Fired Karl. Made me face him. I wanted to do something for you."

"I can see that."

"I'll pack it away." I hated that my plan had misfired.

"I appreciate that, Stella."

"I'm sorry if I hurt you."

"Not you, the stuff in there. It triggers me."

"I should have talked to you about it."

"We live and learn."

I wanted to ask if he still loved Rylee, but that was an insecure move. "There's something I need to tell you."

He came toward me. "You're not pregnant, are you?"

"What?" I flinched as he rested his hand on my belly.

"Are you?"

"No."

Disappointment flashed over him. "Ha, that's a first."

"What is?"

"The idea of having a baby with you didn't make me want to throw myself over the ridge."

I brushed off his hand. "Well, I'm not."

He considered me intently. "What other bomb do you want to share?"

"I want to return to Pendulum."

He walked by me, heading back toward the house.

Following on his heels, I reentered the kitchen.

He peered through the glass oven door. "I'm starving. That smells incredible."

"It'll be ready soon."

"I'll cook for us, too." He beamed. "I attended a cooking class with Greyson. You should have seen us. Made a mess every time. I think the instructor couldn't wait for our course to end."

He'd masterfully changed the subject.

I placed it back on track. "At Pendulum, they know who you are there. Anywhere you go. Any room. Any scene, they'll be on their best behavior. You need someone who can move about with ease."

"A spy?"

"Yes."

"It won't be you."

"You can't stop me."

"Actually, I can."

"They halted your contract, Jake." I watched him carefully.

"Rylee told you?" He gave a knowing nod. "Still a no."

I closed the space between us. "I'm not standing by knowing there are women there against their will. I refuse to let someone suffer like Elle."

"Or you."

"Exactly. Someone like me. Or AJ."

"Maybe I'd have agreed before."

"Before what?"

"Before I…fell in love with you."

We held each other's gaze.

"Don't bring it up again." His words were delivered in a masterful and rousing tone, but I found them equally annoying.

"It's the only way you'll own Pendulum. You need the women in your life to help."

"Is that right?"

"A dominatrix—someone loyal—can move amongst the VIPs and not attract attention."

"You think that person is you?"

"I know it is. And deep down so do you."

CHAPTER FORTY-FIVE

Jake

A FTER A DAY SPENT AVOIDING MY OFFICE, I FINALLY WENT inside the room.

I needed to access my Mac to check my emails. Atticus, Greyson, and I were ready to launch a new offensive at Pendulum.

Stella hadn't had a chance to undo her surprise yet. She'd underestimated the agony her good intentions would trigger. She was still young, but Rylee should have known better.

I sat in my swivel chair behind the desk, surrounded by a variety of football memorabilia—those echoes of my past I'd masterfully avoided up until this point.

Leaning back, I resigned myself to looking at it all one more time before we packed it away. Maybe auctioning it off was a reasonable idea.

On the opposite wall hung a poster of me, the frame covering my safe. In the photo, I was launching a ball across the field—the very throw that helped win my first Superbowl. The player who'd caught it, Lenny Lawrence, had won MVP that year. Rightly deserved, too.

I should reach out to him to see how he was doing, see if he would be up for joining me for a beer.

While admiring the trophies, I felt a surge of emotions as I recalled each precious time I'd been awarded them over my career, the wins first celebrated in the locker room with bad boy banter—the support from each other enduring after losses as well as victories. Times we'd honored coaches who'd come and gone but had left their indelible mark.

Maybe I'd looked at this the wrong way. If this was a shrine to the team who'd enriched my career, my life, too, then all this would be easier to sit with.

On the top shelf of the bookcase sat a framed photograph of me when I was nine with Dolphins legend Dan Marino—my childhood hero. When I'd shaken his hand, he'd told me that I had an impressive grip. The glint in his eye had conveyed to me that following my dream was worth it.

And it had been.

I was beaten up—a lot actually—but I'd had the time of my life.

Next to my hero's photo was a snapshot of me receiving my own MVP award, proving I'd been the kind of man who always gave his best. A man who protected his teammates at every turn, every play.

I was surrounded by mostly good memories here. The kind of memories that made the bad times fade.

Stella appeared in the doorway holding a box.

I motioned to her. "Come in."

"Nice desk."

"I remember you bending over it." I pointed to where that had been, and also recalled tying her up and threatening her life. God, I'd put her through it.

She raised the box. "I'll deal with this now."

"How do you mean?"

"Or later if you'd like?" She gestured to the memorabilia. "I'll put it away."

I looked around. "I'm reminiscing."

She walked into the office. "This was my idea. I invited Rylee and persuaded her to help me. I want you to know it was my fault."

"What's your point?" I leaned back.

"I'm to blame."

"I always need some excuse to punish you."

"Maybe I'll punish you."

"I didn't fuck up."

"Ha!"

"Come here." I wanted her to come sit on my lap.

I wanted to breathe her in, brush my fingers through those dark strands and then run my mouth along her elegant neck.

She didn't move. "I know she may stay in your life romantically."

"What are you talking about?"

"I respect that you prefer an open relationship. That having several partners at one time is probable."

"Who have you been speaking with?"

"You're kind of known for that."

I stood and rounded the desk to get to her. "I only want you."

"But I know you need more."

"What do you want me to say, Stella?"

"I shouldn't have mentioned it."

"Well, you did. And, also, all this—" I took the box out of her hands and threw it down. "Can stay for now."

"You're sure?"

"Shut the fuck up."

"You shut the fuck up."

"Are you trying to arouse me?"

"I'm trying to talk with you about something serious."

I grabbed her wrist and pulled her toward me. "You must know by now what you mean to me."

"I interrupted you in here—"

"You're not getting it, Stella. You interrupted my fucking life. You came out of nowhere like a hurricane to blow out all my doubts about ever finding love. You make me happier than I'd ever imagined.

Knowing you're in this house, where I can find you and spend time with you is everything to me. I'm obsessed with you."

Her eyes widened in horror.

She hurried from the room.

Okay, that wasn't how I'd guessed her response to my speech of the year would go. Standing here, replaying the words I'd shared, I couldn't understand what had thrown her. Unless *she* was the one who wanted an open relationship.

And that was a hard *no* for me. That thought alone had me staring at the wall as though I'd been struck by lightning.

I followed Stella into the living room.

She stood in the center, hugging herself, clearly shaken.

"What's going on?" I asked. "Something you want to share?"

She drew in a sharp breath. "You need to know something about me before you let yourself fall in love with me."

I tutted because it was too late.

She spun around. "I killed Lance."

I hesitated, recalling what I knew to be true. "Atticus was in the room. He had his hand over your eyes. Story corroborated."

"I lured Lance to the sixth floor."

"You knew what they'd do to him?"

"I overheard Atticus saying that whoever went up there, never came down."

This was a woman brave enough to do what we'd failed to, which meant she'd carried the brunt of it.

"That makes me responsible for his murder." She searched my eyes to see if this changed the way I felt about her.

"Lance hurt you, Stella!"

She looked away. "Still."

"He walked a knife's edge. He always did. It was inevitable."

"I didn't know what else to do."

"I failed you."

"You came for me, despite the risks. You turned up in Le Chambre."

"I'd go to the ends of the earth for you."

"In Le Chambre, I knew what they'd done to him. And yet you and I had sex like it hadn't happened."

"Pendulum killed Merrill. You did nothing wrong."

"Lance wanted me to discover the sixth floor. I took him up there knowing how dangerous it was."

"Again, not your fault. He should have known better."

"But—"

"He kidnapped and threatened the life of your brother," I snapped.

"Still, doesn't that make me as bad as him?"

"God, no, Stella." It hurt me to see her hurting. "You don't really think that, do you? Anyway, what *they* did to him probably saved countless others who would have suffered at his hands."

"But what does that make me?"

"Someone I love."

"Do you, though?"

"We're still getting to know each other, but I've spent enough time with you to sense we have something special."

"I need to go back," she said. "To Pendulum. I need to see every single woman go free."

"We can discuss it."

"Lance wanted to know who your fourth partner is," she said.

"We knew that would be an issue if they found out there were four of us."

"They'll go to any means necessary to discover who he is."

My chest tightened as I realized that she knew.

Reading the expression on my face, she gave a nod. "I worked it out."

I raised my hand not wanting to hear Cole's name. "Stella, it's essential his name is never mentioned."

"I'd never tell anyone. He's the reason I'm standing here with you. I owe him everything."

"I wanted to come to you after I dropped you off at your brother's," I admitted. "Giving you up was the hardest thing I've done." And in so many ways, even harder than learning to walk again.

Learning to love, truly love—that was worth fighting for.

She came into my arms.

Bringing her into a tight hug, I whispered, "It's over for you as far as Pendulum is concerned."

"I'm still in this fight."

"I don't want that for you."

"I'll never be able to repay you for saving AJ. Being a part of this is how I try."

I planted a kiss on her forehead, and in that moment, I silently swore to do everything I could to make her happy. "Trust me, we've got this."

She hugged me as though not wanting to let go. "I've changed. I refuse to move through life in fear. I'm not that woman anymore."

"Now that we've cleared all that up, will you at least let me have my moment?"

She looked up at my face. "What do you mean?"

"You interrupted my declaration of love." I winked at her.

"Love." It sounded exquisite the way she said it.

Looking into her eyes, my world once more righted itself on its axis.

I wanted to be the kind of man who deserved her. She had discovered a faint light shining within my sinister shadows.

"This is me claiming you," I said sternly. "Let there be no confusion or doubt. You're mine."

For a man who doesn't have a romantic bone in his body—or so I'd thought—that wasn't bad at all.

For the first time in forever, I surrendered to a feeling of peace.

I had to admit now that I liked having my office display my achievements—the inspiring collection of football memorabilia reminding me how far I'd come.

I'd worked hard for it all.

I deserved to savor it.

And I would prove to Stella that I deserved her, too.

Still, what I had planned for her could destroy everything we'd moved toward until now.

But there was only one way and that was through.

CHAPTER FORTY-SIX

Stella

WITH MY HAND IN HIS, I FELT THE POWER OF HIS strength as he led me onward—blindfolded.

I liked this game, this feeling of handing over my control to this man. I was fast falling for him. If these feelings were true, if I let my heart completely open, this would lead to love, I was sure of it.

Was it too soon to admit that to myself?

I wasn't sure. All I knew was that Jake had me thinking of him all the time. He anticipated my needs. He offered me the strength in my life that had been missing. I hardly recognized myself. No longer the quiet girl who hid away, I was living life to the fullest and my future had never been brighter.

More than this, he'd forgiven me for deceiving him and in so many ways, he'd rescued my life from spiraling out of control.

With Jake wearing a black tuxedo and me in an exquisite silver beaded bodice, we were the perfect couple to play within…Chrysalis?

I wasn't sure, exactly.

A door opened. We walked on through, and I heard it close behind me.

With bated breath, I waited for him, trying to pick up clues from the sounds around me.

Melodic notes rose from speakers, hinting that Jake was preparing a session for us. It made my heart beat faster as I recognized the lovely piece being played—"Experience" by Ludovico Einaudi. Jake would play the song in his car as we drove through the canyons.

When my blindfold came off, a jolt of panic whooshed into my chest when I recognized this dark chamber—we'd returned to Pendulum.

But not on my terms.

I'd demanded my return, yes, but now, as I inhaled the heavy air of the lower chambers, I realized my mistake as the music flowed around us. The exquisite notes elicited something ethereal, something magical, as though he knew that bringing into the room a piece of *us* and our time together would soothe me.

But he wasn't Jake now.

He stood before me as De Sade, morphing into the Dominant who'd earned his vicious name. His dark reputation was a crown he liked to deny he deserved and yet he wore it so well. Though well-respected and loved dearly by his friends, his penchant for pain made him a worthy opponent to any man here. Nothing scared him, it seemed.

We were alone, standing within the same chamber of my nightmares.

I couldn't move, couldn't breathe, frozen in time and space as I contemplated my next move. One that, if executed wrong, could cause me to lose this man if I showed fear or doubt or even confusion.

Along the far wall was a mirror. That was new, too. I caught my expression of fear and quickly pulled back on my reaction, wanting to hold on to these roiling emotions until I was ready to share them.

The scent of sandalwood was drawn deep into my lungs as I sucked in this unsettling quiet. I tried to pretend none of this mattered—that it wasn't within this room where Lance had captured and then secured me to the St. Andrew's Cross, holding me on the precipice of pain and dangling me over the edge of torture.

De Sade stepped back into my line of sight and shadows danced across his handsome face. He was closely observing my reactions.

"Where did you go just now?" he whispered, drawing me out of my trance.

A knot of terror burrowed deep in my chest as I endured the harrowing memories swarming around me.

"You wanted to come back to Pendulum," he said, his voice gravely.

Was he punishing me for my insistence?

Yes, it was true, but not *this* chamber.

I bolted toward the door.

He shot toward me, cutting me off, trapping me between him and the exit, his tall frame looming over me and his firm, muscular body pinning me there. He was all heady cologne and masterful dominance, setting my body alight with need and want and everything in between—arousal that verged on being suffocating.

"I know what happened in here," he said softly.

I'd tasted true fear when imprisoned with *that* monster. There was no way to forget that hour of turmoil, not knowing if my brother was alive or not. But going ahead with whatever Lance wanted because all choice had been lost to me.

He's gone, came that reassuring whisper that had found me since his passing.

The man could no longer hurt anyone. I'd seen to that. Escorted him from this very chamber toward the elevator that took him all the way to the sixth floor, sealing his fate.

De Sade's tone remained even. "You proved you can survive anything. Face anything. You're empowered. There are no enemies except the ones inside your mind."

That wasn't strictly true. This place was still filled with evil men, but I'd thought long and hard about joining De Sade in his pursuit to turn this place into something wonderful.

Something like Chrysalis.

I pleaded with my eyes for us to leave.

He stepped back, gesturing that I could go if that really was what I wanted. He was giving me the chance to bolt out into the night air to the freedom I desperately needed.

Then I saw it.

A vast chandelier hung above the center of the room, a new addition to this chamber. A bluish light glinted from its tiny droplets and showered everything in shards of brightness.

A touch of class. A familiar symbol of something sacred had been brought into this dark space, representing what can be achieved by good and honest men. They really could create a place like Chrysalis here. Where consent was sacrosanct and submissives were treated with dignity.

"Take back the power you lost in here." De Sade's voice sounded distant.

He strolled over to the back wall, reached for a whip and brought it down. The exact one that had been used on me before.

I thought back to that time on Lance's yacht when my power had first begun to fade, my life turning into something terrible.

As my eyes fully adjusted to the darkness, I made out different shapes lurking in the shadows. Sinister designs revealed themselves to be nothing more than exquisite furniture pieces transforming the room. All of them new, all of them symbols of beauty. A woman's touch? Or perhaps designed by men who knew that lavish eroticism set the tone with alluring designs to welcome and not induce fear like before.

De Sade was right. The way out, the way through, had always lain within this chamber—coming back to the place where it had happened and rewriting history.

Making the space ours and ours alone.

"My sweet limerence," he whispered, "you're my new obsession. And I never see that ending. Let me heal you."

I wanted that so much.

"I regret not claiming you from the very start," he admitted. "I could have protected you."

I'd deceived *him*, that was the truth in all this.

I wanted my session first, and my eyes told him that.

"Show me what you feel," I said, my voice low and husky. "Show me what you see."

His brow furrowed as he thought on this. "Martyrdom?"

"Yes."

"You're not there yet, Stella."

"But I am ready to host a session with you here. At Pendulum."

"This was never about me."

"I need it to be," I reasoned. "It's you and me. Yin and yang. A perfect balance between giving each other what we both need."

He mulled this over and then nodded. "Maybe another time."

He denied me with those confident words. But I wasn't easily swayed.

"I consent to…" *What exactly was he offering?*

"If you forget your safe word," he said, "which is likely during the session, screaming 'stop' will suffice."

My flesh tingled with the possibilities, with these unfolding moments that fell like the colorful leaves of autumn. He was lulling me into his world, seducing me into a trance I found hard to resist.

I slid to my knees, assumed the pose of a trained submissive, surrendering to him, respecting that whatever he did to me would be pitch-perfect in all the right ways. The dark pain I craved would be delivered with his expert touch.

De Sade reached out his hand to me, inviting us to begin. I pushed up and followed him toward the St. Andrew's Cross.

He studied me closely as he secured my arms to the bars, his expression reflecting empathy for what had been done to me before.

Heart hammering, I felt myself closing in on panic as those memories flashed into my mind, haunting and taunting me like the cruelest nightmare capturing me in its thrall.

He had to know how this room made me feel.

Peering upward to the ceiling, I drew strength from the exquisite chandelier above, with the blue and gold that seemed to say I was safe now.

You're under my protection.

Let the light in.

This was De Sade's way of helping me reclaim myself, just like any woman who needed to reclaim her mind, body, and soul from her past.

At first, De Sade played with locks of my hair, teasing the long strands, coaxing them, bringing a tingling to my scalp, helping me to relax as my trust unfolded.

His hand moved to the nape of my neck where he gently massaged the tension away, his palm hot against my skin. Gliding lower over my shoulders, his hand kneaded the taut muscles there, too, intuitively knowing what my body needed.

All that had gone before, all that had happened to me, was morphing into something else. That experience of being drawn into this world had led me to this lifestyle, and then it had led me to *him*.

This life, this existence, was seeing me transformed into a woman I only now could become. Like sculpting marble, these cuts I'd never have chosen for myself were now revealing the true me.

I felt empowered and peaceful, a sense of the divine welling up inside me.

De Sade lulled me into the scene, whispering words conveying his affection, his patience not something I'd expected as he continued to build my trust. That's what this was about—creating an atmosphere in which I'd thrive.

He offered an exquisite balance of sensations as he whipped my flesh, stroking, slapping, coaxing my skin to enliven. Then, as though knowing my secret yearning, he tapped the leather between my thighs, touching my clit and causing it to throb as it responded to the snaps of his punishments, swelling with delight as it reacted to his teasing.

With gentle and yet firm fingers, he peeled apart my labia and used the curl of leather to tease me there. The sensations felt delicious and dreamy and had me spacing out from the flawless caresses.

Then he stepped back, having given me what he knew I needed. The session was progressing in a seamless fashion.

The nipple clamps he applied to me were a delicious relief,

sending sparks of pleasure and a pinch of pain into my areola as the tight buds were captured within small metal prisons, bringing a continuous pang and making me feel needy and wanton. I had to force myself not to come from the titillating pressure.

That would never do, not when trying to prove myself as a submissive of the highest caliber—one fit for a Dom of his standing.

He tweaked my captured nipples, which were already bursting with sensations, then he leaned forward and suckled them, drawing one and then the other into his mouth, taking his time. The thrill traveled to my pussy, holding me in that blissful state.

His kisses traveled up my chest and he nuzzled into my neck, his soft mouth teasing me.

As the evening unfolded, I reveled when De Sade used the electric wand over me, gradually increasing the level of shock until I was close to passing out when it reached the height of the pain level. Yet it was bearable, and as I adjusted, I found myself craving more of this heady dopamine release that surged through my veins.

He worked methodically around me, applying lube to a sex toy and inserting the silver butt plug that he twisted around and around for what felt like forever, until my thighs trembled and became damp with arousal.

As though in a dream, I felt straps coming around my body as he secured me more tightly to the bars, making it impossible for me to break free.

In a startling flash, I was flipped upside down and my thighs were eased apart, so I was completely on show, my pussy totally exposed. As the contraption was elevated, my sex was directly in front of his face, which meant he could do anything to me down there. I was powerless to resist his advances.

"This cunt belongs to me," he said. "I'm going to prove to you that I know what it needs." He slid two fingers inside me. "This hungry pussy has been left wanting for too long. But that time's over, little sub."

His words left me trembling.

The sensations of his gentle fingers as they glided in and out of me caused me to tremble all over.

"I love how well your body opens up to me, baby." The pressure of his touch increased to a brilliant tempo. "Like a wildflower in the rain, and you're the rain, too. So damn wet, sweetheart, so damn ready."

His fierce desire to own this part of me continued as he inserted a third finger and, at the same time, he reached around and pulled out the butt plug and then eased it back in, fucking me like this with the small device as his mouth clamped over my labia, teasing, avoiding my most sensitive area like a cruel game of denial until I was thrusting my hips furiously, trying to get him to suckle so I could find relief.

"So ravenous for my cock, baby," he purred. "Thirsty for what only I can give."

"Yes," I managed to say.

But De Sade had already stepped back, walking away to find another tool to torture me with exhilaration. This time he chose two devices, one held in each hand, the first a vibrator and the second a dildo that delivered electric pulses. He used them on my arms, beneath my armpits, across my breasts, methodically covering my entire body with those alternative methods.

Aroused and spellbound, the tension inside me rose and fell with each punishment. I was desperate for relief as he stood before me again while I focused on the terrible panging between my thighs.

Again, he eased two fingers inside me, widening my labia with his other hand as he began licking my clit, one stroke several seconds apart. He drew out the pleasure even more slowly, peering down at my upside-down flushed face as though garnering amusement from my delicious suffering.

He stepped away.

I let out a howl of frustration.

"That's it, little one," he said gruffly. "Let me see your pussy. You're begging for my cock to bury deep."

"Permission to speak!"

"You must trust me to know what you want. Know what you need."

"Thank you, sir."

As though sensing that I wanted this to go on forever, he dragged a chair across the room and sat in it to gaze at me like I was an art display on show, and he was merely admiring his masterpiece. I was just that—dripping with sweat, my pussy soaking wet and left wanting and my nipples beaded.

He leaned forward. "Feel that euphoria?"

I gave a frantic nod, as though this was my chance to convey how much my sex burned with desire for his touch, his control, his ability to let me find relief.

He pulled a lever and there was a click as a board appeared on which I could rest my head. He placed a pillow beneath me, as though proving I'd be like this for a while longer—how much longer, I wasn't sure. But him making sure I was comfortable proved there was more time ahead like this, with me captured and vulnerable and at his disposal.

I realized the pain he'd delivered had been minimal. What he had so far brought to this session was endless bliss as he continued to lull me with his dominance.

He kept me like this, upside down and exposed for over an hour, focusing all his expertise on intense play, fingerfucking me, using a dildo whenever he pleased in between, just him and my pussy connecting in a profound way as he slowly teased me there by flicking and vibrating the soft tissue. With each stroke or slap or flicker of a fingertip to my clit, he held me in suspended animation as he made it clear this was as much for him as it was for me—adoration of my womanly self by a renowned Dominant.

Time dissolved and I no longer cared about it. No longer needed anything other than this, *him*, the chamber now a chrysalis for me.

We lost time together as he continued to perform edge play with that desperate little nub, like a pianist knowing exactly which key to play, which note to tap just so, as his tender fingertips beat out their perfect rhythm.

Then, as the end of the hour drew close, he leaned in and suckled at last on that overly sensitive nub.

I again begged for his cock and this time he rewarded me with it, unzipping his pants and holding it out for me to wrap my lips around his lengthy girth.

Like this, with me upside down still, our exquisite sixty-nine position would probably be something to behold from afar, my head bobbing as I drew him all the way to the back of my throat and gloried in the way his mouth possessed me, his tongue circling with a brilliant beat as he guided me all the way into oblivion.

My throaty moans echoed around his cock as I was finally permitted to come, sucking his heat as we fell together into a sublime realm.

Somehow, I swallowed him down from this upside position. Franticly shuddering as he devoured me in ways that sent me spiraling within. Both of us sharing these exquisite and sacred moments. Filled with so much emotion, my heart might burst.

Bound and captured by this man.

Bound to *him*.

This session was about trust. About finding my way, about me insisting I was ready and him believing this to be true.

This was about a shared respect, a love that knew no bounds. About healing and forgiveness and discovering a rousing indulgence.

Finally, I was released from the St. Andrew's Cross. De Sade guided me to a private bathroom, *en suite*, where we took a shower together. He washed my body with a sponge smothered in a luxury lotion and caressed me tenderly. Taking his time to make me feel nurtured and adored.

"Is there anything else I can do for you?" he asked with devotion.

Afterward, I sat in a robe by a fireplace, and he brought me some hot tea.

De Sade left to reorganize the chamber, telling me he would return soon.

He was giving me private time to come down from my high, and giving me time to think, too. Exhaling in a heady rush, I knew that room no longer held any fear for me. New memories had been forged into the divine.

As I dried myself, I became aware of a presence.

With my towel wrapped around me, I looked up to see Rylee standing there, holding a long box.

A jolt of uncertainty hit me.

"I hear you went back in *that* room?" she said.

I guessed that when Jake had booked the chamber, Rylee had found out about it. Then again, she was a VIP member here. She probably knew what went on behind closed doors.

I shrugged. "I had to."

"You're braver than me, Stella," she said with kindness. "It's no wonder he loves you."

That made my breath catch in my throat.

"One day at a time with him," she said. "He'll burn you up, but something tells me you'll like that." She raised the box. "You have the chamber for a few more hours. I thought this might help you in ways you can't even imagine." She rested the box on an ornate table.

Strolling forward, I lifted the lid and peeked in, my eyes going wide at seeing the outfit she'd brought me to wear.

I gave a nod, reassured that we'd reached this place in our friendship. "Thank you."

"You'll look amazing in it."

"Boots, too. You thought of everything."

"Let me know if there's anything you need."

"Actually, there is," I said. "Please ask Atticus and Greyson to come down here."

She gave a knowing smile.

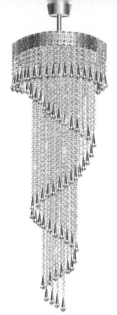

CHAPTER FORTY-SEVEN

Stella

AFTER RYLEE LEFT THE BATHROOM, I TOOK A BETTER LOOK at the latex outfit. The expensive bodysuit would cover me from head to toe in sensual, shiny black material—and it came with a full-face mask.

I pulled on the one-piece suit, pleasantly surprised at how comfortable the high-heeled boots fit. I looked the part of a dangerous Dominatrix. In the mirror, I saw a startling image of me with the black mask covering my entire face and head—my eyes peered back at me, my excitement reflected.

My flesh ignited with arousal at the thought of what lay ahead. Of what I might get away with doing to him. If I could convince De Sade this was even happening.

I made my way back to the chamber.

De Sade was cleaning the St. Andrew's Cross. He heard me enter but didn't look my way at first.

When he raised his gaze to meet mine, he paused for a beat, and then recognized me, his lips turning up at the corner.

"Where did you get that?" he asked.

I stepped forward. "You brought me here to regain my power."

Let me do just that.

His eyes widened as he focused on the doorway.

Atticus and Greyson had entered—both dressed suavely in black tuxedos. Being tall like Jake, they filled the space with their intimidating presence. Both men were seasoned Doms who were willing to take on the world.

"Everything okay?" he asked at their interruption, and then he seemed to notice the way they weren't reacting to me.

He quirked a smile. "Do I get a say?"

He knew before they even made a move on him what this was—it was his fantasy come to life.

They were on him lightning-fast, each one taking an arm and dragging him backwards toward the central table. He struggled a lot, actually, but they managed to strap him down, tearing off his clothes as they went.

I helped them, too, by easing off his shoes and pulling off his socks. As they continued to secure him, I hung his suit on a corner hanger.

When I turned to look at them, De Sade had a ball gag in his mouth. The "attack" had appeared violent and cruel, yet his erection proved he was seriously turned on, his cock bobbing heavily as it curled upward with pre-cum offering another clue.

Mesmerized, I watched as they continued to secure him completely, pulling leather straps across his body until he was immobilized.

With their work done, Atticus and Greyson turned to me with respectful gazes.

Atticus approached me and said quietly, "Want me to wait outside?"

"We'll be fine."

"Remember," he said, staring into my eyes. "There's no such thing as too much pain for him. Just make sure he can always breathe."

I gave a nod.

After they left, the room was quiet and still. I braced myself and approached the table to face his wrath.

Easing out the ball gag so De Sade could speak, I asked, "Do you consent?"

"To what, exactly?" he snapped defiantly.

I felt a stab of guilt, recalling the session he'd just given me. This felt cruel, like a dark betrayal. Doubt settled around me, swirling with tendrils of regret.

He needs this, came that inner voice to guide me.

He likes this—obsessively so.

I'd been advised that he could become hostile and act defiant. The art was in reading what was truth and what was fantasy.

De Sade had told me that, for him, getting into the mood to fuck was through excessive pain. That only when he reached that place of dark arousal could he discover the pinnacle of his desires.

"Do you consent?" I asked again, this time my voice husky with desire.

He glanced away, looking annoyed as though thinking this was a waste of time.

"Safe word?" I coaxed, bravely ignoring his arrogance, his belief I didn't have what it took to get him there—to that sacred place of intensity.

I grabbed his chin and turned his face to look at me. "I've been taught by the best."

"Really, who?"

"I had a private session with Cameron Cole himself."

Cameron hadn't touched me, nor me him, but he'd instructed me, and I'd been honored to practice these dark arts on dominants of Cole's choice at Chrysalis.

I'd excelled and passed his approval with flying colors.

I was ready for this, for him, and for everything that might arise during the hour.

De Sade's smile faded as he realized what that meant. The two men were both connoisseurs of the dark arts, but Cole was the master and if I'd been instructed personally by him, then I had to be more than capable.

De Sade held my gaze for the longest time.

Then a look of resignation crossed his face, as though trusting I had what it took to take him all the way into rapture. Or maybe he was just humoring me.

Just as he'd done, I selected music for his session, deciding on a song by The Irrepressibles—"In This Shirt." The moody, ethereal piece floated out of the hidden speakers, setting the tone, leveling the mood as I set about making this a positive emotional experience for him. More music like this would follow to maintain the atmosphere. An otherworldly experience would ensue.

Something he'd always remember.

Yes, I'd locked him in that torture chamber back at Chrysalis, but this was altogether different.

"No safe word." He opened his mouth, indicating I had permission to reinsert the ball gag.

A thoroughbred of a man lay on that central table, with long toned limbs, taut muscles straining. He was so tall that his feet reached the end of the table. A superb specimen of a creature. The leather straps digging into his flesh delivered their own kind of discomfort.

I couldn't allow his exquisite physique to intimidate me or throw off my focus. Still, it was hard to drag my gaze away.

I stood in the presence of perfection, knowing full well what a profound privilege it was to host a session with him.

Being given the responsibility of his trust, I sensed the sacredness of this moment. I wanted to continue to excel as a Dominatrix through his entire session. I wanted to make him proud, have him see me as a worthy opponent.

As a worthy switch.

Just as I'd been trained, I used measured and cautious timing as I prowled around him, adjusting the straps as I constantly checked his reaction, building anticipation, creating an atmosphere of control.

I began by teasing.

A slew of words left my lips that at first felt foreign as I berated him, ordering him to obey, pleasantly surprised with how well he slid into subspace with my verbal torrent of words.

"How you respond will prove your worthiness," I said sternly.

Utilizing a sharp pinwheel to sensitize his skin, I ran it over his body to enliven his flesh. Next, I used flips of a whip as his trust in me grew, his eyes sparking with delight while I bestowed the right pressure and the right beat of strokes, proving to him he was in expert hands.

And then I fell into a dark trance when I dragged over the larger leather whip, using it on him in ways I'd never envisioned myself doing—not on someone I adored, or cared about. But with each strike he shuddered into the luxuriousness, his erection growing harder still, like iron, fully engorged and so huge I sensed he was enjoying being edged with pain.

The atmosphere around us crackled as the tension between us morphed into something beyond words as we left the world outside.

As I dragged the cat-o-nine-tails across him, he thrust upward as though begging for me to use it on his cock. I did, gently at first, cautiously, and as that area reddened, I observed pre-cum dripping from him onto the strands of leather.

He gave a nod; permission for me to go harder on him.

My hand clenched that monstrous cock, as though it had personally beckoned to me, and I stroked it lovingly, and then increased the pace until his entire body was shaking with desire.

Then I let go and stepped back, admiring the way he trembled.

This bonding between us felt far-reaching, like a war between us that we were also fighting together, as I faced the challenge of fulfilling a man's deepest craving.

Now and again, he struggled against my dominance, fighting my will, testing my strength, my power, but as I held on to this control, he eventually gave all of himself over to me, which sent him deeper and deeper into a trance.

I lubed up the butt plug and brought it over to him. His eyes watched me intently, and when I released his lower straps, his legs fell open inviting me.

"Lift," I said, and as he raised his hips a little, I inserted the plug gently into his asshole, twisting it in and seeing his ass welcome the pressure. His thighs trembled, and his eyes sparked with rapture.

Again, I resecured the bindings.

The nipple clamps went on easily and pinched his small buds just so, and I knew the euphoria surging through him would be significant.

With a flip of a switch, the bed vibrated and shook him violently, shaking that plug inside, no doubt, and sending him over the edge.

Again, I used the cat-o-nine-tales over his flesh, prowling around him as my mighty steed vigorously shook. I took my time teasing and taunting, and now and again stroking his cock with it.

Glancing up, I saw that the chandelier was flickering its blue lights upon him, glinting over his entire body.

And it hit me like a lightning bolt.

I was that chandelier. The chandelier was me.

It represented the light of a soul, and this was our connection, true and honest and fulfilling with a brilliant dance of sparkles to light our way.

I pushed the button to stop the table from vibrating, and then shimmied out of the latex until I was naked except for the mask. Then I climbed onto the table and straddled him.

Lowering myself onto his impressive girth, I ground my clit along his length, backwards and forwards, making his skin slick with my arousal. Stroking myself, I took my own ecstasy from his cock by grinding, twisting, and drawing in every way I needed and with everything he deserved.

His eyes were wide with need and lust and desperation.

When he could bear it no more, I positioned the tip of his cock against me and sunk low onto his full length, fully penetrated by his shaft. Then I rode him hard, clinching him with my pussy, rising and falling fast, coaxing him toward his reward.

Like a wild creature, I continued to torture him, only this time with pure erotic intoxication. "Do not come until I say," I ordered.

He gave a weary nod.

The orgasm snatched my breath away, and it was easy to forget time and place, using him like this, making him feel like that's all he was, just a conduit for my pleasure.

His eyelids grew heavy, jaw slackening, lips trembling, proving I'd hit a nerve. Proving he felt used—and from his widening eyes and arching neck, proving he loved it.

I proceeded to demean him verbally. Each sentence designed to deflate his overblown arrogance, a quality I actually found admirable.

Which seemed to enliven him even more, his hips thrusting fast against the straps, strong and powerful and out of control.

"Make me come again, you freak," I seethed.

He became wild and uncontrollable, a bucking stallion, his hips rising high as he forced himself deeper inside me until I was holding on for dear life, trying not to be thrown off as another orgasm snatched away my breath and sent me hurtling into nothingness. He was so deep now, so hard, so furious in his pounding of me.

My own voice sounded distant as I managed to shout out an order to him. "Come!"

He shot his heat inside me, flooding me, and it was messy and forbidden and again sent me into heady trance. Inside my mind, I rolled down a lush hill until I met a waterfall, and it poured over me its exaltation until I was bathed completely in bliss.

My breathing was ragged as I climbed off him and removed his ball gag. I released his bindings, too, and he sat up and brought his legs to the side of the table, hanging them over the edge.

I watched his reaction.

He lowered his head, his breathing eventually slowing.

When he seemed ready, he slid off the table, carefully removing the butt plug from himself and throwing in onto the table.

Then he looked at me with a sexy smirk. For once, he was speechless.

He dragged me into a hug.

"I'll keep improving," I whispered. "I'm still getting used to… *hurting you.*"

Those weren't the right words, but he knew what I meant.

He kissed the top of my head. "I can take more than you realize."

Resting my forehead against his chest, I knew I'd continue to find my confidence and truly bring him the level of pain he desired.

"Teach me how to do more to you."

"Stella, consider that a date."

"You're magnificent," I breathed.

That made him grin, as though the adrenaline was finally wearing off and he could think clearly.

I stared past him across the shadowy room.

Staring back at me was a masked woman glaring in my direction.

I screamed.

De Sade jolted protectively and pivoted to look in that direction.

"It's you!" he realized.

I gasped at my foolishness and burst out laughing. Both of us were howling at the ridiculous scenario of me have been scared of my own reflection.

He brought me into another hug.

"It was worth it just to have you do that," he teased.

I leaned into him, heart still hammering over that scare, and blurted out, "I love you."

The words spilled out before I could help myself.

"I know," he said. "I'm very loveable."

I slapped his arm to chastise him, searching his expression to see if he felt the same way.

"Of course, I love you," he said, his voice still heavy with lust. "You're intolerable and I can't get enough of you."

I glared up at him. "That's not very romantic."

"I'm obsessed with you," he said. "It's quite a feat to capture the heart of a man like me."

And I knew it was, because Jake Carrington was the most profound man I'd ever met.

I led him away, back to the private bathroom *en suite*, where I would commence the aftercare where I would check in with him emotionally and show my deepest affection in ways words couldn't convey.

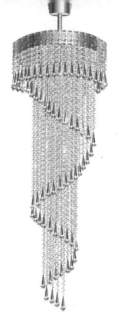

CHAPTER FORTY-EIGHT

Stella

I RETURNED TO PENDULUM THE FOLLOWING EVENING empowered and ready to take on the patriarchy.

I was intrigued to be back here so I could discover more about this club. I intended to do good work here and be a part of something important.

The plan was for me to get to know the submissives, discover who was here against their will and who were genuinely into the scene— and then report all I'd found to Jake.

I blended in perfectly by wearing my glamorous dominatrix corset, along with a masquerade half-mask to hide my identity. The sensual high-top boots I had on reflected a blend of sophisticated sexuality.

I was here on my terms this time.

To my left, the room behind the glass window remained empty. The St. Andrew's Cross was gone. It was the very room where I'd first met Jake.

The Four had made a small step in their progress. For now, there'd be no more auctions of submissives.

I wasn't afraid.

If anyone approached me and made me uncomfortable, they'd get a whip to their thigh—a Pendulum "fuck off."

Many of the men here pined to be dominated. In their own lives, they wielded money and power, and yet here, they were able to surrender and let go of all that stress and tension they were forced to carry in their positions of authority.

This club offered the kind of control that kept them pacified, kept them coming back for more.

I'd learned many things about myself over the last month or two—mainly that I savored being a voyeur.

Standing at the back of the ballroom, I observed a session between Atticus and a fully masked submissive. He had her stripped down to a thong, her breasts exposed, her nipples erect. Her arms were stretched wide, wrists bound inside the metal cuffs of the St. Andrew's Cross where she was positioned upon the stage.

Together, they were in sync, enraptured with each other. It was as though no one else was in the room. Master and sub shared the same trance. Atticus used his talents to keep her in subspace, delivering her orgasms as only an intuitive Dom can, and respecting when she needed recovery time. He knew when and where to touch her to rev her up again, make her jaw go slack, her body tremble. I watched as she shuddered her way into bliss again and again.

Glancing left, I saw Greyson and his submissive Amelia, a petite blonde. They were just as enthralled with the performance.

Stealing glances their way, I noticed they looked like they were in love.

Atticus, Greyson and Jake had come around to the idea of having loyal friends here who could move about covertly. But Greyson had insisted Amelia stay out of this. She was to remain at his side.

"Here you are," said a familiar voice from behind me.

I didn't need to turn around to know it was Jake. "Here I am."

"They're just about perfect."

"Who do you mean?" I glanced left because both couples shone with affection for each other.

"All of them, I suppose," he said.

"Not jealous?" I said softly. "Amelia used to be yours."

He wrapped his arm around my waist. "No, because it freed me up to make you mine."

"Correction," I said, my tone sultry. "You are mine."

"We can agree to own each other."

"I'll consider it," I said with an edge of humor.

"Tonight, I'm the Dom."

His words sent a shudder through me. Switching was as natural as breathing for us. Depending on our mood, or what we each needed, we offered fulfillment on every level.

And tonight, according to De Sade, he ruled supreme.

"In case you're wondering," he purred in my ear, "that's what I'm imagining doing to you later."

"Thank you, Master," I said softly. "Push me hard."

He let out a growl of approval as his hard cock dug into my lower spine, his body warmth welcome in the coolness of the room. It was a privilege no other man would experience because I'd promised him our bond was unbreakable.

Greyson and Amelia moved closer to us.

Everyone's focus remained on Atticus and his elegant sub.

"Who is that with Atticus?" asked Greyson.

De Sade answered with caution. "I have no idea."

Greyson was affectionately playing with Amelia's hair. She turned and leaned into him, giving him a tight hug. Then she excused herself and hurried out—to the restroom, I assumed.

Greyson walked closer to the stage, and I refocused my attention there. "Does she belong to Atticus?"

"I don't know," said Jake. "With Atticus it's hard to say."

Since we were standing at the back of the room, the audience wouldn't see me reach behind and grip Jake's erection through his pants. He became rock hard in my palm.

"Did I give you permission?" he asked huskily.

"No."

"Brace for punishment."

"What do you have in mind?"

We were in the heart of danger, and it stirred my arousal. With my heart racing and adrenaline surging through my veins, I was alight with searing desire.

De Sade slid his hand around my belly and reached between my thighs, caressing me and sending that first jolt of pleasure through me. He circled the sensitive nub teasingly, making me wetter still as he guided me into a delicious trance.

"Your cunt needs to learn to obey," he said, his tone stern.

My head rested back against his chest.

"Relax," he soothed. "You've forgotten this pussy belongs to me."

My wetness coated his fingers now so that he could easily slide two inside me. His thumb beat my clit, too, capturing me in this dominant hold that had me swooning over his supremacy.

"Know what happens when you disobey?"

"Show me." I jolted when he pushed deeper inside me.

"Your pussy is tight around my fingers. It's begging for my cock."

"Yes," I said breathlessly.

"But that level of pleasure comes with a price."

"I'll do anything."

"I'm the one who owns you. I want everyone to see that."

"Not yet," I said.

We had to maintain a clandestine relationship for now.

"You're wearing a mask."

"Patience."

"Scream, or don't scream, when you come. Decision is yours."

His fingers resumed, this time with a brilliant beat on my clit as he pounded me inside with two fingers. His other hand reached around and slid beneath my corset to squeeze a nipple. I shuddered with a pleasure so intense my legs struggled to hold me up, which forced me to brace against him as his fingers pummeled me inside—his remarkable strength keeping me on my feet.

A shocking scream tore through the quiet. It was as though Atticus had somehow timed his sub's climax to match mine.

I didn't care if anyone turned their heads and witnessed me writhing, my jaw slack as I surrendered to a blinding orgasm.

He let me come down gradually from the heady pleasure.

Eventually, he let go.

I glanced over my shoulder at him.

He quirked a smile. "That's your first punishment of the evening."

Something else I'd learned about myself was this ability to reach the heights of bliss and then recover with an extraordinary swiftness.

Again, I leaned back against Jake and savored his hug.

Greyson approached us again. "Can you check on Amelia, please?"

"Sure," I said. "Where did she go?"

"The bathroom." Greyson glanced at his watch.

"Be right back." On the way out, I turned to glance at Jake.

My gorgeous Dom was willing to fulfill my every need. His eyes stayed on me until I was out of the room.

I made my way to the restrooms, wanting to freshen up, too. I looked forward to getting to know Amelia better.

Halfway down the corridor, I saw Amelia being escorted away by Jewel Delany. From the way Jewel was coaxing her, something didn't look right.

Jewel had been kind to me when I'd first entered this world. Meeting me for lunch and encouraging me to get closer to Jake. That right there should have sent off alarms. She'd wanted me on the inside with the men who were taking over this place.

The two women both made good progress down the hallway. I continued to follow from a distance.

Jewel paused before that familiar bar. It was an interesting choice to enter the private space—the same one where I'd done shots with Elle before she'd been dragged off.

Maybe they were going in there to talk privately.

Seriously concerned for Amelia, I continued to follow them. There wasn't time to go back to tell Greyson.

By the time I reached the bar, they'd walked through it.

I knew the way they'd gone and what it led to. My throat tightened with terror as I opened the door and peeked down the hallway.

Jewel stepped inside the secret elevator, guiding Amelia with her. Of course, Greyson's submissive wouldn't know this was an elevator. Or that she was in danger. She probably assumed this was an official meeting with no sinister undertones. Because Jewel was a respected dominatrix.

A shiver went down my spine.

The elevator doors closed.

I followed in their footsteps and stood where they had seconds before, waiting for the elevator to come back down.

I'd been banned from coming to this end of the club for obvious reasons. But right now, I didn't have any choice.

I'd been warned *they* needed more time to gather intel. Time to investigate names and connections and root out evil on the sixth floor, discover which members frequented this part of the club.

And now, I could share that Jewel was one of them.

As soon as the doors opened, I stepped inside, my hand sweeping over the wallpaper for the invisible button and soon finding it.

Nothing happened.

And then I felt movement.

My heart raced as I ascended.

I was second guessing myself, knowing that this was madness. Still, Jake knew I was able to enter these places. Guests would have recognized Atticus, Greyson, and Jake. But not me.

If you visit the sixth floor uninvited, you don't make it down.

The warning bells rang in my ears, but I refused to let Amelia suffer the same fate as I had in Le Chambre. Become part of *that* ritual.

Once out of the elevator, I hurried down the red carpeted hall with the familiar pillars on either side, taking a sharp left at the end.

Pressing my ear against a door, I listened to the chatter, then opened it a little to see submissives preparing for a soirée. I'd witnessed the kinds of things they were exposed to, and I wondered how many of them were here voluntarily. My eyes scanned the room for Amelia.

Elle had been one of these girls.

This was me taking my power back.

I entered the room, ignoring the glances my way, and approached a red door.

I opened it enough to peek through and saw Jewel pulling on a blue robe. It was the same one worn by the three people I'd witnessed sitting on thrones during the ritual where Lance had been condemned.

Amelia was on her knees, waiting and looking confused.

During the ceremony, I'd heard the voice of a woman giving an order for Lance to be dealt with.

It was her.

Jewel had been one of the robed elite in Le Chambre. All that time I'd believed she was just another member.

She was the instigator.

Then I realized, this was likely the woman who AJ had witnessed aboard Lance's yacht. The woman who personally brought these women here.

She'd killed Lance because of what he knew about her. She'd used his yacht and implicated him in the crime.

Jewel put on her black death mask, the exact one worn by the person who'd gestured for the others to kill Lance Merrill.

My heart skipped a beat at the sight of that sinister beak.

Amelia glanced my way, recognizing me. She pushed up and came over to the door.

"You have to come with me," I said urgently.

"I've been chosen," she said, eyes bright with trust.

Bullshit. Jewel was tricking her. And maybe it was because Amelia was with Greyson.

Jewel called over, "Who is it?"

Amelia turned to look back at her. "I'll be right back."

Over Amelia's shoulder, Jewel locked eyes on me, sending a shiver of terror through me.

Amelia stepped through the door, and I quickly slammed it shut.

Grabbing her hand, I dragged her with me, both of us bolting back down the corridor. I hated leaving the other submissives behind as we fled.

We soon made it back to the elevator, and it seemed like we waited a lifetime for it to rise to the sixth floor.

"What's going on?" asked Ameillia.

"You can't be up here," I told her.

"Jewel is a VIP."

"Why did she bring you up here?"

"She wants to introduce me to someone."

Oh, God. It *was* for that dark ceremony I'd been forced to witness.

Finally, the elevator doors slid open and we leaped inside, my fingers scrambling to find the DOWN button.

I saw movement down the corridor.

Jewel Delany was heading fast toward us with her robe billowing behind her like it had come alive. Her threatening mask made her look like the queen of death herself.

My fingertips found the button and pushed it.

The doors slid closed.

Just in time.

I let out a deep breath and gripped Amelia's hand. "When the doors open, you need to run," I told her. "Don't look back."

"What's going on?"

"We have to get to Jake and Greyson."

The ride down to the ground floor seemed to take forever.

As soon as the doors opened, we sprinted along the corridor, navigating around the other guests who watched us with stern curiosity, some ordering us not to run.

We ignored them and made our way back into the ballroom.

There was no one on the stage now. Atticus and his submissive had left the room.

We hurried toward Jake and Greyson. They turned to face us, their expressions showing concern.

"What happened?" Jake led us into a corner.

I spilled the words. "Jewel took Amelia up in the elevator. She told her she was going to introduce her to someone important."

"Greyson." Jake motioned for him to come over.

As he approached, his expression turned to dread. "Where did you go?"

I peered up at Jake. "I got her out."

"You went up there?" Jake's tone was full of fury.

"I had no choice. Listen, Jewel is one of the robed chancellors on the sixth floor."

If he knew this, he pretended he didn't. "Are you both okay?"

"We're fine."

Greyson pulled Amelia into a hug.

"Jake," I said, my voice trembling. "Jewel gave the order for Lance to be murdered."

Fear flashed in his eyes. "Just tell me Jewel didn't see you."

He took in my terrified expression.

"We have to get you out of here." He turned to Greyson. "Find Atticus. And make it quick."

COMING NEXT

CHANDELIER SIN
Book 2
Chandelier Sessions

A power struggle is underway for control of Pendulum.

When priceless secrets are at stake, nothing is off limits. No sin is too great. And no one is spared.

A man must risk his life to rescue the woman he loves. But the true danger is another who claims her as his own.

Passion will push all to the brink.

ALSO BY
VANESSA FEWINGS

THE ENTHRALL SESSIONS
ENTHRALL, ENTHRALL HER, ENTHRALL HIM,
CAMERON'S CONTROL, CAMERON'S CONTRACT,
RICHARD'S REIGN,
ENTHRALL SECRETS, ENTHRALL CLIMAX,
ENTHRALL ECTASY AND ENTHRALL SHADOWS
&
THE RAVISHING—*With Ava Harrison*

&

PANDORA'S PLEASURE
MAXIMUM DARE
PERVADE LONDON and PERVADE MONTEGO BAY
PERFUME GIRL
THE STONE MASTERS VAMPIRE SERIES
Also,
THE ICON TRILOGY from Harlequin:
THE CHASE, THE GAME, and THE PRIZE

&
THE CHANDELIER SESSIONS
CHANDELIER DREAM
CHANDELIER SIN
TBD

ABOUT THE AUTHOR

Vanessa Fewings is the *USA Today* and international bestselling author of the ENTHRALL SESSIONS and THE ICON TRILOGY from HarperCollins along with many additional novels.

ENTHRALL has been optioned by Passionflix!

Her books have been translated into other languages around the world. She now lives with her husband on the West Coast with their rescue Foxhound, Sherlock.

Vanessa can be found in The Romance Lounge on Facebook, Instagram, and TikTok. She enjoys connecting with fans!

vanessafewings.com

Made in the USA
Monee, IL
19 September 2023

42976886R00201